JAMBEAUX

JAMBEAUX

LAURENCE GONZALES

HARCOURT BRACE JOVANOVICH
NEW YORK AND LONDON

Requests for permission to make copies of
any part of the work should be mailed to:
Permissions, Harcourt Brace Jovanovich, Inc.
757 Third Avenue, New York, N.Y. 10017

Printed in the United States of America

Library of Congress Cataloging in Publication Data

Gonzales, Laurence, 1947–
Jambeaux.

I. Title.
PZ4.G649335Jam   [PS3557.O467]   813'.5'4   79–1824
ISBN 0–15–146038–8

First edition
B C D E

Original songs quoted in this book:

"High Rise" (page 55), "Two-Hundred-and-Fifty-Knot Blues"
(pages 80–81), "Jambeaux" (pages 92–93), "You Can't Miss Her" (pages
138 and 159), "When It Hits the Fan" (pages 197 and 268), "Old Song"
(page 208), "Recondo" (pages 246–47).

Lyrics by Laurence Gonzales
Music by Philip Gonzales
All original songs copyright © 1979 by
Laurence Gonzales and Philip Gonzales
All Rights Reserved.
Jambeaux (TM) is a trademark

Grateful acknowledgment is made to the following
for previously copyrighted song lyrics:

Essex Music, Inc. for "A Whiter Shade of Pale." Words and music by Keith
Reid and Gary Brooker. Copyright © 1967 Essex Music International Ltd.,
London, England. TRO—Essex Music, Inc., New York, controls all publi-
cation rights for the U.S.A. and Canada. Used by permission.

Thanks to Janet Bailey and to all those who provided information, assistance, and refuge—especially my brother Gregory.—L.G.

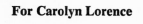

For Carolyn Lorence

JAMBEAUX

-1-

Page had only one rule about his house: telephone before stopping by. And ever since he'd bought the place in Michigan, no one but a handful of adventurous reporters had broken that rule, and they'd backed out of there double time looking over their shoulders at a shotgun. Recently there had been no phone calls, no visitors at all, just the long, self-imposed silence. So it was almost too much of a coincidence that Page found himself leaning against the garage by the sprawling house the day his younger brother Steve showed up. It was like a premonition.

Steve parked the car on the wide concrete apron and got out casually, pretending to ignore his brother, as if he showed up every day about this time, as if it hadn't been months since they'd seen each other. Page, too, feigned indifference as Steve hauled a small suitcase from the trunk. Steve was smiling as he approached.

"We hang trespassers around here," Page said, barely loud enough for Steve to hear.

"Yeah, well, hang this." Steve elevated his middle finger, exhaling an icy fog.

The two brothers regarded each other with bemused suspicion for a moment and then turned toward the house. From the front it was sometimes hard to tell them apart. From behind it was impossible. They both walked alike, as if it were a great deal of fun, an act of defiance or mischief.

"So how are you?" Steve asked as they reached the door.

"I'm gone be all right," Page allowed thoughtfully, leading the way into the spacious living room. It was a room full of light. The bookshelves and windows ran nearly floor to ceiling on three sides, and the light poured in, cutting every figure in sharp shadow at midday. Page went behind the bar and came out with two beers. For a moment the brothers stared at each other across the room, like gunfighters across a town's main street—a grin and a what-the-hell, with blood and smoke hanging in the balance. They both knew what was coming and neither was sure who should begin. Finally Steve laughed nervously and dropped his eyes.

"Sorry I didn't call first."

"Tits on a bull," Page said. "It's good to see you." He lobbed a beer at Steve and it tumbled lazily in the air. Steve plucked it out of flight with a casual flash of his hand.

"Thanks," Steve said, and walked over to the fireplace. A twelve-inch gold record hung on the wall in its frame, another next to it, platinum. And another. And another. Farther along the wall was a framed poster, a frozen moment of enormous energy. A blurred crowd of forty thousand people or more stretched out and away. About three-quarters of them were marked by an orange light, like biblical pictures of the Pentecost in which the Holy Ghost manifests itself with tongues of fire. It was the rock and roll salute: thousands of lit matches held aloft. The scene was dark, the overall image indistinct, but at its center was one bright spot of fusing, vicious light, and inside that light was a lone figure, fixed there like a methacrylate insect, screaming into a microphone at the top of his lungs, a guitar strapped around his neck. Behind him in the darkness were four other men at their instruments. Steve recognized the tiny man at the center as Page, howling out his trademark: Rock and Roll, which Page pronounced as four syllables: Rock and Row-Wool! That cry had become so identified with him that he could say it and bring an audience to near hysteria without even playing a note. At the top the poster said LES BEAUX JAMS. At the bottom, in its characteristic sunset-colored, black-bordered logo, was the band's name—JAMBEAUX—and beneath that, in tiny type, ENIGMA RECORDS, 900 NORTH LA CIENEGA BOULEVARD, LOS ANGELES, CALIFORNIA 90069.

"So there it is," Page said, watching Steve study the poster. "There you have it."

"There *what* is?" Steve turned to face him. "What's all this shit I'm reading about you quitting music?"

"There you go, Coach. The fossil has retired is all."

"You can't quit," Steve insisted, his voice no longer playful. Page just shrugged and opened out his hands with a tilt of his head. "They said you had a falling out with Perry," Steve pressed.

"You know it's much more complicated than that," Page said,

thinking of gray and stately Perry, owner of Enigma Records, rich as a sheik with or without Jambeaux. "Perry and I separated on amicable terms"—Page smiled—"which is to say my terms, which is to say I quit."

"What I figured." Steve sighed and squinted out the enormous windows. "He'd have mentioned it if you'd had a fight."

"Did you talk to him?" Page was surprised. He hadn't talked to Perry in months.

"Gotta look out for myself, you know." Steve shot Page a signifying glance so sharp and fast it was like a switchblade opening. "Still," Steve said thoughtfully, "it's really a shame you talking about quitting. You're at the top of your career, man."

"*Was* at the top of my *former* career," Page corrected. "And anyway . . ." Page trailed off, thinking, How am I going to explain it to this kid?

"Damn, Page, you're only thirty years old," Steve insisted.

"And you're only twenty-one. Look, you want to be a star, go right ahead. I've been, thanks."

"So what about the contracts?"

"I don't know." Page grimaced as if someone had just reminded him of an old bill that was coming due. "The other guys are still talking about going ahead with another record." He cut his eyes to Steve. "But I'm out of it. I'm through. Fuck the contracts."

"If you think so." Steve drank off part of his beer and watched as Page walked to the vast windows facing Thousand Moon Lake. Far across the white expanse a deer took a tentative step out of the forest and onto the ice, delicate as a ballet dancer. A grouse exploded into flight over the lake. It took up a glide pattern, smooth and low, then disappeared into the tree line.

When the phone rang, Page actually jumped.

"Old war wound?" Steve needled him. Page gave him a dirty look and went to answer the phone.

"Butch, you lecherous motherfucker," Page drawled into the handset, "who gave you my phone number? This is a national security matter, Senator. DEW-line. Can't you leave an old man to die in peace?" He paused, laughed, then his face went dark. "Oh, no you don't, Senator." He waited again. "Not on your life, man, when I want to see you, I'll find you. I'm incommunicado, remember? What's the matter, don't you read the fucking papers? Yes, of course I still love you." He stopped again and then finished.

"Yeah, yeah, I'll think about it, but that's all. And if you come around here without calling, my attack maggots will get you, don't forget that. All right, take 'er easy." Page hung up and sat across from Steve. He lit a cigarette and blew the smoke out into the room. The light worked its infinite hieroglyphic permutations in the air.

"So exactly why *do* you want to quit?" Steve asked.

"Well, you just have to go through it to get the full picture." Page sighed. "It's not all that simple."

"All the violence, huh?"

"What?"

"You know." Steve imitated an announcer's voice: " 'The grisly saga, blah, blah, blah . . . ' "

"Shit." Page laughed. "I don't know. It was a lot of things."

It had been a nice journalistic hook for the music writers. When things got dull, they could always crank up another story about Jambeaux, the drugs and violence and sex and music, they could fill it up with more than was actually there, never quite getting it right, even though what was actually there had been plenty.

"You might as well tell me," Steve said. "I mean, I want to grow up to be a star like my big brother." He grinned at Page.

"Fuck you," Page said. And then he thought, Maybe I will, maybe I will just tell him and then he'll go away and leave me alone. "I guess," Page said, "you've got to go right back to the beginning. I can probably mark the exact night when things began to fall apart—which was the same night things began to come together."

"Say again?"

"Here's the way it was." Page got himself another beer and settled into his chair. "Me and Link were playing Galveston, a for-sure shit detail to say the least. But the whole time we really wanted something more, we wanted the best. The best, bar-none band around, period. I had this sound in my head, I'd heard it for years. Shit, even before I went to Vietnam. And when I got back it didn't change, it just sat there singing until I thought I'd go crazy." He laughed but it was bitter and ironic. "Maybe I did."

At times when Page and Link were playing in some true low-life nightclub, Page would isolate the sound they made together and try to match it with the one in his head, a different sort of music, voodoo-miracle, Zodico-reggae, Cajun swampjoy, a delirious, giddy death-boogie. When the saints go marching in, Mardi Gras death-on-the-streets funereal rock and roll. He could never pin it down, never explain the grim exuberance, the built-in paradox of joy and grief, and years later neither could the critics. He only knew it was love, love at first sight.

At the height of it all, Page often felt rabid and dislocated when he talked to high-powered executives or hangers-on from Los Angeles or to the writers who chased around after concerts and showed up at the parties (Oh, the parties, Page would think, please don't make me go again, anything but another party, box me up and ship me home). These people simply had no sense of the hideous jihad it was for all musicians, and perhaps in particular for Texas musicians—that was why so many writers recounted the most lurid stories with such relish, nothing like vicarious danger, blood and fire seen through smoke.

He particularly remembered the rock critic from *The New York Times* asking in all sincerity, completely incredulous, "You mean your band members carried *guns?*" as if he were asking whether they carried smallpox. Page had smiled at him and pointed to the bodyguard standing calmly at the door of the dressing room. "In the old days we had to do his job ourselves."

The critic looked puzzled and went on, "I understand your bass player, Link, is quite a rabble-rouser," and Page practically pissed himself, it floored him, the man's total inability to comprehend how it was back then. Jesus, it had only been a few years earlier. Man, man, Page had thought, this guy doesn't even read the damned newspapers. Page had just decided that the quickest way to get rid of him was to tell him some harmless story he could print.

But now there was another story going through Page's mind and he was tempted to tell it to Steve, maybe put him off this whole thing. The story was old and yellowing now, the edges curling even as Page remembered it, remembered sitting there one evening watching Link unwrap a brand-new Colt Mark IV .45-caliber pistol from its Cosmoline paper. Page asked Link why he had bought it.

"Little business," was all he had to offer.

Page watched with increasing curiosity as Link replaced the grips with checkered walnut, removed the pistol's hammer, and substituted a 1927 government model. And Page thought, There's gonna be a lot of slow walking and sad talking in somebody's hometown if this keeps up. Those were combat modifications. Link sat in the kitchen and held the piece as if to shoot it, drawing the slide back over and over. Each time he drew it back, he stopped to file a bit of metal from the hammer spur until it no longer chewed into his hand.

With each modification, Link's mood worsened. Page watched him enlarge the ejection port and the well into which the magazines are fed.

"Christ, Link," Page demanded, "what in hell are you going to do with that?" Link just looked up at Page sadly, as if to say, What the fuck do you think I'm going to do with it, asshole? Then Link replaced the standard thumb safety with a King Speed and installed a Pachmayr mainspring housing so that the butt would fit his enormous hand better.

Page stood around the pistol range and watched Link fire the weapon over and over, magazine after magazine, getting the feel of it, making neat little chewed-out circles in the silhouette targets, first over the heart and then right in the center of the face. The sun was going down when they left the range. Link bought a box of KTW ammunition, a carbon-steel bullet with a Teflon covering that literally detonates inside the body cavity, producing consistently fatal wounds. The cartridge was loaded up to the maximum power the .45 frame would stand, loaded so high that it tended to knock the rear sight loose.

As they rode out of Houston toward Conroe, Link finally explained about his girl friend, Terry, and what the local Conroe pimp had done to her when she refused to work for him. He told Page about the cigarette burns, the broken nose, the brace she was wearing around her neck, and the tubes running into her arms and up her nose as she lay now in Methodist Hospital from a depressed skull fracture and who knew what else.

Page was just behind Link and to his left when they went through the door to Silky's apartment. The force of Link's foot took the lock off its mount and split the door. Silky weighed about three hundred pounds. He smiled when he saw Link, a panic smile —he knew trouble when he saw it standing six feet five inches tall. Silky stood, Link raised the .45 and said simply, "This is from Terry."

Silky's head turned into a fine, pink spray and the wall behind him splashed with red and white matter. The roar of the weapon rocked the apartment and threw Link's hand high into the air. Silky was dead before he even began to fall, but Link brought the .45 down, aimed again, and fired, this time catching Silky just over the heart. The entire quarter of his body exploded, the arm and shoulder slamming against the wall as if thrown there, and the enormous man spun around like a blowup clown toy. Again Link's hand came into position and just as Silky hit the carpet, another shot ripped through the right side of his back, making his great bulk jump and scattering bone across the room.

Without a word, Link and Page got back into the Cadillac and drove home, stopping only once along the way to drop the .45 into the San Jacinto River.

Page shook himself from his thoughts and turned back to Steve. Well, maybe he'd tell him that one some other time. He wasn't in the mood today.

"Anyway"—Page sighed and stretched—"me and Link decided to crank it up finally. I suppose we just got tired of playing that shitty nightclub on Galveston beach."

⊦2⊦

As Link drove toward Galveston Island, Page could smell the salt and fish from the Gulf. He watched the swampy land on the outskirts of town and tried to figure it: either the ocean was gradually taking over the land or the land was trying to take over the ocean. Scattered here and there were houses on stilts, attended by the gutted, rusting hulks of cars and pickup trucks half buried and corroding in the salt-slush and sand. There were even a few newer condominiums up on science-fiction stilts like some *War of the Worlds* inventions. To Page, or to anyone who cared to look, it was clear that whoever had taken the trouble to put his world up on stilts like that surely lived in fear of the sea. And those rotted cars were proof that whatever the sea didn't get in its long, devastating sweep across the island, why, the salt air would police that up too in the aftermath.

Along the main road into town, the ghosts of once-elegant,

sprawling, New Orleans–style mansions loomed over prefabricated houses, long history and new silence. An island originally inhabited by cannibals, it was now gone to whorehouses and run-down gas stations, and those were wiped away with casual regularity by hurricanes.

A monolithic seawall ran along Seawall Boulevard, sloping down from the street to an embankment of granite boulders that stretched away to flat, sandy beaches. The loose sand would swallow a car up to its rocker panels if the driver wasn't careful. And Galveston on a Saturday night was not exactly famous for careful drivers.

All weekend cars prowled Seawall Boulevard, cruising the length of the beach, stopping to discharge vomit or urine or two or more enraged customers bent on assaulting one another. Summer of '74 and just the ride into town was enough to drive a man to drink. Page already sounded weary as Link turned toward the beach.

"This is God's country," Page said. "He just comes back to claim it from time to time."

The seawall itself was impressive testimony to the endless struggle between men and the ocean. The embankment was there to stop the sea on those frequent occasions when it shrugged, sending a wall of water slamming across the island. Page felt a twinge of satisfaction in the certain knowledge that, with the inescapability of all natural wonders, a hurricane in the megaton range would some day cut across that Gulf once again and wipe the slate clean.

But tonight was just an ordinary Galveston evening, the temperature soaring to giddy stroke levels, the air an overdone gumbo of fish-rot and salt. The place where Link and Page played was nothing more than a slab of concrete surrounded by walls of stout bamboo and hung with a sign that said RIPTIDE RENDEZVOUS. But it was a big club, decked out for serious business. It was what Page called "an in-earnest, for-sure, full-bore, go-ahead, hard-boogie, rock and roll nightclub."

"Saturday night." Page sighed as they entered, and added with a shrug, "Rock and Roll." It was a verbal tic he had picked up years earlier on another continent, when choppers used to take them out on assault missions. According to procedure, after they passed a certain point beyond which the platoon was committed to fighting, someone would shout, "Line of departure. Lock and load," and everyone would chamber a round and slam home the bolt on his weapon. But the first time Page went on such an assault, he thought he heard the man shout above the batting of the rotors, "Line of departure. Rock and Roll!" and it stuck with him.

The club smelled of beer—before and after being metabolized— and of stale tobacco smoke. It permeated and nested in the bamboo fiber like maggots festering in dead flesh, and years later Page would sometimes imagine that he smelled it on himself.

Link went to the bar and Page moved toward the stage. It was a confusion of hardware: microphones pointing their heads attentively this way and that, horns lined up rigid and military in their stands, great banks of gaudy, vinyl-covered amplifiers and speakers in outrageous colors—metalflake crimson, skyblue sparkle, orange sunburst, and massacre red—a bramble of electrical cord that made it nearly impossible to navigate the stage floor. An imposing walnut Hammond B-3 with two Leslie speakers stood off to one side next to a black, speckled drum set resembling a rare, gawky bird, all chrome legs and beak. And placed here and there, the electric guitars and basses, bright sci-fi psycho fantasies that looked more suited to producing death rays than music. Saturday night, and when it came to making noise, they definitely had their technology lined out.

Page made his way past the hardware to the back of the stage and reached up to hit a switch. He had to admit that, even in this nightmare place, a stage full of space-age instruments came to life in the floodlights. The metalflake custom speakers glowed like candy and the flat-bodied electric guitars burst like astronomical phenomena. The brass horns were complex rivers of molten gold, formed into streams and switchbacks by supernatural craftsmen. The stage had a make-believe, festive quality about it.

Page felt a surge of excitement as he took out his guitar. He strapped it on almost tenderly, the way a locked-on junkie ties off before firing up: oh, blessed relief. But not for long. That same sound started up in his head, he'd heard it for so long now that it took a lot of chemicals just to turn the volume down. He knew he was going to have to play a job tonight and it sure wasn't going to match that music—his music. Tonight it was going to be basic, prefab nightclub fare. It was like being horny and in love and a thousand miles from her—you were going to hate yourself in the morning when you woke up with someone else.

"Gone be a crowded motherfucker," Link said as he came across the room with two beers. Page took a beer, drank off half of it, and exhaled loudly.

"We ought to get these assholes to honor that damned contract," Page said.

"I wouldn't bother them if I was you," Link warned. For several summers now, Link, Page, and so many other Gulf Coast musicians had been signing union contracts that guaranteed them scale or better, while in reality the club owners paid only half of that figure—in cash, no questions asked.

"We ought to sue them, the union'd back us up," Page said.

"You're crazy, you know that?" Link shook his head. "The union would fold under you so quick you'd fall flat on your ass. And then you'd never work this strip again and probably just for good measure they'd break your fingers so you couldn't play guitar."

"Shit," Page said.

"Look what happened to Jimmy Blackwell."

"They did kind of mess him up, didn't they?"

"You know why?" Page said nothing. "Because Jimmy got this wild hair and decided, screw them, he was going to start his own nightclub. He was just asking for it. No cigarette machine, no jukebox. He ordered his liquor from another distributor. And he paid union scale on union contracts."

"They don't scare me," Page said.

"Then you missin' some components, Little Buddy. They scare *me*, and I'm fearless."

Page shrugged and went back to his instrument. He plugged his guitar into the amp and adjusted the knobs. He traced his fingers lightly across the strings. And then something happened that was all out of proportion to this delicate movement: a stretch of Galveston beach four hundred meters long exploded with a sound like an electronic whip cracking, the real thing, essence of rock and roll. Up on the seawall, although Page could not see it, puzzled heads turned as the club gave off its eerie, semitonal cry. The manager of the Riptide Rendezvous had the right idea. Other club managers up and down the island hated him because with his two bands, each sporting nine horns and megawatts of brutal power, he could blow everything clear off the beach.

"You know, Little Buddy," Link said, "we got enough equipment in here to fill the Grand Canyon."

"If you were as full of downers and beer as they are, you'd need it this loud just to hear it."

Link hauled his bulk onto the stage and strapped on his bass. Page played an E and Link tuned to it, the throaty bass sounding like a gong struck in some great hall in hell. The club had started to fill at the first sound of Page's guitar. And when it filled on a Saturday night, it filled quickly and to capacity. People were now taking up positions at the various bars inside, mostly slack-limbed men at this point, leaning with that hip-shot indolence peculiar to hard-core white trash.

Page watched a couple make its way across the room. The short, lean, tattooed man wore a western hat, decorated shirt, tooled boots, and tight jeans. The overall impression fell somewhere between ersatz cowboy and borderline fag, though if you had suggested that to the customer he would have taken you outside for a roll in the sand and a deep puncture wound. The girl was bigger in both dimensions, with massive breasts. Her blonde hair was elaborately sculpted and sprayed into place, and she walked as if speaking some exotic sign language with the top half of her body. Soon the couple was swallowed up in the Saturday night crowd that was flowing in.

There was a seemingly endless procession of couples, singles, hookers and crooks, oil riggers, cat operators, jerks and truckers, waitresses, secretaries, clerks and bookies—Cajun, Indian, Cowboy, Freak—losers and loners and hungry women, dandies, dudes, cops and robbers, veterans of wars both foreign and domestic, the lean, the mean, the hairless and legless, stoned and sober, straight as Interstate 10 and crooked as a refinery catwalk; they came alone or with reinforcements, in groups of two and three, in armies and cadres—small attack units of swinging dicks and vast divisions of pussy. For it was Saturday night and they had come to slake their thirst for noise and booze and sex and action, love and death and human contact in all its most graphic mutations. They came and reeked of sweat and piss and beer and all the glorious, livid discharges of their animal couplings. They came in their manifold ruttings and rubbings to squirm in the arclight and obliterate the horror of it all. But Page knew why they really came. In the final analysis, they came to boogie.

Page and Link left the stage and huddled in a corner to drink beer and just watch it all come down before their first set.

"I don't think I'm gonna make it through the night." Page's voice shook. "I'm getting too old to take this shit."

"Then take this shit." Link held out his hand. Between his thumb and forefinger was a dark, elongated capsule bearing pharmaceutical hieroglyphics and the numbers 18-875. Page recognized it as an old favorite: the notorious Penwalt twenty-milligram Biphetamine, so dark in color it was popularly known as a Black Molly or Black Beauty.

"Ahhh." Page smiled. *"La Negrita."* He opened his mouth and Link dropped the capsule in like a priest administering the holy sacrament.

"The Black One," Link said.

"Our Lady of Sympathomimetic Amines." Page swallowed it with beer. When he opened his eyes he was faced with a young, very drunk girl.

"You're Page," she said. She had a vague, farm-girl prettiness somewhere behind her stoned expression. Page nodded and smiled uncertainly. "I think y'all's is the best band on the beach."

"Who do you have to fuck to get a transfer outta this chicken-shit outfit?" Link asked the ceiling. Page just thanked her and asked her name.

"Melanie," she said, listing to one side.

"Are you alone?" Page wanted to know. She didn't answer at first. She stared at him, admiring his high cheekbones, the deep skin tones, the great cloud of dark hair. Page dropped his eyes, thinking, Yep, she's definitely one of them, another Gulf Coast casualty, a genuine mattress-backed sweetie from Bossier City or Lake Charles or Pasadena. Or from Texas City, where the effluvia poured into the air by the oil refineries were so thick and potent that the residents walked around in a constant, demented drunk. Page felt he was losing his grip. He'd been doing this for too long.

"Yes," the girl finally said.

"Well, Melanie," Page began uncertainly, "we're going up there and play some of that music now, but I'll catch up with you later on."

"I'll be right over there." She waved vaguely and lurched away into the crowd. Page turned to see Link frowning.

"What's wrong with you, shitbird?"

"I wouldn't fuck her with *your* dick," Link said.

"You'd fuck anything that's warm." Page laughed, a little too high, a little too easily. In another twenty minutes he felt the Biphetamine kick in. His heart went into a canter. Oh yes, oh yes, nothing finer. Page always imagined it was what fighter pilots felt when they popped their afterburners.

"Rock and Roll." Page now felt the speed grip him as if he'd grabbed a high tension line. "I feel good enough to *kill* somebody." Link's laughter was drowned out by the ambient crowd noise. The club was revving up its generator and all it needed was a little rock and roll to complete the circuit, then watch the sparks fly.

"Line of departure, Coach." Page pointed to the band assembling on the stage. He and Link fought their way through the people.

To get things rolling Page called "The W. S. Walcott Medicine Show" by Robbie Robertson. Page and Link set up the bass and guitar intro, a syncopated, slap-hammer, plunking lead. The drummer came in pumping, sizzling, as Page took two steps forward until his lips nearly touched the Shure microphone. He grimaced as if he had some really bad news to tell, then sang the rawboned, rangy melody. Link stepped up to his mike to sing the harmony part in an incongruously high, warbling tenor. Page watched the people and listened to the band behind him. He felt the guitar humming in his arms and put his voice on the line. It came back to him a thousandfold, 130 decibels of it, raking up and down the beach.

The people were moving now, jerky and ataxic, as if a mad scientist had created a bad benzodiazepine dream that danced. Page surveyed the entire scene with a detached, almost innocent horror, listening to his own voice (Who *is* that guy singing?), hearing the second trumpet player honking out of tune (Where did we dig up that dude?). He tried to concentrate on the sound he and Link made with their instruments, with their voices. He desperately wanted to hear it, for sometimes, against the holocaust backdrop of this band, Page was able to focus, filtering noise, and even transplant himself and Link into some mythical band that could do no wrong, the band he had always heard playing in his head.

He held the sound for only seconds at a time, though, as he

called another tune and then another, rushing through the set.
" 'Whiter Shade of Pale,' " he hollered behind him and stepped
back to let Link sing. Link's voice came down a fourth and belted
out the old overused song. "We skipped the light fandango /
Turned cartwheels 'cross the floor."

The set wore on and got old very fast, nothing like stale music
to make you want to pack it all in. When it finally ended, Page
took the microphone. "Evenin', folks, thank you. I think the drugs
are beginning to work"—light ripple of approval from the crowd
—"so stay with us. The Hurricanes'll be up here in a minute to
play a set while we take a short beer and speed break, so don't go
away." And Page thought, Do, do go away, far far away, all of
you, as the band played a fast breaktune behind him. Someone
handed Page a card and he said, "One more announcement, we
have a tan Chevy, license number DZQ eight six three, that's block-
ing some cars, would the owner please move it? All right, now, we
be right back." They wound it up quickly and scattered to different
corners of the club, eager to get away from the stage. When Link
came over to the corner with two beers he saw that Page was
shaking.

"You all right?"

"Man, I don't know how much more of this club I can take.
Look at me." He held out a hand and it trembled visibly.

"Man, they just a bunch of *kickers*." Link slapped him on the
shoulder. "No sweat. Just play is all."

"I don't know, I think we better find something else to do pretty
soon." He thought for a moment. "Maybe I could get some nice
quiet work, like smoke jumping."

When they mounted the stage half an hour later, it was worse.

" 'Sympathy for the Devil,' " Page called. The song just about
matched his mood. Besides, it was long and he wouldn't have to
think for a while. After that he went through some old favorites for
the Louisiana crowd—Otis Redding, Bobby Blue Bland, The
Temptations. But then it hit him again, about halfway through the
set: that sound. That Sound. At times he had even spent long
afternoons writing out parts for the musicians so that he could
teach them one of his own songs, but the actual *sound* was never
there when they played. Now he longed to hear it and knew he
wasn't going to, not tonight, not in any damned Riptide Rendezvous, you better believe it.

The whole routine was wearing on him like metal fatigue; a plane will shake and shudder only so long before an engine just falls off one day on the airstrip. Page was on the razor edge of nightclub fatigue. Some people had other names for it, shell shock, environmental anxiety—Page didn't care what they called it, he wanted out. As the last song wound down, Page took the microphone again.

"Thank you, folks." His voice came through the sound system like that of some delirious god, panting across the little island in foot-high letters. His eyes scanned the acres of flesh. The only thing that kept back the nausea now was the Black One coursing through his veins. He was about to start his standard rap when he spotted the couple he'd seen earlier, the ersatz cowboy and his busty girl friend. He watched with mute wonder as the girl opened the cowboy's fly and started working him over with a skillful, vigorous fist. It was the first time Page had seen a handjob in this club and couldn't quite believe she was doing it. He felt Link lean over his shoulder and whisper with astounded reverence, "Well, I'll be dipped in shit."

"All right!" Page hollered into the microphone. "Don't let your meat loaf, Cowboy." Page felt himself slipping now, as if some internal gear had just ground itself smooth. It was not as if Page hadn't seen some strange things in nightclubs; it was the cumulative effect that was finally getting to him, and this most recent abomination pushed him further than he had ever gone. Now the girl's head was thrown back in hysterical laughter—a bad laughter, the kind heard in the halls of mental wards. The cowboy was hunched over, trying to get his pants back together. Page wanted to turn away but he couldn't take his eyes off the couple.

"Yes, sir," Page went on, "we got a *man here* just got his *lizard whipped!"* No one could ignore that. The room coughed up a cosmic, surreal chuckle and outside, people began to force their way into the club to see what was going on. "That's right, *stud.*" Page pointed at the man. The audience tried to follow his finger but the club was far too crowded for anyone to see past the immediate neighbors. "How'd it feel?"

"Great!" the cowboy yelled, and his girl friend nearly collapsed with laughter.

"Well," Page said with a savage grin, "I've got *twenty bucks* here says you two won't do the *crocodile rock* right there on the floor." Page pointed as if aiming a weapon. Link moved up closer behind him, seeing him skittering across the icy surface of hysteria now.

Page's challenge had cracked across the beach like the sound of artillery and heads turned toward the club with dim, reptilian curiosity. Inside, a low, dangerous roar went up from the crowd, which grew larger and louder as more people tried to get in the door.

"Let's have it," Page screamed into the microphone. "GIT SOME!" The girl covered her face in a giddy gesture of embarrassment, while the cowboy waved his hands in the air like a champ entering the ring. At last Link closed the set down, pulling Page away from the mike. The other band mounted the stage and the club manager tried to make his way through the crowd as the cowboy and his girl actually went through with it. She hiked up her skirt gingerly, pulled down her panties, and lay on the filthy concrete. The cowboy dropped his jeans and began going after it, pumping and jumping spasmodically. Page passed close enough to drop two ten-dollar bills on the cowboy's back before Link led him into the night air. The club roared its approval like a Roman coliseum. Page shook uncontrollably and something deep in his chest split painfully.

Link kept him out on the beach for half an hour until they had to go back in for the midnight set. Page thought they should just leave—fuck it. "I'm warning you," he breathed, wide-eyed, "I can't predict what's gonna happen up there."

"You gone be all right," Link said. "Just one more set is all."

"It's your ass." Page shivered, freezing in the ninety-five-degree heat.

And when they began again, Page started calling the fastest, loudest numbers he could think of, one after another. He screamed at the microphone in a weird alien voice until he was hoarse and the trumpet players were begging him to slow down and call an easier tune.

"Eat shit," Page hollered at them. "If you can't play good, play loud," and he launched into yet another hard, fast song, wearing the crowd down, actually working it, as if by sound alone he could force them to dance themselves to death. His voice went out to them like a directed-energy weapon, lethal and unrelenting. Without realizing it, he was singing better than he ever had. The crowd was going wild, but Page couldn't tell. He stood there in the white-hot light, screaming and sweating and shivering.

And then something shifted deep inside him—an enormous piece of emotional cargo loose on the deck—and the wall of pretense collapsed then and there. He turned around to call the last song of the set and Link could see that Page was practically blue. He gave Link a sick grin and grabbed the microphone before naming the final number.

"Oh *my*," he said, hoarse and weary. "We lit that *hard boogie light*, didn't we now?" The crowd roared at him and it shook him. He hadn't noticed they were paying attention. "*My, my.*" He sighed. "We gonna *slow it down* a little. Might play a little number called 'Rivers of Babylon.' Might just *do* that." He was breathless and a pool of sweat had formed at his feet. "Oh, yes, *yes!* And if we did, it might just go something like *this.*" He raised his hand in the air and when he brought it down, the other guitar player hit it. As he sang, no one had any idea how far over the edge he had really gone. Even Link, who had seen the brutal ugliness on Page's face, didn't know. Link stepped up right beside Page and sang harmony:

> But the wicked carried us away captivity,
> Require from us a song.
> How can we sing King Alfa song
> In a strange land?

As the band headed into the out portion of the song—a jumping, jangling, heartbeat rhythm—Page grabbed the microphone and in that same exhausted, detached-panic voice, began a speech that shook the club to its concrete foundation.

"*Rock and Row-Wool!*" he screamed, smiling like a skull. The crowd howled its approval. "Do you like good *music?*" The people exploded in a sea of noise. "Are you having a good *time?*" Again, the ripping cheer. "Well, that's all right, my, yes, and do you think we should get paid *union scale?*" The audience was in a mood to approve anything he said, even if it didn't understand what he was talking about. "So do we, *so do we.* That's why we're through signing *union contracts* and getting paid *half what's coming to us.* Because we *Rock and Row-Wool!* Am I right?" The crowd shouted, *Right!* "And all you boys from the *attorney general's office,"* Page shouted. "You been hanging around here long enough to know what's going on. How's that *investigation* going? Figured out where these clubs get their *liquor* yet? Had any liquor trucks hijacked lately?" The crowd was laughing, but near the far end of the club, two men in suits practically dropped their drinks. "That's right. How about it, *Clovis Younger?* How about that skimming operation out in *Vegas?* You getting enough coming through here so you think you might pay *us* some of that *laundered money?* Might pay us *union scale?* Why don't you come on up here and say a few words to *Uncle Sugar* about the taxes you pay on your casinos? Or maybe about the *illegal casinos* in Lake Charles or Beaumont? Or about that *cocaine deal* in the Bahamas? Or about Jimmy Blackwell's problem with fire insurance these days?" The two men in suits were moving through the people now and the club manager was trying to fight his way to the stage. The crowd screamed and laughed, oblivious. "Don't you just know it," Page went on, *"nothin' finer.* We got one full-bore *operation* going here, don't we? How many people we got here tonight from *Treasury* and *Organized Crime Section?* Come on, boys, raise your hands now, let's have a show of hands, we know you been out here every night for two months, now. Just ask *Clovis.* How many sets of *books* you keep here, Younger? Two? Four? And let's don't forget *Bob Bunker."* At the back of the club a heavyset bouncer moved steadily toward the back room, crushing people in his path. "I know this all may come as a surprise to you," Page continued, but at that moment the club's electrical system went out as the bouncer threw the main power switch. In the darkness, the two men in suits were still somewhere out in the crowd, trying to shoulder their way through. The club manager was making progress, shouting and waving his arms frantically. And Page felt an odd, inappropriate calm overtake him, like hearing a surgeon say, "Now, count backwards from ten. . . ."

Page tried to explain it to Steve. The boy had been a musician since he was a child, a real natural, but once Page cut the trail, things had gone more easily for Steve. Now Page figured there were a lot of things he didn't know about that trail. How it was possible for a man's will to be completely broken by it all, at every level of the game, from street musician to superstar. In that regard, Page and Link had been lucky. By the time they decided to start the band, they were not broken and they had no major attachments. They lived on very little money, but there was the consolation that they could walk away from it anytime they wanted. They both understood that a musician's life is one great economic disaster, nothing to worry about, chapter eleven, chapter eleven, chapter eleven, memorize it, it was written for you. A musician doesn't get and hold a job. He plies a trade, itinerant and vagrant all his days. He plays a series of gigs, some more steady than others, all finite, and nothing in his life carries the vaguest hint of stability except death or surrender. If he keeps at it long enough, his hearing begins to go, his liver, even his brain, then good luck, a musician getting old, twenty-six going on sixty, sometimes he can get so frail they can't even sweep him out of the street afterwards. He becomes like a feather, and on a clear day you can see right through him. Page had never seen anything sadder in his life, except maybe in Vietnam, where the children and old men were like shocked and profoundly baffled ghosts. Yet he had refused to let it wrap its skeletal love-and-death arms around him.

That last night at the Riptide Rendezvous things changed. "I don't know if they got better or worse," Page would tell Steve later, "but they sure got different." It wasn't just another lost gig in the long line of lost gigs since Vietnam had coughed Link and Page back into the World. Their last night in Galveston, landmark time.

When Page awoke the following morning, the only thing he could remember about it was Link's hand pulling him away from the microphone and the club manager screaming at him from beneath the stage. Now Link wandered around the living room of their Houston apartment, trying to find his new set of bass strings. Page asked him what had happened.

"Oh, nothin' much." Link pulled the cushions from the sagging couch, searching angrily. "Thirty bucks for new strings, where *are* those suckers?"

"What happened?" Page asked again.

"Fucker said he'd get us." Link looked at Page. "You got on their case about all that Maf shit. You really had 'em going, too."

"Oh, shit." Page ground his knuckles into his eyes. "You think we need some reinforcements?"

"Tits on a bull," Link muttered, opening and closing drawers.

"What else?" Page sat heavily on the disheveled couch, as discouraged and depressed as he could be, yet somehow glad to be out of it, to know he wouldn't have to go back to the Riptide Rendezvous.

"Oh, there was that Melanie chick you met. She caught up to you while I was getting our stuff from the stage and you was out in the Land Yacht humping her when her boyfriend showed up."

"What?"

"Yeah, I just happened to come out there. I think he was fixin' to kill you a little bit, too."

"No shit."

"They was pretty haired off, her boyfriend and two others. Kind of calmed down, though, when I showed 'em my bidness." What Link called his "bidness" was an Ithaca Auto & Burglar, a cut-down 20-gauge shotgun that had been sold in the 1920s for home protection. It was small enough to stick in your waistband.

"I'm really sorry, man." Page hung his head.

"No sweat." Link smiled tolerantly and went to take a shower. Page just sat there looking around the living room. The apartment unit was on Timmons Lane in one of those TraveLodge-style complexes that had been thrown up in ever-expanding fairy rings around Houston as the city grew outward, uncontrolled. Link and Page had shared the furnished apartment for some time now, and it had taken on the character of so many bachelor musician apartments. It had two bedrooms decorated in ascetic motel style, airless and lightless and cluttered. It always smelled of tobacco and grass and stale beer, just like a nightclub. The tangerine rat fur of the rug came out in great hanks, like hair off the head of a chemotherapy victim. The thin Sheetrock walls transmitted sound with remarkable efficiency.

The shades were drawn tight against the hammer heat of the Texas latitudes, shrouding the room in half darkness through which Page made out the litter of ashtrays, dirty dishes, clothing, sheet music, records, toys, manuscript paper, female underclothes, used guitar strings, cigarette papers, magazines, and assorted trash from McDonald's or Church's or pizza places—the musician's C rations. Page knew there was no beating it. It was as if entropy crept in every day at dawn and rattled their world: the second thermodynamic law of Rock and Roll. Page shivered in the air conditioning, slowly coming to the realization that something would have to be done. The same fatigue that had thrown his panic switch last night manifested itself right here in this apartment. How low could a man sink? He didn't even have the inspiration to pick up after himself.

"So what do you want to do now?" Link came in toweling himself dry.

"Start a band," Page said without hesitation.

"Never happen." Link didn't even look up.

"Oh, yes." Page leaned forward. "This time I want to do *my* songs. You and me. We put together a band. We make a demo. We do the entire number, you know, money, fame, satisfaction." Page smiled. "Nookie." Link was not amused. "Come on, we know all the musicians you'd want to know. And they're just pissing it away in clubs, too, hating every minute of it, making shit money . . ." Page trailed off, seeing that Link was ignoring him. "Well, goddamnit, Link, I don't know about you, but I just don't have anything to lose in trying. I've bottomed out." Page went to the little kitchenette and started some water boiling for coffee. He looked back at Link, who met his eyes and laughed.

"We gotta work somewhere," Page offered. "Might as well be our own band."

"Well." Link shrugged. "You know me. I'll try anything."

"All right." Page smiled. "Now who's the best guitar picker in town?" He paused. "Other than me, of course." He knew where his main strength was: that voice, that rangy angel tenor, and those songs he wrote, songs that worked.

"Lotta good guitar pickers in this town," Link said. "Charlie."

"The Country Cowboy." Page nodded. "Beautiful. But not quite what I need."

"There's Cliff," Link offered.

"The Polish Terror. He's certainly right up there. But there's still another sound I've got in mind. . . ." Page rubbed his chin, thinking.

"And then there's . . ." Link hesitated. "I mean, if you're really looking for the *best,* no matter what. You know, Scoop *is* the best."

"Oh fuck oh dear," Page said with genuine regret in his voice.

"The Elusive Missouri Professor of Death? Doctor Scoop? You've got to be kidding. He could screw up a wet dream."

"But he *is* the best guitar picker."

"There's that," Page agreed. He sounded almost sad, as if he could look down the long tunnel, past forming the band, past the disasters and horrors, down the intolerable road to something— something he couldn't put his finger on, like the feeling you get meeting and falling in love with a woman so lovely it hurts to be around her because you know that somewhere along the line it will change, turn and coil back on itself, and end. And all you can do is hope the termination won't be too swift or the payback too brutal. But the sound of the music Page wanted to make—like the face and body of that woman—was too great a temptation.

"There it is," Page said after thinking it over. "I guess if we can work the Riptide Rendezvous, we can work with Scoop again."

"What about horns?" Link asked.

Page shook his head emphatically. "No, no, I know exactly the sound we should have. I'm not goddamned Count Basie, you know. We want a light assault team. Search and Destroy Rock and Roll. Para-Music Insurgency. Mobility is the key. You, me, Scoop, and someone who can play, let's see, woodwinds, keyboards, maybe a little percussion. All rolled into one. We don't want to be hauling eleven guys around."

"You don't ask for much, do you?"

"I have in mind, God help me—" Page laughed and shot his eyes to Link. "I have in mind a name that contains five letters and has been known to instill chronic shakes in teenage chicks and turn level-headed club owners into serious Valium addicts."

"Butch!" Link yelled. "You want to work with Butch again?"

"Gotta admit, the Senator fits the bill."

"Best," Link mused.

"Best damned saxophone player ever fell off a stage." Page remembered the incident, blood on the dance floor, the odd ways saxophones can bend when anesthetized humans fall on top of them from a height of four feet.

Link just nodded.

"There you go then," Page said, as if he'd struck a gavel.

"Drums?" Link asked, but Page could tell he already knew.

"No selection whatsoever."

"What I figured."

"The British Commando." Page laughed hollowly. "Captain Blye. No one else's gonna measure up in this outfit."

"There it is," Link said.

"You better believe it."

They put out feelers and located Butch the next afternoon at the house of a girl who claimed to be nineteen but couldn't have been a day over fifteen. After much cajoling they got him to agree to come over. They were waiting when he blew through the door.

"Anybody can't tapdance is a queer!" Butch shouted as he sashayed into the living room, tiptoeing around the detritus and waving his arms like a vaudeville imitation gone wrong. Though Link and Page were immersed in the task of arranging a song, they both leaped to their feet and began a frantic tapdance. It was an old Special Forces joke.

Tall and lean and broad in the shoulders, Butch sported a full beard and a well-trimmed mane of dark, straight hair. There was a slash of white in his black beard. Its origin was a closely held secret—one night it just happened, and he had never revealed what dark encounter caused it. When he grinned, he showed a perfect set of large, sharp teeth, supplied to him at a reasonable cost after he knocked out his own in the fall from that stage. His tweedy sport coat made him look more like a graduate student than a musician, an illusion betrayed only by the solidly crazed look perpetually on his face and the way his eyes tended to revolve in their sockets with agitated, giddy lunacy. Page called him the Mormon Senator because he came from Salt Lake City and had the bearing of a politician.

Page and Link had met Butch near China Beach where he played in a band. That, as everyone knew, was just a cover job— Butch had picked up his dress habits at Princeton and had spook written all over him. But his preference for music and women and drugs, combined with his lack of interest in the Mission, had easily let him out of that sort of work. He had stayed so consistently stoned and drunk in Vietnam that Link and Page used to laugh and laugh, calling him their only confirmed kill, a real war casualty. In fact, at Da Nang they had arranged for an ambulance to take Butch to and from his gigs, death and rock and roll.

Butch went to the refrigerator to look for something to eat. He came up with a spike-heeled shoe. Page and Link just shook their heads and laughed. Butch settled for a beer. He drank off about half of it and sat heavily on the couch.

"Somebody tried to kill me last night." Butch sighed.

"Put him outta his misery, I hope." Link smiled.

"Nope, was a girl. Attacked me with a full ounce of cocaine in one hand and a quart of rum in the other. Armed to the teeth, she was. Mercifully, I passed out before any serious damage was done." He grinned demonically, thrusting the white streak in his beard at them. "But I'm hurt. Hurt bad." He drank off the rest of the beer and went to get another.

"Yeah," Page said casually, "me and Link took drunk last night, too." Page got up and opened the shades. He had to see at least a sliver of daylight before night fell. He missed the light all the time, but the musician's life-style was hardly geared to sunshine. He looked across the courtyard. The two-story building formed a U around a swimming pool, some sun-scorched grass, and a few mangy palm trees. Page could see one of his neighbors, Cyndi, sitting in a plastic lawn chair by the pool, sunning her magnificent body. He felt a knot of longing form in him and turned from the sight.

"We got fired," Link said.

"Woo-woo!" Butch jumped up, threw his arms out awkwardly, and did a little dance step.

"We're going to start a band," Link added.

"What a novel idea."

"In a way it is," Page said.

"You bet." Butch feigned sincerity. "You bet. I'm sure none of these poor dumb fuckers ever thought of *that* before."

"Scoop's going to play lead guitar, Blye is going to play drums. I'm playing rhythm guitar, writing the songs, singing most of them too. Link here is playing bass. Everybody will sing some, of course. Backup vocals and leads on some songs. And we just thought you might want to be the point man. Saxophones, flutes, keyboards, a little Pre-Cussion, if you know what I mean." Butch's expression changed from one of cynical amusement to one of admiration. And then, after some thought, to one of mild horror.

"You're gonna play with Blye *and* Scoop? At the same time?"

"No, asshole, they're gonna play on Tuesdays and Thursdays

and me and Page're gonna take Mondays and Fridays." Link shook his head in exasperation. "Of course we are."

"How come we called you." Page yawned absently, as if it happened every day. "We're going to cut a demo with them."

"Jesus." Butch went to get another beer. "You're not planning a bank robbery or something?"

"Just music," Page said. "Specifically, Mr. Senator, I'm planning to put together the best damned band in the country and quit fucking around. I don't know how much you dig blowing yourself out at the Astro every night, but I'm goddamned sick of it myself. I'm also partial to money and all that good shit. I'm tired of this mess, too." He waved his hand at the apartment. "So I'm going to get a band together and get a record out. Start making some sound I can live with. Maybe even stop living like a pig." The last words he spoke with such uncharacteristic viciousness that Butch recoiled.

"I'll be freeze-dried," he said.

"You with us?" Link asked.

Butch regarded the two of them. They were serious. He turned to watch the failing, brilliant afternoon and thought about his alleged job. Yes, the Astro Club, folks, an enormous cinderblock hole with a football-field-sized dance floor of Plexiglas squares lit from below with blinking colored lights, where the frenzied masses danced nightly. Butch thought of his club owner, who had the fetching habit of getting paralytic drunk and shooting out the lights. He considered the weariness, the tired old songs, tired old pussy, tired old cowboys, hotter than a two-dollar pistol on a Saturday night. And he saw, yeah, fuck it, he had nothing to lose either. Anyway, what was he going to do with a steady income? Buy butterfly spreads on the silver futures market?

"Well?" Page asked.

"Why not?" Butch said as seriously as he could, but the three of them just laughed.

"We really stepped into it now." Link clapped his hands together.

"Better get Damage Control." Page laughed.

Butch picked up the phone and punched the buttons in a hasty businesslike fashion. "Damage Control!" he shouted. "We need immediate assistance. We're taking on weirdos."

"All right." Page took the phone from Butch. "Now we gotta get Scoop to agree to this thing."

Butch drew his eyebrows into a concerned bramble. "I thought you said you already *had* Scoop."

"Well, shit." Page grinned maliciously. "I had to get *you* to agree to it first."

"Goddamn! Fuckin' con man!" Butch slammed his fist into his thigh, turned to Link, and pointed at Page angrily. "He'd rather climb a tree and lie than stay on the ground and tell the truth."

"It'll be all right." Page dialed. "Scoop'll jump at the chance when he sees what we've got going."

"Yeah," Butch said facetiously. "He'll run like a scalded dog."

"Fuck." Page put down the phone. "No answer."

"Didn't he get sent up for an armed robbery charge?" Butch asked.

"No," Page said. "He got some kind of psychiatric deal where he has to spend Friday and Saturday nights in jail after his gig. I don't know how he worked it, but he just takes a Tuinal and sleeps through it."

"I know where he is." Link rubbed his chin, thinking.

"Where?" Butch asked.

"The Burning Spear."

"Burning Spear, man," Page said as if it were perfectly clear that anyone who would go there had something wrong with him.

"Let's go talk to him, I guess," Link said.

"Rock and Roll." Page sighed.

When Page swung open the apartment door, the hot air was like a physical pressure against his face and chest, as if he had opened the gates of hell. The heat of Houston can waste you in a few hours—definitely stroke country.

"I'll be right along," Page said as they passed near the pool.

"Don't get hung up." Link continued walking toward the parking lot as Butch followed, giggling over his shoulder at the lovely body stretched out on the lounge chair by the pool.

Page approached Cyndi from behind, admiring her hair—it was so black, batwing black, it glowed almost blue in the sun. It fell around her back and shoulders in sharp contrast to her white skin. No matter how much time she spent in the sun she did not tan.

"Not much light left," Page observed. Cyndi looked up from her magazine. She had a small nose and beautiful Italian features. Her lips pursed involuntarily, like a lipstick advertisement.

"Hi, Page," she said with a sleepy smile. "What's going on?"

"Nothing much. I'm forming a new band." He said it as if he did it about that time every afternoon.

"How nice." Cyndi sat forward and stretched luxuriously. As she lifted her knees, Page had a deep yearning to get down and place his head squarely between her legs.

"Are you going to be around later?"

"Yeah." Cyndi yawned, stretched like a cat, and Page had to look away. "Roger's out of town." Page knew that already; her husband was home only on weekends. Cyndi spent weekends assuring him of her iron-clad faithfulness and weeknights screwing her favorite boyfriend—at this point, Page. The marriage had been a youthful mistake and Cyndi had long ago outgrown the man, who would never grow if what Cyndi said was true. Roger's psychotic jealousy rendered him impotent most weekends, which made Cyndi hornier, which made him even more jealous—a complete neurotic circuit.

"I've got to go." Page bit his lip. "I'll be back in a couple of hours."

"Come by." Cyndi swung her feet off the chaise longue and placed them in the withered grass. "We'll eat at my place."

"Sure," Page said, thinking, Anytime, *en-ee-time*. He hurried out to the car, already sweating through his clothes. When he jumped into the shotgun seat of the Cadillac, the icy, metallic breath of air conditioning threw him into a fit of shivering. Page lit a joint.

"Get any?" Butch asked, and the white slash in his beard seemed to give off an evil light.

"Shut up and take your medicine." Page held his breath and handed Butch the little cigarette.

"Whatever you say, Page." Butch inhaled eagerly and passed the joint to Link, who drove with one finger. When they finally stepped into the furnace heat again, they were laughing and joking.

"But first," Butch said as they loped across the crushed-oyster-shell parking lot, "oh, man, we *have* to get something to eat."

"Shit," Page said, but he and Link followed Butch into the 7-Eleven Store fifty yards from the Burning Spear. Butch was overwhelmed by the array of goodies inside.

"Oh, man, let's get some of these pigs' feet."

"Gaa," Page said, holding his throat.

"And potato chips, man." Butch gathered up a large bag in his arms, along with a bottle of pigs' feet that looked like a formaldehyde laboratory demonstration specimen. "And a six-pack."

"Hey, numbnuts, they serve beer in the club." Link took the beer away from Butch and replaced it in the cooler.

"Right, right. . . ." Butch nodded at the profundity of what Link had said.

"How about these cupcakes?" Page taunted.

"Yes, oh, wow." Butch took two packs of cupcakes.

"You like sardines?" Link winked at Page.

"*Sardines, man,* adore them. King Oscar Norwegian sardines in oil. But then we must, absolutely *must* have some crackers." Link and Page just grinned at each other as he filled his arms until he couldn't carry any more. When he dumped it all on the counter the bill came to $11.75, and Butch had to borrow $2 from Link.

Just as they were leaving, a gum-snapping high school girl walked in. She smiled vaguely at them as she drifted down the aisle. Butch did a fast one-eighty and headed off in her direction, his eyes revolving wildly in their sockets. "All right, turdbird." Link got Butch by the arm and spun him back to the door, but Butch's head continued to face in the other direction like an owl's.

The Burning Spear was barely a shack, four walls and not much else. Its front faced Fannin Street near the four-lane underpass that crossed below Holcome Boulevard. It was fitted with a large glass panel that allowed a street view of the back of the stage, presumably so the casual passerby could see the intense action in the club and be drawn to it. In reality, the casual passerby, seeing the dismal, airless hole that it was and the crowd that frequented it, kept right on going.

This afternoon the club was nearly empty. As soon as they entered, the three men saw Scoop sitting at the bar, his skinny body wrapped around a beer like a pterosaur protecting its offspring. Scoop didn't acknowledge their presence when Page ordered three beers. "Shot and a beer for Scoop," Page added, and Scoop finally looked up. He was a weatherbeaten young man with long, hay-colored hair trailing down his back. Obviously of midwestern white-trash origins, he had the look of a slightly rakish, mildly deranged ferret. When he heard Page place the order for him he began to smile. When he saw Link, his smile widened, revealing a jagged escarpment of discolored teeth. When he saw Butch, the smile vanished and he said with a gasp, "Get thee behind me, Satan." Before anyone could react, Scoop was up and out the door.

"Scoop," the bartender whined ineffectually, "cain't nobody here have carry-outs." Page was quick and caught him in the parking lot.

"Unhand me!" Scoop tried to wriggle out of Page's grip and spilled beer on both of them, his eyes glowing like those of a proto-madman dredged up from some medieval dungeon.

"Cut it out, Scoop, I just want to talk."

"Not in the presence of that, that . . ." Words failed him.

Page sighed and looked off across the street in frustration. He brushed at the beer Scoop had spilled down the front of his shirt and began again. "How would you like a garbage bag full of cocaine?" Scoop nodded vigorously. "And how about hordes of insatiable teenage chicks clawing at you?" Scoop nodded even more emphatically and showed his yellowed teeth. "And how would you like to live in a great, huge pad with servants and limousines and avoid honest work for the rest of your life?"

Scoop's smile disappeared and he leveled a suspicious glare at Page.

"I smell a rat," he said. "A largish rat. A capybara even."

"Come inside," Page urged. "Butch is under our control." At first Scoop resisted, but his glass was empty and the afternoon was hot. Page finally seduced him back into the club.

"Now just keep your mouth shut, Butch," Page said as they entered the Burning Spear. He got Scoop settled on a barstool with his shot and a fresh beer and patiently explained what they had in mind. He asked Scoop if he wanted to waste away in this black rat's nest, and Scoop again nodded enthusiastically: Yes, he thought that was as good a way to waste away as any. Page argued that he was assembling the best musicians on the whole Gulf Coast to become stars, to be freed. But Scoop's considered opinion was that Page was full of shit.

"Allow me to die in peace," he said. It had been his attitude ever since he had finally gotten out of the joint. Before going to prison, Scoop had been a rather well-respected professor of music at the university. He had been put in a Missouri prison on a bogus morals charge by one of his students. He'd given her failing grades and she turned the heat on him as revenge. The sentence was light, but once inside he was uncontrollable and kept getting his term extended until at last he went into a kind of catatonia.

Now he was considered unemployable and was subject to wild fluctuations of mood ranging from paralysis to mad, aberrant behavior and oration. But despite his drug and alcohol binges, he still played some of the most beautiful, moving guitar around. Up and down the intercoastal towns of Texas and Louisiana he was in demand. However, when a man from Lake Charles had come out to the club to offer him double his salary, Scoop had shrugged and turned him down in order to stay at the Burning Spear. And now he repeated his only known ambition in life: "Let me die in peace."

"No, we won't," Page insisted. "I don't so much give a shit what you do, but we need your guitar playing."

Link chimed in, wheedled and cajoled, begged and threatened, but Scoop held firm. He had what he wanted, his little obscure club, his draft beer, the other guitar player, Sonny—he didn't want to make a vain attempt at stardom only to be disappointed when he ended up back at the Burning Spear anyway. Why bother?

So by the time Link, Butch, and Page walked out of the club, there was already a crack in the plan. "So there's your famous band," Butch said. Page ignored him, his mind working as they got into the Cadillac and rode slowly back to the apartment. "Well," Butch taunted, "what're you gonna do now?"

"Shut up, Butch," Link said, wheeling the car around with his little finger. He didn't have to say any more. Butch knew Link well enough to listen when he spoke in that special tone of voice. He knew where Link came from, knew Link was the kind of person who got what he wanted. In Vietnam, where helmet and flak jacket graffiti were raised to an art, Link had carefully lettered across his helmet cover BY ALL MEANS. It was all he needed.

At one point Link had wanted that Cadillac so much he and some old boys went out and lobbed a brick through the window of a 7-Eleven Store. They took the check-writing machine used for money orders, then broke into a factory office to steal blank checks. They spent all day one Friday cashing them. Link got the Cadillac outright and put the down payment on the big television set in his bedroom. And he quit. The others weren't quite as smart and continued hanging paper until they were caught. Butch knew that story—hell, everybody in town knew, the big joke was to offer someone a check and then tell them it was OK, Link would cosign for it.

Now, as they rode along, even Butch could see that if Link and Page wanted it badly enough, they would get Scoop.

"All right, all right," Butch gave in. "We'll get Scoop. But how?"

"Let's get Blye," Page said firmly. "Get Blye and the four of us'll get Scoop. He'll come because, whatever else he is, he's a musician. And we'll be the only game in town." He paused for a beat. "Besides, we've *got* to have him."

As the three men entered the apartment complex, still discussing tactics, they didn't notice the tan Chevrolet parked outside in the failing light. The two nondescript men who sat in the front seat watched the musicians file past and then drove off.

$$\bowtie 4 \bowtie$$

Page and his friends referred to his place in Michigan as the Ranch, even though it was not really an operation but a residence. The locals had turned up their noses when they first heard that, testily asking, "What exactly is it you raise on your *ranch?*" and giving the word a particularly odious inflection. Page had just smiled and said, "A ruckus."

The afternoon Steve arrived Page's "ranch hand," Red, had come back with three grouse and was now preparing to stuff and cook them for dinner. Page and Steve were still talking out in the living room. A ragged line of empty beer bottles stood on the bar. The smoke from Page's cigarettes hung in the air, shot through with the running sunlight lances like a three-dimensional Cartesian graph.

"You really ought to call Butch back and get him out here," Steve was saying. "I'd like to see him."

"Oh, I might," Page mused. "It'd be all right. I haven't seen him since that last concert tour fell apart." Fell apart! Blew up in his face was more like it.

A few months earlier, just as the news of his quitting was break-ing in the press, some reporter had managed—in spite of the tight security Page had insisted surround him—to get in close enough to ask him one question: the boy had shoved a microphone into Page's face and blurted out, "Looking back over your short but brilliant career, do you have any regrets?" Page had just looked at the boy as if he were stark raving mad, then got into his limo. Regrets? Does the sea have fishes? Sky have stars? Star have regrets? Man, that is one ill-informed reporter.

And now, when he spoke to Steve about it all, he spoke with a measured consideration, as if thinking it through for the first time, as if he were merely offering possible theories of what it had all been about.

"I've got to have something to cut this ethanol," Steve said, taking a phial from his vest. "Want some?"

Page shook his head. "Can't do it no more, Coach."

"Got any whiskey?" Steve asked, needing something stronger than beer to compete with the mighty powder he was about to take. Page went to the bar and got a bottle of George Dickel bourbon and a beer. He set the bourbon beside Steve, who shrugged and fired a spoonful of white powder into his nose. Page watched, thinking back on the mad cycle he had gone through too: some Bolivian to cut the alcohol, some alcohol to cut the Bolivian, Methaqualone to cut the Bolivian, Bolivian to cut the Quāaludes, Biphetamine to cut the Ludes, and on and on until you didn't know whether to shit or go blind. But Page just watched his little brother and shrugged. There was only one way to learn anything important: you had to go through it.

"You know," Page mused, "in the end I probably just ran out of what we used to call the Jesus Factor."

Steve rubbed his nose and made a face. "Meaning?"

"Well, it's just an expression." Page placed his feet on the table, tilted the beer to his lips. "When me and Link were going out on our first Lurps missions, this old officer gave us a little talk. A kind of final warning, you know—five men ride out and only four ride back. And when he'd said everything he could think of, he went, 'And then there's the Jesus Factor. And each man will know how to handle that one himself. It comes *real* natural.'"

"That's real clear."

"Look," Page said, "guys over there would sometimes just know when they or one of their buddies had run out. You'd get that feeling—you'd look at some grunt and say, 'That boy has run smooth out of that Jesus Factor.' Race-car drivers have told me the same thing. Then it's just a matter of time before you walk into it. Step on a mine or be walking point when it comes down, slide into the wrong tunnel—" Page paused, thinking. "Shit, you could run across an airstrip, one of those nifty little VC one-twenty-two rockets comes whistling in. All she wrote, no more Jesus Factor for that one." Page looked at Steve, narrowed his eyes to slits to see if the boy understood.

Steve was just old enough to have had a whiff of the Vietnam War and just young enough so he wasn't quite sure what it had been all about.

"I remember this guy here." Page rolled his head back against the chair. "He was an older guy who had *seen* it, the A Shau Valley, Ia Drang, Khe Sanh, Hill Eight Seven Five near Dak To, you name it. Then one day we stepped into it and only two of us survived, me and him. I never knew dirt tasted so good." Page laughed, but it wasn't funny. "I must have eaten four, five pounds that day."

Page stopped talking. Steve watched him, not sure whether or not to say anything because Page had never talked about Vietnam before. Steve had asked right after Page came back but had gotten nothing; now Page was telling stories Steve had always wanted to hear.

"Well, that was the day Deke's ran out—that was his name, Deke." Page sat forward. "I could smell it on him. I could *see* it, feel it. And sure enough, about two weeks later Deke took it from a Claymore."

"What's that?" Steve asked.

"Check it out." Page pointed to a framed poster on the far wall. Steve got up to look at it. It said, "FOR OFFICIAL INTERNAL USE ONLY, Circular Four, military explosive materials department of the treasury united states secret service" and showed a wide range of destructive devices, including the Claymore, which looked like a gray, rectangular plumbing fixture fitted with spike legs so that it could be stuck into the ground. On the face of the device were letters in bas-relief that said, FRONT TOWARD ENEMY. The caption read, "Claymore M18A1: This rectangular, fiber glass, curved mine is the most effective directional fragmentation anti-personnel land mine in use today. The fragmentation material of the mine consists of 700 steel ball bearings imbedded in a plastic matrix of explosives. These fragments are effective in producing casualties up to a range of approximately 325 feet."

"Shit," Steve said, coming back to the couch.

"The charge goes off," Page continued, "and those bearings actually melt, spitting out at supersonic speeds. It's like getting tied over the muzzle of a cannon loaded with grapeshot. So, occasionally"—he sighed—"the gooks would sneak up on your position, real quiet, through the wire and all that, and turn the Claymores around to face you. So that when they attacked, you'd fire those fuckers and blow yourself away." He paused. "Well, that's what happened to Deke. Fired the thing himself. When I got up there, I thought a whole damned fireteam had taken a hit. But it was just Deke. Deke was all over the place that day."

Page watched Steve swallow hard and thought, Well, might as well tell him something since he came all the way out here. Steve had just missed a time in the 1960s when the war was everywhere. America was insane with war, giddy and high and out of control on it, like some grim new drug. And as with rock and roll, no one could ever agree when it started (there was no Alan Freed of Vietnam). But you could take the mid-fifties and at least have a conversation, Dienbienphu and Rock Around the Clock, Viet Minh and the Crickets. "You know my heart does nothin' but burn! Cryin'!" You didn't have to be Marshall McLuhan to put two and two together and come up with cut time. Shout Bamalama! Rock and Roll!

A mere decade later, kids like Page were crossing the great ocean to put in time as our western defense long-ball hitters, Mondo Recondo, "slippin'-and a-slidin' peepin' and a-hidin'" out into the tree line, painted up like psychotic Fellini episodes, sleuthing alongside the very enemy himself, Victor Charles, Long Range Reconnaissance Patrols, Lurps, Recon meaning anything from a look-see to assassination to full-scale pitched battles or taking someone home for dinner. (Try touching your elbows together behind your back, VC prisoners did it all the time, clever those gooks.)

One niner six eight, the big one. Martin Luther King and black power at the Olympics, Bobby Kennedy and Chicago police riots, the *Pueblo*, Khe Sanh, Quang Tri, Ton Son Nhut, blood on the highway, blood on the sheets. Mickey Mouse turned forty and all of America was chewed over and partly digested by war, over *there* and right here at home, burn down the Mission! "Raaape! Murder! It's just a kiss away. It's just a shot away." War in the country, war in the streets, war in the air, war underground, riverine mobile war—oh, yes, and war on the frigging radio— "Pleased to meet you, hope you guess my name!" The entire country sustained a full-scale conniption over it, and the only difference was that one war was rocket-powered, the other rock-powered. Either way, you were swallowed up by swale and paddy, drugs and combat cosmetics. Busted flat in Muong Phalane or Baton Rouge, just like Roger Miller or Kris Kristofferson or Janis Joplin said it. Page and Link practically busted a gut the first time they heard "Which Side Are You On?" Which side? What the fuck difference does it make? Man, that's beautiful. Which Side Are You *On?*

Page had been drafted and did not resist ("She didn't bat an eye as I packed my bags to leave"—Tyrone Davis didn't miss a trick), but went straight as you could into Special Forces, United States Army, Fourth Division, and then it was Lurps ("Might as well get my feet wet"). They could come from anywhere, Lurps—generally in small denominations, five men at best—marine, army, irregular as hell sometimes. God knew where they got them—motorcycle renegades, absolute religious killers in some cases, farther out on death than Page would ever be on drugs or sex or even music, the genuine article. But they were always legendary meta-killers and absolute survival freaks. Their training was not only secret but actually something straight out of Greek mythology: The Test of Seven Fires, Road of Ice, The Thousand Deaths of Boredom, The Monkeys Invade the Heavenly Palace—nothing was spared in making these boys comprehend that the game was played for sure, for real, for keeps, and far out, they played it that way from Basic on. There was also nothing that could erase where they had come from: It's all right, Ma, I'm only bleeding. They were WWII baby-boom material: Rock and Roll Death Freaks.

Page certainly never forgot. Sometimes, locked to the ground within shitting distance of a platoon of NVA regulars, he would smile and think, It's all the same, a hot wash of enkephalins, stoned on his own natural juices, comatose and ready for anything, trance-panic cool. And then the music would come rolling in: "You can take a little walk down in the park / Steal a little kiss, baby, while in the dark / Don't let your head get wet! Oh, with the Midnight dew, now / In the Danger Zone! Oh, Yeah!" *What a fucking goof!*

He and Link were on the same fireteam and their key to success (success meaning you come out alive) was to be as the very earth itself. The enemy could walk on you and never know it—just like the flower children back home, passive resistance, Tai Chi Chuan, eternally yielding, nonexistent and therefore indefatigable.

Once Page lay on the rain-forest floor near a small group of Viet Cong, and one of the enemy soldiers walked over to his perimeter and threw a small pan of oil on him from a distance of a few meters. It was warm. Page didn't move, didn't even think about breathing. Link was right behind him. They slithered away after a while, the music pounding in Page's brain. It went something like this: "Yeaaaaaahhhhh, been searchin'. I got searchin'. Searchin' every whee-eee-eeech-a-way. . . . But I'm like that Northwest Mounty: You know I'll bring her in some day. Now if I have to swim a river, you know I will. And if I have to climb a mountain, you know I will."

No, rock and roll wasn't the first time Page and Link had been superstars. They had been two of the finest killers over there. And no matter how many times they went out, they just couldn't get over it. They would laugh and drink all night sometimes, just digging it. "Did you see the look on that Gook's *face*, man?" But the laughter wasn't what you'd call laughter unless you'd been there first.

Sometimes at dawn, after a patrol, the music would go more like, "Forget the dead you've left, they will not follow you." Poor Dylan. He didn't know shit about it. Finally Page had to evolve his own brand of music, and when it all shook down there was precious little war imagery left in it. That had been boiled off to the crystal distillation of joy and fear. War to Page was no metaphor. It was the thing itself, everything else just resembled it a little, the same way everything else can sometimes resemble sex. And anyway, Page got off lucky.

He came back in a bad head, sure, but others weren't so lucky, some never returned at all. Others blew their minds in the first, primal sense of that expression. After all, Vietnam was the adolescence of Rock and Roll, the point where it passed childhood and started to grow hair and get ugly and uncontrollable—it was the realized intensity promised years earlier; they were right, our parents, who told us not to listen to that music, it *was* evil, it made us kill.

Anyway, no musician who went over there could ignore it, that sound intruded on the war so much that while the shooting was a relief from music on this side, the music was a relief from the shooting over there. Years later, at the height of Page's rock and roll career, someone named George W. S. Trow, Jr., would put it into a context of sorts, at least for Jagger (Hendrix had his own context, his own metaphor, he was a believer, certified with a tag on his toe): "Jagger's 'demonic' persona was not enhanced by the death at Altamont. . . . The lesson of Altamont was that Jagger was a performer in need of crowd control." Which could have been said about Westmoreland, too, if anyone had been interested in getting down to basics.

The words of the songs were just too damned close to home for anyone to miss it. Even Dylan got in his licks: "There must be someway out of here, said the joker to the thief." And those words only encouraged the sense of irony that already surrounded the war. Once after a long, serious engagement Page heard Bobby Gentry sing, "And now Billy Joe McAllister's jumped off the Tallahatchee Bridge." And he bounced off the walls, screaming, "Yes, yes, man, of *course* he did if he saw what *I* saw last night," while Link just leaned up against the wall of the hooch with a thumbnail of Double U-Oglobe, chuckling hollowly at his little buddy.

Page always heard a metaphysical saxophone player behind the whole thing, riffing to machine-gun fire. Everyone but the generals heard it, and of course they had never heard a saxophone anyway. But there wasn't a swinging dick who'd ever witnessed an F-4 (standing with another Lurp, watching one of those fighters unleash its fury against a field of light, Page had heard this choice one: "Do you realize that's the last sight a lot of good farmers ever see?") or a four-deuce or—God help us—Puff the Magic Dragon who couldn't hear the music. Besides, so much of the war came to you over the radio: the sky was full of death and radio waves. You could hear anything you wanted if you just clipped the antenna right: "Dance Base! Oh, God, Come in, we have forty percent casualties, Oh, Jesus, Dance Base, *Please* come in, man!" And lightly over the airwaves some lieutenant comes on singing, "Same-

same, we lost half a company, Medallion, we copy Lucky Chicken, *hold on I'm comin'!*"

When Page and Link came back into the World, they knew only one thing, they'd have to go some distance to follow that act. There was nothing political about it, the killing may have been interesting but they were tired of it. They wanted to rock and roll. They were through with that war, ready for the next.

Page stopped and regarded Steve. From the look on his face Page thought maybe he'd gotten something across. Page started to go on but Red appeared in the doorway, wiping his hands on a towel.

"Got some bird on the table," he said.

They ate in the kitchen. The flesh of the grouse was moist and delicate, stuffed with rice and nuts and raisins. It had the slightest taste of mint to it. Steve was quiet during the meal. When Red started clearing the dishes, Steve took a plastic bag from his shirt pocket and rolled a slim joint.

"How about a little after-dinner jam?" Steve asked.

"Naw." Page ducked his head modestly. "I'm full."

"I'll sing, you play guitar." Steve got up. "Come on, man, let's just do some old shit like we used to."

"I really don't know. Why don't you play one of your songs. You're the one wants to be the star."

"All right," Steve said, and they went back into the living room. Although his instrument was the bass, Steve also played piano and guitar, as did Page. Steve sat at the concert grand and began working his way up in long, flowing chords.

"You been practicing that piano."

Steve looked over his shoulder and smiled. When he began to sing, it blew Page's mind. It sounded exactly like Page's own voice. He hadn't heard Steve sing for quite a while, and his voice had mellowed and grown hair. He sang a slow-burn ballad, "Close your eyes now, it seems like I'm winning, I won't even ask where you've been." When Steve finished, Page was sitting down.

"Rock and Roll," Page whispered softly. "That is definitely all right."

"So why don't we do a number together, just for old time's sake?" Steve asked.

"Naw." Page lowered his head again. "Maybe later."

"Whatever you say." Steve sighed and turned around on the

piano stool to face his brother. He started to ask a question, but the phone rang.

"Now who the fuck could that be?" Page got up. "I haven't had this many phone calls in a year." When he picked up the receiver, he frowned, then smiled. "Shit oh dear, I thought you were supposed to be in a prison on Ibiza or something. Haven't you drowned yourself yet?" Page strained to listen. "What? We've got an awful connection. Where are you?" Page listened again and then said, "I'm fine, just fine." When he got off he turned to Steve. "That's just too much coincidence for me. That was Blye, man, calling from the radiophone on his boat."

"The Lord works in strange ways," Steve said. Then there was an uneasy silence during which Steve wouldn't meet Page's eyes. But before Page could go on, Steve maneuvered him back on the track.

"So what's all this stuff about the Mafia before you hooked up with Perry?" Steve asked.

"I suppose I should have had you around more often," Page said. Even before Jambeaux made it big, he had rarely seen Steve. After all, when Page was twenty-five, Steve was only fourteen. Now it was going to be harder than ever to explain. "You should have seen some of the types we ran into. Just think of all the possibilities there are for criminal activity in the music business. The cash. The liquor. The drugs. Records have to be shipped by trucks—Teamsters and their lot. The musicians themselves, half the time worse criminals than anyone ever realized. I mean, Christ, Las Vegas. The whole shot. So ultimately, when I cut loose that night, I touched some raw nerves."

"So how come nobody found you floating in the ship channel?"

"Me and Link had a reputation, you know. Coming from where we did. People thought we were pretty bad dudes. I don't know, maybe we were. Anyway, I guess they thought just threatening us a little would take care of it. They just weren't good enough to pull it off."

◄ 5 ►

The evening Page returned to Timmons Lane from the Burning Spear, after Scoop had refused to play with them, Page was ready for anything to take his mind off it. The day had been so brutally hot that the first thing he wanted was to swim a few laps. Cyndi was still sitting by the pool as the sun went down. She watched Page step from the apartment, carrying a ratty-looking towel. Although Page was only five ten, he gave an impression of potential energy. There was an almost simian power in the flat plates of muscle that seemed to hold his body and move it in a slow, indomitable dance. His tan skin and high cheekbones confused people about his origins—Greek? Italian? French?—and the implied power there would generally keep people from suggesting the truth: half-breed. To Cyndi he was a statue, some Michelangelo invention come to life, and she didn't care what they called it.

Page dove, making a flat explosion on the water's surface, and swam steadily for fifteen minutes without acknowledging Cyndi's presence. When he was done, he sat on the edge of the pool and dried his hair with the towel.

"How'd it go?" Cyndi asked.

Page sat staring at the ragged, purple scar on his wrist. He fingered it and shrugged. "I was trying to get Scoop to join up with us but you know how he is."

"Want me to talk to him?" Cyndi asked, getting up.

"Not yet, anyway." Page got up as well. "I'll meet you over at your place."

An hour and a half later, Page and Cyndi had rushed through their dinner and into bed. In the flickering candlelight of the bedroom, they went after it with a fiery determination. And just as Page was easing in out of the cold, the shrill metallic bell of the telephone jolted him like a cattle prod. Cyndi got it on the second ring, listened briefly, and handed the receiver to Page. "Link," she said.

Page took the phone angrily, but Link spoke before he could say anything. "Sorry, really man, but you better get over here right away."

"Goddamnit—"

"No, seriously, right now." Page could tell by the tone of Link's voice that it was no practical joke. He told Link he'd be right along and began to get dressed. "Sorry, honey," he said to Cyndi, who clutched the covers to her neck and didn't bother to ask.

Page hurried out into the hot night, taking the stairs up to the apartment two at a time. When he entered, he saw the two men in suits and recognized them immediately. At the club he had thought they were from the D.A.'s office in Austin, and now he knew how wrong he had been. You could just tell by the look of them.

What have I done? he thought. My music, my sound, my band. It will never happen, we can go around and around on this great wheel of violence and we can do anything we like to put it together, but it will never ever happen. He stood there shaking his head, sadder and more discouraged than he could remember being. And then another thought: he had also gotten Link into it. He had better not collapse on this one. There was no telling what these two were planning to do. Stop feeling sorry for yourself, he thought, you'd better do something before they do. You'll have plenty of time for despair later. Lock and load.

"Siddown," one of the men said.

Page looked around, forcing his throat open. Butch was missing. Page merely noted it and looked at Link, who shrugged. Page had seen that shrug before and he knew what it meant. Give me strength, he thought, perhaps we will kill some gangsters tonight. He sat down on the far right-hand side of the couch, putting his hand by his right thigh. The one who spoke continued while the other just stood there like a refrigerator. It was obvious that they were both wearing guns.

"There are some people who are very, very upset," the man began. He wasn't from Houston, Page could tell that by his accent —or lack of it. Just like in the movies, Page thought, letting his hand move an inch, then another inch. "Some of them have even suggested that you guys are in big, big trouble. Do you understand what I mean?" Page nodded slowly, said nothing. He moved his hand another inch. The man stepped up closer to Page and his backup followed, standing beside him. Both men now had their backs to the bedroom door. Page's hand stayed still. "I'm going to tell you this once, all right? Saturday night two busts came down and some people think it was your fault. You named names. People don't name names and stay around for long. You're playing with serious people. They don't think you're funny." The man paused to let that sink in. Page kept his eyes down, now, not wanting to look. Link was poised, ready. When Butch tapped the barrel of the shotgun on the man's shoulder, he spun so suddenly that he cracked his nose against the muzzle. His partner began to withdraw his revolver.

"Go for it, motherfucker," Butch said softly, grinning at them. "Please, go for it, because I'll put you all over that wall when you do."

The gunman relaxed his grip and slowly put his hands out in front of him. The talker just stood there, frozen. Page slid his hand beneath the cushion, brought out the .45 that was hidden there, and stood up. He carefully, almost gently, pressed it into the talker's ear, released the thumb safety, and drew back the wide-spur hammer. The clicks it made were tremendously loud. The man squirmed.

"Down on the floor," Page said softly. "Real slowly, please."

The man knelt and then lay on his stomach. The gunman did the same under Butch's shotgun. Link now had his Ithaca out and held it over them.

"Who thinks I'm not funny?" Page asked. When they said nothing he jammed the barrel farther into the man's ear and ground it, leaning his weight with the motion, drawing blood. "Who thinks I'm not funny?"

"Younger," the man said.

"Get 'em in the car," Page said to Link and Butch.

"What're you gonna do?" the gunman asked.

"What the fuck do you think we're gonna do?" Link asked.

By the time they reached the beach, the two gangsters were practically hysterical. But Page and Link simply forced them to undress and turned them loose on the beach.

Back at the apartment, Page began to realize that they were going to have to put some distance between themselves and these new enemies they had made. It was time to get down to it, to get out of town. Ideally to get real famous, Page explained to Butch and Link, nothing like a little spotlight illumination to keep the wolves away.

"Oh," Link said after a while, "I forgot to tell you. Blye's in London."

"London!" Page practically blew his drink all over the room. "He can't be in London. We've got to rehearse."

"Well, he is." Link took the joint Butch passed and handed him a bottle of Mescal. He puffed thoughtfully. "While you were ventilating Cyndi, I was on the hot line. Blye is in London."

"Well, goddamnit," Page began but said nothing else.

"Lure him." Butch smiled.

"Huh?"

"Cheese for the mouse," Butch said. "Temptation for the weak."

"Olfactory senses receiving hints of plot." Page leaned forward, his mood lifting slightly. "Go on, go on."

"What is it the British Commando would sell his grandmother up the river for?" Butch asked grandly.

"Indochinese Death Trip," Page offered. "Turkish Analgesic."

"That's a roger," Link said.

"There's your cheese." Butch shrugged as if it were settled.

Page nodded his head and pursed his lips with a sense of finality. He took the bottle from Butch and drank from it.

"You just keep thinkin', Butch," he said. "That's what you're good at."

Butch was so pleased with his plan of action that he forgot about their troubles and tapdanced out of the apartment to go find one of the hundreds of teenage chicks he knew—off on the kooze trail once more.

Later, Link and Page, still celebrating their freedom from work, wound up at the Burning Spear. "Scene of the crime," Page called it. They listened to Scoop and Sonny put out a sound lean and fine-honed enough to break your heart and make you want to start all over at square one. At the break, Scoop hunched toward the bar like a great crippled condor. When he was about twenty feet away, he spotted Page and Link. He made an expression of mock horror. It was late enough in the evening that he was already drunk, and therefore easier to get along with.

"Egads!" he shouted. "Two bone-worthless ridge runners who appear to be blowed outta their collective mind on dangerous chemicals and ethanol! Come to search and destroy in my very place of business." He took up a stool next to Page with great fanfare and ceremony and watched wide-eyed as Link chuckled soundlessly. Looking at him now, Page realized his mistake in having approached him in the afternoon when he was almost sober.

"Found us out," Page agreed.

"And bein' it please yer Lordship." Scoop began a fair imitation of Robert Newton doing Long John Silver, screwing up his countenance and feigning a bad left eye. "What might yer be holdin' this fine evenin'?"

"Had the honor of a visit from the Peruvian Consulate." Page winked mightily, dipping a finger into his vest. "Bein' it please *yer* Lordship."

Scoop raised his eyebrows and his eyes fixed on the little phial in Page's hand. "Indeed, indeed. I'll be havin' a small sample o' yer wares, your Royal Highness."

"Knock your dick in the dirt, Coach." Page slipped the bottle into Scoop's palm, indicating the restroom with his chin. "Just make sure you come back."

"Hey, man," Link protested after Scoop disappeared, "he'll go and blow the whole fucking thing in there."

"You got to pay the cost to be the boss," Page allowed. "We *need* that fucker."

"Shit." Link went back to his beer. "Old Deep Nose there'll put us in the poorhouse."

"Not to worry, Coach." Page patted Link on the shoulder. "I'm softening him up for the kill."

Before Link could go on with his objections, Page looked up to see a real Dickensian apparition—a rail-thin, almost emaciated man as pink as a newborn rat crossing the floor toward them with a vague, dreamy smile. A truly startling cascade of lightning-white hair hung to his shoulders, and he wore dark glasses. Sonny was albino. Sonny was a very good guitar player. Sonny was also a wonderful singer. But most of all, Sonny was a freak supreme. Page and Link loved Sonny a great deal; he was vulnerable and kind and gentle, one of the few musicians Page knew who was any of those things. He loved people and blues and dancing. But most of all, he loved pussy and drugs.

"How it *is?*" Sonny pulled himself up onto the stool next to Page, and the bartender served him a bourbon with a 7-Up back, which was what Sonny drank all night every night. Sometimes he would treat himself to a bottle of Romilar CF cough syrup, a habit few people could understand since all it does is make one crawl around on all fours for three or four hours, unable to speak or see.

"We sneakin' by." Page placed a hand on Sonny's shoulder, gently.

"Sonny," was all Link said, but he touched the word with such unguarded tenderness that he didn't need to say anything else.

"Heard you're getting a new band together," Sonny said. His head moved constantly, the way a blind person's does.

"Tryin'," Page said. "Want a little Peruvian Brutal?"

"Oh, man!" Sonny exclaimed, flushing even pinker than normal, visibly agitated. Sometimes he could work himself up to the point where it appeared he might disintegrate from sheer excitement. As his head wobbled, a spotlight caught Sonny's sunglasses and produced sharp explosions of light. "Oh, *man!*" he said again.

"Guess he does." Link laughed, enjoying Sonny's unbridled enthusiasm.

"Man!" Sonny said and hugged himself in ecstasy. He pulled off his dark glasses and squinted around the club. Without the glasses he was blind, even in the dim light.

Scoop returned and hop-skipped around the group. He slapped Sonny on the arms and shoulders and Sonny's long, pink fingers went up to protect his face. Scoop laughed. "Peruvian *Dreamfuck,* Sonny," he taunted.

"Gimme, gimme." Sonny giggled as Scoop continued to torment him before finally giving him the phial. Sonny unfolded his immaculate, emaciated form like some rare snowbird. With great grace and care, he loped slowly across the dance floor toward the restroom. A few minutes later he emerged even pinker than before. His sunglasses were back in place and produced slow detonations of light across the distance to the bar. Sonny passed by the stage and grabbed his Stratocaster from its stand. Then he ambled back to the bar and climbed up onto his stool.

His pink fingers opened and closed hypnotically as if he were consciously trying to make a special, complex pattern in the air, a pattern he couldn't quite get right. Then his hands floated to the guitar and began playing soundlessly, his fingers disappearing in a blur of crimson activity. Suddenly, an expression of surprise crossed his face and he grabbed his head as if it were going to explode. "Oh, man!" he said. "What *is* that shit?"

"Moche Mystery." Page smiled. "Four-thousand-year-old mystery." Page watched Sonny try unsuccessfully to contain himself and couldn't help smiling at him, shaking his head. Everyone loved Sonny. Whatever shit was coming down, Page always felt better when he saw Sonny. Sonny just enjoyed his life so much.

"Oh, man!" Sonny was still holding his head, rocking back and forth, Parkinson-like. "Oh, *man!* That's almost as good as *pussy!*"

"Hey, Sonny." The bartender shook his shoulder. "Phone." The man offered him the handset and Sonny finally came out of it.

Page and Link watched him nod and listen. His smile vanished. "Hey, come on, man," he said in an irritated tone. He listened again, holding the phone away from his ear for a second as if the noise was painful.

"Hey, man," Sonny said, "don't fuck with my head. Who *are* you?" There was a pause and then his voice turned very snide. "Yeah, and I'm a Chinese Aviator," he said and hung up.

"Who was that?" Link asked.

"Some joker." Sonny shook off the ill feeling. "Said he was Phil Shorter from New York City and wanted to fly me out there so he can *manage* me." Sonny said the word as if the man had offered to sodomize him. Then Sonny looked very seriously at Link and said, "That really frosts my ass. Now, why would anybody pull that shit on me?"

"Maybe it was him," Page suggested. He had heard of Phil Shorter and he knew that up and down the Coast Sonny was a legend. *Rolling Stone* had even written about him. He had cut some local records and people loved them, but, like Scoop, he preferred the obscurity of the Burning Spear.

"Shit." Sonny dismissed the notion, rubbed his hands together, and, like magic, was back in his fine mood, hard to keep a stoned man down. He picked up his guitar and his fingers flashed over it once more.

"Sonny." It was the bartender again. "Same fella wants to talk to you again." Sonny squinted at him to make sure he was hearing right. He looked to Page for confirmation and Page just shrugged. Sonny took the phone greedily.

"Hey, listen, man." His voice had a keen edge to it. "I don't know who you are but I don't like this kind of joke, all right? I mean, I don't know what's in this for you, but I wish you'd just blow it off." There was another pause while he listened. "Hey, no offense, man, but fuck you." Sonny slammed down the phone. "Goddamn!" He sounded almost sad now, though he was grinning and shaking his snowy locks in such a childlike way that Page could only laugh. Sonny, his concentration shot now, went to the stage to put his guitar back in its stand.

"You think that really was Phil Shorter?" Link asked.

"*Some*body oughta get Sonny recording," Page said with a shrug. "Somebody will, sooner or later."

"How come we don't try to get Sonny to come on with us, then, if Scoop won't come?" Link suggested.

"You kiddin'?" Page shook his head. "No way. First, Sonny's worse about this fuckin' place than Scoop. Second, he's a blues guitar player. Don't get me wrong, he's among the best. But it's, you know, Muddy Waters stuff, slide guitar, Robert Johnson. It's not the sound we need. What we need is that man there." Page pointed now to Scoop, who was lurching across the dance floor. Page watched him with a weary, resigned expression on his face, thinking, Yeah, sure, that's what we need, that human wreck who only happens to play guitar just the exact, perfect right way we need it played. And Page stopped in mid-thought, snapping his fingers. He turned to Link. "That *was* Phil Shorter," he said softly.

"Say again?" Link cocked his head to one side.

"It *was*, it was Phil Shorter on the phone. I know it. And I know just exactly how to get Scoop away from here."

"How?" Link looked at Page suspiciously.

"I'm going to call Shorter and tell him the only way he's going to get Sonny to believe it's him is to come out here and give Sonny a plane ticket and take him away. Otherwise, Sonny'll just keep thinking it's one of his friends playing a joke on him."

"You don't want to do that," Link said. "They take Sonny out of here, they'll chew him over in a month's time. They'll ruin him, lookit him." Link pointed over to the stage where Sonny was getting up to play again. He looked like a schematic, translucent angel.

Scoop came up just then to get his beer before the next set. When he saw Link watching Sonny, he jabbed him in the ribs. "Lookit him. Isn't he bee-yoo-tee-ful, man? *Look* at him." Then Scoop danced off to the stage and Sonny began singing.

"See," Page said, "as long as Sonny's here, we'll never get Scoop away from him. Scoop is fucking in love with him."

"But you know what'll happen if you call Shorter and he really comes out here and takes Sonny away." Link stopped and looked at Page and saw that it was no use trying to talk him out of it. "Well," Link said, "don't say I didn't tell you."

"Hey, Ritchie," Page called for the bartender.

" 'Nother drink?" Ritchie asked.

"No, you got that guy's phone number Sonny was talking to?" Ritchie handed him a piece of paper, then the telephone. As Page dialed he watched Link.

"You fuck," Link said, only half smiling. "You low-life fuck."

"Some days you eat the bear." Page grinned with determination. "Some days the bear eats you."

⊣6⊢

"Still," Steve said to Page, "I can't see anything—anything—as a reason for tossing a career out the window. I mean, not one like you've got."

"You sound like somebody's mother." Page laughed. "Career? Who the fuck cares about careers?"

"You used to," Steve said. "You just finished telling me. *Had* to start the band. The sound wouldn't let you alone, blah, blah, blah." Page ducked his head and shrugged.

"Yeah, well, all right." He thought for a moment and began again. "Did I ever tell you about Jan?"

"I can't keep track of every post you piss on, brother."

"Right after that episode with those two hoods we left to skinny-dip on the beach was when I met her. Word came down through one of Butch's cop friends that these bad men were seriously gunning for me. Well, that made me real happy so I gracefully left town. Decided to take a little time off, see what'd happen if we let things cool down. So I went to stay at Willie's in Austin—that was before he got super famous, of course."

The day after Page arrived in Austin, the weather turned mercifully cool and bright, and he strolled over to the University of Texas campus just to see the sights. He saw them, in spades. First he spotted a long-legged palomino lady sitting under a pecan tree, reading a book. She wore a skirt and was tall and lovely. Then Page turned a corner and saw another, perhaps even more beautiful, talking with locked-on interest to a young man. A hundred yards beyond that, he saw yet another. Man, man, he thought as he walked on, looking over his shoulder, I could hack that *any day.* What am I doing working in these nightclubs with all these strange people?

For the next few weeks he stayed around the university and actually met one of the palomino ladies. Her name was Jan and she was tall and intelligent. Her apartment had large windows that took in the light from the south. Jan kept potted plants hanging everywhere, which she watered carefully with a brass watering can, first feeling the soil, then pouring in a thin stream of water, softly cursing spider mites. She had prints of Vermeer and Paul Klee and Magritte on the walls, neatly framed. Coming from his place on Timmons Lane, Page was amazed by the graceful ease with which Jan maintained her work and was still able to empty an ashtray or take him to the laundry, where they washed clothes and sheets and pillow cases, which Jan then ironed. She cooked and Page washed the dishes, wearing her apron. She played Mozart and Bob Dylan, Bach and Leon Russell. She had a classical guitar, and some nights they would sit up drinking wine by candlelight and Page would play on the soft nylon strings, singing one of his songs to her. Other nights they would lie in bed and Jan would read T. S. Eliot to him: "Teach us to care and not to care, Teach us to sit still." He only stayed with Jan for two weeks but years later it would seem like an entire era in his life. At the end, he realized that he was faced with a choice between Jan and his band. Reluctantly, he said good-bye to her, to her veal piccata and her bottles of white wine with French names.

"Page must go," he told her the night before he left.

"I had that feeling," Jan said. He had told her all about the band and she had listened intently, quietly, watching his eyes light up like those of a child describing an adventurous new game or the violent beauty of fireworks. "I can tell you're going to make it. You're obsessed with it."

Page almost asked her to come with him, but he knew that wouldn't be right for so many reasons. Page wouldn't survive in Jan's apartment and Jan wouldn't survive out there. Page left, and the first time he ever heard the word "love" used in connection with their relationship was years later, when she sent him a card. "Dear Page," it said. "I don't know if you'll remember me. You lived with me for two weeks in Austin in 1974. I just wanted to say I told you so. Congratulations and I hope you're doing as well as they say. Merry Christmas and have a good 1979. Love, Jan." Page had stared at the word "love" for a long time. Then he phoned her and learned that she was married and had a kid. Again he was tempted to ask her to come out to see him, but he didn't.

"Now," Page told Steve, "I still to this very day have some serious second thoughts about that lady. There was some kind of quiet there, some kind of ordinariness that I've never known. Everything in my life has always been extraordinary. And for two weeks I was treated to what it's like to be really ordinary and content with it. Well, now I'm rich, I'm famous, and I've seen a lot of shit go down. But I still wonder if things wouldn't have been a lot different for all of us if I had just stayed there in Austin and said, fuck it. And I can't say I made the right decision, either." Oh, he knew all right. You can never make those choices right and at the right time. But in the end, this was one of the central points he was trying to make to Steve, the knowledge that somehow he was different from the others because of his secret need for quiet, for daylight, for a simple home, a place to go, for something that was for once not outrageous.

It wasn't until years later that Page realized that the most seemingly insignificant things about those two weeks had made him continue thinking of Jan: getting up in the morning and going to bed at night, some kind of selection all on its own, so simple, so important. Not having to stay up and out until three or four or dawn. Sitting in Jan's apartment watching the ten o'clock news and then going to bed and reading until he fell asleep, curled beside a beautiful lady. Then waking with the sun streaming in, seven o'clock in the morning, the eggs and bacon, the hot coffee, a shower and a clean shirt. An entire day before him. A man can do goddamned near anything with a beginning like that.

He should have known. He told Steve about sitting in the dressing room at Madison Square Garden just before going on, thinking, My God, what have I done? What am I doing here? It's midnight and I haven't even started work yet, I'm ripped out of my brain and half drunk and a thousand miles from home. More: I don't even have a home. Where is it? L.A.? Texas? Michigan? It depressed the hell out of him and once again he had thought of Jan and what he had walked away from. Even now, talking about it with Steve, it began to eat at him.

Red came into the room carrying a stack of mail. "Want any of this shit? Something here from Perry and a lot of crap from the rest of the world."

"Lemme see the thing from Perry." Page held out his hand for the envelope. When he ripped into it he found a card with a Van Gogh snow scene on the front.

"Premature Happy Birthday," it said. "I'd really like to get together and talk now that you've had some months to rest. The entire crew sends best wishes, you're over the hill now. As ever, Perry." He handed it to Steve.

"Hey, I forgot, you've got a birthday coming."

"Old as God." Page took the card back. Then his head came up. "You know, if you just looked a little more like me, I could send you out there and Perry'd never know the difference."

"Would I get to screw all the groupies, too?" Steve grinned.

"All the nookie you can eat."

"You want the rest of this?" Red held up the mail.

"Naw," Page said, and Red left the room.

⊢7⊣

When Page returned from Austin, he was rested and ready for work, but Link was gone. When he hadn't shown up by midnight, Page decided to get some sleep so he could work on new songs the next day. When he awoke, he wasn't sure where he was, wasn't even certain what year it was. At first, before he opened his eyes, he thought he was in Vietnam. Then he became convinced he was back on the road with another band, in another time—about five months after Vietnam, when he and Link had gone out with some true originals, genuine undiluted criminal insanity cases, passing for rock and rollers. Back then it had been tough to remember he was on earth, forget about being in Law and Order America— stateside—free at last, free at last. Going out with them had been a kind of purge—Page and Link had never talked about it, but they didn't need to. They both knew that the only thing to do was run if they were going to escape that awesome depression you'd get coming off a rip like Vietnam. The only selection was no selection at all: more action, taper off gradually to avoid withdrawal. So they had gone on the road for some of that rock and roll music, line of departure, lock and load.

Those nights had repeated themselves like a loop from a bad reel of movie film. Back then there had always been some brute-force, last-minute way of peaking out one level above the previous day: all-night acid marathons, pinned to the eyelids, poorly remembered, blurred and out of sequence. Somewhere a girl lay in the center of the dining-room table, pulling her own trigger as entertainment while everyone ate. (Where was it? When they'd traveled with those crazies to L.A.? Yes, he could remember the enormous rains that season—or was that the monsoons? Was it houses sliding off the hills above the Canyon, chic and doomed, or the officers' mess at Khe Sanh blown away with the incoming rounds?)

Page got up and went to the shower, determined not to be sidetracked by the psychic sewers backing up on him. When he emerged into the chill, brassy air of the apartment, he flipped on the big television set in Link's room so that he could hear it while he made coffee. Page deduced from Link's absence that he'd found true love the previous day. As he absently worked in the kitchen, he distinctly heard a lady newscaster's voice announce cheerfully that Houston was due to be hit with a "long line of scattered brains." It made him jump so badly that he went into the room to look. It was only the weather lady. Obviously she had said "rains," and he had heard it wrong—no small joke there, haha, the old war wound: some guys came back with trick knees. Page had a trick mind.

Page switched it off and laughed hollowly at himself. He didn't like the sound of that laugh, he'd heard too many guys laugh just like that coming back from some horrible contact in the forest, and you never wanted to hear the explanation behind that laugh. While the coffee dripped out of the machine, he drank off half a quart of orange juice, then made a place on the low table next to the couch, sweeping everything onto the floor with a bare forearm. He laid out manuscript paper, pencils, guitar, coffee, Camels, ashtray. That same old sound was there, full of the swamp, the island dreams. Page couldn't shake it, he'd heard it even in his sleep. It was time to get it out.

He sipped coffee and began writing a song. He desperately wanted to begin rehearsing the band but a voice in his head had one comment on that subject and it was an old familiar phrase: never happen. Not, that is, until someone spirited Sonny away from the Burning Spear so that Scoop would leave, not until Blye could be lured away from London, not until they could rent a place to rehearse, not until . . .

Page sighed and sat down to write a song that had started to burn in his head, spinning there like a cell about to divide. He jotted lines, crossed out words, retraced his steps, and noted chords beside some lines. Occasionally he referred to his guitar to play something out. He drank cup after cup of coffee and let the Camels burn down to nothing in the ashtray. After a while, he felt the generators kick in: caffeine overdose. The humming began deep in the neurological power plant, deceptive because it was really powerful enough to light a city of dreams. He felt a kind of distilled excitement as he wrote several verses, rewrote them, made musical notations on the ledger paper, working off the ugly morning the way you'd work off a bad hangover by running a few miles. And after a time, he sat back to look at it, with no idea what it was, what it meant, whether or not it would fly.

> High Rise
> High Rise
> Look at her staring
> Look at those eyes
> She's so far up
> She's stopped caring
> They say it's so pleasant
> Up in your High Rise.
>
> High Rise
> Up in the sky
> Watch out the sun
> Don't burn out your eyes
> If it falls
> She'll surely die
> In her
> High Rise . . .

By the time the phone rang, there were seven verses. He had reworked it twice and knew the rest of the revision would have to come in vivo, whenever that might happen.

"Hello."

"Page, lad? Eh?"

"Blye! Where are you?"

"Jesus wept, son, how are you?" The voice was thick with British chop, high and full of street life. "Caught the midnight outta London. I'm at Houston International doin' fuck-all. Do we have loads of fifteen-year-old chicks jiggling about?"

"Goddamn!" Page was elated. "Listen, Link's gone out somewhere. I don't have the Land Yacht to pick you up."

"The wot?"

"The Hog," Page said clearly. "Link's Cadillac."

"Haw! Fok! Right, riiiight. Well, no danger of that, then." It was a broad, casual phrase Blye used often, a verbal tic.

"Get a cab," Page said. "I want to start rehearsing right away."

"Rehearsing wot?"

"Never mind, just get over here."

"Gosh, sure, super," Blye said. "Splendid."

After hanging up, Page paced the room, unable to focus. It had worked. He'd taken another prisoner.

Blye, Blye, he thought, a definite asset on any light, mobile team, dangerous music, dangerous habits, wicked fun. Blye had proven himself more than once around Link and Page in that venomous Houston scene. Captain Blye, they called him, for he was always at sea. They had met him after he wrecked a yacht that belonged to Aristotle Onassis. He was supposed to ferry it across from Antigua to Greece, but he had hired such an incompetent crew that they wound up in the Sargasso Sea, where the Cuban Coast Guard boarded them and informed them that they could go free if they just got out of Cuban waters. Blye proceeded to navigate from there straight into the maw of a tropical storm working its way into the megaton class. He washed aground somewhere near Corpus Christi, where he promptly abandoned ship. He hitched to Houston and stayed two years the first time. Page was fondly reminiscing when the phone rang a second time.

"What's hap'nin'?" Link sounded relatively relaxed.

"And where in hell are *you?*"

"Me? Well, shit, I'm right here." Link laughed. "Judy's place."

"Come on, shitbird. I don't know any Judy. Where are you?"

"I'm out here on some little ranch ridin' horses and gettin' my goober eat," Link drawled proudly.

Page fought back a laugh. "Well, Blye has A-rived. He's on his way from the airport right now."

"Beautiful. That's really beautiful, man. I mean it. Un-fucking-credible." Page could tell that his enthusiasm was not infecting Link.

"All right, come on. Where are you?" Page asked.

"Well." Link sighed heavily, then said, away from the mouthpiece, "Oh, hey, honey, watch it, careful. That's it."

"Link!" Page put his hand over his face. "What's going on there?"

"Well, I already told you. I'm gettin' my goober eat."

"Right now?" Page sat down.

"Right this fucking minute." Link chuckled roundly and then a female voice came on, giggling, high and sweet as hash oil: "And is it ever *gooood!*" And Link dissolved into easy, rolling-thunder laughter.

"Well, I'll—" Page began. He took a deep breath. "See if you can't figure out where you are so you can get out here by the time the sun goes down. Maybe we can do a little rehearsing and all that happy shit."

"That's a rog," Link said.

An hour later Blye came through the door, five feet seven inches of taut, squat muscle, charging head-on into the room. He wore a muslin shirt open almost to the waist. His abdomen protruded, not from fat but from stance, like a round mahogany drum. He was tan and weatherbeaten from his days at sea; his hands were calloused and his reddish-brown hair was prematurely thinning and flecked with gray. Page leaped across the room as Blye came in and there was a good deal of backslapping before they settled down to talk.

"Haw! Fok! You look bloody fucking *super,* lad. How *are* you?"

"I think I'm gone be all right, Captain." Page grinned. "I mean, I've consulted some experts in the field and they say I'm gonna pull through."

As Page stood admiring how fit and tan Blye seemed, he noticed that Blye was sweating. It didn't appear to be bothering him particularly, but big drops crawled down his cheeks and fell to the floor, even though it was sixty-eight degrees in the apartment. Page didn't know how Blye had gotten hooked on heroin; the facts of the story always came out different. But he must have been on a plane for quite a while, and Page could see that he was going to need some kind of medication soon.

"You all right?" Page asked.

"Hmmm . . ." Blye mocked introspection, looking at the ceiling. "Haw! All right?" He looked as if he were up to the utmost mischief and not about to let the hilarious secret out now. "Mmm. No danger of that, eh?"

"Wait," Page said, going into the bedroom. He returned with his palm outstretched. In it were two methadone Diskets. Blye sighed, visibly relieved.

"Health and stealth," he said and popped the tablets into his mouth. And although the sweating didn't stop until an hour later, Blye immediately launched into a lengthy narrative of why he'd had to throw a foretopman overboard at high sea on one of his recent trips, punctuating his monologue with demands for Page's assent: "Eh? Am I right? Bloody fucking awful, these foretopmen. Don't you think?"

Blye had a gravel voice and when he laughed it was as if he had been trying not to, as if he had just done something horrid to someone and couldn't help thinking it was funny. And when the laugh came, it was loud and explosive. When he'd heard Page's plan—heard the names Butch, Scoop, Link—he held it as long as he could before starting in. "Haw!" He jumped up and began pacing. "Fok! Super. Splendid, lad. What say we phone a barrister now and save some trouble? Eh? Am I right? Be in jail in no time flat. Aw, fok. Never mind, I haven't been in jail since Maui anyway." He rushed across the room and faced Page squarely. "It's about bloody time someone here took charge, you know? Let's get to it, then. Where are the girls?"

"By the way," Page said, "nobody has foretopmen anymore, Blye, you know that."

"And a good bloody thing, too, eh? Might've missed him otherwise."

By sundown they were reunited with Link and Butch, and the four men drove over to the Burning Spear to try Scoop again. At a stoplight Butch fell in love with a girl who was apparently waiting for a bus. He leaned way out the window to call to her.

"Hey, little girl," he said forlornly, "please, man, I'm in *love* with you, wouldn't you like some Quāāludes?" Link pulled through the red light, zoom. Scratch one groupie.

"Jesus wept." Blye laughed. "Hasn't changed a bit, has he?"

As they entered the club and surveyed the dancing couples, Blye's eyes lit up and he began to whisper to Page, "Jiggling bottoms, look at all the jiggling bloody bottoms, will ya? Blye must have one, must have two. Mmmm. Haw! Fok! Jiggle-jiggle."

When Scoop saw Blye, he was so pleased that he didn't even try to run from Butch. The five men crowded up to the bar, ordered beers, and jabbered at each other excitedly. Page was quiet, watching them talk. They're acting like a band already, he thought, and they don't even know it yet. Look at them.

"Lookit him, lookit him!" Scoop said excitedly, holding Blye by the arm. "Isn't he gorgeous? Gad Zooks! How are you?"

"Haw! Fok! How *am* I?" Blye hollered. "How bloody long've you got?"

Page noticed Butch watching something across the room with uncharacteristic intensity and followed his gaze. "Who's the dude with Sonny?" Butch asked. Sonny was speaking with a man they'd never seen before.

"Don't know," Page said, his interest growing as Sonny smiled and waved his arms and talked. Then Page saw the piece of paper in Sonny's hand and realized what it was. "I'll be right back." He crossed the club, fighting through the dancers.

"Page, Page," Sonny said breathlessly, "this is *Phil Shorter,* man." Sonny emphasized the words as if he had introduced Buddha. Page took the airline ticket Sonny was waving around and examined it.

"Pleased," Page said to the man and handed Sonny the ticket. "So when're you going to New York?"

"Tomorrow." Sonny rocked back and forth. "He says we're going to be on Columbia Records."

"Far out." Page nodded, thinking, There it is. Not only would Scoop have to play with them, but Ritchie wouldn't have a band. And sure enough, at the end of the set, it sank in to Ritchie, the club manager: this stranger, this New Yorker, was taking away the main attraction, the man who put people on the dance floor. And then he freaked and flew around the club in a fury of questions.

Page just watched, shrugged at the questions, ducked his head innocently, let Ritchie work himself into a frenzy. And then he put forth his proposition.

"You let us rehearse here in the afternoons. We'll play the evening gig until you can get someone else."

"No, no," Ritchie said immediately. "You guys are trouble. Isn't nobody suppose to work with you after that shit in Galveston."

"If you think so." Page smiled. "I hope they like it when they hear you aren't even bringing in customers in the evenings."

"Wait, wait." Ritchie grabbed Page's arm as he started to walk away. Ritchie didn't know what to say. Page just looked at him. "Are you ready to play a gig?"

"Christ, no." Page laughed. "We've never even rehearsed this band. But we've all played together a lot over the years and we all know the same boring old songs. So at, say, two thirty tomorrow, if we come in here and work on it, we could have enough tunes to get us through the night. And anyway, what other choice do you have? Maybe if we bail you out of this problem, those assholes will go easy on you for working with us. We don't want trouble any more than you do."

"Well, you certainly got a peculiar way of lettin' people know that."

"Yeah, well . . ." Page walked away. He knew Ritchie would come around. And years later Ritchie would look back on that moment with secret regret and a mild sense of confusion. He would spend more than one dead-heat afternoon half drunk, pointing to the taped sound coming from the speakers and assuring a customer, "Yeah, I gave them boys their start. Right here in this club." At the moment, however, Ritchie wasn't sure if he'd just been saved or screwed.

On the next set Blye sat in with Sonny and Scoop. He was up there bringing the stage to a new life with a sound as exquisite as an ingenious method of torture. Like his explosive laugh—the laugh of someone trying to stifle a laugh but failing because it is *so fucking funny*—his playing had a quality of evil jubilance, a black and terrible exultation. It was exactly what Page wanted, exactly what he'd been hearing for so long now.

Even Scoop heard it and smiled as he played along, and it gave Page some hope. But at the next break Scoop was practically in tears with the realization that Sonny was leaving him alone, that he was not going to be allowed to die in peace at the Burning Spear.

Page took him by the shoulder, and it was as easy as he had expected, like leading the wounded to a corpsman. "You get to stay at the Burning Spear even in the afternoons. We'll be rehearsing here and everything." Scoop darted his eyes left and right like a confused animal and Page felt him twitch. But Scoop didn't have any choice. Years later, thinking back on it, Page would see that if any of them had had a choice in the matter, the band probably would never have been formed in the first place.

Naturally, there was a celebration that night—of Sonny's big break, of the consolidation of the new band, any excuse for a party. They wound up at Sonny's house drinking and smoking and gobbling up whatever potions and pills they could find lying around, until a gray light came creeping around the edges of the drapes and doorways like an extraterrestrial force seeking entry. Page remembered five hollow-eyed girls in there somewhere, but their faces were just vague blurs.

"Jesus wept." Blye wandered around the room. "Look at me, will you? Starkers. Back on the warpath, how did I get to America? I want to know. I want answers! Am I beautiful or what? I want to know now. Am I not gorgeous? Let's have a garbage bag full of Indochinese annealing powder for this poor lad."

"The Captain is out of his fucking mind," Butch announced.

"Oh, no beastly danger of that." Blye lurched forward, lost his balance, and sat softly but suddenly on the floor. He looked around as if wondering how he had gotten there, and said, "Super. See-you-pah!" Then he simply began chanting, "Entropy! Entropy! Entropy! I'm a victim of entropy!"

Butch's dead-reckoning navigation across the room toward Page made it look as if he were walking on a waterbed.

"What'll we call it?" he asked Page. Earlier he had tried to convince Page that they should tie up one of the girls who wanted to go home but Page had managed, even in his drunken condition, to explain to Butch that this was against the law and therefore not such a sound idea. Now Butch didn't want to go home, and Link and Page had been trying to get him to comprehend that they had to rehearse the next day.

"What'll we call what?" Page stood at a marked starboard list.

"The band, man."

Page moved up close to inspect Butch's eyes. "You lookin' real fine, Coach. You eyes nearly as red as mine."

"I'm about fucked up like a ten-dick dog." Butch smiled weakly.

"Let's call it Jambeaux," Page said with conviction.

"What's that?"

"It's nothing, that's what it is. Jambeaux." He spelled it for them.

"So why should we call it Jambeaux, then?"

"Now how the fuck should I know that?" Page asked indignantly. "Can't you tell I'm drunk?"

"You musta got it somewhere."

"There's a Swahili word, *jambo,* that means hello." Page lost his balance and found Link beside him. Link straightened him up.

"Why Swahili?" Link asked.

"Because musicians are the niggers of the artistic world. And the *e-a-u-x* ending makes it sound Cajun or *look* Cajun, dig it? That's the sound I been talking about, Afro-Jamaican-Cajun funk."

"I can fade that," Link said.

"And the word *Jam,* too," Page continued. "You know, sounds like you're jammin'."

"Jambeaux." Butch weaved, half in a trance. "Yeah, and the French, *Les Beaux Jams.*"

"Right. What do you say?" Page turned to Link.

"I can definitely feature it."

"Jambeaux," Page repeated. He didn't remember much more of the evening. Somehow they all got home. At least he knew one thing: he wouldn't be having any of those dreams that night.

⊢ 8 ⊣

Link popped out of bed at one in the afternoon and began crashing around the apartment. He shook the couch where Blye was sleeping.

"Haw! Fok!" Blye shouted, instantly awake. "Splice the main brace! Avast, me bloody beastly fucking hearties!"

Once he was sure that Blye was on his way, Link picked up the phone to call Scoop and Butch. By the time Page appeared, gasping for breath from the cold shower he'd taken, Link had made coffee and scrambled eggs. Page's stomach lurched against his ribs at the smell of food, but he ate anyway. They had a lot of work ahead. The party was over.

"I'm hurt bad," he muttered.

"Good bloody thing, too." Blye rummaged in his seabag. "Mmmm. Look what we've uncovered here. Beastly treasure." He held up a foul-looking bottle of rum. "Absolute guarantee with this stuff. It'll keep termites out of your fence posts for twenty-five years or your liver back. Here, lad." He offered it to Page, who turned pale and shook his head. "It'll put you close to God." Blye took a big, bubbling swallow from the bottle and sat down to eat, expelling a great blast of wind fore and aft. "Drink up, girls, there's sober people in China. Haw!" And he launched into a manic monologue, punctuated with stabs of his fork and explosive laughter.

"No permanent brain damage," Page observed, opening and closing his fist before his eyes to see if his extremities still worked.

"You really stepped into it last night, didn't you, Little Buddy?" Link chuckled at him.

"Let's see," Page muttered, "assault with a deadly weapon, possession of controlled substances, illegal use of firearms, willful and wanton cruising with intent to get weird, disturbing the poontang —man, the charges are definitely mounting." Page paused to inspect Link for signs of damage, but there were none. "Amazing," he said. "Little party didn't bother old Link, no sir. But you wait." Page pointed a forkful of egg at him. "You just wait, Coach. They'll get you."

After breakfast they went to Butch's place. He had apparently showered, dressed, and lapsed into a profound coma. A girl who looked about eleven years old wandered in from the bedroom, yawning and rubbing her eyes, stark naked. When she saw the home invaders dragging Butch out, she let go with a yell like a cat set afire and locked herself in the bathroom. As they half-carried Butch, all he could say was, "Whatzit? Whozit?" and they just laughed.

"Damn," Link said, "you're sure not *acting* like a star."

"Ladies and gentlemen," Page intoned, "the Esteemed Senator from Utah."

"Whozit?"

They found Scoop slumped against the wall of his apartment with a Lone Star beer in his hand, fast asleep, naked except for sunglasses. He looked like a drowned ferret. Half an hour later they had him propped up on the stage at the Burning Spear.

Soon the sounds began to come through the thin club walls and blossom out onto Fannin Street. The bell-like guitar and bass notes, like the call of some futuristic satanic church, beckoning to the faithless. The slash of a Zilgian cymbal, the crisp crush roll of a snare. Finally, the great golden bird, the molten honking of Butch's tenor saxophone. The beauty is on duty, Page thought, listening to Butch play over Link's hellgong bass line.

Page didn't realize the microphone was open when he started to speak. "Rock and Roll," he said, and the sound lashed across four lanes of traffic. He cut the switch and spoke to the band, laughing. "Line of departure, boys. Lock and load. Time to play some mew-zik."

Blye came from behind his drum set to roll his bell-bottomed jeans up to his knees so they wouldn't get in the way. He wore a towel around his neck and was dressed in the same muslin shirt.

"How about 'I Shot the Sheriff'?" Page asked. "In A?"

"You singing lead?" Link was changing the cord that ran from his bass to the amplifier.

"Yeah," Page said.

"Where's my flute?" Butch searched through the jumble of instrument cases and wire. When he found the slim black case and assembled the silver tube, they all tuned to the piano.

They began the song three times and Page stopped them. The harmony was wrong. Page, Link, and Butch were carrying the triad and someone was off. So Butch sat down at the piano and played out the parts until they had them right. They began again. Page stopped them once more in the middle of the song and asked, "Captain, say, you want to put an extra rimshot in there where I say 'Deputy' on the end of three?"

"Super, yes. You mean like this?" Blye made two explosive sounds, using the head and metal rim of the snare simultaneously like sixteenth-note gunfire.

"Yeah," Page said. They tried it again and this time ran all the way through. Link's bass line moved up and down the lattice of sound like a muscular vine. Blye's drums were crisp as autumn in

Michigan, covering fire with heavy artillery in the background. Scoop's guitar solo was a laser-guided missile, still on the drawing board but pure essence of rock and roll. And the rangy flute Butch played, humming over the actual note, was like a jungle lizard watching the entire operation, heavy-lidded, missing nothing.

There it *is*, Page thought, as he tuned his ear like a wire, that *sound*. Rough and raw as it was, blurred around the edges of someone else's song, he heard it, embryonic, pulsing.

When they finished, even Scoop was smiling. They had actually played a song together. It wasn't much, it was terribly unpolished, but the peculiar sounds of those five men mixed like the strange ingredients used in gumbo—bats and roof rabbit, file and alligator and unheard-of spices. It would clearly take a while for the flavors to blend, but the smell that filled the kitchen was dizzying.

Page knew the feeling: like the very first time he'd taken down a girl's underpants. And the woman in this case was endless, boundless. However crude the initial grope, they had made music together. And he could see the others had heard it too. But there was no time to savor it. Jambeaux had to play five real sets that night, for money, to a live audience. The whole thing had suddenly ceased to be theoretical. Raw or not, it was a working band.

" 'The Night They Drove Old Dixie Down,' " Page called. "Key of C."

"You want me on organ?" Butch asked.

"No, piano, remember?" Page played the five-chord intro on his guitar to illustrate.

Butch went over to the club's old, beat-up piano. "Is this thing miked?"

"I don't think so." Link crossed the stage and moved two of the boom mikes over to it. Butch played the five chords and shook his head in dismay.

"Man," Butch said, "this really blows it."

"Come on," Page said. "Let's play the son of a bitch."

"Oof!" Butch said, ringing into the introductory chords as Blye kicked the first note with his bass drum.

"Yes, yes," Page said into the microphone, ignoring the sad sound of the piano, digging it, it was *their* sound. He came in rolling: "Virgil Cain is my name and I served on the Danville Train." Scoop filled with subtle, discreet bursts of guitar until they went into the chorus: "The Ni-i-i-ght they drove Old Dixie down."

"Hold it!" Page shouted, and the music machine rolled on under its own momentum. *"Hold it!!"* Finally it ground to a halt. "We've got those harmony parts all fucked up. I'm singing the three there."

"Yeah?" Butch leaned around to look at him.

"You should be on the tonic." Page plucked a C on his guitar. "I'm on the word *night.*"

"Ni-i-i-ght...." Butch sang a C.

"Right, and you're on the five." Page turned to Scoop. "G, right?"

"I was on the tonic," Scoop said.

"Sing the five next time around, Geee?" Page sang the note, tilting his head to one side, questioning. Scoop nodded assent.

"Link, you're doubling the fifth?"

"I was doubling you an octave up." Link sang in two steps, two distinct notes, modulating, "Niii-iiiight," and explained, "D and then C."

"Ahh...." Page smiled. "There you go. Fine." He turned full around to nod at Butch and Blye to begin again. This time when they hit the chorus the voices were all there, right on the good notes, and Page wanted to leap up and down because it sounded so slick. He felt a shiver of pleasure run through him and then he just sang it out, whooping at the end of the song. *"Rock and Row-Wool!"* he shouted. A few songs later, they were so intent on the music that the applause took them completely by surprise. Scoop jumped clear off the stage. When he realized what was going on— that some customers had come in and were drinking beer and having a good time—Page looked around at the others to see their reaction. Link was grinning wildly.

"Pucker, motherfucker." He laughed at Page. "I didn't even *see* 'em."

"Oh, this is gonna work." Page said it like a prayer. "I can smell it. Nothin' finer, nothin' finer."

They rehearsed through the afternoon, the excitement so high they didn't even take a beer break. Ritchie sulked around, out of their way, not wanting to have to face up to Page saying I told you so. Page had promised him a bonus of real customers in the afternoons, and this was the largest afternoon crowd Ritchie had had in months. After a five-hour rehearsal, the band had enough standard nightclub numbers roughed out to get them through the night's work, however haltingly.

By the fourth set of the night, they were exhausted. Flubbed notes began to creep into the performance. They were short on material and had to go back and repeat some songs from the first set. But Page just grinned through the pain, there it was, his band, he could hardly believe it, it had been so many years now. When they ended the night with "You've Lost That Lovin' Feeling," Page had to fight to keep his throat open to sing harmony behind Link's bold, warbling, gravel tenor. And when they left, no one wanted to party that night.

They awoke refreshed the next day—not a hangover in the crowd—and Page made arrangements for an early rehearsal that was more concentrated, lasted longer, and left them with the feeling that they might actually be gaining on something. The crowd at the club was larger than the previous day's, but they played as if nothing in the world existed but their music.

By the third week of this, they were skating through the night's work, packing the house. Page began springing his own tunes on the audience. Jambeaux was averaging eight hours of playing a day and Page talked Ritchie into letting them play only four sets a night for the same money. He could hardly refuse. Business was too good.

After six weeks of solid playing, Jambeaux had become a single organism, all systems functioning with graceful interdependence. They had become obsessive about it and constantly discussed new songs, endlessly going over the tiniest problems that arose. They rehearsed new harmony voicings while riding in the car and even got into heated arguments about such minutiae as an additional half-beat rest somewhere. But the thing began to tighten down, the spaces closed so that nothing could slip through. It was a seamless entity. And as they put together each new song that Page wrote, it was like watching a pyrotechnist assemble a shell for a fireworks display—these pellets here, this powder there, wrapped tight as a drum—so that when it finally detonated high in the sky, it would be in perfect symmetry. A fiery chrysanthemum, a megawatt elegance of balance and color with an afterburst that could bring you up shorter than an adrenaline bath.

And another process took place that was so subtle and gradual Page almost failed to notice it. One day he awoke with Cyndi in his arms and realized he had all but moved in with her. He was sleeping with her four nights a week when her husband was out of town, and it brought a kind of stability into his life. She began to come to the club with the band, to sit and listen each afternoon for an hour or so and act as a sounding board for Jambeaux.

"Cyndi," Link might call across the club, "now listen to this line and tell me if you think it's better than the first one we played." Then she would wait attentively and make a decision.

"You're turned up way too high," she'd tell Butch. "The saxophone is overpowering the backup vocals."

"Thanks," Butch would call, and they'd make the adjustment. Page saw it as a measure of some real devotion that Cyndi gave up her time to help them. And in a way it frightened him, but then that little edge of sanity was important to him. And he would inevitably catch himself thinking about Jan in Austin—maybe he was just trying to re-create a little of that.

Even Butch seemed slightly more under control. True, he wasn't the most disciplined member of the group, and twice he showed up late for rehearsal. But those two times the band's reaction had been so swift and brutal that he began coming on time even when he was only clinically alive, occasionally dragged there by whatever girl he had been with the previous evening.

And as one rehearsal blurred into the next, the days and nights ran together and the weeks whipped by them like a breeze. Gnawing at the back of Page's mind was a growing concern about the silence of those Galveston boys. If those bad-asses are so haired off at us, he wondered, why don't they just do something?

He tried not to worry about it, and then one day came the realization that there was nothing left to do with the band. His next move had arrived: studio time. That sound he'd been hearing for so long in his head was no longer just a notion, it was something anyone could come into the club and hear for the price of admission: the real thing, *that sound*. Now all Page had to do was get it on tape. Then maybe they could get out of this town and forget what had gone down.

Scoop almost crawled down into his boots when Page announced that they were ready for the demo sessions. But Page talked to him and assured him that the studio he had chosen was every bit the shithole the Burning Spear was. "You can even bring some roaches if you like."

"But we're not ready," Scoop whimpered.

"Nothin' to it," Link said. "We got it snaked."

"There it is." Page shook Scoop's shoulder, smiling at his ferret-faced innocence and terror. "There it is, Professor."

⊣9⊢

"There it is." Page pointed to the deer, touching the phrase with a special reverence and delicacy. He and Steve had gone out early to look for deer deep in the woods around the Ranch. And there they went in their weird, silent, uncanny animal way, seeing, smelling, hearing things people would never know. When the deer were gone, Page said, "Let's get some breakfast," and they began the long march through the snow.

"Say," Steve said, "you know what I saw a few months back?"

"What?"

"A rerun of the 'David Frost Show' you guys were on." Steve giggled.

"Oh, God." Page winced visibly. "That was awful. Just awful."

"I was on the *floor*, man. That hokey little videotape of you guys poling a flatboat through the swamp and *singing* at the same time . . ."

"Oh, no, man, let me up. Shelly talked us into that. We never should have done it."

"Just like some pseudo-Beatles regurgitation." Steve enjoyed putting the screws to Page. "Really slick."

"Please, Coach, don't even remind me. That was an old tape. Honest, I didn't mean it. And Frost, what an asshole."

Steve needled Page about it all the way to the house. Half an hour later they sat down to fried eggs and potatoes, bacon, English muffins, raspberry preserves, orange juice, and coffee. A Labrador retriever who had been sleeping in the corner came up to the table occasionally to beg for food from the newcomer, and each time she approached, Steve did this bit: "That's a revolutionary dog. I've been teaching her Marxist tricks. Watch. Smash the state, Lilly!" He spoke in that high, quick, inciting-to-riot tone people use with dogs. "Go on now, go smash the state! Retrieve the power structure! That's a girl!" And the dog, completely confused, would wag her tail, look expectantly at him, and then wander off to her corner. Page laughed every time.

After breakfast, Steve plucked three lemons from a bowl in the center of the table. Page watched, impressed, as his brother stood and began juggling.

"Where'd you learn that?" Page asked.

"I don't know." Steve shrugged and flipped one lemon behind his back and high into the air, catching it without losing a beat.

"Pretty good," Page allowed. "You're just a natural entertainer, aren't you?"

" 'Oh, de camptown ladies sing dat song,' " Steve began, then sat back down, tossing the lemons into the bowl.

"You ought to work that into your act," Page said.

"What act?" Steve sounded disgusted. "I don't even have a fucking record contract yet."

"Well, if you actually decide to go on with this foolishness, I'm sure Perry could work something out," Page said, thinking, Let's talk about something else, leave him alone. Then thinking, Well, he came here. I didn't force him to come. And: Page, you are evil. Would you actually do that to this kid?

Steve changed the subject. "You know, you never said what happened with those Younger people. All that trouble. They didn't just drop it."

"Oh, no, no, nothing like that." Page gave Steve a signifying look and then told him about the afternoon he, Link, Butch, and Cyndi were sitting around the apartment discussing harmony voicings for a new song.

"Well." Cyndi stretched and got up from the floor where they were all poring over the lead sheets. "I've got to run some errands." She put her hand in Link's hair and said in a sweet mocking voice, "Link, Huh-nee, kin I borrow your car?"

"Only if you get us some beer," Page put in.

"Sure," Link said. "Anytime."

"It's a deal," Cyndi said to Page. "What kind?"

Link looked at Page, who said thoughtfully, "Mil-ker-hoonah."

"What?" Cyndi laughed.

"Miller," Butch said. "Mil-ker-hoonah. It's like, you know, like vodka, for example. Vod-ker-hoonah."

"You guys are nuts," Cyndi said and left.

Three minutes later she was back. "Your car won't start," she told Link. "I think somebody ran into it, too."

"Oh, shit." Link started to get up.

"I'll take care of it," Butch said. "Just get that damned harmony part right, will you?"

"If somebody run into my car, there's gonna be a shooting in Houston tonight," Link said.

But when Butch came back, Link and Page both knew they had bigger troubles than a dented car. He walked slowly over to the couch and sat almost carefully, setting a paper bag on the table.

Page and Link just watched, seeing that he needed a minute to put it together. Then Page realized what was missing. He jumped to his feet.

"Where is she?" he demanded.

"I sent her home," Butch said weakly. "She's all right."

"Lay it out," Link said. "What is it?"

"Goddamn," Butch said. Page opened a bottle of whiskey and handed it to Butch, who took a halfhearted sip. "When're we getting this thing finished?"

"What do you mean?" Link asked, puzzled.

"We gotta get out of town." Page and Link waited for more. "I went out, and sure enough somebody's run into your front end. Smashed it pretty good. And like Cyndi said, it wouldn't start." He stopped talking for a moment and looked like he might throw up. He swallowed some more whiskey and went on. "So I opened the hood to see what's happening and . . ." Butch touched the brown paper sack on the coffee table very gently. Neither Page nor Link had particularly noticed he was carrying it when he came in. The bag looked like someone's lunch, crumpled and grease-stained. It smelled of almonds. Page spread open the crumpled top and peered in. Link watched him closely.

Page turned white. Link already thought he knew that smell, recognized those grease stains. He leaned over and looked into the bag and saw the ten-inch-long cylinders with their casual inscription: DANGER DUPONT EXPLOSIVES RED CROSS + EXTRA 40% STRENGTH. He saw the coils of Primacord, the connectors, and the pencil-thin brass cartridges, crimped and stamped with the legend: BLASTING-6.

"Oh, fuck," Link whispered hoarsely. "Let's get this outta here. This shit's sweating." The oozing of the dynamite had produced the almond smell and the greasy stains on the bag.

"I mean, I turned the fucking *key*." Butch shivered.

"How come it didn't fire?" Page asked, shuddering hard when he realized that it would have been Cyndi sitting there with her legs torn off. Oh, my God, he thought, why did I get her involved in this? He was only beginning to understand how strong his concern for her had become.

Butch wandered around the room, holding the whiskey bottle by its neck. He took a drink and coughed. Then he leveled an evil stare at the two of them and broke up laughing. Link and Page just stared. Eight sticks of 40-percent dynamite between them, primed and ready to blow. It wasn't funny. Then they too began to laugh. For in the face of it all, what could you do? The choices were minimal: you could flip or fly. Submit, there it was. Finally, Butch got hold of himself and told them.

"Fucker ran into you," he began, but then blew whiskey across the kitchen, laughing. "Ran into you and knocked the battery cable off. So when I turned the ignition—" He slid to the floor, out of control. He just sat there giggling high and scary, the tears running into his beard.

It took a while to bring the situation under control and by that time it was understood that Butch especially was among them—a certified, card-carrying, dues-paid member of the band. Page phoned Cyndi and learned that she was all right. The implications of it—that she would have been in the driver's seat when the dynamite went off—had not completely sunk in. Or else she was braver than they were.

While they were trying to figure out what to do, Blye came charging in, head down, ready for action. He was carrying a fifth of hundred-proof Wood's Navy Rum from Guyana, some odious black creosotelike liquid that only hard-core sailors could drink. On the bottle was a picture of a weathered old seaman with the quote, "Splice the mainbrace!" below, and it advertised, "Finest old Demerara."

"Haw! Fok!" he shouted as he came in. "Mmmm, let's have a bite of this, then." He opened the bottle and took a healthy pull. "Put hair on your knees, yes, yes, here you go, girls, have after it." He waved the bottle at them and failed to register their mood.

"Say, wot's this?" He grabbed at the paper sack violently and Page nearly fell over himself getting away from him. "Oh, haw! Super! Dynamite. Gosh. . . ." He looked at them, puzzled. "What're we blowing up tonight, then? Anyone I know?"

Page was in the corner, his hands over his head. Link shook his head back and forth, chuckling, and Butch just sat where he was, incredulous.

"I think you better sit down," Link said finally. "And leave that goddamned bag alone."

"Gosh, sure, super." Blye sat on the floor and passed the rum bottle to Butch. "Here, lad, you look like you need this. Wot's up?"

Link explained it to Blye, and Page broke out the last of the Bolivian. The DuPont Red Cross package sat on the coffee table as they dipped little spoonfuls of the powder and chattered to one another softly. Finally, Page caught Link staring intently at the sack. Page shot him a malevolent grin, all teeth and terror.

"Well, shit." Link smiled modestly. "It makes me damned nervous is all. That fuckin' thing's all ready to go. All she needs is a word. I don't even like to *look* slantwise at weeping dynamite."

"We'll think of something," Page said confidently.

"Oh, right," Link blustered, "riiiight." He turned to Butch, animated. "Fuckin' Recondo here thinks he knows it all. Fucker doesn't know shit about explosives. One time in Nam, this lieutenant goes, like, 'Take this C-Four and blow down some of them trees.' So Page gets him a case of M-Five-E-One and goes over and puts like *eight pounds* around some tree. Blew the leaves off everything for two clicks in both directions. His tree was still standing. So like now he goes, 'We'll think of something.' Riiiight."

Page was laughing, embarrassed.

"So what do you want to do with it, Coach?" Page asked Link.

"I know what *I* want to do with it." Butch jumped up, pissed. "I want to give it right back to them." He stomped across the room. "They can't fuck with us like this. Let's bring it right back to them."

"Fok!" Blye jumped to his feet. "Certainly, yes, bloody taste of their own medicine. I mean, that's no way to treat a bird, now, is it?"

"Shut up, Blye," Link said with good-natured disgust.

"Right-o." Blye laughed and sat back down to sip his rum.

"What do you say, Coach?" Page asked Link. "The Senator has spoken." He knew he had started the entire pissing match and he knew it wasn't going to end just because the bomb didn't go off. But he didn't want to foment the revolution unless the others were willing and eager. "It was your car, Link," Page added.

"Why the fuck not?" Link stood heavily. "They ain't gonna leave us alone. Might as well give 'em the message. Besides, Blye's right. It would have been Cyndi got the grease on that one, and that ain't no way to go."

"Yeah," Blye said. "Fuck 'em if they can't take a joke."

"Well," Page said, "let's get that battery cable back on." At first Page and Link had trouble convincing Butch and Blye to stay home, but Link put his foot down.

He fingered the Land Yacht around the corners on those cushy shocks as Page gently—tenderly—cradled the package in his lap. Page breathed as softly as he could, whispering, "Gawd, don't run no traffic lights. Gawd, don't run no stop signs. Gawd, don't hit nothin', Coach," all the way across town, while Link cooed at him like an animal trainer calming a skittish cat.

Clovis Younger lived in River Oaks in Houston. He'd bought up Pine Valley Court off Lazy Lane and taken over more than an acre and a half in the vicinity of the terminus of Troon Street. He owned a nice restaurant on the outskirts of New Orleans where they served the best cold asparagus soup in the South. Clovis Younger also owned—or controlled—numerous gambling casinos, every major whorehouse, and a good deal of the cocaine and heroin traffic along the eastern Gulf Coast. He held the quitclaim deed to the Riptide Rendezvous and had enough traction with arms dealers to outfit dim-brained professionals with factory-made dynamite. He was under investigation for possible illegal campaign contributions in the 1972 presidential election, and rumors had been circulating that he might be heading for Costa Rica soon. He was under nonstop scrutiny by the Treasury Department and the Attorney General's office. Link and Page and Butch could have gone after the lower-echelon hoods, but this smelled like a Clovis Younger operation from start to finish. For even in his own underworld circles Younger was known as a mad dog.

Link wheeled the Land Yacht over Westheimer, up Kirby Drive, and through the winding, tree-lined streets of River Oaks. He idled up the arcaded drive to the house with his lights out and stopped just clear of the searing circle of security lamps.

"Now, don't waste no time," he said to Page. "I don't want any contact here tonight."

"Not to worry," Page said and got out with the care and grace of a ballet dancer. "I'll just be a second." Link watched as Page blended into the tree line. Before he had the car turned around, Page was back, saying, "Go, go! Let's go!"

Link pulled out onto Lazy Lane and hummed away to the south on Kirby Drive, back out toward Richmond and Timmons Lane.

"How'd you hook that thing up so fast?" Butch asked when they walked in.

"Didn't," was all Page said.

"What d'you mean you *didn't?*" Butch was incredulous.

"Don't you understand anything? If I hook that thing up and Younger comes out in the morning—or, say, his teenage daughter comes out in the morning—and blows that Lincoln all over River Oaks, you'll have your bomb squads and feds and every cop in the city out there. And out *here.*" There was silence. "But this way, with that package sitting under the hood and the ignition wires cut. . . ." Page grinned and held up a pair of needle-nosed pliers. "Why, old Younger comes out and tries the engine. Won't start. And he opens the hood and does just like you did, Senator."

"Haw!" Blye stalked around the room. "You goat! You absolute monster! Be *reasonable,* Page. All he did was try to kill your girl friend."

"You goddamned devil," Butch said with admiration.

"No rest for the weird." Page lit a cigarette, and his hand shook ever so slightly.

Years later, hearing this, Steve laughed and laughed. "You *are* evil, Page," he said. "But why would Younger try a trick like that? I mean, after all, bombing? It doesn't make sense."

Page just shrugged and shook his head. No, of course it made no sense, these guys are *crazy,* haven't you heard the stories about gangsters? They're all true, mad, lurid Dark Ages Inquisition nightmares, stories of people kidnapped and tortured in hotel basements in Las Vegas for days before being shot through the head or simply being allowed to expire from loss of blood or shock. Torture with strange instruments, too, no ordinary mischief, no ordinary hit, grisly, wildly imaginative torture and death, push his face slowly into the element of an electric stove and see how he likes it. Shit, Page would explain, a little package of dynamite wasn't even clever for those types. And anyway, Texas just spawns these types, *Blood and Money*, Dean Corls–Roman Polanski inventions. Must be in the climate, in the earth, in the water.

"Well," Steve asked, "didn't your little trick just bring down the shit that much quicker?"

"Well." Page smiled, sipped his coffee. "We were kind of wondering about that ourselves there for a while. I mean, we figure, OK, next thing he does is drop the big one, right? Surgical nuclear strike or something. But it turns out he goes out and opens the hood. And goddamned if he didn't have a heart attack."

"Right *then?*"

"Way I heard it, he took a real shock when he saw that dynamite. And he took to bed for the day, sick. Next day he's working in his garden or some shit and he dropped like a stone. 'Course I imagine he had one coming anyway, you know, bad pump and all. You don't just have a heart attack like that unless there's something already wrong with you. But that's what I'd call pharmaceutically pure, reagent-grade luck, not even stepped on once."

"Talk about your Jesus Factor." Steve shook his head.

"Yeah. And it was a good one, too. He didn't die, but it put him real close to God, they said. Spoiled his whole fucking day. Also, we heard later from the cops that Younger had some real nasty shit planned for us, sorry 'bout that." On this last phrase Page raised his eyebrows and smiled. "Of course, he did manage to hurt us some when he recovered, but we got over that."

They sat in silence for a while. Red cleared the dishes and put them in the dishwasher while Steve looked around the enormous room. The ceiling was probably twenty feet high. An elaborately decorated wooden-bladed fan hung above the kitchen table on a long brass chain. Above the sink where Red was working, the windows went all the way to the ceiling. The whole room took on light, seemed to draw it in with a suction.

The telephone broke the silence and Page flinched. "I'm gonna have to get another bell for that thing," he said, getting up to answer it.

"Little touchy." Steve smiled.

"Hello," Page said. "No, he's not here right now, can I say

who's calling? Oh, I'm afraid he isn't giving interviews." Page sounded like someone's secretary, but he craned his neck around to face Steve and gave him a conspiratorial wink, making an insanity swirl with his index finger at his temple. "I'm afraid not, not to anyone. Sorry I can't be more helpful. Sure, I'll give him the message. 'Bye."

"What was that?"

"*Playboy* magazine." Page smiled and sat down. "Interview, profile, blah, blah, blah, yadda, yadda, yadda. You know, same old bullshit." Page rested his chin in his hands. "Ought to do it, too, you know. One time Hefner had us out to his house in California. Mmmm! Did I eat something *good*." He shook his head, reminiscing. "Wish I could remember her name."

"What happened?"

"Well, that's really getting ahead of the story."

"So be it." Steve shrugged. He got up and stretched. "Mind if I practice for a while?"

"What're you going to practice?"

"A little bass, a little guitar. I've been trying to build up my guitar chops lately." Steve started for the living room. A few minutes later the sound of his bass-playing drifted in. Damn, Page thought, listen to *that*. He could almost hear Blye's drums crackling behind it—that old sound. It was so spooky it made Page want to get up and leave. But he sat through it, thinking, No, it's just Steve, it's all right. Then: Ought to call Perry. And: No, leave him alone, let him dig his own holes, look what you did to Sonny, strung out in some New Orleans hospital on smack and MDA for eight months running, unable to play, a miracle he came back at all.

"Sure sounds fine," Red said.

"Yeah." Page sighed, thinking, Sure sounds like someone I used to know.

"Butch called while you was out," Red said. "Said he wanted to come visit."

"Yeah, I talked to him once already. Told him I'd think on it."

"I don't know, Page. Haven't seen him in months."

"Yeah, maybe I should." Page thought: Can't stay holed up forever, then: Sure I can. Fuck it.

When Steve put down the bass and began playing guitar, Page went in to build a fire.

"Say," Page said when Steve stopped to tune the guitar. "How's that girl friend of yours, what's her name? Jeanie?"

"Oh," Steve said casually, "she's dead." Page nearly fell into the fireplace. "Hey." Steve laughed. "I was only jacking with you, she's fine." He set down his guitar and watched Page shake.

"You fuck," Page said, "you absolute fuck."

"Sorry." Steve still couldn't help laughing. "I didn't mean it."

"I really can't believe you, man." Page sighed heavily. "I mean you're worse than I am."

"Say, I'm sorry," Steve said again and flipped off the amplifier. "Get your guts up. Anyway, you were supposed to tell me about all that happy shit in the recording studio so we could get to the good part."

"The good part?" Page asked.

"About Hugh Hefner and all the pussy."

"Oh," Page said. "Oh, yeah. Well, recording was reasonably smooth, I mean, considering that we didn't know what the fuck we were doing. I suppose it sounded OK for a first try at a demo. There was this guy in there we knew from one of the bigger studios and we got him to listen to the songs. So he fronted us some time at his place to mix down the tapes. You know that Chocolate Bayou Studios? It's pretty popular now."

"Of course I know it."

"Well, back then he was just getting started, trying to draw business, inviting all the bigwigs to check it out. He had all the latest equipment and a good engineer. So he offered us some time in the mornings when no one else wanted to get up to play. Of course, that's where Perry came in."

⊣10⊢

Chocolate Bayou Studios was luxuriously appointed in a restrained and tasteful manner: subdued lighting, paneled walls, deep, warm-colored carpeting, anechoic. Perry Holden stood in the hallway outside Studio C looking as slick as a platinum dagger in his gray suit. His female assistant stood on one side of him as he spoke to a nervous-looking man in his thirties. Directly behind Perry stood another assistant, disinterested and lethal as a Secret Service agent. Perry's tone of voice was gentle—almost sweet— but conveyed so much venom that the man he addressed stepped away. Perry moved forward to close up the distance again.

"Don't correct me, Dale, I know what I'm talking about. I said they cannot press a high-quality disc. And I'd also like to know who you had master that thing. True Value Hardware? They sent us a reference lacquer that sounded like some of my old Billie Holiday seventy-eights. Dale, don't you understand what I'm saying to you? Everything about this has been a fiasco. I asked for Japanese PVC and you got me Tenneco. You took the job to CBS and they pressed far too many records on one stamper. I said we wanted these metal mothers to be destroyed after they're used. Dale? Are we speaking the same language?" The man lowered his head and did not respond. Directly behind Perry the male assistant removed his sunglasses and polished them. "Didn't I say I was willing to pay up to seventy-five cents per unit for this pressing?" Perry waited, but the man still said nothing. The female assistant did not react at all. It was as if she were alone in the hallway. Dale started to speak but Perry cut him off. "Dale, let me go on, please." Just then a low, eerie sound came through the door from Studio C. Perry cocked his head for a second, then continued.

"I very clearly stated that I wanted these pressings done in no less than twenty-nine seconds each. I know that everybody is doing it in twenty-three seconds. Listen, I can hear with my own ear a transduced undulation in the pressings I've got. They're not letting them cool long enough and they're shrinking and warping. We're losing the upper range on these discs." Perry again stopped to listen to the music coming from Studio C. Dale tried to speak, to defend himself somehow, but Perry waved him off, concentrating on the music. Then he went on. "Now, look, this is extremely simple, Dale. I want you to go back to square one. I want you to call Doug Sax at Mastering Labs. I want a decent lacquer to hear, and I want it soon. Very soon." Perry looked at his watch. "Then I want you to call Bert Morstein at A & M. He knows what he's doing. I want him to tell us what he's doing with his quad discs. I want to know if everybody in this country is dead set on turning out second-rate discs." Perry was distracted again by the music from Studio C. He turned on Dale, glaring. "Who's in there?"

The man lit up, relieved to have something to say. "Nobody," he said with disdain, "some local group. Nobody important." He tried to smile.

"*You* don't know what's important, Dale," Perry said softly. "That's good music. Sloppy but good." Perry examined the man carefully but the man only averted his eyes. "So call CBS and tell them we're out. We don't work with them again. Is that clear?" Dale nodded and walked away, defeated. Perry faced his female assistant. "Doesn't that sound *odd?*" He turned toward the nagging sound and cocked his ear to the door.

"Certainly does," she said. "Sounds good."

"Let's have a listen, then." Perry smiled at her and walked into the control room. Page was bent over the board with the engineer and didn't notice the visitors. Perry and his assistant stood unobtrusively in the corner watching the engineer move the knobs and levers and dials.

"Can I just hear the bass track alone?" Page asked, and the engineer replayed Link diddying up the scale. "All right, let's hear it through once like it is. There's still something wrong."

There was a brief introduction to set up the rhythm—not quite reggae/voodoo, not quite Cajun; blues chords but very little true blues sound. It was a jumpy, cheerful sound with a kernel of death at its center. Then Page's voice came in, right on the edge between giddy and scared, singing "Two-Hundred-and-Fifty-Knot Blues."

Wind shuffling up the runway
Snowballs coming outta the sky
Some people say it's the only way
Lord help me,
I'm about to fly.

Maybe the captain is crazy
Wish I was outta this seat
They say the mechanics are lazy
If it's true we're all dead meat.

I see the ground disappearing
The sweat's running into my shoes

I can't seem to get my bearings
I've got the Two-Hundred-and-Fifty-Knot blues.

They tell you it's under control
I've heard those famous last words
They've got me body and soul
Locked in this big iron bird.

Just a blip on some radar screen
I can see the headlines now
Some two-hundred-ton machine
Fell out of the blowing snow.

As the music wound along, as the solos snaked in and out, skipping and loping through the frequencies, Page's voice took on a
strained, panic quality and listening to it, he could almost feel the
plastic armrests in his clenched fists. Somehow the control booth
appeared to him like the cockpit of an airliner—the big window
facing the studio, the board with its knobs and dials and lights.
Even the fresh smell of plastic and petroleum distillates reminded
him of the kerosene smell of an airplane. It was eerie.

Finally the tape came to the end, which would eventually be
faded out:

Oh, no, no, no
This is no way for me to go
We'll never land I know
Folks down there are in for a show. . . .

"Drummer's miked wrong," the engineer said matter-of-factly.
"Sorry, man, but you know where we put these tracks down."
Page shrugged helplessly.
"Page, there's just not that much I can do with tracks like these.
It sounds like your drummer didn't even have any cans on. Listen,
he's dragging."
"Don't bother." Page waved him away. "Same thing happens on
'High Rise.' "
"I'm going to try the Marshall Time Modulation bit on 'High
Rise,' but on this one I'd re-record it if I was you."
"Goddamnit, Phil." Page was starting to lose his patience. "You
get us the studio time, we'll record them till snow flies in Del
Rio."

"Excuse me," Perry interrupted politely. Page turned, surprised that anyone was behind him. He saw the man—a well-dressed, gray-haired man, neat and distinguished. Then he looked at the woman and felt something take the wind out of his sails. He would never be able to say later exactly what caused it: the brown hair— stepped and swirled and shining; maybe the odd, deep, drowning-green eyes, like layer upon layer of intricate design. Or the precision-perfect features, bone fine and motile, lit from inside like a living lantern. It could have been the body—oh! months later Page would make her laugh at his antics about it, as he attacked her, declaring that if God had intended for her to remain un-aroused, He wouldn't have given her that body.

But now Page was quite simply arrested by the sight of her. He tried to pay attention to the man, who was talking, but he was having a problem of focus. A hand was being extended to him.

"Sorry." Page smiled slightly. What did he say?

"I said, I'm Perry Holden. I own Enigma Records. You've heard of Enigma Records?"

"Oh, yes," Page said. It got his attention anyway. He looked for the first time into Perry's face and wondered, What's this dude doing *here?*

Page had heard of Enigma Records all right, only one of the most magical independent recording companies around. And, of course, he had heard of its owner. An industry magazine profile of Perry had been headlined "The Midas Touch." By the time he had started his own label, Perry already had a reputation in the business: not only did he have an uncanny precision and accuracy in finding what would fly on the market, but he was an oddity among those high-level powers in the music industry, because he produced all his own artists. It was difficult to say where he got the energy or time. ("In a rare and graphic demonstration of Einsteinian Relativity," one music critic had written, "Holden seems to have neared the speed of light and therefore, while we get older at recording sessions, he gets younger, actually appears to *gain* time by spending it.")

Page had also heard the guarded references to the enormous power wielded by this unassuming, mild-mannered man, heard of the Maf ties, the rumors of distribution wars and Teamster in-fluences and chains of nightclubs owned in partnership with famous rock and rollers who let certain people dust off their dirty money in a cash-intensive business, money skimmed (some said) from casinos in Las Vegas.

Rock and Roll: it was common knowledge that the $2-billion-a-year industry had that gray miasma leaking from it the way any megabusiness does at some point in its development. But the details were always cloudy in that euphoric reticulum of the entertainment world. It was a masterful sleight of hand: drink up, Ladies and Gentlemen, notice that at no time do my arms leave my sleeves. Like some cosmic clown, the lighthearted hollowness and mindless good humor of rock and roll disarmed even its most tenacious investigators, who, passing through to the inner circle, inevitably failed to realize that inside that circle was another circle, and another inside that. And another. All of them half-silvered mirrors. Reporters could rush around looking until their batteries went dead, and people like Perry would just smile and nod and roll out another platinum disc. For if the rock and rollers were the grunts of the industry, the light assault teams, then the Perry Holdens were the Ellsworth Bunkers or the William Westmorelands of it all, conducting their esoteric strategies from electronic maps.

"This is Jill," Perry was saying now, and she took Page's hand. He felt as if she'd just given him an injection of a drug he'd never tried before, a big rush and a boss feeling. Page felt a paradoxical sleepiness overtake him.

"Love the sound." Perry indicated the console. He didn't bother to mention to Page that the recording quality was pretty awful.

"Thank you," Page said and thought, You're going to have to do better than that. Get it to-*geth*-er. "That's great," he added and felt like an ass.

"Unique sound," Jill offered. "A little like that Louisiana music, what do they call it?"

"Zodico," Perry put in.

"Zodico, yes," she said.

They talked for a while about Zodico music, "migrated with the Acadians from Nova Scotia to Louisiana in the 1700s," Perry told Jill, "mixed with the African music from the blacks who lived among the Acadians and ended up as what they call Zodico."

"Where did that word come from?" Jill asked. Page could think of nothing to say and concentrated on keeping his mouth closed.

"No one really knows," Perry said. "I think Bob Palmer once

suggested that it was a mispronunciation of *l'haricot* because there's an old Cajun song called 'Tes Haricots Pas Sales.' "

"Well, there's something of that sound in it," Jill said.

"But not exactly," Perry said. "Something else too . . ." He let his voice trail off, musing. "You have others, I presume." Perry brought his head up, fixing Page in his gaze. Page stared blankly. "Songs," Perry suggested.

"Oh, yeah, oh, yeah, we're just trying to mix four right now. I mean, actually, we could record maybe ten or twelve, but we were sort of putting together a little demo. And I'm always working on new songs."

"You're the writer?" Perry asked.

"Yeah, I write all the songs, at least so far. I sing them. I do the initial arranging on paper and then we just work it out in rehearsal until it sounds right. But it's really a complete group thing. I mean, it's not *me*." He poked himself in the chest. "It's a band. It's the whole band."

"What's it called?" Jill asked.

"Jambeaux," Page said, then spelled it.

"Meaning?" Perry asked, turning to Jill with raised eyebrows. "It does sound Cajun."

"It's supposed to." Here Page laughed, shrugged modestly, ducking his head. "It really doesn't mean anything. We just sort of came up with it." He explained the various meanings it might have, as he had to the rest of the band the night he came up with it.

"I like it," Jill said. *"Les Beaux Jams,* nice."

"Yes," Perry said. "Has some mystery."

"Enigmatic?" Jill laughed lightly at her own joke but the laughter hit Page like a hammer ringing an anvil. One voice in his head was saying, Man, there it *is*. Another was singing that age-old song: Never happen. And a line came to him that he knew would become a song. The lines always came to him at such odd times. *It's an age-old song Mother Nature sings*. He filed it away for future reference.

Perry asked how long they had worked together, and Page explained that they had been playing off and on for years, but that this particular mixture was new.

"Is Jambeaux working somewhere?" Perry asked.

"Yes." Page grinned, embarrassed at the thought of the Burning

Spear. "Just a ratty little club. We needed a place to play so we just took the first thing that came up. Just a place to rehearse, really."

"Do you mind if Jill comes to hear the band?" Perry asked, and Page's head came up: Mind? Would I *mind?*

"Not at all." He tilted his head to one side, squinting at the man. "Any-Time." Then he smiled. "Of course, it's not a very *nice* place."

"I'm used to it." Jill laughed. "You should see some of the places Perry's sent me into."

"Oh, I have. I have."

"I'd come myself," Perry apologized as they went out into the hallway where Perry's driver/bodyguard waited, poised on the balls of his feet, looking like a lot of potential energy. "But . . . business." Perry said it as if everything were revealed in that one innocuous word.

Then Page was alone in the hallway with Jill, wishing he had shaved that morning, wishing he had dressed in something other than an old T-shirt that bore a skull and the legend: COURAGE NOT COMPROMISE.

"Mind if I listen?" Jill pointed at Studio C.

"No, no," he lied. He knew he wouldn't be able to work with her watching but he wanted her near him. Half an hour later he had clearly demonstrated to the engineer that his working day was over by screwing up in every possible way. Jill stepped forward.

"I'm making you nervous," she said. "I'll leave."

"No, no." Page shot out of his seat. "Stay."

"I can't." She smiled—almost laughed at him, really. He was acting like a teenager on his first date. "Look, I've got to take care of some business. Let's have dinner tonight."

"I thought you'd never ask." Page ducked his head.

Jill laughed. "I'll pick you up at six." Page gave her the address and she left. He watched her all the way down the long hallway. The ballet of muscles under her skirt nearly hypnotized him.

"Page." The engineer came up behind him. "What in hell's wrong with you?"

"Fuck oh dear," was all Page said.

"Listen, do me a favor. I've got Bobby Bland coming here in an hour. Why don't you go home? I'll see you tomorrow."

Page was so distracted by the encounter he didn't even notice the tan Chevrolet parked in the studio lot as he left. An hour later he was bouncing off the walls of his apartment, beer in hand, jabbering away at Link, who sprawled on the couch and punctuated Page's mad monologue with an occasional chuckle, enjoying the desperate antics.

"Man, man," Page said with wide, childlike eyes, "I'm in *Love*, man. She is so *Beau*tiful! Oh, God, what am I going to do? I. Am. Suffering. I'm honing bad."

Even though Page frequently went into streaks over women, Link could see that this was different. He could tell Page had a major case of it. When Page went to the shower to get ready for dinner, Link began thinking about Cyndi and how that little matter would shake out. He had watched her and Page become closer and closer over the months, drawn together by accidents of proximity and need, neither admitting it, neither even asking for it. And now Link just wondered.

"Just remember," Link cautioned as Page dressed, "she's just another woman. She looks good today and she's real smart and all that good shit, but don't let it put you uptight. You just in *love* is all."

"Yeah," Page said sternly, his brain going, Yeah, yeah, and the atomic bomb, like the slingshot, is just another weapon, don't let it put you uptight. You just remember that, Page.

At five minutes to six Page stood on the curb, impatient and nervous as a cat, squinting up the street in the running sunlight. When the limousine appeared, rounding the corner, Page wondered, Now, what the hell could that be? He had a moment of panic, thinking Younger himself had come to get them, and reached for his waistband. When it stopped in front of him and a driver got out to hold the door, Page looked at the man as if he'd made some terrible mistake.

"Get in." Jill laughed from the dark interior. "You're letting out my air conditioning."

Page just stood there and through some crazy quirk of his mental pathways made a connection with the first day he was taken out in a chopper, when he'd had this reaction: This machine has come down here to pick *me* up? Oh, no, it's *got* to be much worse than they said it was going to be. In Vietnam he'd had no choice and now, in Houston, he simply pushed the thought from his mind. He got in and pretended nothing unusual was happening, even when

Jill hit a button and a glass partition slid up, sealing them off from the driver. Even when she smiled tenderly at him and touched his hair with her fingertips.

"How are you, Page?" she asked as if she'd known him for years. "Don't be so nervous."

Haw! What a joke. Nervous? Shit. He felt like he was going to need a respirator in a minute.

The land frigate eased silently away from the curb and Page told himself that he really, really wanted to be a star, yes, and he'd better start rehearsing for the part now. No time like the present, sitting in a limousine for the first time in his life, next to Jill.

He could already feel the great machine churning out its power —not the car, but the entire mechanism atop which he was sitting. It's like that moment when an airplane physically gathers itself for flight, no turning back, just hope to God they've got it together up front. Page fidgeted, unable to think of anything to say. He fingered the telephone before him with detached fascination. Man, he thought, a telephone in a *car?*

"You need to make a call?"

"No, no." Page pulled his hand away, embarrassed. "I've never seen a phone in a car before."

"A bit tacky, isn't it? There ought to be someplace you could get away from the damned thing."

"Oh, *no,*" Page said breathlessly. "I love it, really. Nothing finer. Wish I had to call somebody."

Jill laughed. "Tell me all about Jambeaux."

Page gave her a short history of the band. The talk was small, but each time Jill looked at him and smiled in that special way, he felt as if they'd been eyeing one another across a room for ten generations.

One of the few places where a musician is treated well is in restaurants. When they arrived at Pino's, the owner charged out to greet Page enthusiastically.

"Page, Page, what have you been doing? I've heard there was some trouble. . . ." The little man stopped short when he saw Jill. He straightened and said with a slight bow, "Miss, you are welcome here. Especially in the company of Page, who is like a brother."

"Thank you." Jill smiled at the man, who was clearly eager to please them.

"Come, come, come," he said, "I will personally show you to your table." Pino made a great spectacle of bringing wine and menus and jabbering excitedly at the staff until he was certain everything was in order at Page's table.

"None of my business," Page began when Pino had left them alone, "but what's a guy like Perry doing in a brand-new studio like Chocolate Bayou?"

"Mick got pissed off at the people at Criteria in Miami." Jill sipped the wine Pino had brought and nodded her approval. "Mick said he didn't want to record there. So, naturally, word gets out, and he gets offers from Wishbone, Caribou, Island, LeStudio, Mediasound, Ice Nine—all the usual suspects. But he was in a bad frame of mind, I mean anybody would have done it for him, and frankly, anybody could get *their* sound on tape."

Page drank off half his glass of wine, wondering, Is she talking about the Mick I think she's talking about?

"So he decided he wanted to try one of the newer studios, and Chocolate Bayou seemed to be pretty nice from what we'd heard. Perry wanted to see for himself." Page watched her, smiling.

"Mick, eh?"

Jill laughed and looked into her wine. "Yeah," she admitted, a little embarrassed. She really hadn't been name-dropping, it was just reflex. "*Mick.* Or Michael if you're fucking him."

"Are you?"

"No. He's, uh, not my type."

Page let it drop when the food arrived. He had a thing about Italian food. "Carbing out," he'd heard it called. And now he went at it with a purpose, maintaining just enough conversation to keep Jill laughing. He ate and goofed and Jill nearly ran a mouthful of wine down the wrong pipe.

"Ah, Italian ops, nothing finer," he said, poking around in a plate of pasta. "Chop ops, mmm, how come the Italians can't fight? Too much chop ops."

"Ops?" Jill asked.

"Operations, man, delicacy ops, pasta ops, nothing finer." And he remembered something Jan had shown him in Austin, some of the little poetry he remembered from that period. It had been in the front of an F. Scott Fitzgerald book: "Then wear the gold hat if that will please her and if you can bounce high, bounce high for her too, until she cry, 'Lover, Gold-hatted, High-bouncing lover, I must have you!' "

During a lapse in the conversation, Page happened to drop his eyes to his plate with all its tomato sauce spread around and he took such a bad flash that he felt a fiery olfactory hallucination seize him. He turned away abruptly. No matter how much time he put between himself and those days, he was never less amazed at how quickly a beautiful moment could turn ugly when your guard is down. It took his breath away.

"What's the matter?" Page heard the voice as if from a distance. Page focused on Jill for a second and then defocused again. She had seen his face go through the spectrum to a sick green. He knew that but couldn't respond, persistence of vision: that kid from Delta Company in the wrong place at the wrong time. Page had been lighting the kid's cigarette when the sniper round took him squarely in the head. And he tried for weeks afterwards to wipe off what had erupted into his cupped hands, what had spattered across his face and chest like a hot, lurid insult. He developed a rash after a while from washing, until that same old voice had come to tell him that he could wipe away his chest and hands and face, and then he could wipe away the bone beneath his face, finally the brain matter under that, and even then it would never, ever occur: "A little bit of soap will never wash away these tears."

"Are you all right?" Jill seemed truly worried.

"Fine, fine," Page lied.

"You lie." Jill's manner was authoritative. Clearly she wasn't fooled by his attempts to recover his equilibrium.

"I lie when I can." Page tried to smile as the busboy removed the exploded head he'd seen in his food. Jill wanted to press it further but changed the subject instead, asking about the other band members. It gave Page a chance to make all the standard jokes about the Senator, the Captain, the Missouri Professor of Death, and Jill laughed until her sides hurt. By the time they got back in the limousine, both she and Page were in a good mood. Page launched into an extended warning about the Burning Spear.

"I've been in some pretty bad clubs," Jill assured him.

"No, really." Page gesticulated wildly. "This club is *so* bad, so filthy, on such a low scale that I don't even know how I *play* there.

One time it got so repulsive that Link and I took some of the cockroaches—I mean they have these humongous cockroaches there, probably breed them near nuclear waste dumps, man, I mean they are absolute mutants, you'd better believe it, and they *fly.*" Page gave the word such an odious inflection that Jill couldn't help laughing. "I mean they are—Well, let me just put it this way, if you have a bat complex, you don't want to go *near* this club, because those cockroaches will *terminate* you. All she wrote." Jill was doubled over, holding her stomach, which just encouraged Page to go on. "So anyway, me and Link, we took some of these vampire cockroaches and painted on their backs in white paint EAT AT THE BURNING SPEAR, and we set them loose in the club and some of these people absolutely took a cardiac arrest when they saw that, I mean they just left. It really destroyed them."

"Page," Jill gasped, "you are really something. Cockroaches! Oh, I love it!"

With no warning, Page moved across the seat and kissed her. And she kissed back, putting her arms around his neck while his mind went, Man, man, you could have just queered the entire fucking scene with a move like that, oh, God, what is this? She could have killed you, but what's going on? As the Continental limo spooled along the steamy streets with its oblivious android driver, Page knew he wasn't back in his apartment sound asleep only because this wasn't the sort of dream he had.

"What's that?" Jill asked softly, curling her hand back around his waist against something hard—not a human part. She pulled away from him and asked again, "What is that?"

"What? What's what?"

"This." She grabbed for it but Page moved away, laughing.

"That's a back brace." Page looked away. "I'm paraplegic. War wound."

"A back brace." Jill smirked to let him know she thought he was full of shit.

"Yes, and if you believe that, I've a nice piece of property you might like to buy, just about a hundred miles south of New Orleans."

"Why do you carry it?"

"You've been in L.A. for too long." Page began in earnest now. "This town is populated by actualized killers. They're truly crazy.

Give you an example. You heard about Sonny and that Phil Shorter deal?"

"Yes. Do you know him?"

"Old friends." Page crossed his middle finger over his index finger to indicate the degree of closeness. "Anyhow, we were at the PapaBurger—great little Northside burger joint—and some simian reptile comes out, sees Sonny's white hair, and goes, 'Hey, faggot!' And Sonny, being a sweet guy, goes, like, 'Suck dirty swamp water through a pigmy blowgun.' Next thing we know the fucker throws down on us with a *firearm*." Page said it as if he had never fired one before.

There was a pause.

"What happened?"

"We lit him up." Page grinned sheepishly, shrugging.

"Lit. Him. Up," Jill enunciated.

Page looked at her as if it were hopeless to try to explain any more than that. They rode in silence, her hand in his, all the way to the club. Page watched Houston go by, thinking, Gee, it sure looks better from inside one of these things. No wonder they use them.

At the club Jill planted herself in a corner and didn't move for the rest of the night. Page hadn't told anyone but Link that she was coming.

"Goddamn Sam," Link whispered to Page as they mounted the stage. "Guess you weren't—uh—ex-*aj*-er-atin'.'"

"Shhh." Page put his finger to his lips.

Page strapped on his guitar, tapped the mike with one finger. It made a pop and he leaned into it: "This Is Dedicated to the One I Love." He sounded husky. Then he added, "Rock and Row-Wool!" Blye struck his snare drum once solidly and Link drove into the song with his bass. Each time the break came up, Link sang the line in a high, warbling falsetto, odd for a man his size, and Page came in below, staring across the dark smoke and scum air. When it was over the people clapped. Jill clapped.

"Thanks for the clap," Butch said into his microphone, and Page gave him a dirty look.

From there it was just so fine. They moved through the night like a full-bore circus passing through a small town, the people still spinning when they were gone. (What hit me?) It was one of those nights when no one could do anything wrong, because Page's enthusiasm and his high were so infectious that the third set even saw Scoop dancing and jiving. They were so wrapped up in it that Page almost failed to notice the two men in suits enter the room.

They had approached the club from its dark side away from Fannin and came quickly around to the front entrance. They walked over to the bar and, looking as if they meant business, took Ritchie aside and gestured stiffly at the stage. Ritchie looked very uneasy during the exchange. The two men were still barking at him angrily, when one of them stopped and grabbed the other's arm. Page tried not to stare, but he couldn't take his eyes off them. The two men whispered at each other intensely and then one of them spun on his heels, as if he were exasperated, and walked out. The other followed reluctantly. Page had no idea what to make of it and by the end of the set he had become so caught up in the music again that he didn't think of it again until much later. Besides, there was Jill in the back of the room, and Page was drawn to her. Each time their eyes met, he wanted to leap off the stage.

At the end of the third set, Page and Link sang "Shake," hard and fast, and the crowd went wild. When the song ended, Page stepped up to the microphone. The applause was deafening. Behind his back, Butch leaned around to grin at Blye, who waved his drumsticks back at the Senator.

"Thank you, ah, you're so sweet tonight," Page said breathlessly. The applause continued. "Thank you, nothing finer." He turned around, placing his hand over the microphone, and asked Link, "Want to do our Jambeaux number?"

Link turned to Butch. "Jambeaux, get your noisemakers." When Butch was ready with his Caribbean sound effects, they launched into a new song they had been rehearsing. It was done in a very Jamaican style—intentionally overstylized—and Page sang it with a Jamaican accent while the musicians bobbed around him, jumping and dancing. Butch played his bells and gourds and ratchets, accentuating the reggae effect. It was a nonsense song, purely for fun and dancing. The beat was infectious and the crowd pranced around, grinning and shucking, even though they had never heard the song before.

> Jambeaux singin' in de night
> Singing in the rain

Always singin' of the joy and pain.
Is your daughter on the street?
Are your birds in flight?
Watch out! Jambeaux comin' home tonight.

Jambeaux man gonna make you happy
Jambeaux man gonna make you fly
Never can smoke too much Jamaican
Mebbe get arrested
But at least you're high.

After three more verses, Jill thought: Now, how am I supposed to make an objective decision on this one? Perry's going to have to make up his own mind. By the end of the night she felt drained. Even the normally jaded crowd had gotten into it: Jambeaux had found its groove, trailing on Page's exhilaration. Four sets and it seemed as if they'd just begun. But the gig was over, and that was all right with Page. They rolled into the breaktune they always used to end the night. It was a hard, fast, rocking jazz-form with walking bass, over which Page could talk. He took the microphone in both hands, sweating happily like a fighter who'd won.

"Thank you, thank you!" The crowd was actually screaming. "Remember, Tuesday night is free beer night. We'll be playing from eight to midnight." He spoke in gleeful gasps, gulping air after the workout. "Y'all come and get Di-*Rek*-Ly down with Jambeaux." He pronounced the word *Jom-bo*. "Once again, Link on bass." He turned and smiled at Link, who diddied through an arpeggio at high speed. "The Mormon Senator from Utah, Butch himself, on flute, tenor, alto, clarinet, bassoon, piano, organ, synthesizer, guava, ratchet, bells, xylophone, and, of course, probably on drugs too—did I miss anything?" Butch smiled, put the tenor to his lips, and played a fiery sheet of notes. "The Missouri Professor, dead but too dumb to stop playing, Scoop, lead guitar." Without moving a thing but his fingers, Scoop lashed out at the people, who applauded wildly at the fancy guitar licks. "And of course, direct from London, the Mideast, Barbados, and the Caracas Penitentiary, the British Shock Troop Commando, Captain Blye on tubs." Page turned around to face Blye, who exploded in a fury of motion and sound. "Yours truly," Page said, "call me Page, Page." And the band roared into a final chorus of the bass-walking jazz break theme. Then they shut it down quickly and killed the stage lights.

When he got to Jill's table, she jumped up and hugged him. "It's really something." She beamed. "You've really got something special there, Page."

"Call me Page." He grinned. He knew it had worked.

"I haven't had that much fun in a long time." Jill threw her hair out of her face with a shake of her head.

"How come I done it." Page shrugged modestly. "Come on, I want you to meet the band."

When he was introduced, Link puffed up a little and announced, "I shore do appreciate your comin' out here, ma'am."

"Please don't call me ma'am," Jill said. "I'm only twenty-six."

"Yes, ma'am." Link grinned obligingly, as Page introduced Blye.

"Gosh, charmed, super," Blye said breathlessly, wiping the sweat from his face and neck with a towel that was already soaked.

Butch moved right in, grinning maliciously. "As long as I've got a face, you've got a place to sit," he said earnestly to Jill. Page just about took a stroke.

"Ooo"—Blye backed out of the way—"no bloody danger of that."

"Goddamnit, Butch!" Page screamed, rolling away from Jill and facing off with the crazed saxophonist. Jill thought it was funny, but Butch saw Page's expression and moved back. Those teeth were expensive.

Scoop hung back and nodded slightly when Page got around to introducing him. And all of them were thinking roughly the same thing. Maybe Page had been right after all. Maybe they really would have to go out into the real world and play that music. There was the flat, fast rush of enlightenment, like, Oh, man, we just played an audition for Enigma Records, dig it! Then the thought: Good Lord, it's a good thing we didn't know or we would have really fucked up, and then: Oh, no, we *definitely* blew it, remember that rimshot I missed, that note I hung on for too long, that harmony on some song where my voice wavered from the pitch? Holy shit, it's all over now.

Link, however, was as unflustered as usual. Page thanked whatever rock and roll gods he prayed to that he had let the band sleep through the day, that he had gone to the studio alone. For Page knew Jill had just seen Jambeaux at its absolute, uncut best, rested, sober, in the groove. And even the dumbest of musicians wouldn't have asked the question they most wanted answered: Are we going to get to record on Enigma and be stars with a big *S?*

Page managed to disengage Jill from the band and ask her if she would like to go have a drink somewhere. She said yes, knowing what he meant by asking her out for a drink—shy Page, even after all these years; he laughed with her, seeing that she was not about to be fooled by that but that she appreciated the delicacy nonetheless.

As the Lincoln pulled away from the Burning Spear, a light autumn drizzle had started to fall and Link, Blye, and Scoop stood there oblivious to it (Butch, clothes conscious, was trying to brush the drops from his jacket, impossible task). They stood with their mouths open; it had knocked them clean, smooth out.

"Make fuckin' believers outta you yet," Link said softly when the taillights had disappeared down the misty road.

⊶11⊷

When Page and Jill first arrived at her hotel suite, they had a drink and talked nervously in the living room. It was classic: they tried to tell each other their life stories in the space of an hour. And, of course, they were both thinking the same thing: When and how? Is it time yet? Is this the right moment?

"Do you like it in Houston?" Jill was asking.

"What's your sign?" Page asked and Jill laughed. "That's what they say in California, right? What's your sign? Want a back rub?"

"That's what they say." Jill nodded.

"I'm a vertigo," Page went on. "Vertigo with a moon in escrow."

"Also slightly mad." Jill stood up. "And, yes, I do want a back rub." Page stood up to meet her. In her arms, Page felt the form of her body, lean and strong and at the same time fragile. And where their bodies touched, he felt a pure, singular energy arc between them.

In the bedroom, Jill turned off the lights and left Page standing there, blinking in the darkness. He heard the movement beside him, the hiss of material, the delicate clink of a belt buckle, the zip of a zipper, and then the single word, "Page," said in a way that shook him out of his daze. How can something so old be so original, he wondered, ultimate, basic, million-year-old sensation, so uncomplicated, there's no time like the first time, uncut essence of pleasure there in the Bible blackness above this warm lady in that exquisite ballet of muscles, until he heard nothing but his own voice, repeating over and over the syllable, "Jill, Jill, Jill, Jill."

Shortly after dawn the thunder woke them and they sat up in bed, watching it all come down.

"They're playing our song," Page said.

"I love a good storm." Jill stretched and Page saw her, cast momentarily in the strange glow of lightning, the only perfect breasts he had ever seen, neither large nor small.

"Nothin' finer." Page slipped out of the bed and went to open the window and watch. It was a bleak dawn with heavy, occluded black clouds moving fast and low across the half-lit morning. As he watched, a crooked shaft of lightning stitched its way down the sky, illuminating the sheets of rain driven by a gale-force wind. "Rock and Roll," Page whispered reverently. He was glad to be fifty miles inland and not on Galveston Island now. Jill crossed the room and wrapped her arms around his waist. The thunder clapped against the window and then rolled across the city, shuddering away in waves. Page hoped silently that the Riptide Rendezvous would take a direct hit this time.

"Mother Nature," Jill said softly.

"Mother Nature," Page repeated. "Yes, Mother Nature." He suddenly spun away from her and disappeared into the living room.

"What're you doing?" Jill squinted into the room and saw him take hotel letterhead from the writing desk and sit down with a pen.

"I just remembered something." Page began scribbling. "You go on back to bed. I'll be right along. I've just got to write this little thing. I'll be right there." Jill saw that he was lost in the task. She shrugged, yawned, and went back to bed. Later, she vaguely recalled him crawling in with her, but she didn't wake up.

It was well after noon when Jill rolled over and placed a kiss on Page's forehead. He opened his eyes.

"Buzz," he said.

"What?" She laughed. Page was not really awake.

"Buzz," he repeated.

"Are you a little bee?" she asked, as if talking to a child.

Page didn't answer. He just reached out and pulled her to him. "Time for your physical therapy," he muttered.

She laughed and rolled over on top of him. Page pulled the sheets around her, and it was after one before they left the bed.

In the shower together, they soaped one another and Page just stared at her body. She looked like a dancer.

"I've got to say," Jill began, "I've never seen that kind of dedication, especially in a musician."

"What kind is that?" Page asked.

"Leaving a lady like me in bed alone—to write a *song?*" Jill smiled and scrubbed Page's back with a washcloth.

"I guess I get kind of weird when I write," Page said. "It's my thing."

"I guess."

"That and singing and playing."

"And physical therapy."

They ordered breakfast, which was brought on a cart and laid out on the table. When the waiter left, they sat down to eat but paused before starting. They looked at each other for a long time, their eyes locked together, sharing a half smile, that look only two people recently in love can have, where just the looking passes so much gentle energy back and forth it can bring on tears.

"Damn," Page said reverently, shaking his head. He started eating with exaggerated cowboy vigor. "Goddamn, woming." The storm had ripped away the haze and ozone, and now the day was razor sharp and autumn cool.

"I have to go back to L.A. today," Jill said.

"What I figured." Even so, Page felt a twinge of loneliness. That was quick, he thought. Jill got up and crossed the room. She came back with her briefcase and took out a business card for Page.

"I'll probably call you tonight," she said, "but you can call me collect anytime you like."

"You better watch it or the phone company'll shut you down."

She stood over him and the light hit her eyes in a certain way. Page looked at them and then remembered the previous day, noticing that deep green jungle-snowflake pattern, layer after layer of overlapping kaleidoscopic color, like looking through fathoms of green and brown.

"That's it," he said. "I was wondering what it was."

"What?"

"Your eyes." He took her face in his hands and drew it closer. "You and I have the same eyes." He led her into the bathroom and they stared in the mirror at each other's eyes.

"You're right," she whispered, touching his cheek.

Back in the living room, they sat sipping coffee in silence, watching each other. Finally, Jill laughed involuntarily.

"So what's going to happen?" Page asked.

It was the first time he had mentioned the unmentionable—Jill knew Page was not asking about their embryonic relationship. She also knew that she was going back to L.A., and at the moment, the only way for Page to get there was for Enigma to call him. And if Enigma didn't want Jambeaux, Page could just stay in Houston. He would have to hawk his demo and that was an old story. It could take a month, a year, maybe two. Maybe never. The music business was a grim joke; you either got fucked or fucked over, laid or laid out on a stainless-steel table. Screwed or screwed down until you couldn't move without hurting somewhere. Some people liked to think being a musician was fun; it was something like the way southerners viewed colored people back when, those happy darkies with their wild, funny ways, oh, to be so carefree, but nobody'd ever told it, not the way it was. Talk about double-double binds, if you were content with your own miserable lot, like Sonny, they'd snap you up and digest you so fast you wouldn't even get a chance to thank them. And if you were not content, you probably weren't good enough anyway. Page had seen that final chord come down far too often to kid himself about what might happen, yet all musicians had that ability to suspend disbelief, suspend suspicion and even reality, long enough to extend a hope. It was all propaganda, right? Them, not us. It can't happen here. How then could Page possibly hope to make it? Well, there were other strengths and weaknesses that often transcended rules and statistics, and there was always the quantum mechanics of luck when the strengths ran out, there was the Jesus Factor too, if you wanted to call it that. And now all Jill could say was that she didn't know, truly didn't know. She didn't want to offer him any false hopes, though she knew she had already done that by sort of falling in love with him, not too cool.

When the limousine discharged Page back on Timmons Lane, he assumed he was in for some good-natured ribbing about Jill. He didn't know the first thing about it: when he walked in, they were waiting like wolves, and they set upon him as if they were famished. Page quickly realized that they had assumed that if everything "went well" between him and Jill, Jambeaux would be home free. And it was a major letdown when Page was noncommittal and brooding. Butch had expected there to be a limousine for *him* by today.

"Now look here, you dumb motherfuckers," Page shouted, "you been out in this Houston sun for too long."

"Wow, man, he gets his first ride in a limousine and we're a bunch of dumb motherfuckers," Butch said. "Well, fuck that shit."

Link sat on the couch, paring his fingernails and pretending he didn't hear. Blye stood at the kitchen counter sipping coffee and smiling at them. "That's the spirit, girls," he said quietly. "Let's tear this whole bloody thing down for good." No one paid him any attention.

"You don't know the first thing about how the music business works, Butch," Page flashed at him.

"Jump back, Jack!" Scoop mocked. "Man, he spends one night with some record company flak and he knows the record business."

"Fuck you, man." Page whirled around. "I don't know how it works either, but at least I know it doesn't work *that* way. Whatever went on last night between me and her doesn't have anything to do with any damn deals. She's not a flak, anyway. She's got a lot of power. But this dude Perry Holden is big. He sends her out, *maybe* he comes to hear us himself. And then if he likes us, *maybe* he does something about it. We're not the first band he's ever heard."

He stopped. Jesus, he thought, looking at them, they might actually get violent. But there was only quiet, until the air-conditioner thermostat cut in with a resounding *thunk*. If it had gone unspoken before, it was clear now that Page was the undisputed leader. But it also brought him up short, because now the responsibility was on his shoulders. Where it had been a vague notion before, full of jargon and hope (form a "band," cut "demos," become "stars"), it was now much more than that: Enigma Records had come and heard them and had liked them. And they were believers now, hungry believers too. They had seen the limo and all of a sudden Link's damaged old Cadillac didn't look so sleek anymore. Where before, working the Burning Spear and recording at a ramshackle studio was a thrilling, electric novelty in their grinding existence, now they had new, more stirring images in their heads and the lust for them. The first shot's free, just like they say.

"Man," Butch continued, "I think your attitude has really gotten out of hand. Who do you think you are?"

"Hey"—Page turned his palms out and faced off with Butch—"what are you talking about? You get fucked up on Quaaludes or booze or coke every day and barely make rehearsals, while I've pushed this thing along as hard as I could, every step of the way. Just what the fuck do you mean, who am I?" He put his finger in Butch's face as Butch flushed red. "Who the fuck am I? Who the fuck are *you*, motherfucker?" The veins popped in Page's forehead.

The only one who hadn't said anything was Link and now he spoke, unfolding his massive body from its position on the couch.

"All right, that's enough."

"Who are *you*?" Blye shouted at Link, making fun of Butch.

"Shut up," Link said. It was all he needed to say. He said it so evenly and with such clarity that everyone—even Page—did just that. Link looked around the room to see if anyone was going to go against him. "All right," he spoke quietly. "Now we aren't going to go fighting like this. We've made one little contact, that's all. That don't mean we have to go gettin' so haired over it. Maybe it works, maybe not. Page says the guy heard the stuff in the studio and liked it. Great. The chick said she liked what she heard at the club. Great. But that don't mean we gotta go tearin' each other a new asshole. Ain't we in this together? Page didn't do nothin'."

"Jesus wept, Link," Blye started in. "No, no, let's have after it here. Here, here." He grabbed an umbrella that was leaning against a wall. "Now, here, Butch, lad, you take this—" He tried to place it in Butch's hand but Butch shied away, embarrassed. "There's a lad." Blye went over to Page. "Here, son, here's a grapefruit spoon, now, good for removing eyeballs and wot-not. Little enucleation for the starkers crowd, eh?"

"Shut up, turdbird," Link said, and Blye went back to his coffee.

"Gone loony in one night," Scoop said, slapping himself in the head. "Egads."

"And *if.* . . ." Link smiled broadly now, expansively. "If this lady happened to take a shine to Page, why, what harm could come of that?"

"Indeed," Scoop piped up. "It couldn't hurt if she happened to receive an injection of Doctor Page's Elixir of Life, guaranteed to cure feminine complaints."

"Haw!" Blye jumped forward. "I heard that it was an intramuscular injection. It must have been painful."

"Gad Zooks!" Scoop said. "Fucking medical miracle, this boy."

"Yes siree." Butch came over and slapped Page on the back. "A wonder he can stand up." And Page started to chuckle with them, ducking his head, embarrassed, as the whole cadre disintegrated into giggles. They went back to the club and put in four solid hours of work.

-12-

When Page returned to mixing the demo, Butch wanted to know why they even had to send it. After all, Jill had heard them play. How come this Enigma guy didn't just make up his mind? Page knew it was never that simple. Jill and Perry knew a good thing when they heard it, but they were cautious too. And during the barrage of phone calls and letters she and Page exchanged, through the haze of affectionate language and longing, was the distinct message: send the demo. Perry wants to hear it. And to the rest of the band it seemed that when Page wasn't playing the gigs or rehearsing, he was either talking on the phone with Jill or tinkering with the mix at Chocolate Bayou.

It was a good week after his first night with Jill before Page could deal with Cyndi again, and it wasn't easy for him then. But that was his fault, not hers. She had never expected anything from him, certainly not some kind of exclusive franchise and especially not with her stormy marriage. And when she learned that he was in love, she just laughed and laughed. "Poor Page, poor silly Page." He was so taken aback he didn't know whether to be offended or grateful.

When Cyndi and Jill met later and became friends, Page was once again mystified. "Page," Jill explained matter-of-factly one night, "we love you. Don't you understand? No one can have you. I'm not really sure anyone would want you. But that doesn't mean we can't love you or have fun with you." Jill's words just compounded Page's confusion, but at least gave him a hook from which to hang it. In addition, they gave him an uneasy feeling that was never to leave. "I'm not really sure anyone would *want* you." That buried itself deep and stayed there.

But the simple request for the demo presented problems that were far from simple, and it kept Page more than occupied. Chocolate Bayou yanked them from the mixing schedule, having filled the morning time slots with paying customers. Page had to await whatever time was free. And the sense of urgency only increased as Page realized that the sound was never going to get there—that it would not match the sound he had always heard. The original tracks just weren't good enough, and even the best of engineers had to have something to work with. Page felt trapped. Every time one of the band members insisted he let the demo go, send it out, he practically blew up. He knew it wasn't going to get any better. But he continued to tinker with it, refusing to admit that perhaps he was stalling or that he was terrified of rejection if the demo didn't live up to expectations.

On top of that, Page could not help wondering about the Younger people. What about those two men in suits who had come into the Burning Spear the night Jill was there? It wasn't until much later that he knew the whole story, but he and Link discussed it frequently.

"I mean, the papers said he had a fucking heart attack," Link said at one point. "But that doesn't mean they're just gonna shut down. Something's going on."

"I know," Page said. "I don't like this either. I'd almost rather have them come out and do something. This silence is getting me weird."

"Between that and this demo, it's no wonder you're spooked."

"Nothin' to do but wait," Page said.

"And get that demo out there," Link reminded him.

They didn't have to wait long. The steady and unrelenting silence and delays had settled on them like a bad contract and even Page ultimately agreed to send the tape out to Los Angeles. Fall was upon them and they had borrowed about all the time they could.

By then they were pretty pleased with themselves, glad it was finally over. (Years later, Page and Link would bust a gut over that one: "*Over!* Whew! Man, we were beautiful, weren't we?") But naturally, there was a small celebration the night they finished the tape and Page slept late the next morning. He had gotten drunk and talked to Jill all night on the phone, just like he was in love for the very first time.

"Fucking the duck," Link said to Blye in the morning. "Goddamn, Page's on the phone all night with that chick and now we got this tape ready for her and it's almost noon and what's Page doing? Fucking the goddamned duck. Didn't even have the energy to go over to Cyndi's after that phone call. Man, old Page is in the gap." Link had tried with no success to wake Page.

"Back in the cut," Blye offered.

"Sawing the fucking logs." Link smiled.

"Copping the bloody *Z*," Blye added. "Haw!"

"Crash Central." Link was chuckling, too.

"Oh fuck oh dear." They both turned to see Page standing in the doorway.

"Well, I should hope to kiss a pig," Link observed.

"Oh, lad," Blye said mournfully, "give us your name and we'll put it on the list." Page just looked puzzled. "The critical list," Blye explained.

They turned Page around and directed him toward the shower. Half an hour later they were walking out the door to drive across town to United Parcel.

"Oh, wow," Page said as they stepped into the sunlight. "Man, somebody loves us. It's so *cool*." They started across the parking lot.

"Gosh, marvelous." Blye grinned up at the solid blue sky. A norther had come through during the night to cut away the pollution. So far, fall hadn't been much better than the death-camp summer, and the cool weather was a perfect treat. At first, when Page felt his senses suddenly sharpen, he thought it was the air. Then he realized that the sound he heard was a suppressed machine pistol, firing. It was all instinct after that, his mind even identifying the weapon: Skorpion—you never forget the sound of a weapon once you've had it fired at you. It was instinct, too, that he didn't hit the ground immediately, instinct or intuition, for he simultaneously reached for his waistband and turned to mark Link's position. But it was too late. Link took it in the leg first, the slugs ripping away flesh and clothing as Link crouched toward the pain. As he began to go down, a second burst spun him, that bad dance—it caught him in the right shoulder even as Page dove to cover him with his body.

At the same time that the motion seemed to stop, Page felt as if he were going at a devastating velocity, his brain overloading with the input. He tried to see where the fire came from but all he saw was the mild light reflected from the cars. He felt the asphalt, slightly warm from the sun. He smelled the tar and felt the hot, slippery wetness beneath him and suddenly realized the ultimate simplicity of the situation: Shot, Page thought, Link is shot, and even though no more than a second or two passed from the time he dove on top of Link to the time he went on, Page would always remember it as a lingering, moist embrace as he wallowed in Link's blood. Actually, he hadn't even fully landed on top of Link, when he saw them thirty yards off—oh, my God, those guys in suits—and knew what he'd done: he had done it to Link, gotten him into this thing, blown the lid off, and there it was. He remembered an instant in which he had the nearly irrepressible urge to put his head down on Link's back and lie there. It was almost a sleepy feeling. But then the pieces snapped together inside him and something completely other took control from him. To the men who were shooting it must have appeared that Page reacted almost instantly, but he would never recall it that way.

Page heard the metallic clack behind him as Blye unlocked the safety on his .45. Page already had a revolver in his hand, and they emptied their weapons in the direction of that tan Chevrolet. In a fury of point shooting Page put his first round right between the horns of the man on the left. The slug caught him just above the right eye and the top of his head was gone, leaving his machine pistol spinning in the air before it clattered to the parking lot. Both Blye and Page poured fire into the chest of the second man, who also had a Skorpion. The man slammed against the car, making a wet sound with his back, which had split wide open. As he slid to the blacktop, he left a two-foot-wide red message on the tan exterior of the car, and his weapon came to rest between his legs, upright. And just as fast as the thing had taken control from Page, it let him go, let him down completely, abandoned now, all his defenses gone and all he could feel was the shock lashing through him in waves.

His panic suppressor was so completely blown then that he nearly shot Butch, who had come flying out of the apartment with a shotgun. Page's hands were covered with Link's blood and he held up his revolver helplessly, tears running openly on his face, an ill and alien wail coming from his throat. Kneeling beside Link, Page finally let the revolver drop from his hands, but he couldn't touch Link or even form a thought. Link's face was pressed against the asphalt, making his lips pucker. He drooled onto the ground and Page just knelt there and shook as the sirens began in the distance. Link made a gurgling sound as Page tore off his own shirt and tried to stuff it into the gaping wound, but his hands were shaking so badly that he couldn't hold it. As he fumbled it again and then again, he just stopped and extended his hands into the air. He was covered with Link's blood.

He seemed to remember looking down at himself during the ambulance ride and seeing the red liquid all over his bare chest as it dried and flaked. He heard the wailing, but couldn't decide if it had been the siren as they screamed through the streets toward the Houston Medical Center or something coming from his own throat.

At the hospital they got an I.V. into Link and he started to mumble, and then continued all the way into the operating room. They never really got him under, and even when they removed the bullet from his thigh and all the fragments from his shoulder, he just kept gurgling and stuttering strange phrases to the doctors.

"Put him under," the surgeon said to the anesthesiologist.

"I'm trying, you want me to kill him?"

"Goddamnit!"

"What's he saying?"

"Shut up."

Page paced outside the door, chain-smoked Camels, and tried to stop shaking. This one had taken him down to the nucleus, it blew right through him, clearing out any protective mechanisms he'd had for dealing with emergencies. The doctor's voice sent him into a fit of shuddering.

"Is he your brother?"

"Yes," Page said.

"We'd like you to fill out some forms and the police want to talk to you." Page followed the doctor meekly and sat through hours of questioning. The police, of course, knew what had happened—they had the best information in town, in fact. But officially, all they had was two unidentified bodies. The word would eventually go out—two men firing on innocent bystanders who returned fire, which, under Texas law, was what a Houston policeman would call Mighty Fine. You don't shoot back, it's going to be him filling out those forms.

And then the FBI and the Attorney General's boys came, making their Orwellian suggestions: "We'll provide you with a new identity if you are willing to testify," and Page, in spite of himself, laughed until the tears ran again, out of control, high on grief. Oh, Lord, a new identity, a brain transplant was more like it, what a fucking riot! And ultimately, what could they do to convince Page? His mouthing off in Galveston didn't mean anything, just another crazy half-breed ranting and raving, drunk again, hearsay, hearsay, hearsay, *et cum spiritu tuo, laus tibi,* Link, *visibilium omnium et invisibilium.*

"Must be PCP," one of them said, and Page heard it as if from a long distance. They thought he was stoned.

"Or LSD," another remarked.

"He'd make an awful witness, either way," the voice admitted, and they finally left Page alone.

As soon as they had gone, he fell asleep. He found himself standing in a cemetery. Perry was there, Jill was there, Cyndi was there, the whole band was there. Except Link. Page looked out across the field of gravestones and saw a statue of an angel atop a large monument. The angel had its arms stretched outward and down toward the grave beneath it. Its right hand had been broken off. Then Page looked over and saw Link's mother and knew that Link was there—right in that casket they were lowering into the hole. He awoke with a jolt, coming out of it all at once with full force. It was nearly midnight. He rushed back to the operating room. The surgeon assured him that Link was not going to die, that he had some serious injuries but he was going to pull through just fine and no, they would not let Page see him.

Returning late to Timmons Lane, Page found Cyndi waiting up for him. He would not talk to her, and she just sat and watched him drink with bitter determination. She said nothing until he fumbled in his jacket pocket and brought out a little plastic capsule about two inches long. It said on the side, STERILE. NON-PYRO. MONOJECT 200 PATS APPLIED FOR 26 × 1".

"Page, you're going to kill yourself with that," Cyndi protested.

"Jess," Page said and dropped the hypodermic needle, "Jess gone pop a little something here, sweetie."

"Page," Cyndi said as he unwrapped the Becton, Dickinson & Company Super-Ward Tuberculin syringe, "where'd you get that?"

"Made a little visit to the hops-pistol," Page said, then laughed at the mispronunciation. "Horse-pistol," he added.

"Come on, now, Page." She reached for it but Page pulled away with such ferocity that she left him alone. He assembled the rig, took out a small paper of heroin, cooked it up, and then injected the liquid under the skin of his arm.

Cyndi sat up with him until nearly noon. She tried to talk to him, but mostly just watched him nod off and grin a bad grin, one that scared her. When he finally passed out, Cyndi got a cleaning pail and filled it with ice water. She dumped it on him, and he exploded out of the apartment as if he'd been shot from a cannon. He stood panting by the pool, half naked in the bright daylight, stoned and out of his mind. Cyndi screamed almost hysterically, "It's not your fault, Page. Will you please stop blaming yourself?" But Page just went back in and stared out the window.

A few days later, Page realized that the surgeon had been right, Link was not dead, was not going to be dead—he was, in fact, the same old indefatigable Link. He was stronger than most people, not merely in his ability to lift a weight or throw a punch, but constitutionally stronger, with some kind of deep, swamp-bred toughness. Stories had always circulated about him and they kept the image intact. One afternoon, for example, Link got behind about forty milligrams of Biphetamine at a picnic and decided he'd try his hand at waterskiing. He skied from Port Arthur to the Bolivar Peninsula, about fifty miles.

"Boy's strong," people commented.

Another afternoon—stoned again—Link was driving along the

Eastex Freeway and rolled his car. He was probably clocking about six bits and naturally he wasn't wearing a seat belt. The car rolled seven times. Link held himself in place by gripping the steering wheel and walked away from a wreck that looked like a bunch of beer cans that had been run over with a lawn mower.

"Boy's *mighty* strong," people had said.

So it didn't surprise Page that as Link's hospital stay wore on, he began to get more and more recalcitrant. Link just didn't take well to bed rest, and after two weeks he began raising considerable hell. The administrator of the hospital called Page one morning to inform him that the chief surgeon had told Link that under no circumstances should he be discharged, whereupon Link had torn out one of the balusters from the bed and hit the man over the head with it.

Page rushed over to calm Link, and there was a lot of grumbling among the staff about the psychiatric ward ("Disturbed," they called it) but Page put on his best businesslike manner and assured the staff that his brother would remain under control. He gave Link a stern lecture, explaining that these people were *crazy* and that they might actually lock him up if he continued assaulting the staff. "You'll be healed up soon, and you can get out of here," Page said. And then Link told him what the surgeon had said.

"He *what?*"

"What the fucker said." Link was colorless now, a look Page had never seen on him. "Said it wasn't no way I was gonna play any bass again."

"Oh," was all Page could say, and he sat on the edge of the bed as if they'd just come and put the dimes on Link's eyes. They sat there for the longest time, until it became too much for Page, and he started to look around the room for something to kill. When he finally turned to look at Link, it was the first time since Link had lost Terry that he had seen tears on Link's face.

"I cain't move my fingers." Link's voice was hoarse, and his jaw muscles contracted rhythmically.

A few days later, Page was sitting on the bed again when Jill walked in. Page knew he should have been ecstatic, but he just couldn't react appropriately. He hugged her and mumbled something about being glad to see her. Page had already told her on the phone what was going on with Link. Jill walked over and put her hand on Link's face.

"Hello." Link tried to smile. "All washed up," he said.

"No." Jill pulled her hand away. Her voice was a little shrill, but it was in control. "Now, listen, I don't want to hear any of that shit."

"Doctor said he won't play bass again," Page said.

"And what do doctors know? I don't want to hear it. I won't even discuss it." She was flushed and quivering, angry. "Link, I don't know you that well, but you don't strike me as the type of person who'd let doctors make decisions for him."

"Wasn't doing a whole lot of that the other day," Page muttered and heard Link chuckle proudly.

"Kinda put the hurt on one old boy here." Link smiled now, a real smile.

"Damned right," Jill said, almost too forcefully, and Page watched her, thinking, Something else is bothering that lady. "And I don't want to hear any more about you being washed up. You've had a couple of weeks to recuperate and you expect to be out there knocking them dead again." Jill paused. "Anyway, Cyndi sent the demo and Perry likes it. So you'll just have to figure a way around this problem."

But even before Page could become excited about the news, he was stopped: Do what about it? Faith healing? And also Page could tell that something else altogether was troubling Jill, something more than Link's problems.

"I've got to talk to you," she said to Page. He shrugged at Link and followed her out.

"What's going on?" Page asked on the ride away from the medical center, but Jill did not answer. She just drove the rented LTD in silence—no limousine this time. Page leaned back in his seat and rested his head. Fine. Let someone else take control for once. He was exhausted and just beginning to feel it. They rounded the drive by the statue of Sam Houston, then parked and walked into a stand of pines. Page hadn't noticed her carrying a newspaper until she handed it to him.

"What's this?"

"Read it." She turned and walked a few feet away.

He opened it and saw the two-column picture of Clovis Younger under a banner headline: REPUTED MOB LEADER SLAIN.

"Oh, my God." Page's eyes showed white above and below the iris. He read the story through, then read it again. Police said it had to be an inside job. Someone Clovis knew. Six shots to the head. Twenty-two-caliber. Obviously a silenced weapon, since the maid was in the house and did not hear the shots. No, she had not seen anyone enter or leave. Found him in his library, cigar still burning.

"Who did it?" he finally said to Jill's back. She turned around slowly. Her face was stiff, different.

"How the hell do I know?" Jill said, irritated. "But I think you ought to know that the people you've made angry are not just ordinary street hoods. You may have inadvertently gotten yourself into a bad position with these New Orleans mob types but you're—"

"Wait a minute," Page interrupted, putting his hand up. "New Orleans? This was a Galveston thing."

"See what I mean?" She sounded weary, as if she wanted to be on another subject. "It's all part of the New Orleans operation, beginning to end. Big old plantation money. Houston Mafia, all of that." She sighed. "You don't want to know. Besides, even I don't know very much."

"You didn't—" Page began, pointing at her.

"God, no." She grimaced. "Jesus, Page. And I don't know who did. I haven't spoken to anyone at all about the death of Younger. I just figured you hadn't seen the paper."

"I guess not."

"But I want you to know that the little war is over, understand? I don't want Link out there starting it all over again. Do you understand that? No shooting?"

"All right." Page's mind was reaching into places he knew it should not go: What? Did she say all that? He wondered what had become of the woman who had seemed so surprised by the sidearm he was carrying that first night in the limo.

"And I want you and the band to come to the Coast as soon as you can. You should be out of this area."

"What about Link?"

"I don't know." She dropped her shoulders as they started back toward the car. They walked through the woods, entering and leaving patches of light and shade. Page watched her face, now lit, now in shadow, and it brought to mind the forests of Michigan with their magic, dappled, sunshot eeriness. He took her arm.

"We think we can do something with Jambeaux. That's all. I don't know about Link."

"I'm not using another bass player, if that's what you're thinking."

"Don't be a child, Page."

The hair on the back of his neck rose, and he let go of her arm but said nothing.

"Look." She stopped and turned on him. "Link is wonderful. I've listened to bass players for a long time and he's among the best. But what are you going to do?"

"I don't know," Page admitted reluctantly.

"I want you to bring the band to the Coast," Jill said.

"I will," Page whispered, then faced her directly. "When Link can come."

"Well, Perry is waiting for you." Her voice was calm now, and Page's head came up fast.

"He is?"

"What do you think I'm doing out here?" She took Page's face in her hands and shook him. "He wants to sign you, Dim-o."

"Me?"

"Yes."

"What about Link?"

"Perry is interested in *you*." She let go of him and moved on. "He wants you and the sound you've made. Now, the band is obviously a part of the sound. But it is your music, your voice, your songs, that he wants, and if you have to use another bass player for a while, then it doesn't matter to Perry."

"It matters to me," Page said again. "How many times do I have to say that?"

"No one can force you to work with Perry," she said. "But you can't just quit because of Link."

"Hide and watch."

⊢13⊣

That afternoon, Jill phoned Perry to say she was taking a vacation for a few days, which she hadn't done in five years. Page lay on the bed with her, his head in her lap. He stared at the ceiling and listened to her half of the conversation.

"There's a real problem with Link, though," Jill said. "These two are like brothers." She smiled down at Page, pushing her fingers through his hair. Page smiled back and mouthed the words, *You better fucking believe it.* "It's going to take some pretty subtle magic," she added, as if joking, and Page smiled, nodding vigorously.

"And are you not subtle and magic?" Perry asked.

Jill knew what Perry meant and was glad Page couldn't hear. She tried to keep up her smile but Page noticed the change in her expression. Jill and Perry had always been very close, but now she sensed her loyalties were being slowly, painfully divided. And the two dividing forces were so strong she felt they might just draw and quarter her before it was all over.

"Let's go see Link," Page said when she hung up the phone. "What'd Perry say?"

"Nothing," Jill lied. "He's interested, like I said. He's worried about Link."

The hotel was not far from the Houston Medical Center. When they arrived, they found Butch, Scoop, and Blye crowded into Link's little semiprivate room.

Scoop had an acoustic Martin D-45, Butch was playing alto flute, and Blye was manufacturing strange percussion sounds on an instrument Page had never seen before. The three set up a regular, jumpy heart-rate rhythm that dipped and jived in and out of sync like a two-sectioned beast loping along in the jungle. The three instruments blended and booted out sympathetic notes that dragged along an empire of emotions, like drawing a long strand up from your throat. Link was humming when Page and Jill came to the door and they paused there, silent. As they listened, the tune's structure and function became clarified and purified until it held a standing wave, like rhythms in water, and Link sang, his voice as ragged and shocked as the naked face of a cliff in New Mexico, red-rough and bloodshot as the iron-rich escarpments:

> Got a bird that whistle
> Baby got a bird, honey got a bird that sang.
> Got a bird that whistle

Mama got a bird, *child* got a bird that sang.
With-*out* Corinna
Sho' don't mean, sho' don't mean a natch'l thaing.

It was the last straw for Jill and she turned from the room with her hand over her face. In the hallway Page took her in his arms and held her as she first sobbed quietly, then broke completely. Page led her away to the car. When he got into the room at her hotel, she continued in explosive spasms, and all Page could do was hold her and repeat over and over, "Oh, baby, I *know*."

Later Page awoke in the dark, startled, disoriented, his brain sizzling with ugly flashes. He shook himself awake, stepped lightly from the bed and stood there for a few seconds. Jill lay breathing deeply but irregularly—Cheyne-Stokes demented sleep of depression. Page went to the dark bathroom and returned.

Back in bed, they moved together like spoons nesting in a drawer. He reached over to the clock-radio Jill traveled with and switched it on to help him get to sleep. The radio glowed yellow and purred to life, whining Steven Stills's guitar and voice:

> Blue blue windows behind the stars
> Yellow moon on the rise
> Big birds flying across the sky
> Throwing shadows on our eyes
> Leave us
> Helpless, helpless, helpless . . .

Ain't that the truth, Page thought. Jill stirred and pressed harder against him and then, slowly, carefully, he was inside her. Heeelllllpless. The next morning he wasn't sure if she had been awake or asleep. Jill was up on one elbow, leaning over Page, saying over and over, "Buzz. Buzz," trying to wake him, when the phone rang.

"Hello?" Her voice cracked. "What? He *what?*" Jill's voice was unfocused but shrill. Page felt something was dreadfully wrong but couldn't move. Finally, he broke through the sleep and rolled over.

"What is it?" Page asked but Jill didn't respond.

"We'll be out in a few minutes." She hung up, dialed again, and spoke curtly into the phone. "Yes. I need the car now. Room fifteen hundred. Ring when it arrives."

"What? What?" Page was moving out of the bed now.

"Link's gone." She jumped out of the bed and went directly to the shower. Page followed and got into the shower with her, the hieroglyphics of sleep tattooed across his cheek.

"What's your friend up to now?" She sounded annoyed and worried.

"That's Link for you." He accepted the soap from her. She was scrubbing herself, trying to keep her hair from getting wet. She moved to let Page get under the stream of water. Look at her, he thought, just look at her. He felt himself falling in love with her all over again.

"Fuckin' U/A," he said through a breath of water.

"What?"

"U/A." He soaped himself.

"What's that?" she asked curtly, then: "Lemme rinse myself."

"Unauthorized Absence." Page got out of the way and Jill moved under the water. He hugged her as she rinsed. "Goddamn," he said. Just the feel of her was enough to make him crazy.

"I'm worried," she said, not responding to his affection.

"Oh, Link does weird shit like that all the time," Page began. "He used to—" Then he saw her face and stopped. He backed off and looked at her. Her expression. Oh, no, he thought. Not *that*. "You don't think . . ." He didn't even finish the sentence.

"I don't think anything, but I'd sure like to locate Link. And fast."

"Holy shit." Page hadn't even thought of that possibility.

The panic ran like quickmatch that day, eight hundred feet per second, easy, explosive in nature, especially with the headlines slapped inches high with Younger's death. A real professional job, they kept saying. They ran the news for days, milking it for all it was worth. And where was Link?

The fear had raked the band into small heaps of neurons by evening, raked the emotions there rather haphazardly, as if the job had been done by a spastic. Jill came to the gig that night and they sounded terrible. It was bad enough that Link *couldn't* play with them. The whole night was dominated by the thought that Link *wasn't*, period. Part of it was the substitute bass player. The only one they could find for that night had been working a day gig and playing nights to support his wife and kids. He was basically competent but he was exhausted from going seventy-two hours without sleep, and he had never played with Jambeaux before. In addition, the band's emotional energy was running very much against any substitute for Link. It was like having your wife die and watching as the government agency sends the B team in that evening to service you. It stank.

During the third set the bass player actually fell asleep in the middle of a song and Butch had to kick him to wake him up. An organ player known as the Deacon had come in to hear Jambeaux and walked over to Page at the break. Page was drinking heavily at the bar.

"Hey, man," Deacon said.

"Hi." Page glared at him unintentionally.

"Man, where'd you get that bass player?"

"Oh, he's just sitting in," Page said. "He's been working a day gig, hasn't slept for three days. He's a security guard."

Deacon's eyes lit up with intense interest. *"Where?"* he asked excitedly. Page couldn't help laughing. But he didn't laugh when he went up to finish the night. The sound was truly awful. Even Jill found herself wondering if there really was a future in Jambeaux without Link. Maybe Page was right.

It was the night Cyndi and Jill got to know each other for the first time, and later Page was to wonder if it weren't this megacrisis situation that made it possible for the two women to move so easily into the relationship with no edgy feelings. They literally clung together that evening and with slow, careful determination got drunk. It was not nice. Page got drunk as well and later had a meaningless, incoherent fight with Jill, about nothing. He was sent home, where he first tried to get into Cyndi's apartment but found her equally drunk, equally depressed. In an irrational rage, Page cursed her and went back to his own apartment.

He found the other three men shouting at each other about whose fault it was that they sounded so bad that night. But when they noticed Page standing in the doorway, they all stopped. They understood the significance of his presence there, away from Jill. It was a bad time for Jambeaux.

Page wasn't able to say much in favor of the next day either. Link's mother called from Kemah, having just heard the news that Link had been shot and had disappeared.

"I don't know, Page." She spoke in a sad, slow, cracked old Texas voice, and he could just imagine her shaking her head. "Every since Link's daddy died," she said, measuring her words carefully, "I knowed something like this was agonna happen. When you and Link was in Veet Name, I just knowed he was agonna get his self kilt. But now, I just don't know, Page. I'm at my wit's end, and I don't know what to do." She paused and Page could hear her wheezing. His eyes filled and defocused. He remembered sitting at her kitchen table with Link while she cooked them brisket and beans and homemade bread and admonished Link to get his feet off the table. Now Page didn't know what to say to her.

"I'm just glad Link's daddy isn't alive to hear about this. I just know they kilt Link. I just know it."

"No, no, ma'am." Page heard his own voice in the handset as if it were someone else's. He pressed his knuckles to his eyes and fought to keep his throat open, to speak. "Link didn't like that hospital at all. I'm sure he just ran away." But he wasn't sure, he wasn't sure at all.

"I just don't know, Page," she croaked. "I always knew Link would come to a bad end, every since his daddy died. I always tolt him not to play that music. And now I just don't know what I'm agonna do."

Page didn't know what he was going to do either. He also didn't know about Judy. Later he remembered the phone call from Link that came just as Blye arrived from London, when Link had been out on a ranch somewhere with a girl who had horses. But when she drove up to Timmons Lane a few weeks later, Page didn't remember her. Page was sitting by the pool, talking to Jill and Cyndi, and when he saw the van pull up, he wondered whose it was. When a woman stepped out and began pulling a Fender PianoBass from the back, Page stood. And when he saw Link emerge, he practically fainted. When Page realized that he wasn't seeing a ghost, he stood up and glared at Link as if he were going to kill him. Link, smiling and tanned, didn't even notice at first. He just sashayed over, Judy following along, both of them looking proud and pleased. When Link got up to Page, his expression collapsed.

"What's the matter?" Link demanded, expecting to be welcomed with open arms.

Page hauled back and slapped him across the face so hard that Link lost his balance and sat heavily on the grass. He was so utterly stunned by Page's reaction that he didn't even try to move.

"Well, what the fuck was *that* all about?" Link boomed, his eyes glowing, his expression combative and hurt. Page and Link had never exchanged blows before.

"Where in the motherfucking hell have *you* been?" Page screamed at the top of his lungs with such ferocity that Link recoiled.

"Well, what the fuck is it to *you?*" Link shouted. The women tried to calm the two, but the exchange continued.

Page turned to one side, as if he were speaking to someone else. "What is it to me?" he mocked. "What is it to *me?*" He turned on Link. "You big dumb asshole! I only shot two people to save your fucking life, that's all. And then you disappear in the middle of some pissing match with these lunatics. And we don't hear from you for weeks." Page was out of control, and Jill said nothing as she watched him rage on. "And you're asking what is it to *me?* You goddamned ape!" He started walking off toward the apartment, shouting, "Nothing! It's fucking *nothing* to me."

Link sat heavily on the lawn chair, stared straight ahead, then glared at the grass and fumed, feeling his face burn. Jill rushed after Page and Cyndi handed Link a beer, which he sipped at, staring sullenly after Page. "He'll get over it, honey," Cyndi said softly.

It took Jill about half an hour. She and Page had made up the day after their fight—they had both known they were drunk—but now she had to contend with his explosive temper again. It didn't often come on Page, but when it involved someone close to him, he could have an extremely short fuse. He felt as if Link had abandoned him, betrayed him, and made fools of the entire band —as well as of Jill.

When the two of them were brought together, Page apologized. "I'm sorry I hit you," he said. "I thought they'd—"

"I know," Link said, putting his hand on Page's shoulder. "Cyndi told me. I didn't figure on it. It was a real dumb thing to disappear like that."

"What the fuck." Page hung his head.

"How come I did it," Link explained, "I got this thing." He gestured at the equipment. "I didn't even think about it. I just had to get outta that hospital before I went nuts, and then Judy, here, she got this idea. You know, I'm left-handed and all? So she bought me this thing. Come on, lemme show you."

Like most of those musicians who really come from down under —and Texas shrimp-boat towns were right down there—Link played a number of instruments. He could play guitar quite well. Drums fairly well. And keyboards very well. Judy's solution to the problem was simple. She'd bought him a Yamaha B100-115 amplifier and a thirty-two-key Fender PianoBass, which he played with his left hand—his best hand anyway. When he and Page had set up the amp and the keyboard, Link dove into it with skill and fury, and Page lit up. He was blown away.

"Well, I'll be dipped in shit." Jill laughed at them, imitating Link.

Judy stood proudly with her hand on Link's shoulder. "You should've seen him practicing," she said. "He was up before the *horses* every morning."

"Can you feature it?" Link was like a child, glowing once again. The time at the ranch had done him good.

"Man, a one-arm bass player," Page mused, "big drawing power there."

"Very sexy," Jill said.

"*Very,*" Cyndi said. "You want to have dinner with *me* tonight?" she joked.

"He's having dinner with *me,*" Judy said. And in truth, it was this little woman, to whom no one had paid much attention so far, who had brought Link out of it.

And though Link wasn't exactly playing up to the technical level he was used to, he was on the job that very night, popping that hellgong sound that was his trademark. It was still a little rough, but there it was, nonetheless.

-14-

"Oh, man, I'm going to *die*, wow, help me," Steve shouted, grinning and reeling around the house with Page laughing after him. "Good God! Kee-riiist!"

"Get back here, you shitbird," Page called after him. "You're just stoned again," and he broke out laughing again, calling back into the other room, "Sorry, Royal, but I *am* my brother's keeper."

He finally got Steve back down on the couch and had him shut up. This lady he called Royal stood there and shook her head, unable to control her laughter.

"You two are crazy, you know that?" she said.

"I'm in love!" Steve shouted and Page cuffed him playfully.

"Shut up, maggot, or I'm going to have Red tie you up in the barn."

"God help me." Steve giggled and took a sip from his drink.

"I've read about you rock musicians," Royal said. "I'm getting out of here."

"You don't have to go," Page pleaded.

"Oh, yes, I do." She flashed a set of teeth that would have been perfect except for the space between the incisors. "Anyway, Red and I are going to the movies tonight." She looked at her watch and waltzed out.

"How the hell does Red get so lucky?" Steve asked.

"Boy, you don't stop messing with that redskin's woman, you're gonna find yourself leakin' precious fluids," Page said evenly.

"Well, what do you expect, bringing a lady like that in here?"

"You're stoned, you know that? You're just fucked up." Page sat down and watched the fire.

"No, man, that's not it at all; if you can't see her, you ought to have an overhaul." Steve exhaled heavily. "Damn!"

"Shit," Page said, "you should see her *sister.*"

After Royal had been gone an hour, Steve began to calm a little. Lilly came into the living room, climbed up on the couch, and promptly went to sleep, groaning with pleasure as Steve scratched her neck. Page and Steve had spent the last couple of days wandering around in the woods, talking and generally doing nothing. Steve made Page take him into town, and it was a shock to Page to realize that he hadn't been to the little village since he got home from that last tour. In town everyone waved and said hello, and the shopkeepers couldn't do enough for Page and his brother.

"Dang," one of them might say, "you look just like your brother. *Just* like him."

"Lucky son of a bitch." Page would smile and then ask after the man's family or animals or whatever seemed appropriate.

Steve insisted on going into the record store to buy a Willie Nelson album, against Page's better judgment. Sure enough, inside, three high school girls accosted them immediately.

"You're Page, aren't you?" the first one asked, snapping gum between silver braces. "If we buy your record, will you sign it?"

"Say, I've got something you can sign." Steve began grabbing for his fly, but Page cut him off with a wave of his hand.

"Don't mind him," Page said, "he's my brother. He's just on leave from the mental hospital."

"Really?" one of the girls asked.

"Oh yes, oh yes." Steve puffed up his chest. "I ice-picked my grandma to death when I was ten, been in stir ever since."

The three girls backed off, not sure whether to believe it or not.

"Naw." One of them smiled. "You're putting us on."

"Sure we are," Page said.

"No, really." Steve moved in close. "Hey, how'd you three like to come out and see the ranch?"

"Can we?"

"Shut up." Page glared at his brother. Then he turned to the three girls and said, very gently, "We're just on our way out of town. If you went out there now, there wouldn't be anybody there but the armed guard and the dogs."

"Armed guard?" one of them asked.

"Now, go get that record." Page motioned toward the record rack and the girls went off in a flurry like doves scattering from a wire. "Listen, numbnuts." Page turned to Steve. "Will you give me a fucking break?"

"Aw, you been holed up too long." Steve ducked his head just the way Page would. "I'm trying to liven up your existence a little."

"I believe I've had enough livening up in the last few years to hold me a spell, thank you. Now let's get the fuck back to the Ranch before we both get arrested."

When they got back to the house, the phone was ringing. Page picked it up and was immediately sorry he had.

"Perry," Page said wearily. "I thought we had settled everything."

"Not quite everything, Page," Perry said, his voice both smooth and sharp at the same time, like quicksilver. "Anyway, never mind, that's not why I'm calling. I just wanted to know if you received my card, and I wanted to send my best wishes."

"Well, thanks," Page said, thinking, Look, I was born at night but it wasn't last night.

"Say," Perry said casually, cheerfully, "mind if I speak with Steve?" There was a long silence while Page's mind raced ahead. But he just handed the phone to Steve with a look that said, Whatever it is you're up to, just be warned. . . . But Steve turned away, his wild mood uninterrupted. Page could glean nothing from Steve's side of the conversation.

As soon as he'd hung up, Steve put on his Willie Nelson album as loud as it would go, which on Page's equipment was pretty loud, window-breaking loud, at least. Then he said he'd like to call Butch.

"No you don't," Page said.

"Shit, I just want to say hello." Steve picked up the handset. "I mean, if you won't let him come over, at least I can say howdy."

Page left the room and Steve jabbered over the phone with Butch for half an hour before coming out into the kitchen, where Page was sipping coffee and talking on the other line. After Page hung up, Steve started right in again. "Come on, man, let's play some mew-zik, yeah! Rock and Roll! Remember?"

"No," Page refused flatly. It wasn't easy to refuse every day like that. Steve was awfully tempting as a musician. And he was right. He and Page could make some fine music together. But Page had been through it. It would have been insanity for him to reconsider at that point (Page told himself), just plain insanity.

Steve made his *pro forma* stab at getting Page to play with him, then practiced bass alone for half an hour. Page came out to watch the fire. "I was thinking about something you told me the other day," Steve said. "All that underworld stuff. It just doesn't make any sense."

"Never said it would." Page lit a Camel, striking a kitchen match on his jeans like a cowboy.

"How come they didn't just shut you down back when you were at the Burning Spear?"

"Well, that one night those dudes came in, that first night Jill was there? That's what they started out to do. They were going to give Ritchie an alternative, either get us out of there or start looking for fire insurance or prosthetic kneecaps or something like that."

"Don't sound like much selection to me." Steve went over to the fire and poked it, then threw on another log.

"I found out later that one of these two guys recognized Jill because he had been in L.A. one time on behalf of Younger to see Perry. So he saw her and figured that whatever was going on, if Perry had somebody—like his right-hand person—in there, he had better check with the boss before stepping in over his head."

"But then how come Link got shot if Perry was so fucking scary?"

"Because he was scary to little street hoods—maybe even to big gangsters. But Younger was a realized mad dog and he was power crazy. The Mexican heroin dealers in Houston called him *Cochiloco*, which means crazed pig. You've got to understand these people. They think they're God. And so Younger—at least as far as what I heard—goes like, 'Well, fuck Holden, we're gonna get those fuckers.' Next thing we know, the shooting starts. Of course, next thing Younger knows, he's got six bullets in his head."

"You think Perry did that?"

"Hell, no." Page sounded impatient. "I mean, I don't think anything, know what I mean?" He smiled thinly at Steve. "All I mean is that Younger was crazy and really stepping out of his bounds, not just in Link's case; I mean, this theme ran through his whole business empire. He had more powerful enemies than anybody could safely have. So I don't know who shot Younger or why, but what he did to us was just part of his pattern. Psychomotive. Out of control."

"Jesus." Steve shook his head. "What finally got you to L.A.?"

"Me? Or the band?"

"You, didn't you go there first?"

"Yeah." Page thought a minute. "What got me there was pussy."

-15-

Enigma Records headquarters was located on La Cienega Boulevard in Los Angeles, but Perry Holden did not work there. His own offices were in an elaborate house situated high on a bluff overlooking the Pacific Ocean. Standing in the cool, sunshot living room, Page tried to keep from staring at Perry and feigned interest in various artifacts on the bookshelves. So this is it, he thought, this is Malibu. He fingered a metal statue of a discus thrower. It was obviously old. The thrower held a penny instead of a discus. Eight inches from the ten-inch-tall figure was a metal container with a slot in it. Page pushed a lever, and the discus thrower launched the penny right into the slot with a satisfying clank.

"Did you see the penny?" Perry asked. He stood slowly and walked to the kitchen to draw beer.

"No," Page admitted. Although Perry spoke in a very neutral tone, his words seemed to convey a great deal more than he actually said. Page tried to get a handle on it but couldn't.

"Indian Head," Perry called from the kitchen. "Nineteen-oh-seven." He returned and handed the beer to Page, who tasted it and gave Perry an odd look. "It's all right?" Perry asked.

"Yeah, fine. It just tastes familiar. Like a beer I used to drink somewhere."

"And what beer is that?"

"I think it was called Point," Page said. "But you wouldn't—"

"But I would. Stevens Point, Wisconsin."

"How did you know?"

"More to the point"—Perry smiled—"how did *you* know? You're from Texas."

"My stepfather used to take me fishing and hunting up in Wisconsin, Michigan—big Hemingway complex."

"Los Angeles is so boring. Even Malibu is boring." He gestured at the magnificent room and went to look out the glass doors. The ocean raked the beach a thousand feet below. "Lou Adler lives down there," Perry said absently. "Very boring, people always coming by, gawking at his house. I've always preferred Wisconsin. But business . . ." He didn't finish his sentence.

If you are extremely powerful and have untold amounts of money, the world works in strange ways—the ways you want it to work. You barely have to tell it what to do, so attuned does it become to your wishes, needs, whims. The slightest hint and the world seems to follow you like a heeling dog. A snap of the fingers could be dangerous, for it might cause an earthquake. People could get hurt. That is why those who are savagely rich and powerful move so slowly. Perry moved as if humans were blessed with infinite life spans and he therefore found it unseemly—irrelevant—

to rush or move quickly. No sudden gestures. Serenity is the best policy. His tendency toward care and discretion even colored the way he spoke. He did not generally refer to things as "far out" or "fantastic" or "incredible." Those were loaded words, too extreme for Perry. His words didn't need to come equipped with baggage because he had freight of his own to impart to them. Perry didn't get "ripped" or "wigged out" or "blown away." Most of the time, all he needed to muster was mild amusement. Page hadn't known that, of course, when Perry said he "loved" the sound that day in Chocolate Bayou Studios. Had Page known at the time, he would have been "blown away."

"I have this amusing little place," Perry said after he and Page had discussed the Great Lakes states at length. "It's in Wisconsin. Perhaps sometime you'll come out there. Sandra will probably be out there. We can all ride horses."

"Sandra?" Page asked.

"My wife." Perry smiled. "Sometimes I forget that everyone hasn't met her. Sometimes I think she knows more people than I do." He laughed gently to himself. "Of course, *no* one knows more people than I do."

There was a silence while Page drank his beer. His mind raced as he tried to think of something to say.

"I was sorry to hear about your bass player," Perry said finally. "What's his name?"

"Link." Page nervously lit a cigarette.

"What are you going to do?" Perry asked.

"He's got a keyboard bass." Page leaned forward. "You know, he's a real natural musician." Page felt an odd combination of fear and anger growing inside him. He felt foolish trying to sell a one-armed bass player to one of the world's biggest record moguls, but goddamnit, Link sounded like Link again. "He's playing a Fender PianoBass," he said weakly.

"Doesn't have much range," Perry observed dryly.

"He sounds awfully good," Page said ineffectually. He wanted it to work so badly he didn't know whether to get on his knees and beg or take the man by the throat. "We could even have one custom-built with an extended keyboard."

"There's that," Perry mused, placing his fingertips together in front of his face. Then he said something apparently irrelevant, as if he'd just thought of another subject and had lost all interest in

Link. "You know, I think bluegrass is going to happen to rock and roll the way folk happened, the way country and western happened —and is going to happen even bigger. The way jazz is happening to rock and roll." He paused. Page just stared at him as if he were nuts. Perry looked thoughtful, almost puzzled, as if trying to solve a knotty problem. "Or maybe it's not that these things *happen* to rock and roll. Maybe it's that rock and roll happens to these things. Suppose rock and roll is gradually taking over all other forms of music, like a virus of some kind that imparts its own genetic material to a host cell." Perry paused. He had completely disarmed Page. "At any rate, I'm not sure *when* bluegrass will happen to rock and roll—or rock and roll happen to bluegrass— but I do believe it will, sooner or later. Perhaps it will happen if I make it happen. Perhaps next year, but I don't think so." Perry looked to Page for a reaction but Page just smiled, laug˙ed tim- idly, and sat there. "But," Perry continued, satisfied with Page's silence, "I do think *you* will happen as well."

Page's eyes widened. It was as close to the subject as they had gotten so far. He said nothing.

"Clearly, rock and roll has already happened to you in a very big and significant way. This unusual sound of yours, Cajun, reg- gae, Gypsy, Zodico, whatever it may be." Perry stared at his tented fingers, then destroyed the tent. "So now as I see it, you must happen to America—you must happen to the world," he said. "I think I'm going to have a beer." He left Page staring at the empty chair with his mouth open.

Page got up and went to the glass doors. Just under them was a strip of garden a few meters wide and beyond that, a drop to the sea. A Mexican gardener came by, hunched over, peering at the ground cover as if he had lost something. He disappeared around the house. Page looked at the sun dropping more quickly now into the sea. This must be it, Page thought, and he searched himself for some reaction. Come on, man, you must feel something, right? This man is telling you he's going to make you famous. Isn't that what everyone wants? Riches? Standing knee-deep in nookie? Ain't that just like an emotional reaction, Page thought. When you want one, they're never around. He was grinning when he sat back down.

"What's funny?" Perry asked as he returned.

"Nothing." Page smiled.

"Well, you have good reason to smile." Perry sat in his chair. "This whole adventure should be very amusing." He sipped his beer delicately. "Do you really think Link can play well enough to make it work?"

"Yes." Page tried to control his voice. "No question. Like I said, the only difference right now is the range, and that can be fixed."

"What about that sound he gets, that kind of—" Perry sought a word. "Like chimes?" He sipped his beer and looked away, out the glass doors, at the sea.

"We used"—Page laughed—"we used to call him King Gong. It sounds like five hundred little gongs ringing behind a song."

"Right." Perry smiled. "Precisely. Gongs."

Page smiled back at him.

"So what about it?"

"What about what?"

"Does he sound like that, still?" Perry turned and squinted into Page's eyes to see if he was going to lie.

"Well." Page dropped his eyes. "It doesn't sound *exactly* the same."

"You know," Perry started as if beginning yet another conversation. "I know a bass player who sounds very much the way Link *used* to sound."

"Link still sounds good." Page flashed a hard look at him. He didn't like the way Perry emphasized the past tense, as if Link were dead.

Perry held up his hand. "I'm just saying that Jaco Pastorius sounds very much like him. He's really quite good."

"I'm glad to hear that."

"You wouldn't consider—"

"No, I wouldn't."

"All right, all right." Perry smiled, picked up Page's glass, and went to refill it. "It was only a suggestion. I'd like to give you every possible option." When he returned with the beer, he said, "When can I hear Jambeaux with the keyboard bass?"

"I'd like some time to get Link used to playing that way." Page drank, looked out over the ocean. The sun was hanging out about twenty degrees off the horizon, fusing red-orange heat. "A couple of months, I'd guess."

"You should consider leaving Houston." Perry gazed out over

the ocean as well, giving the sentence no inflection at all. Page shot him a glance, but Perry wasn't looking. "It must get tiring after all this time. Maybe you'd like to go somewhere quiet to rehearse for a while?"

"Absolutely." Page smiled, thinking, This guy is really about as slick as they come, lookit him, just look at him.

"I know a place in Wisconsin. An amusing place not far from the Illinois border where you could set up to rehearse. They have a little studio there."

"That's going to be awfully expensive," Page said. "We don't exactly have any spare capital. We blew everything on that demo."

"A shame," Perry said. "It's a pretty dreadful demo."

Page was shocked. Perry had said he liked it. The shock must have shown.

"I mean, it is relatively clear from the demo that it was done in a low-quality studio by musicians who don't know how to record in studios." Perry smiled at Page's dismay. "This place would give you an opportunity to learn to record in a studio properly and at the same time you could rehearse enough songs to make an album." Perry let that sink in. "Enigma would, of course, take that money out of your advance."

"Advance?"

"Against future sales. You would need to sign a contract."

"Sign a contract." Page made the flat statement as if he were half asleep. He yawned. That old reaction setting in. "Yes, of course. Sign a contract." Page couldn't have been more profoundly confused. This isn't the way it happens, he thought. There must be more than this, right? It's got to be more complicated.

Well, it did and it didn't happen that way in the music business. As Perry knew—and Albert Grossman and Phil Specter and the rest knew—it could happen any way it happened. Anything at all could happen in the music business. And you could succeed or fail in so many different ways that nothing was unusual. More to the point, nothing was ordinary either.

We don't even have a manager, Page thought. We'll get completely fucked. He knew how it worked. You sign a contract, they sell a quarter of a zillion records and then send you a bill for $200,000. It was no joke. It happened all the time.

"I mean, I've got to talk to the rest of the band, naturally." Page stalled, while a hundred horror stories rushed through his mind.

Most musicians knew the stories and Page didn't want to become another one of them. And Page was thinking, Right, wow, far out, you've come all this way and here the guy is talking about signing you, and you're having second thoughts, great, they'll love you for that.

"Naturally," Perry said and then looked at his watch as if he had something to do.

"Where'd you get that?" Page asked, noticing the make of Perry's watch.

"Get what?"

"The watch." Page hadn't seen one in a long time.

"Jimi Hendrix gave it to me," Perry said. "He was with the Hundred and First Airborne, you know."

"Yeah, every grunt in Nam knew that. Also, everybody wore those watches. Government issue, nonrepairable plastic watch." Page smiled. "Best damned watch I ever had."

"What happened to yours?"

"Got it blown off my wrist." Page chuckled that sound that wasn't really a laugh, then held out his left arm for Perry to see. Perry raised his eyebrows when he saw the long, red scar. "A mine went off. I was knocked down into the mud. Looked up to check the guy in front of me and he was holding down five different positions." Page shook his head wearily. "Dust one."

"Shame," Perry said.

"Yeah." Page looked down at his beer. "It was a damn nice watch."

Perry just looked at him.

⊣16⊢

When Page returned from L.A., he found Link sitting in the living room, squeezing a tennis ball. At first Page just dismissed it, but then he noticed the total concentration on Link's face and realized that Link was using his right hand. Link didn't even look up, and Page watched in silence.

"Have you talked to the doctors lately?" he finally asked.

"Tits on a bull," Link said, the sweat beading on his face. His fingers only moved about an inch but he was doing it. As the days wore on, Page watched with increasing interest as Link worked the ball every day for hours, then worked the arm with a weight. He had started coming home from the gig and going straight to sleep, getting up at seven thirty in the morning to work out. One morning, out of curiosity, Page got up, too, and watched Link suit up and take off across the parking lot at a steady trot. When he asked Judy, she said he had worked up to six miles a day.

"Perfect physical shape," Link explained later. "I figure if I'm in perfect physical shape, I'll have my best shot at it. I mean, if I'm gonna take a shot at it, I might as well go the whole route." Link gradually became a stone fanatic about it. Judy stayed around him all the time, just watching him work, fixing his food, sleeping over when the ride back to her ranch became too much trouble. And when Judy moved in with Link, Page moved in with Cyndi, although if anyone said anything like, "Oh, you've moved in with Cyndi," he would duck his head shyly and say, "Naw, I'm just stayin' over there to keep outta Link's way." Cyndi's husband had finally left for good. Actually, she had thrown him out after he nearly killed one of her boyfriends. He only showed up once after that and he left in a hurry when Page leveled a .45 at him. These days, Page didn't go around with anything short of a .45 and one of those neat little stiletto picks they gave the nightfighters in the bad old days. It looked like a piece of wire with a handle, but it would go right through bone. Page knew Younger was dead, but he'd had too many close calls not to be a little edgy.

Back over at Link's apartment, an incredible metamorphosis was taking place. Judy was taking control, redecorating, cleaning, ripping out that ancient tangerine rat-fur carpeting. She knew the Gulf Coast well enough to realize you had to have something to do during those bitter, midwinter days when a constant dismal drizzle put everything into abort-mode. She explained to Link that she had to keep busy somehow: "You don't gotta worry so much if you think about killing your family, you just want to get a little concerned when you start inventing *really strange ways* to do it."

Page and Link watched her haul in a big sanding machine and refinish the wooden floor that had been buried beneath the carpet for so long. She was short and rounded and quite strong. She wasn't thin but she had a double-take figure and charged around getting it all done, a real can-do woman. When she'd finished, she cocked her head to one side, threw out her hip, and sneered at her work, a hand at her waist.

"Lookit her," Link whispered gleefully. "Ain't she a sight?"

Blye had gotten his own apartment by that time, as well as his own supply of methadone, gradually tapering down the dosage to get completely clean.

And Jill. Page had gone to L.A. so quickly and alone because, as he explained to Steve, he wanted to see Jill. But he had only seen Perry, and it was no small thing to him when Perry told him Jill had gone to Cleveland to hear a new group. For one thing, Page simply missed her—he thought she might have stayed just to see him. For another, it hadn't really registered with him that Jill was dealing with other bands. He knew it was her job, of course. He just hadn't faced up to the demands it must make on her time. Before he went to L.A., Jill had been all his, had belonged to Jambeaux. And now, back in Houston, although Page was getting calls from her every other day, he was made a little jealous by the fact that she spent as much time talking to Cyndi as to him. But when Jill and Page did talk, she begged him to come to the Coast, and Page would only say, "Soon, soon." They still hadn't found a manager, even though Jill explained over and over that they didn't need one. "Get a lawyer if you like." And Page balked.

On Valentine's Day it was sleeting in Houston, the first time in years that it had been cold enough to do that. But nobody minded, as they left for the gig. Link was going to play his string bass again for the first time since he was shot.

Page had watched him finally work his arm above the shoulder, had seen the glee on Judy's face, had watched Link crush tennis balls and then go to a spring hand exerciser, then to a wrist machine. And at last, Page watched Link fit a flat pick between his thumb and forefinger and begin picking guitar again, slowly at first, playing scales. Starting from ground zero. But each morning he was up at seven thirty or eight, working that electric guitar, silently, with no amp. And then the bass, flat-picking bass, until one morning Page wandered over from Cyndi's to find Judy practically beside herself and Link grinning there with his bass in his arms. The little amplifier glowed and Link said, "Listen." Then he hit some licks and there it was: that old hellgong sound.

Page was so excited he called the doctor who had done the operations on Link's arm. When he told the surgeon that Link was going to play electric bass at the Burning Spear, the doctor postponed a family trip in order to watch. In spite of the worst weather of the year, everybody was acting like he was on the beach at Biloxi. When the doctor walked in and took his seat—incongruous among the degenerates in his three-hundred-dollar suit—Link stepped up to the microphone to call the tune himself.

"This one's for Doctor Blankenship," he said proudly, and they rolled into an old number Link and Page had often done together. It was the first time they had done it since leaving the Riptide Rendezvous, but it had been so ingrained in them, cellular memory, that Otis Redding couldn't have done it better. "These Arms of Mine," so full of pathos and energy it made you want to get down on your knees and bite the nails out of the floor planking, and when Link put out that sound, when Jambeaux twisted it up so tight that the slightest touch would shatter it, when Page sang the harmony behind it all, it threw the grief switch on the entire club, like running a current through it.

The doctor nearly shorted out. He couldn't believe it. He rushed up to the stage and pumped Link's arm vigorously, asked him if he would come to the hospital so he could show the others, maybe appear at a seminar of residents. Link mumbled, embarrassed by the attention, but declined. The doctor asked him to keep in touch and went out into the sleet.

"We gonna teach you to play that thing yet," Page said, and they launched into the rest of the set. Jambeaux sounded as fine that night as it had ever sounded, they did fifteen original songs to a roaring drunken crowd. Even Sonny was there, passing through on his way to California, and after the gig he ambled over, some futuristic mutation of man, no longer in need of pigmentation because he spent all his time in rock and roll dream caves.

"Link." Sonny smiled tenderly, extending his hand.

"Hey." Link smiled and touched Sonny's shoulder while he shook hands.

"You're gonna make it." Sonny turned to Page. "This is sounding righteous."

"Thanks, man."

"Bodacious," Sonny added. "Somebody told me Perry Holden's been talking to you."

"That's right." Page jumped down off the stage. "I think he wants to sign us."

"Do it, man, do it." Sonny looked around and saw his driver, who waved and pointed to his wristwatch. "Listen, I gotta run. You get to New York, be sure and call."

"Right," Link said. "You be fussy, now."

Link decided not to go straight home, as he had been doing for months. Everyone agreed it was finally time for a party. But as they were packing up, they were approached by a man wearing a leather vest and gold chains around his neck. He asked which of the musicians was Page.

"That's me," Page said. The man appeared to be in his fifties and Page regarded him with distaste and suspicion.

"My name is Shelly Silver," the man said. "Artist's representative. I understand Enigma Records is thinking about signing you."

"Where'd you hear that?" My, Page thought, word sure does get around.

"I'm from L.A. You hear things."

"What can we do for you?" Page already didn't like him.

"I want to represent you," Silver said. "What's holding you back from signing with Enigma is not having a manager, right?"

"Not really. We're just getting the band ready. We had a little problem here and there. Anyway, we don't need a manager to sign a contract."

"Yeah, I heard about your problem with, uh, Link? Your bass player?"

"How do you know about Link?"

"Word gets around."

Page finally insisted that they were not interested. The next day he got a call from Jill, who told him he was making a big mistake in not signing Shelly Silver to be Jambeaux's manager.

"How do you know about this?" Page asked. He was beginning to think he was the only one not tied into this hot line.

"I'm the one who told Shelly to call you, Dim-o. He went out there because I *told* him to go out there." Jill spoke as if she were talking to a child.

"Oh," Page said. There was a pause. "But I don't like him."

"That shows good judgment," Jill said patiently. "He would back a car over his mother for a dollar." She paused to let that sink in. "But," she added, "he's the best there is. He's a known miracle worker, Page. They call him the Silver Fox. He'll get you a great tour, he can put you into places no one else could. So will you please stop acting like a child and get out here?"

"We'll be out there soon," Page said ineffectually.

"Page, it's almost spring, and that means if we start now, we won't be out till summer, which is not the best time to release a record. I want to see you and Link and everybody out here at the end of the week."

"We don't have enough money." Page was losing ground fast and knew it.

"I'm calling for tickets now. And I'm wiring you some expense money. No," Jill said before Page could object. "Don't tell me: you don't know how to get from the airport to here. Fine. We'll have a car pick you up. We also have a little house for you to stay in. So do it, all right?"

And Page sat there with the phone in his hand wondering why he was hesitating. They were ready, he had to admit that. He knew, though, he just knew, that was why. It was right there within his reach and he couldn't articulate it. He had this sudden, backed-up flash and remembered lying face down in water with machine-gun fire etching the air above his head, so close he could hear the buzz of the bullets, thinking, Can't we just talk this over first? And now he wanted to say, "Take me home, I want to go *home.*" But he had no other reasons to stay. Jill was right, as usual. Nothing to it, just get on that plane.

"All right," Page said softly, thinking, Why? Why am I feeling so low right now? Every musician in the country would give his left nut for an invitation like this. We're going to be stars, man, famous, rich, important. Why is it all so depressing?

"Page, get the boys together and pick up those tickets. I'll have the expense money to you tomorrow morning."

"All right," Page said again. "I'll see you in a couple of days."

He told Link and Link grinned shyly. "You think I'm sounding good enough?" he asked.

"Never sounded better. A fucking medical miracle." Page tried to smile but it just wouldn't happen.

Even Scoop had come a long way and didn't mind too much the idea of going to L.A. The band had been very good therapy for him, and even to Scoop the old routines were getting a bit boring.

When Page told Blye, he puffed out his cheeks and raised his eyebrows for a moment. He finally exploded with laughter. "Yes, of *course,* we'll all get some of that marvelous California sun, Jesus wept, man, think of it. The ocean, the open bloody ocean! And that health-giving California heroin! Fok, yes, lad. Let's have after it."

"Think of it," Butch said with awe. "Think of all the thirteen-year-old chicks who will want my *body!*"

When Link told Judy they were finally going, Page said she could come along if she wanted. He knew, after all, that without her, there would be no Jambeaux, at least not with the sound Page had always heard.

"Shit." Judy grinned and dug her toe into the floor like a cowboy. "I got too damned much to do out on that ranch without going on the road with a bunch of half-crazy musicians." She smiled at Link. "Some of us *work* for a livin', you know."

So they packed it up, packed it in suitcases, packed their instruments away. They even told Ritchie good-bye. There was almost a note of friendliness there when they finally parted company.

"You guys done real good by me," Ritchie said to Page.

"Thanks, Ritchie." Page smiled at the weird little man. "I appreciate your taking us on back then. I know it musta been kind of dangerous at first."

"I'll never understand why those gangster types never came back." Ritchie still looked a little scared, as if someday they might come back, as if he might spend the rest of his life waiting to find out. "They threatened me one night and they just disappeared, right in the middle of a sentence. Never saw them again."

"Who knows?" Page shrugged. It wasn't until much later that he found out. "Anyway, thanks. I hope things work out for you."

"Yeah, good luck." Ritchie shook Page's hand and never saw him again, except once or twice on television.

The day they were to leave, the sun came out unexpectedly, and the temperature soared into the sixties. Page wandered out to the pool, where Cyndi was reading. He had just finished moving all his things out of her apartment. She had helped him for a while, but then decided she didn't want to see any more. As he approached, she folded the magazine in her lap and looked up at him, raising her sunglasses onto her forehead. Page never ceased to admire how pretty she was.

"When will I see you again?" she asked. She looked drawn and worried. It had all happened so quickly. For months and months it had been all talk. Sure, Perry was interested, and sure, there was Jill, too, hot on the case. But to Cyndi, Perry was a distant theoretical entity, not a real person, and Jill was just their friend, someone she and Page knew and loved, not a powerful record-company executive. And now that it was happening, Cyndi couldn't quite adjust. After nearly nine months' containment at Timmons Lane, the band had all but cleared out of Houston in two days. Things were just moving too fast. ("We got to the top so quickly," Page would say later, "my nose bled.")

"I don't know." Page sat on the edge of the chaise longue and put his hand on her leg. "I don't know what they have planned for us. The contracts are all drawn up. They want us to sign and then go into a studio somewhere and start laying it down. Then we go on the road, I guess, and they release the record. So I don't know."

"Can I come out and see you on the road?" She asked it with such childlike sweetness that it practically broke Page's heart. He realized that during this wild, weird time, she had provided something for him that he had never had before. If he had tried to get it from Jan in Austin, probably just the fact that he was trying would have made him fail. But unconsciously he had found it in this most unlikely woman. And without even thinking about it, they had both backed into a warm, subtle relationship that some might even call love if that locution hadn't become so devalued.

"Of course." Page emphasized the phrase perhaps too strongly. They both knew it would be difficult, if not impossible, to see each other from then on. She would (they both knew) fly out to some godforsaken town—Memphis or Toronto or Cleveland—and spend a few days with Page, have a reunion with the boys. And then she'd come back to Houston, to her alimony and her swimming pool.

"Saddle up!" Link called from the balcony outside the apartment. He stood by the rail, grinning in a T-shirt, the sun gleaming on his forearms. He was sweaty from the work. "Let's get this show on the road."

"Be right there," Page called up at him, smiling. He turned back to Cyndi and they embraced, gently and without sexuality, like brother and sister, and Page whispered her name.

"Color me gone." Page jumped up without further ceremony and roared around in a fury of action. Then they were gone—just like that—and the ratty, brown, grassy stretch around the pool was silent except for the sound of the stunted palm trees rustling in the breeze now and then, and Cyndi flipped the pages of her magazine without really seeing what was on them. She turned once only to look up at the balcony from which Link and Page and that wild old, bad old bunch had disappeared, and the history of that place took her in the throat, suddenly, closing off her breathing like fingers around her neck. She turned away, thinking, I'm going to have to find another place to live, and she lay back, lifting her face to the first tentative sunlight of the season.

-17-

"You *fool!*" Page laughed softly at Steve, shaking his head in despair. He turned back to the window where he had been watching the truck bounce along the trail. At least he knew one of the things Steve had been up to. "Now, what else have you done?" he asked with a sigh.

"I invited *The New York Times*, too," Steve sneered.

"You *fool*," Page repeated and went to get a beer and slouch in his chair by the fireplace. But when Butch burst into the room shouting, "Anybody cain't tapdance is a queer!" Page got up and tapdanced.

"You filthy maggot." Page shook Butch by the shoulders. "You've brought venereal disease to the Indians, now, haven't you? Admit it, you have, haven't you?"

After a few minutes of this, Butch sat down with a beer and Page took stock of him. He hadn't changed that much, though the white slash in his beard had begun to take over the entire lower half of his chin. He still wore his tweedy sport coat and high-collared shirt, but now he looked more like a professor than a graduate student, or perhaps like a senator from Utah.

"What'd you bring that shit for?" Page asked when Red came in carrying Butch's instrument cases.

"I get lonesome without them." Butch grinned.

"I heard that jazz sax stuff you did, that was pretty fuckin' good," Steve said.

"I'd always wanted to do a solo album," Butch said. "So I figured if I couldn't play with this dumb fucker"—he jerked a thumb at Page—"I might as well cut my own record."

"Sell any?" Steve asked.

"Oh, yeah, yeah." Butch rolled his eyes. "Let's see, my mother bought one . . ."

"What I figured," Page said.

"Well, I didn't exactly do it for the money." Steve watched Butch's expression and saw the slightest hint of a smirk there.

"Oh." Steve shook his head up and down. "Ohhh, I get it. I know why you did it, you sly lecherous son of a bitch."

"You got his number." Page laughed. "Definitely got that boy's call sign."

"Because teenage chicks have to go change their panties when they hear that old saxophone sound, is that it, you golden-tongued devil?"

"Well." Butch chuckled immodestly.

"You clever horse." Steve laughed.

"What about you?" Butch asked. "What have you been doing?"

"Oh, I've been tryin' to get my asshole brother to quit fucking around and get back to work."

"Never happen," Page muttered.

"So"—Steve ignored him—"I'm just going to have to go it alone."

"You'll be sorry," Page said.

"Yeah," Butch said seriously, "I'm so sorry when I get into my red Porsche Turbo Carrera that I cry all the way through fifth gear." He looked up gloomily. "And last fall when I spent a month skiing in Zermatt, I couldn't hold back the tears as I blasted down into Italy for lunch." Butch hung his head in mock sorrow.

"Yeah." Steve glared at Page, who just shrugged; fuck 'em if they felt that way.

"Well!" Butch popped to his feet and rubbed his hands together. "Let's do something."

"Let's play some music," Steve said.

"Come on, Page," Butch said. "Get your fucking git-box."

"Yeah, fuckin'-A right." Page jumped up and rubbed his hands together. "Let's play some of that music."

"All *right.*" Steve smiled and went to pick up his bass.

"You guys just warm up a little first, I gotta help Red for a minute."

"All right, we'll be hot when you get back," Butch said, sitting at the piano. Page began lacing his boots as Steve and Butch got it together. He didn't want to play, but he didn't want to act like an asshole about it either, always whining that he wouldn't play. In part, that was why he didn't want visitors. Because he knew he would constantly be on the defensive. So he just agreed to play, knowing he wouldn't. Easy. Still, he couldn't shake his curiosity about how they would sound. That bass line in particular. And Steve's voice.

"Hold on here a minute while I check the angle of the dangle," Steve said. "Gimme an E."

And Page listened as they cranked into a long slow intro that sounded all too familiar for Page. He had gone deep into the woods to achieve some semblance of silence and now he was hearing so much in what they played, it was so resonant with history, he thought he would have to leave the room. That old sound, for one thing, strung so tight on such a fine wire he felt if he touched it his fingers would fall off—Steve must have been born into it, because there it was, that bass line dropping straight and smooth to infinity. And then when the actual song began, his worst fears were confirmed: Steve's voice came on throaty and tenor as a tuned racing engine, singing a song Page had written for Jill years earlier, one of his favorites, one he never ever wanted to hear again.

> Living together
> On the same wavelength
> Her wit and her beauty
> And her fragile strength
> Through the islands of enemies
> The weak and the lame
> She comes shining
> Again and again

When Butch hit the harmony behind Steve, Page got up abruptly and left the house.

When Page returned, Butch and Steve were drinking beer and snorting coke in the living room. ("Destroying the evidence,"

Butch called it.) Butch's solo album was playing and every time his saxophone ran through a particularly impressive lick, he would jump up, move the needle back, and say, "Listen, listen to this. Isn't that something?"

"Butch, you egomaniacal degenerate, will you please sit down and help me destroy this evidence like a good criminal?" Steve pleaded.

"Well"—Butch looked up as Page came in—"lookie here, it's fucking Lord Jim."

"You guys want any *food?*" Page asked with a grin. "How about a couple of big, thick steaks?" He could see from all the way across the room how wired they were. They probably wouldn't eat for days.

"Shitbird here talks like he never did any coke before," Butch said to Steve.

"Hey." Steve was truly stoned. "You're acting like I'm supposed to know everything before I even start."

"Say again all after 'know,'" Page said in a radio operator's voice, and sat down by the fire. He took a bottle of whiskey from the hearth and unscrewed the cap.

"I mean," Steve said, rubbing his nose, "like as if you knew it all right from the beginning, like right now before it even starts for me I'm supposed to look into the future and see how things are going to go for me."

"Well, shit," Page said and put the cap back on the whiskey without tasting it. In a sense he did have some foreboding. He didn't particularly want to try to explain it to Steve right now and Butch knew what Butch knew, no one had to tell him anything, he never wanted to know anyway. But Page could remember that first day they arrived in L.A. and the ensuing days. And he could certainly remember the day they finally got down to signing the contracts with Enigma and Shelly. He especially remembered the light in the living room of Perry's Malibu house. It was a failing, running red light.

Page stood at the bookshelf, sipping champagne and looking at the little discus thrower. He took the penny from the statue's hands and examined it. Another Indian Head penny, dated 1898. He turned around to face Perry.

"Nice," Page said, "eighteen ninety-eight."

Perry smiled at Page and lifted his own glass. *"Chapeau, Jam-*

beaux," he said, and around the room the boys stood and raised their glasses. Shelly Silver walked in from the kitchen, snagging a glass along the way. He had Jill in tow. Page had been watching her and Shelly and did not think much of the easy familiarity with which they talked and looked at each other and touched. But then everybody in L.A. seemed to touch everyone else. It was as if people there were not convinced that other people actually existed and therefore needed to touch each other all the time as a reassurance.

Page, too, raised his glass and felt oddly afraid, as if something awful were about to happen. He told himself it was natural and tried to ignore it.

As soon as Jambeaux arrived in L.A., Page saw they would need a lawyer, and the only way he knew to find one was to ask Perry or Jill or Shelly, which would be like having no lawyer at all. Finally, he had hit on a solution and phoned Sonny, who asked Phil Shorter, who recommended a Los Angeles attorney. The man told Page that the actual structure of the deal Shelly and Perry wanted to set up was not unlike the one Sonny had gotten. Essentially, they were going to sign a contract with the manager—Shelly —who would in turn sign a contract with Perry. Now the lawyer sat quietly at the side, waiting in case someone needed him. He had approved the contracts as amended. There was nothing left to do but sign. Page felt his skin go cold, and every time Shelly rested his hand on Jill's hip he had the urge to jump up and break a chair over his head. But after days and days of negotiations, listening to the drone of the attorney's voice explaining each salient point of the contracts to him over and over, he had just been worn smooth, the way a sharp piece of glass will be blunted in a gentle surf.

The sun dropped into the Pacific beyond the cliffs of Malibu, ninety-three million miles of it, running red across the roaring beach and Page slumped into his chair, wondering, Why? Is it just jealousy about Shelly pawing at Jill? No, that's ridiculous, look at the old fox. What then? Are all these people conspiring to screw me? No, probably not. They just want to make money. Then you're just a fool, right? Fuck it, he reached for the contract in front of him, noticed that Perry had provided an actual quill pen for the occasion, dipped it, and laughed. Line of departure. Rock and Roll.

"Hold it," Shelly said, and Page looked up. He was blinded by the pop of a strobe as a photographer he hadn't even noticed before took his picture at the moment of signing. He was so nervous he almost hit the floor, old white phosphorous memories, Man, man, don't ever do that to me again; and later when he saw the photograph, the expression on his face reminded him exactly of one Link had snapped of him as he jumped out of a chopper under fire at some godforsaken landing strip, flat-out, unguarded panic.

As soon as they had signed the contracts, Blye got up holding a glass of champagne and started in again, "Jesus wept, man, that made me tired, I say we all need a vacation, we've been at this too beastly long, know wot I mean?" Perry chuckled soundlessly, but Page wasn't laughing. He took Jill's arm and asked her if they could get the fuck out of there, fast. She took one look at him and nodded.

Out at Jill's house, overlooking the San Fernando Valley's shimmering lights, it didn't take Page long to get over his grim mood, wine and home cooking and love, don't forget love. Jill reassured him that he was going to have a fabulous time, that Jambeaux was going to be big, "perhaps bigger than anything Perry's ever done," she said, cutting up cocaine on a marble slab.

"Jesus," Page said softly.

"What?"

"I'm just beginning to realize. It's starting to sink in. We've really stepped into it this time, haven't we? We're really going to do this."

"What was your first clue?" She handed him a silver tube. He took two generous lines, then leaned back and sighed, long and weary. "Oh fuck oh dear." The rest of the evening it was like watching it all happen to someone else, hovering over the San Fernando Valley in some cosmic, out-of-body pleasure center, riding the neurological tidal waves into sleep.

The following day, business really started. Perry and Shelly sat them down and launched into discussions of a cover concept and artwork, photographs and dental work.

"Wait a hold on here one minute," Link said. "What're we talkin' about the boogin' cover for? We ain't even got the record to put in it."

Shelly laughed. "The hardest thing of all is the cover; we have to start now."

Scoop tried to keep his lips together as he asked, "What did you say about dental work?"

"Your lovely teeth, Scoop"—Shelly grinned, showing his caps— "they look *awful*. They need to be fixed. This is show business."

"I don't fucking believe it." Page looked at the ceiling.

"Sure, sure," Butch said, "look at these." He grinned, baring his teeth for Scoop, who looked as if he might crawl under the table.

"Bloody right," Blye said. "Have 'em all pulled out is what I say—"

"You too," Shelly said, and Blye shut up.

"I'm not going to no dentist," Scoop said. But he did. He and Blye both, and it was truly remarkable what a difference it made in Scoop's appearance. He looked like a college student. A crazed, maniac, ferret-faced, ridge-running college student, who might have escaped from a penitentiary. But a college student nevertheless.

At one of the meetings Perry brought up the subject of some new equipment for them. "Things have changed," he said as they sat in the living room. Page wandered over to the tap and drew himself a beer. "The way it's done now is with small units, light, quick-response units. These little amps produce a very fine sound but not much power. So they in turn are miked and recorded. Even in the big concerts now, they don't use large amps for the instruments, they use enormous sound systems like Northwestern up there in Oregon uses—you must have seen them at outdoor concerts. Then the musicians are miked through their amps and that sound is fed through the larger system."

"I like it," Page said. "I like it. It fits. Light assault rock and roll, like I always said. Mobility is the key to nobility."

They spent a couple of days looking at equipment before they settled on Twin Reverbs for Scoop and Page and a Fender Studio Bass Amp with Built-in EQ for Link. They were learning.

But not all the learning was on their part. Jill and even Perry may have thought all the trouble was over, but Jambeaux had a lot of layers of history to get through and if, in the coming years, there was to be decreasing evidence of violent behavior and a proclivity toward trouble, it most certainly wasn't going to happen overnight.

The band went down to the Roxy one evening to hear a new act that was supposed to be knocking everyone dead in L.A., and they got pretty seriously overserved. Blye waved vaguely for a waitress, trying to get another drink, talking too loud, saying things like, "If that's what they call music, we're in the wrong town, Jesus wept, listen to that cunt, will ya? Beastly awful, someone ought to put the poor bastard outta his misery." And Butch chimed in behind him, "Who *is* that guy? Give us a break. He's so bad he could drive a hungry dog off a meat wagon." Eventually, a largish bouncer-looking gentleman approached.

"You boys want to leave?" the man asked. He was about Link's size and wore a suit.

"And who the fuck wants to know?" Blye asked belligerently.

"All right." The bouncer saw he had a wise-ass on his hands and grabbed the back of Blye's chair, but Page came up fast.

"Say, you wanna blow it out your ass, buddy?" Page watched as the color drained from the man's face. The man couldn't believe this little character had said that to him. Page saw the man's shoulder tighten and knew what was coming next, but even drunk, Page moved so quickly that the man dropped as if Page had been wearing a cestus and went down in a heap without a sound. Then three others seemed to materialize out of nowhere, three big ones with nightsticks, and Link took the first one with a left to the side of the head. The man never saw it coming. A second bouncer brought his nightstick down across Scoop's neck and put his lights out. Page picked up a wine bottle and hit the man so hard with it that it appeared to explode, twinkling green crystals in the smoky light, as the fey Los Angeles crowd shied like horses in a burning barn.

In the wagon on the way to jail, Link chuckled at Page and said, "I gotta hand it to that singer, he may not've sounded so slick, but he sure didn't stop playin' when the shit hit the fan."

"Musta had some of that nightclub training," Page said, holding his ribs.

They were out of jail so quickly that it made Page wonder about Perry. They never even had to show up in court. Who in hell *is* this guy? Page thought.

"Fucker's slick," Link allowed.

"Fucker could talk tenpenny nails out of a pine plank," Page said. But they forgot about it soon enough; there was too much else to occupy their time.

⊷18⊶

"Oh, wow, oh, *man,*" Page said as they entered Ice Nine Studios in Wisconsin for the first time. "Man, look at this *equipment.* Oh, Christ, what's this?"

"Jesus wept." Blye laughed. "Wept bitter tears."

"Lordy," Link said, turning full circle inside the control booth to get the whole cinemascope picture.

"Astronauts," Scoop muttered, his eyes wide. "They've made a mistake, man, they think we're Ass-tro-knots." He spun around and shouted, "Hey, man, there's been some mistake. We're only musicians. We don't want to go to no moon!"

Page laughed. "God, I don't know if we're up to this."

"Hi, fellas." The engineer came through the door carrying a diet pop. He was thin, thin, thin. ("Dude's so thin," Link said later, "takes two grown men to see him on a clear day.") He wore very tight pants and high boots. His light brown hair was perfectly sculpted and possibly even sprayed. He carried a filter cigarette in a cigarette holder and a clipboard under one arm. "We've got this thing booked solid for you for the next six weeks, so we can just mike everything the way we want it and then leave it."

"Rock and Roll," Page whispered to no one in particular. He focused on the engineer, smiled, and extended his hand. "I'm Page."

"I'm Tom," the engineer said. "This is my assistant, Holly." He stood aside to present a young lady in jeans who definitely got the band's attention, though they were in such awe of the studio that no one said a thing. "You guys relax," Tom continued. "I want to mike the drums first and it may take a while. Blye? You wanta get into the pagoda there?"

"Sure."

"Say," Page said. "Would you mind telling me what some of this equipment is before we start?"

"Sure, oh, absolutely." Tom lit up. He even set down his Tab, which he wouldn't do often as the sessions increased in intensity. He clearly warmed to the job of initiating a new band into the wonders of music technology.

The console sat like a giant mahogany desk before the great

glass window that looked out into the studio area, where the musicians would perform. Above the console, set into the walls, were two massive speakers. Tom pulled a speaker cloth free with the ripping sound of Velcro adhesive, revealing the components of the studio speakers. "Urei monitors."

"What's Your-Eee?" Link asked.

"United Recording Electronic Industry." Tom smiled. "It's an Altec Six-oh-four, fifteen-incher with a built-in exponential horn. It's double-woofered and time-aligned so that the highs and lows arrive at the mixing board simultaneously. Really fabulous sound, like wearing the world's biggest earphones." He replaced the speaker cloth and moved to the console. "This board is about the latest thing. M.C.I., J.H. Five Hundred series, twenty-four-track, of course. This is the Five-twenty-eight with automated mixdown. It's an eighty-thousand-dollar item. The machine is M.C.I., too, and the two-track is the trusty Studer quarter-inch mix-down."

"How much are the speakers?" Link asked.

"About twenty-four hundred." The board itself was desk-high and had three swivel chairs set before it. The desk-top surface of the console was a nightmare of electronics—sliding rheostats, tiny black knobs, little lights and switches, and a garble of technical labelings that defied interpretation. The surface was canted toward the engineer's chairs, and the twenty-four tracks ran, from left to right, up and away from the near edge, each forming a straight, thin line of components and functions. "The board has a Spectrum Display in red and the amber forty-five-fifty," Tom went on. "This whole area here is called the Audio Display Function. It replaces the ordinary VU meters." He indicated a line of vertical slots—like a back splash on a counter at the far end of the track modules—in which yellow lights would jump up like a liquid suddenly filling a tube, as the music played. He punched a series of buttons and a song came on. For every instrument there was at least one slot—one channel—with its own yellow light. As a note was hit, the light jumped up to a level indicating the peak force of the note, then gently dropped off as the note died out. Attack and decay. Tom let them watch that for a moment and then turned off the tape. "Then there's all kinds of other machinery here. You'll pick it up as you go along. This is just a patch bay." He pointed to a well about a foot square on the far right of the board that contained a tangle of patch cords. "Each channel here has a reverb circuit in it. The pathway of the music is as follows: fader, equalizer, tape, monitor, level, reverb, effects, and pan. Of course you can monitor from anywhere in the signal path."

"What's pan?" Scoop asked.

"You know." Tom made a motion with his hand, passing from the right Urei speaker to the left one. "It pans the sound from one side to the other, like a camera pans."

"And," Blye inquired, "I trust the fader fades?"

"You got it." Tom smiled. "The level is just that, sound level— volume. Reverb is an electronic analogy to an echo chamber. Don't worry. You'll get the hang of it. I know it sounds complicated, but you don't have to know all this right now. That's what I'm here for."

"Doesn't anybody just record anymore?" Link asked.

"Oh, sure." Tom picked up his Tab and took a long puff from his cigarette holder. "We had Woody Herman in here, the entire band. They came in, did the song twice, and said, 'All right, that's it.' Sounded pretty damned good, too. I think they may have over-dubbed one sax solo or something like that. But most rock is done a step at a time. It's really orchestrated."

Page was leaning over the board, reading little legends he didn't understand. COMM FEED TO SEND BUSSES 1-2, 3-4, 5-6. MONITOR MUTES, with the cryptic L.F., R.F., L.B., R.B. labels below. What the fuck is that? Page wondered. MONO, SOLO, TRIM, he read. All right, he thought, if you think so. Tom was going on, to the left of the console, showing them some of the gadgets and toys. "I'm not going to try to bother explaining all of the bells and whistles here until we use them, you'll see what they do when we turn them on, like these limiters, harmonizers, filters, limiter-compressors, digital delays, the good old Marshall Time Modulation Effects Machine —that changes tempo without changing pitch. And so on. It would take too long to explain it all. Let's go out into the studio." Tom opened the heavy double doors that separated the control booth from the hallway and the band followed. "Anyway, in here, time is money. Your money."

The hallway, like the rest of Ice Nine, was done in deep-toned paneling, with indirect track lighting. In the hallway was a Coke machine that dispensed Tab, Coke, Sprite, Stroh's beer, all in bottles, all for thirty-five cents. Another machine beside it served up candies and cookies, and another offered fruit juices. As they moved toward the studio, Page noticed Butch hanging back, preparing to make his move on Holly.

"Come on, shitbird," Page said, taking his arm and smiling at Holly. Butch reluctantly followed the others into the studio. There was an impressive clutter of equipment and cable strewn around the floor. In a far corner was the "pagoda," an enclosure with triple-glass windows in which Blye's drum set had been assembled. Facing the pagoda was a gleaming ebony Baldwin grand, nine feet long. But the first object of Page's attention was a great picture window facing out into the forest: Light, man, he thought, northern light. Page picked his way among the cables and stood looking into the woods. There were only small patches of snow here and there and clearly the battle was over: spring had arrived.

"Rock and Roll," he said softly. "Nothing finer."

"We got a Yamaha Crystogram Electric Keyboard here, C-Three Hammond organ, Fender Rhodes piano, the Baldwin electric harpsicord, a Mini-Moog, all this percussion equipment, and these other keyboards and synthesizers." Tom droned on and on about the technology in his studio, until they finally just wanted to get started. Neumann U-87 microphones, $750 each, outboard equipment, blah, blah, blah, it was a blur of information. At last Tom turned to Blye, who had wrapped a towel around his shoulders and rolled up the cuffs of his pants.

"Wanna get into the pagoda and we'll begin?" Tom asked.

"Right-o," Blye said and got behind his drum set. He kicked the bass drum and grinned, looking up at the ceiling. "Bloody all right, will you look at this? What's it do, digest me?"

"That"—Tom smiled, holding the door—"is eight feet of anechoic tuned fiber glass above you, Blye."

"Haw! Fok! Bloody good fucking thing, too!" Blye started in, but Tom closed the two-foot-thick door, effectively silencing him. Tom returned to the control room and then the rest of the band began the wonderful process of waiting and waiting while he tried to get Blye's drums miked properly. He used five tracks for the drums, some seven microphones in all, and it took quite a while to do it correctly. The only distraction for the other musicians was the terrifically exotic Holly, who moved around the studio, following Tom's commands to move this or plug in that, adjust this, remove that.

Beneath the M.C.I. logo on the big board was a tiny circle of screen, behind which was a hidden microphone. Neatly lettered above it were the words COMMUNICATE FUNCTIONS; below it was a button, labeled COMM. Tom hit the button and said, apparently unflustered, "Want to try that once more, please?" They had been at it for four hours, and Blye was no longer in such high spirits. Everyone was exhausted from sitting, but Tom just turned to the other band members with a smile and a shrug, as if to say, Sorry 'bout that.

"Mind if I take a walk?" Page asked wearily. "I'm about to come unwrapped here."

"Go ahead," Tom said. "We'll be at least another hour from the look of it." Tom checked his watch. "All you guys, take a break. Take a walk around. But try and be back by, say, five thirty and we'll set up the rest of this."

"Gawd." Link stood heavily and followed Page out. Page stopped before the vending machines, searching his pockets for change. It was the first day of recording, he had done nothing but watch Tom say over and over into the little microphone, "Rimshot, please. Holly, want to move the bass drum mike out a little? Bass drum, please. Bass drum, please. Again. Again, please. Again," until he thought he would lose his mind.

"Link," Page finally said, exasperated. "Have you got any change?"

"No." Link ran his hands over his pockets.

"Holy Christ." Page turned from the machines. "Let's get the fuck out of here."

"That's a rog." Outside, the rolling Wisconsin land was deep in mist. The ceiling was down as far as it could come without being ground fog. There was a knifelike chill in the air, and Page pulled his windbreaker around his throat and felt a stab of loneliness. He wanted to go home already. As they walked along the blacktop road away from the complex that housed Ice Nine, Link took in the land, shivered, and asked, "What the fuck did they put us all the way up here for?"

"Jill said they wanted to keep us out of trouble." Page shook his head. A hundred yards off in the tree line he saw a pheasant flush and glide low into the woods. "Picked a good spot for it," he observed.

Ice Nine was situated on a large tract of forested, hilly land, and a blacktop road led from the recording studios to a collection of cottages specifically designed for the musicians, two of which had been allocated to Jambeaux. Link and Page had the smaller one. It was patterned after an A-frame, with one bedroom enclosed just off the kitchen, another in the loft, overlooking the living room with its floor-to-ceiling windows facing into the woods. It was done in unfinished, rough-hewn timber, and a proper complement of sound equipment was built into a bank of bookshelves on one wall. There was even a Fender Rhodes electric piano for arranging and composing.

"You could do a whole lot worse than this," Link said as they entered the cottage.

"I guess," Page said. He went to the refrigerator, which the housekeepers kept stocked with a variety of food and drinks. On the white door a previous occupant had left a message for whoever might find it:

> Love is Blind.
> God is Love.
> Ray Charles is Blind.
> Ray Charles is God.

Page laughed and took out two beers. He went over to the fireplace, which hung like a great, black inverted funnel in the living room.

"Let's build a fire," he said to Link.

"We'll just have to go back to the studio." Link accepted a beer. "I sure hope this recording business gets a little more, uh, interesting."

"We're just bummed out because we haven't been doing anything," Page said, but he knew he hadn't convinced himself. Link said nothing to help him along either, until Page turned to face him. "Link, why the fuck is it I'm feeling so bummed out?"

"Got *me* by the short ones." Link walked to the window and looked at the forest. "You been a little crazy ever since we got on that plane from Houston." He turned around. "Hey, don't worry, you'll be all right once you start playing again. You just ain't been playing, that's all. I mean, we aren't exactly cut out for sitting around talking to record executives."

"Then we're in the wrong business."

The doorbell rang and Page got up to answer it, saying, "That must be Butch and Scoop." But he opened the door to a United Parcel Service deliveryman with a package.

"Sign here," the man said, giving Page a clipboard. Page signed it with a puzzled expression and took the box.

"What is it? What is it?" Link asked excitedly.

Page took the Buck knife from his belt and sliced the tape. Inside the box was a magnum of Dom Perignon with a ribbon around the neck and an envelope attached. Page opened the envelope and read the card.

"Love to my boys," it said, and Page recognized Jill's scrawl.

"A class act," Link said with reverence.

"And *look here.*" Page held up the little origami paper that was attached to the note. Another little note was attached to it. It said, "I hope I can trust you not to overdo this." Page didn't need to open the origami paper to know what was in it.

"A *real* class act," Link said.

"God, I love her." Page grinned. "Here, you better hold onto this." He gave Link the coke.

"See, I told you you'd feel better." Link slapped Page on the shoulder. "What do you expect, a thousand miles from home on a cold day in a weird place? Naturally we're gonna feel a little out of it. Man"—he shook his head and smiled—"that Jill."

Once Blye's drums were miked, the rest of the setting-up process was simple. Tom wanted to run Link's bass line direct—just to plug it into the console and record off the signal—but Link insisted they use the Studio Bass amp he'd bought, so they miked it. They did the same thing with Scoop and Page's Twin Reverbs.

By seven o'clock the entire band was miked and out in the studio. From there on, all communications with Tom were done through the COMM system. Anything they said—any noise in the studio—was piped directly to the control booth by some fifteen open microphones out there. And when Tom hit the COMM button, anything he said was fed back out to them through their monitor speakers and headphones, which Tom called "cans."

"Scoop, do you like the sound of that new cord I gave you?" Tom asked. "Don't you think that other one was putting out some sort of hum?"

"Yeah. Sounds fine to me now." Scoop hit a screaming, sustained note.

"Page?" Tom asked.

"I can hear it's better," Page said.

"All right, everybody," Tom said finally, "lemme relocate here." He hit a button on the Auto-Locator and then hit another. The thick reel of tape spun, then stopped. "OK, I'm ready, what's the title?"

" 'Jambeaux,' " Page said with a grin, "by Jambeaux."

" 'Jambeaux,' take one, tape is rolling," Tom said, picking up a clipboard on which he wrote the title, time, and tape counter numbers. Then he pointed at Page, who was watching him intently, and Page pointed at Blye, who popped the song off to a start. Butch came in beneath with his noisemakers. This is it, Page thought, this is the moment we've all been waiting for, we have contact, we are Go, there is a launch window. His mind raced ahead to stardom.

"Hold it!" Tom hit the COMM button and stopped the tape. "Hold it."

The band stopped. "Let's go again. Butch, leave out the noisemakers. Link, straight bass line to start, no frills. Let's try to get down a real basic rhythm track on this. We can overdub all we want later on. Blye, you keep doing what you're doing, the drums sound great. Page, you want to do a scratch vocal, will that help?"

"I wouldn't mind. It feels funny not singing anything."

"All right, your voice mike's live. Just sing it any way you want and we'll overdub it later." Tom rolled the Auto-Locator and they started the song again.

"Page!" Tom said as soon as the song got going, "Page, hold it! Please. You're on the wrong mike."

"Sorry," Page said. "This one?"

"Yes. 'Jambeaux,' take three, tape is rolling." Tom pointed at Page again and they started once more, very simply. In fact, it sounded nothing like the song they had become so used to playing. It was merely Blye pounding out the rhythm, Page playing chords on guitar against Scoop, and Link putting over a smooth, even bass line with not much movement to it.

"Hold it," Tom said again about halfway through the song. "Page, you're rushing. Butch, you can relax in here if you want to, you won't be on for a while. Once more." He started the tape and Butch just stood there with an expression that seemed to say, What kind of shit is this? " 'Jambeaux,' take four," Tom said, and pointed at Page again.

Page was ready to fall over by midnight, when he heard Tom say, incredibly, " 'Jambeaux,' take twenty-seven." Page saw him point but he just stood there. "Page? Take twenty-seven, please. Tape is rolling."

"I'm beastly dead." Blye wiped his face, but the towel he wore had been soaked hours before.

"Me too," Page said softly. He looked over at Link and laughed weakly.

"Light's on but nobody's home," Link said with a smile, unstrapping his bass.

"You guys need a break?" Tom asked brightly.

"Boy," Butch said, "old Tom's quick."

"Take a break, guys," Tom said and turned away from the console. He met them in the hall. As they came straggling out, he took a good look at them and laughed. "I guess we'll wrap it for the night."

"I *guess*," Blye said. "I've got blisters on me feet."

"All right, how about noon tomorrow?"

"Yeah," Page said, and they dragged out into the night, so numb they completely forgot about the champagne and coke. They just fell into bed, too tired to do anything at all.

Page slept in the downstairs bedroom and Link slept up in the loft. At about three in the morning a quick, deft, king-hell thunderstorm came rolling through the Wisconsin hills like divisions of troops. The explosions woke Page, and he sat with his nose pressed against the window screen, his face getting soaked in the cold heavy rain. It passed through rapidly, with deafening, startling fury, and was gone—as if it had some more important objective to get to. Page toweled his face dry and went back to sleep. And this, he thought, is only the beginning. Maybe Scoop was right after all, maybe we should have stayed at the Burning Spear.

⊢19⊣

The pickup truck was parked in the snow next to the garage, and as Page and Steve climbed in, they laughed at Butch, who was hollering from the house.

"All right, you cocksuckers!" The voice sounded shrill and empty in the icy air. "If that's the way you feel, don't take me along. But you just wait. They'll get you for this!"

"Listen to him." Steve shook his head. "Deranged."

"Let him holler." Page dropped the truck into gear and fishtailed away from the garage. "No way is he coming along with us." He navigated up the drive and turned onto a rutted road, heading across an open field.

"I didn't realize you still saw her," Steve said. Page just smiled and shrugged. A few minutes later, he parked alongside the concrete strip, and they walked out to the yellow Cessna 401. Page walked around, inspecting the control surfaces and landing gear one last time, even though Red had serviced the plane already. Page opened the engine cowlings and checked the oil.

"I thought you were afraid of flying," Steve said as he watched Page's cool professionalism.

"Oh, I am, I am. Terrified of it." Page went around to the left side of the fuselage and opened the door. A set of steps folded out and they climbed in. In the cockpit Page worked the control surfaces, turned the ignition key, and throttled up one engine. He opened a small vent window and hollered, "Clear!" then started the engine. He did the same with the other engine and waited for them to warm up. The roar was deafening, but Page shouted over it. He told Steve about learning to fly. "Took to it like a *bird!* I'm going to get a *Pitts.*" He adjusted the mixture on the engines.

"What's that?" Steve locked his seat belt.

"Acro plane. Do *rolls* and stuff."

"Just what you need." Steve shook his head. "Put a nice *capper* on your *career!* Glad to know you're still *crazy as shit!*"

Page took off the brakes and steered the plane around for taxi. When they reached the end of the runway, he turned the plane so that it faced three-quarters off the centerline. He set the brakes again.

Steve watched, fascinated, as Page ran the engines up to 1,700 rpm. The noise shook every rivet in the fuselage. While the rpm were up, Page checked the alternators and then threw the magnetos, making sure the engine speed didn't drop more than 125 rpm. He exercised the props, checked the vacuum system, trim tabs, and alternate air control, and then rechecked the controls. He opened his cowl flaps and checked again to see that the cabin door was locked. When he completed his checklist, he said, "We're Go."

And then, very quickly, so that Steve felt his heart go into his throat, Page switched on the auxiliary fuel pumps, turned the plane onto the centerline, and ran the engines up to 2,700 rpm.

As the plane gained speed, Page bounced in his seat as if adjusting his position for comfort and better control. Actually, it was simply the nervous motion produced by delight and terror. He watched the speed indicator intently, his eyes wide, his teeth together, as if he were running this machine at a brick wall. At 95 mph, he gently pulled back on the yoke, and the plane seemed to gather itself physically. When they hit 105 mph the craft hunched into flight. Steve gripped his knees and felt the fear lock into him, deep in his throat and thighs, as Page banked hard, climbing out, all skill and motion.

"Rock and Roll," Page said softly to himself.

"What?" Steve screamed.

"Rock and Row-Wool!" Page shouted above the roar, grinning at his brother, who shivered and tried to relax. Page reached under the instrument panel and hit a switch. It activated the tape player and Wilson Pickett came on screaming "Mustang Sally" through big speakers in the cabin.

"I don't *believe* you can actually fly this thing," Steve said.

"Don't worry." Page grinned at him. "If we *crash,* you'll be the first one to the scene of the *accident!"*

Steve just stared at him, wide-eyed.

The flight to Grand Rapids took only twenty minutes, and as they approached the area, Page turned on his radio, listened to the ATIS, and called the local controller.

"Grand Rapids Approach, Cessna Four-oh-one, seven six one four Juliette, nine west with Kilo."

"One four Juliette." The voice crackled over the speaker, vectoring him toward the airport. Four miles out the voice said, "One four Juliette, contact Tower on one two five point nine. Good day, sir."

"One four Juliette," Page said back, "one two five point niner, thank you."

Page got his clearance and put the plane down gently. He hit the taxiway and idled on toward the small terminal building.

"There she is." Steve pointed to a figure standing by the building.

"Goddamn," Page said, clearly excited. "Goddamn."

Page stopped at one of the parking spaces next to another small plane and shut down the engines. Cyndi was already making her way toward the plane, carrying her suitcase, but Page jumped down and ran to her. She dropped her bag, and when he hugged her, she came right off the ground. Steve walked up and took the bag.

"Page, you look beautiful." She couldn't stop smiling and held onto him tightly. Steve hadn't seen Page look so happy since he arrived in Michigan. "Steve." Cyndi took his free hand and squeezed it. "What're you doing out here?"

"You don't want to know." Steve held her hand for a moment and then started for the plane.

"Givin' me trouble," Page said. "Boy come up here to torment me."

"Good." Cyndi walked along, holding onto Page. "Serves you right."

"Gonna end up with the whole family here if we don't watch out. Might be a nice idea, reunion of the survivors of the Jambeaux saga."

"That would be fun," Cyndi said. "Where's everybody? You've got to tell me absolutely *everything* that's happened since I saw you last. Good God, Page, how long has it been, anyway?"

"Too damned long, sweetheart." Page put his hand into her hair—black as ever. "Too damned long. Wait'll you see who we got back at the Ranch."

"Who?" Cyndi asked, but Page just told her to wait.

They were back on the ranch in half an hour and all hell broke loose when Butch and Cyndi saw each other. They hugged and danced around, and Page kept saying, "See? See why I didn't want you along? You would have gotten us all killed, man, my first official forced landing."

"Oh," Butch said happily, "we're gonna have a party." He turned to Steve seriously, as if explaining a battle plan. "Now, get on the phone to the local high school. We need some teenagers."

As Page opened beers and passed them around, listening to the chatter, he realized how glad he was to see Cyndi and even Butch, in spite of what he told Steve. He was beginning to understand how deeply he had grown into his silence and loneliness over the months. He walked over and put his arm around Cyndi.

"You know," he said, "you're the only person I know who had the sense to send me congratulations when I quit."

"Aw," Butch mocked. "You think you're slick, man, but you just watch. They'll get you. Next thing you know, you're going to be at Madison Square Garden again, going, 'Rock and Roll! Rock and Roll!'" Butch did an imitation of Page in a high, nagging falsetto.

"Ooohhh." Cyndi raised her eyebrows and gave them a hard look. "*I* get it. So that's what you two are doing here."

"Yeah." Steve wouldn't meet her eyes.

"Well, you ought to be ashamed. This is probably only the smartest thing Page has ever done." She smirked at Page. "Apart from getting obscenely rich, that is."

"Sure," Butch said, but Cyndi ignored him.

"Now." She sat across from Page. "Out with it. I want to know everything. I want some gossip. Lore. News. Come on."

So Page started giving Cyndi all the gossip and news he could think of, precious little input these last few months, so he had to go back a ways. Page talked himself out and then brought up the subject of dinner, and Cyndi insisted on making one of her specialties, spaghetti. She had made it for Page more than once back on Timmons Lane; it seemed like ages ago. Page helped her chop mushrooms and find the right spices.

"Page," Cyndi said as they worked, "I read somewhere that you're going to make a movie with Paul Schrader."

"Oh, that's a load." Page shook his head. "He got all high off that *Taxi Driver* thing and read all the blood-and-violence stories about Jambeaux. So he decided to make a movie. Said he wanted a real violent, gory rock and roll movie. And like I'm really going to play myself in a movie about Jambeaux. Shit. Never happen."

"I thought it was kind of weird."

When they sat down to dinner, Page tasted the spaghetti and closed his eyes. "Oh, *man,* this is fabulous. What a nostalgia trip." Butch and Steve and Red all mumbled with their mouths full. And sitting there around the big table in his kitchen, with old friends and a fire and food, he felt like he had a family, a family and a place—he'd had just about everything else, but he'd never had that, not in recent memory anyway.

"Have you heard from Link's mother?" Cyndi asked.

"I called her a couple months ago," Page said. "She sounded

pretty good, all things considered. Said she was working at the library or something."

"They have libraries in Kemah, Texas?" Cyndi asked.

"I guess."

When Red began clearing the dishes after dinner, Lilly came to beg scraps as usual. Steve once again did his revolutionary-dog bit and Page couldn't control his laughter. Jesus, Page thought, maybe they're right. He hadn't had so much fun since—Since when? he wondered. Maybe the company is starting to do me some good. They sat around talking and drinking for an hour or so, but Page was eager to be alone with Cyndi. He tried to make conversation, to be good company, but after a while, over Butch's protests, he took Cyndi upstairs.

A winding staircase ran up from the living room, and at the first landing was Page's bedroom with its giant canopy bed on a raised platform. It had been Jill's idea of a bed, but Page no longer thought of that, he had burned that one clean out of his mind. As they undressed, Cyndi and Page could hear the music drifting softly from below, as Butch and Steve warmed up.

"That's one of Steve's songs," Page whispered as they got into bed. "Listen to him. He's good, he's really good."

"Listen to the way he plays bass," Cyndi said softly, pulling the covers up to her neck in the cool room. "It's almost spooky."

"It's very spooky." Page put his arm around her and gently moved her toward him. For a long time they just lay there listening. Page heard his own voice coming from below—it sounded so much like him he could hardly separate it, or maybe he'd become so detached by now that he felt it had never been him at all, that all those songs had been sung by someone else, someone who had now come back to haunt him down there in the living room. And that bass. Page fell asleep hearing that bass.

⊢20⊣

The second day at Ice Nine, the band arrived to be greeted by Holly, who was waiting in the musicians' lounge—a kind of waiting room. She offered them doughnuts and coffee as they sat discussing an arrangement for the day's sessions. Holly interrupted, handing Page three coins with holes in them.

"What's this?" He turned the coins over in his hands. They had Oriental pictograms on them.

"We're going to throw the Ching," she said.

"Ching?" Link asked.

"It's a Chinese book of changes," Butch volunteered.

"That's right." Holly took the book and laid it on the table. "An ancient Chinese oracle." When she said that, Page and Link practically fell out of their chairs laughing. But they threw the coins anyway. ("If she'd-a asked us to stand on our heads," Link said later, "we'd-a done that too.")

"Number nineteen," Holly intoned softly when the coins were cast. "Lin. Approach. The hexagram of Approach means becoming great."

"See?" Butch grinned.

"See what?" Page asked.

"The Judgment," Holly continued. "Approach has supreme success. Perseverance furthers. When the eighth month comes, there will be misfortune. Six in the third place means: comfortable approach. Nothing that would further. If one is induced to grieve over it, one becomes free of blame."

"What's it mean?" Link asked. And while Holly read the explanation from the book, Page was thinking hard, he didn't want to know.

"Let's play," Page said. "That's just a load."

Out in the studio everything was set up and they had twenty-six takes of "Jambeaux" under their belts. The sun had come up clear, and Page just put it out of his mind, Ancient Chinese Oracle, shit. When everyone was situated, Tom sat at the console and looked at them through the vast glass partition.

Although Perry was their producer, he had decided to let them fool around in the studio with Tom for a few days to get a sense of the routines before coming out himself for the serious business of recording. He'd asked them to save all their takes, good or bad: they weren't exactly making a dry run, but they might have to start all over if, when Perry arrived, he didn't like the tracks.

Tom hit the COMM button and spoke: "Why don't we leave that Jambeaux song alone and go on? We can go over the takes we've done later and see what we've got."

"How long does a song normally take in here?" Butch asked.

"No way of saying," Tom said. "I've seen guys do two hundred takes."

There was a collective groan from the studio that poured into the control booth through the open mikes.

"All right, title, please," Tom said.

" 'You Can't Miss Her,' " Page said. He was feeling right, ready to play, the way an athlete feels when his blood is up and he's ready for a hard game.

"Lemme relocate," Tom said, touching a button. There was a wild scream as the tape ran backwards at high speed. He stopped it, punched it forward, and got ready. "Tape is rolling," he told them. " 'You Can't Miss Her,' take one."

Butch launched into the slow, modal piano intro. Blye came in softly on the hi-hat cymbals while Scoop and Page moved through the tactile thrill of the chord structure. Page warbled into the scratch vocal, lean and rangy and heartbroken.

> You can't miss her
> Just you wait and see
> She'll be with you
> Till you're eighty-three
> It'll go on the rocks
> And you'll hit the street
> But you can't miss her
> Here she comes again
> You can't miss her
> But you've missed her all the same.

He went through two more verses and Tom raised his eyebrows in admiration. After Page stepped back from the microphone, the rhythm track continued. Eventually, Butch would play a soprano saxophone solo in this slot, but for now the sound was odd—vacant and bare and strange, like looking at something unborn and horrible, even though you know it will develop into a thing of beauty. A baby may be lovely, but a fetus is not. This, Page thought, is an abortion in reverse. When the song was finished, the band waited expectantly. Tom stopped the tape and hit the COMM button. With no suggestion of emotion he said, "Thank you, all right, once more. 'You Can't Miss Her,' take two." He waited, then added, "Tape's rolling."

"Well, goddamn," Link said. "What did you think of it?"

Tom stopped the tape again and hit the COMM button. "What did I think of *what?*" His innocence was complete.

"The goddamned song, turdbird," Page said good-humoredly. "How did we *sound?*"

"Oh." Tom laughed. "It was perfect. Beautiful. Absolutely gorgeous."

"Then why are we doing it over again?" Butch asked.

"Because we could probably make it better," Tom said. "Don't you even want to try to improve it?"

The band members all looked at one another, shrugged, and Blye said, "Natch. Let's have at it, can't hurt."

Tom hit the Auto-Locator and said, " 'You Can't Miss Her,' take two, tape is rolling."

They played it again, and to Page's surprise, it was better, so much better that they decided to do yet another take.

"I love that one," Butch said. "Let's hear that one."

"All right," Tom said. "Come on in." They sat around the control room, and Tom played back the third take. When it ended, there was a long silence. It was embryonic, but it was clean.

"Even the scratch vocal sounds good, Page," Tom said. "You could use that one on the actual mix if you wanted. I like this take a lot, want to wrap it?"

"Yeah," Page said.

Back out in the studio, Page watched the forest outside the window and saw a small rabbit lift its nose to the crisp air, twitching, listening, all its senses open. He felt a wave of loneliness wash over him and pushed it from his mind. It's going to get a lot worse than this, Coach, better keep it under control.

"Title, please," Tom said.

" 'Two-Hundred-and-Fifty-Knot Blues,' " Page called.

" 'Two-Hundred-and-Fifty-Knot Blues,' take one," Tom said. "The tape is a-rolling." It was a fast song with complicated guitar parts for both Scoop and Page, and they aborted fifteen takes less than halfway through.

"Hold it," Page called after several false starts. "Hold it, Butch, that's a fall-off there, Ba-da-da-Baa-Bow," he sang the piano part. "Just rake it down the keyboard a little there."

"Like this?" Butch played the part correctly.

"Yeah," Page said.

"Well, then the way to do it would be an octave lower—G then A-flat, or else I could do a fast chromatic."

"Try it." Page waited. Butch did it again and Page nodded at him. "Fine. You're going to be behind your own organ or synthesizer there, see? You got a solo. So you can play the same rhythm later over that if you like."

"Oh, OK, let's try it again."

"Page," Tom's voice came through, "Blye is waving at you. You've got your cans off, you can't hear him."

Page turned around and walked over to the pagoda. "What?" He made a face at Blye through the enormous soundproofing, but Blye couldn't hear him and he couldn't hear Blye. Page grinned and stuck out his tongue at Blye, who laughed and smashed his cymbals with a drumstick. Page couldn't hear it but the others flinched and grabbed their earphones.

"Want to watch it!" Scoop hollered.

"Boys," Tom said, "come on, let's get back to it."

Page put his earphones on and Blye asked him about a drum part. Then they went into take sixteen. At five o'clock they still didn't have a good track on "Two-Hundred-and-Fifty-Knot Blues," and Tom called Holly, who came dancing into the control booth. Butch ogled her through the glass partition and whispered to Page with awe, "I'd lay a thousand meters of comm line to hear her fart over a field phone."

Holly's face came up fast. "Oops!" Butch put his hand over his mouth, realizing that the mikes were all open and she could hear every word he had said. "Why me, Lord?" he asked, flushing red.

"Holly," Page said in a casual, friendly tone, "you're going to have to excuse the Senator from Utah, you see, he's a Mormon and he never did speak English too well, so he thinks that's *Moron*, you understand?" He smiled superciliously at Butch, who tried to make himself smaller. Behind the glass, Holly smiled and waved them away.

"Wanta take a break, fellas?" Tom asked. "Holly's gonna get some sandwiches or something."

The band filed into the control room. Butch towered over Holly, apologizing profusely, grinning and jutting his white beard slash at her.

"It's all right." Holly smiled. "They warned me about you."

"Aw, come *on*," Butch pleaded. "What d'you mean?"

"Like I said," Holly explained, palms outward. "It's all right. They told me to watch out for you and I guess they were right." She turned away, leaving Butch to suffer.

"Order up," Tom said. Holly listened quietly and wrote the sandwich orders on a pad. When she came to Page, he tried to hold her with an attentive stare, but he might as well have been talking to a computer for all the reaction he got, and she left to get the food.

The previous night's storm had cleared the day, and the air was razor keen. The sun was starting to drop onto the horizon but the temperature was up, the afternoon almost balmy. Page suggested they break for lunch outside, and by the time Holly returned, they had spread blankets at the edge of the forest. Tom sat next to Link—dwarfed by him—and sipped his eternal Tab, delicately picking at a salad. He seemed to be on a never-ending diet.

"How come you eat that shit when you're so skinny?" Link asked.

"How do you think I stay skinny?" Tom smiled.

"That's rabbit food," Link said, taking a big bite out of a roast beef sandwich and stuffing a forkful of potato salad into his mouth. He washed it down with beer.

On the other side of the circle, Page spoke to Holly. "Can I buy you dinner tonight?"

"No, thanks." She smiled, unflaggingly polite, nibbling on her sandwich. "I've got a boyfriend."

"Well, I didn't ask you to leave your boyfriend." Page laughed. "I just wanted to buy you dinner."

"No, I don't think so." She looked up into his eyes and showed her teeth. "I don't think so."

Page shrugged and looked across the forest. The sun gradually made longer and longer shadows into the woods. Page hadn't figured on celibacy being one of the components of recording a rock and roll record. Weird, he thought, the difference between what people think it is and what happens when you get there. Before he could regroup his thoughts for another attempt at Holly, he heard footsteps and turned to see a largish young lady in a baggy dress waddling over toward their group. As she came closer, everyone looked up, as if a giraffe had just walked out of the forest.

"Oh, no." Holly covered her eyes in despair.

"Who's that?" Scoop asked.

"Local reporter," Tom said, gingerly forking a piece of lettuce into his mouth. "Always coming around to find out who's famous over here. Do you guys want to be famous or anonymous?"

"Anonymous for me," Page said. "What about the rest of you assholes?"

"Fine by me," Link said. "I got nothin' to say."

"There'll be time for that later." Scoop seemed to shrink physically. He might be ready for recording and playing, but he was not ready to be interviewed.

"Hey, why not?" Butch demanded. "I mean, if we want to get publicity and all that—"

Holly laughed. Page looked at her. Their eyes met and held there while they laughed, until Holly caught herself and dropped her eyes.

"There's no cure for you, Senator," Scoop said to Butch. "Your condition is terminal."

"Well, I don't understand why we can't—" Butch began but Blye reached over and cupped his hand over Butch's mouth. They struggled there for a moment and the reporter approached.

"Hi, Tom," she chirped. She had a notebook and a pencil stuck behind her ear. She didn't exactly look unclean, only as if she hadn't given it much thought.

"Hullo, Darlene." Tom sighed.

"Who've you got here?" No one invited her to join them, but she sat down nevertheless.

"Just some local boys," Tom lied.

"I heard Enigma Records had a group in from Texas." Darlene poised her pencil and licked the tip of it—she actually licked it. Must have seen that somewhere in a movie.

Tom shrugged, wide-eyed, as if he didn't know what she was talking about. Darlene turned on Butch and admired his beard for a second.

"Hi," she said to him, showing a row of uneven teeth. "What's your name?"

"Butch." He smiled at her. Holly covered her eyes again.

"Are you with Enigma Records?" she asked.

Butch started to answer but before he could, Blye jumped him and wrestled him to the ground. They struggled there, Blye on top, Butch grunting and spilling his beer.

"Why all the secrecy?" Darlene asked Tom. "They must really be hot if you're not even letting them *talk.*"

"I'm just the engineer." Tom shrugged. "I don't tell musicians when to talk and when not to talk."

"Are you from Enigma Records?" Darlene asked Page.

"Me?" Page smiled. "Lord, no. I'm from Milwaukee."

"Yeah," Darlene said, making a note. "That's really a Milwaukee accent."

"Do you *mind?*" Holly finally said to Darlene, holding up a sandwich. "We're trying to eat our lunch and get back to work."

"Whatever you say." Darlene got heavily to her feet and waddled away. "See you boys in star land."

"Haw!" Blye exploded with laughter. "No danger of that, eh? God, I wonder what she's like in bed, eh? D'you suppose she ever *gets* any? She certainly looks in good enough condition to deck some bloke, wouldn't you say?" Blye made a face and blew beer across the grass. "Fok! What say we rape her?"

When Page entered the studio waiting room the next day, Holly was standing there, smiling sweetly at him. He smiled back expectantly. Then she handed him the local newspaper. In the lower right-hand corner of the front page, the headline read, "Mystery Band Recording at Ice Nine."

"Oh, no." Page sat heavily on the couch.

"And you haven't *read* it yet," Holly said.

"No, and I'm not going to either." Page tossed the paper back onto the desk and walked out into the control room, leaving Holly surprised and impressed. Butch came in just in time to overhear the end of their conversation.

"Lessee, what is it?" he asked excitedly. Holly just jerked her thumb at the paper and followed Page out of the lounge.

A few minutes later Butch came bursting into the control booth where Tom, Page, and Link were discussing different ways to get a decent take on "Two-Hundred-and-Fifty-Knot Blues."

"Play take twenty again," Link said. "I still think you're rushing it, Page."

"Hey, hey"—Butch rattled the paper at them—"did you read what that chick wrote about us?"

"Not now, Butch," Page said.

"But, *man,* it's our first real publicity, I mean people are fucking speculating about us already and we haven't even recorded the damned record."

"Come off it," Page said.

"I know," Link said. "She liked your beard."

"How did you know?" Butch asked, but it was too late—he'd been had and knew it. "Well, fuck you," he scowled. "Really, man, fuck you. I think it's a real break." Page and Link laughed sadly, shaking their heads.

The band spent the first two hours putting down another usable take of "Two-Hundred-and-Fifty-Knot Blues," and then went on to "High Rise." By lunchtime they still hadn't gotten through the entire song without making a mistake big enough to stop them.

"Come on," Tom said, touching the COMM button. "This time I want you to play it all the way through. If you make a mistake, leave it, just go on and we'll punch it in later."

"What's he mean?" Scoop asked Page.

"Punch in?" Page asked. "I don't know."

"It means . . ." Tom began, then wiped his face and said, "I'll show you later. Right now, just play the song through and don't stop for anything."

"All right." Page shrugged.

" 'High Rise,' take thirteen. Tape is rolling," Tom said, and they played it all the way to the end without a mistake. "All right, thank you. Shall we break for lunch?"

"How about lunch?" Page asked Holly in the waiting room.

"We're *all* going to have lunch," she said.

"Come on, you know what I mean," Page pleaded.

"I sure do." She smiled and spun on her heel.

They ate sandwiches near the woods again, but the sky turned ugly halfway through lunch. An abrupt change in wind direction a few minutes later dropped the temperature ten degrees.

"Definitely gonna pee on these hills today," Link said, checking the sky from pole to pole and gnawing on a sandwich. Suddenly he heard a bad old sound, one he didn't ever want to hear again, and it made him feel clammy all over.

"What the fuck is that?" Page heard it too. And then the chopper appeared off in the distance, closing on their position fast.

"Man, I hate this shit," Link said. "Choppers give me the creeps."

"Lookit," Scoop said. "Lookit, he's landing."

"Must be my shipment." Blye squinted up at the sky. "Placed a rush order for piping hot quim from Bangkok."

The helicopter reared back as it approached the studio and settled behind the building. The rotors kept running, then the machine rose, tilted with a sickening rocking motion, as though it were going to lose control, and lifted smoothly toward the west.

Perry came walking around the building with a briefcase, smiling.

"Good afternoon," he said cheerfully. "Tom, Holly, how's everything going?"

"Man, don't scare us like that," Link said.

"Scare you?" Perry paused, shaking Link's hand. Then he smiled down at the hand.

"Choppers," Page said, as if the one word were explanation enough. "Good to see you."

"I told you I'd get here as soon as I could," Perry said, still unaware of what they were talking about. "What have you got for me?"

"Well"—Blye jumped up with his plate in his hand—"you can have ham and Swiss on rye, or, let's see here, there's salami on whole wheat."

Perry just smiled and turned to Tom.

"Three songs," Tom said. "Rhythm tracks on 'Jambeaux,' 'You Can't Miss Her,' 'Two-Hundred-and-Fifty-Knot Blues,' and if we're lucky, we'll have rhythm tracks on 'High Rise' sometime today."

"Not bad," Perry said. "Let's have a listen, then."

In the control booth they listened to selected takes of each song, while Page stood by the glass partition looking into the studio and out the picture window where the forest grew darker and darker as the clouds came in low and ugly. As Perry called for another playback of "You Can't Miss Her," it all broke loose, the rain came in sheets, obscuring everything. Lightning struck, but all was silent through the thick soundproofing and triple glass.

"Page," Perry said, "you're rushing on 'You Can't Miss Her.' I want you to do that one over again."

"Thought it seemed a little easy." Link laughed.

"The others sound awfully good," Perry said. "I'm surprised, frankly."

"I think it's Tom," Scoop said. "He's told us everything to do."

"Don't be silly," Tom said.

"I think it's Holly," Blye said. "I really think she should stay a good deal closer to this entire operation."

Perry ignored him. "Well, do 'You Can't Miss Her' again, but then just go ahead and run through all ten or eleven songs, get them all down, and we'll go back and start from the first again. I think after you've been doing this for a while, you're going to want to re-record some of those early songs."

"Why?" Butch asked.

"Because, when you finish the rhythm tracks on the last song, you'll go back to the first song and realize that you can do it better."

"Do they have annual rates on those cottages?" Scoop asked.

Perry removed his jacket and sat in the chair next to Tom's. "All right, 'You Can't Miss Her,' " he said, waving them out into the studio. But when they got out there, he was listening again to the "High Rise" track they'd just finished, and he hit the COMM button to talk. "Page, I've changed my mind. I want you to try 'High Rise' again. I think I know what your problem is."

"Anything you say, Coach." Page strapped his guitar on and flipped the switch on his amp.

"I want you to slow it down, first of all," Perry said as the band got ready to play. "Butch, I want you to leave out the piano part altogether. We'll put that in later if we need it. I'm not sure we do. I hear a synthesizer, really. We'll see. Scoop, just play the chords, nothing baroque. Just the straight rhythm part. Page, don't even play your guitar this time around. You've got a rushing problem and I want you to get it right. Just try the scratch vocal. And Link, you just do what you been doing. Ready?" Perry turned to Tom. "Why don't you take a break, Tom. I'll do this one myself."

"Sure." Tom got up and sat on the couch behind Perry, sipping his Tab. Perry slid behind the console where Tom had been.

"All right." Perry touched the COMM button. "Ready when you are. This is 'High Rise.' " He turned back to Tom. "What take is this?"

"Fourteen," Tom said.

"Take fourteen, rolling." They began and Perry called, "Hold it, hold it, Page. You're still doing it too fast. Slow it down, please, will you?"

"Right," Page said. "About like this?" And he popped his fingers in time.

"Slower," Perry said.

"Let's try it."

" 'High Rise,' take fifteen, rolling."

In five takes Perry called it a wrap and they went back to re-record "You Can't Miss Her," which they did in one hour. The legend was at work and the band could tell the difference. Although Perry had told Tom he was just taking over on that one song, Tom didn't get back to the board before the night was out. That tinny, hollow sound started filling out as Perry directed them this way, then that, orchestrating the whole thing like a conductor. And Page thought, It's happening, it's really happening. That old sound. Perry's jacket had come off first. Next he took off his tie. Then his shoes. And by the end of the night, he looked completely disheveled, though he didn't seem at all tired and was surprised when Blye pointed out that it was midnight and that they had been going for twelve hours.

"Splendid." Perry smiled. "A good day's work, then. Good night."

As the band filed out, Perry pulled Page aside and asked if he would like to stop by for a drink. Page didn't particularly want to do anything except go to sleep, but he shrugged and left with Perry.

He was mildly curious about what kind of cottage had been provided for His Majesty, anyway. As they entered, Page began to understand something about the privileges of rank. In overall design, Perry's cottage was similar to Page's. But in detail, it was in another class altogether, lavishly appointed and equipped. Indians please use rear door, Page thought.

"What would you care for?" Perry asked.

"Tequila," Page said, sitting at the bar. Perry placed a shot glass and a bottle before him. Cuervo 1800, Page observed, pouring.

"So how's Blye doing?" Perry asked casually, as if he'd just thought of it.

"You didn't have to invite me over to ask that." Page drank his first shot and poured another.

Perry ignored the remark. "So how *is* he doing?"

"Far as I can tell, fine. I'll say one thing, if he's managed to score around here, you should have him doing something more important than playing rock and roll. Anyway, I've personally watched Blye take his medicine every day."

Perry said nothing. Page drank off another quick tequila and started for the door. "If that's all, I'll be getting some sleep."

"That's all."

As the session wore on, Perry gradually grew more and more excited. Page had never seen this side of him, didn't know Perry was capable of it. Tom was left sitting on the couch almost all the time. Of course, he knew Perry was producing the record, so he had expected that, sooner or later, he would lose control to him. Besides, he was learning from the old master himself. So Tom hung around, sipping his Tab, drawing on his cigarette holder, and bringing Perry a new reel of tape each time he needed one. Tom took notes on the clipboard and watched the genius at work. Perry played the band as if it were a single instrument, played the recording console as if it were another.

One day Shelly showed up to watch the recording. Page caught sight of him in the middle of a song, and when it was over, came out into the control room to greet him.

"Shelly." Page shook his hand. "You'll have to pardon me for acting like an asshole back in L.A. I didn't mean to be a prick."

"Don't be silly." Shelly smiled. "I don't know what you're talking about. Listen, we've got a real nice tour lined up already. It's amazing how fast things are going here."

"Tour?"

"Yeah, you guys are going to go on tour with the Eagles. Opening for the Eagles is awfully goddamned heavy for a band on its first album."

"How did you swing that?" Page asked. "I thought we'd have to work into things like that gradually."

"Most people do." Shelly smiled proudly. "Just lucky, I guess."

Page thought, Jill was right about this dude. That's some shit. The Silver Fox, eh?

"Oh, man," Butch began, but Page cut him off.

"Yeah, I know, I know," he sneered. "Teenage chicks."

"Yeah." Butch's eyes revolved wildly in their sockets and his beard almost seemed to glow.

"Well, we'll have time to talk about all this," Shelly said.

"You've got to get back to work. I just wanted to stop by and watch the action for a while. Incidentally, I want to have dinner with all of you tonight. I want you to knock off just a little early. We've got to discuss the album cover."

"What do you mean?" Scoop asked.

"We'll need a photograph, cover copy, all that. I don't know if we've even talked about what the album is going to be called."

"Why, *Jambeaux*, of course," Perry said.

"Of course." Shelly hadn't heard that.

"Let's get back to it," Page said.

"All right, I'd like another take on that, anyway," Perry said.

In the middle of the next take, Page was absently watching the forest when three teenage girls broke through the tree line and approached the window. They cupped their hands to the glass and watched the band. They jabbered excitedly at one another and pointed, grinning. Then two more appeared and then three more.

"Hold it," Page said in the middle of the song. *"Hold* it!"

"What's wrong, Page?" Perry asked. "That was a good one."

Page just thumbed over at the window and watched as Perry looked at the little audience with dismay.

"Gosh, super. Jiggling bottoms," Blye said. "Jiggling beastly bottoms!"

"Let's go find out what they want." Butch got up from the piano.

"Nothing doing," Scoop said. "You'd have us all taken out on a morals charge. No fucking way."

"Perry?" Page called.

"Yes, Page?" Perry leaned over the console, touching the button.

"Can't we have something done about this? I can't work this way."

"I've called Security," Perry said. "They'll take care of it." Then he turned to Tom. "Do you run into this problem often?"

"No." Tom sipped his Tab. "It was that damned reporter."

"What reporter?"

"Holly?" Tom turned to her. "Where is that idiotic article?"

She rummaged around in a drawer and came up with a clipping. Perry read it, his eyes widening. He smiled. "Isn't that something," he finally said. "I wonder if there's some way to turn this to our advantage."

"If there is, you'll think of it." Page was at the door. "Perry, honest to Christ, I don't mind publicity, but don't you think it's a bit premature?"

"Oh, definitely, absolutely. I'm amused, though. I wonder what will happen when we actually turn on the hyperbole machine."

"Maybe we can play off the 'Mystery Band' idea," Page offered. "Maybe people will be more interested if we *don't* crank up the machine—or at least if we keep ourselves at arm's length."

"Maybe." Perry looked up and directed Page's attention to the window, where security guards were chasing the girls away from the building.

Page walked in early the next morning. Holly was drinking coffee in the silent studio lounge. She looked up as he entered and smiled as if she couldn't wait to show Page what she had up her sleeve.

"I forget to zip my fly or something?" Page asked.

"You're going to die when you see this one." Holly handed him the newspaper.

"Not again."

"Worse." She winked, and Page longed to go back to bed today, with her. When he saw a picture of himself on the front page of the entertainment section, he just about swallowed his tongue.

"Mystery Band Identified." He whispered the headline as if it were a warrant for his arrest.

"I told you." Holly seemed to be enjoying his discomfort.

The photo credit and by-line both said, "Darlene Powers." Page recognized the girls from the previous day. Through the long lens Darlene must have used, they almost appeared to be hugging Page, as he played and sang, his mouth open, his brow furrowed.

"Welcome to stardom," Holly said. "They're going to get you, Page, you just watch. I've never seen it start this early or pick up so much momentum so fast. You're really in for it."

"I'm beginning to get that impression."

"I thought that's what you were here for."

"Yeah, so did I." Page put down the paper.

"Aren't you going to read it? It's really awful."

"No, I'm not going to read it."

When Butch came in, Page tried to hide the paper from him. But he quickly found it, and then he wanted to get over to the newspaper offices and give them a full interview with pictures and everything. In fact, if you looked very closely at the photo of Page, you could see Butch faintly in the background, playing piano.

"We're going to have you locked away," Perry explained softly, when he arrived, "if you so much as *look* at a reporter."

"But *why?*" Butch asked helplessly. "Aren't we here to become famous?"

"We're here to make a record, period," Page said.

Butch left the room pouting, and Page came to a major decision: he had Tom call Maintenance to put a shade on the window. One of the things Page liked most was to see out—to see the light, the forest, the outdoors. But that evening they drew the shade, and it remained drawn through the balance of the recording session.

A week later, they took their first day off from recording. Perry had to go to Los Angeles for a couple of days, and they all agreed that they needed a break. For the occasion, Holly invited the band to her house for a cookout. She lived a mile away, in a spacious ranch-style house in the woods. When Page arrived and saw the sprawling patio, the big yard, he wondered where Holly got off having such a spread. Then he met her boyfriend.

When she introduced him to Harry, Page felt as guilty as if he had been having an affair with Holly. He was glad he hadn't pushed her too far. Harry was only about six feet five inches tall and looked as if he could eat trees. He crushed Page's hand enthusiastically, all smiles. He looked like Charles Bronson, and Page immediately saw that he was about as sweet a guy as you could hope to meet.

"Lookit that dude." Scoop jabbed Link in the ribs, pointing to Harry. "He's a fucking *monster.*"

"Looks like he mighta played some football," Link admitted, turning to Butch, who stood nearby, ogling Holly. "Hey, Senator. See that guy who looks like he'd bite the head off a bobcat?"

"Yeah." Butch came out of his reverie.

"That's Holly's *boyfriend.*" Link smiled.

"As I gracefully leave town." Butch did a mock dance step in the other direction. "Jesus!" He stopped to stare at Harry. "I hope she didn't tell him about me."

Link was nobody's fool. He knew his politics, if anyone did. He took Harry aside, holding Jill's tiny origami package in his hand, and said, "You wouldn't care for a toot, would you?"

"I might run a little of that up my nose," Harry allowed, narrowing his eyes to slits. They wandered off to the house to cut up a few rails.

Page stood on the patio, feeling the warm sun on his face. He heard the distant scream of jet engines and scanned the sky, but saw nothing at first. Holly approached, carrying a beer and a copy of *Rolling Stone.*

"Thanks." Page smiled, distracted but still aware of the sound of engines.

"Don't thank me yet," she said, thumbing through the paper. "I've come bearing more news; whether it's bad or good depends on your point of view."

"Not the fucking *Stone?*" Page asked incredulously.

"Look." Holly pointed out a passage near the end of the "Random Notes" section. "And this one you're going to read; it's only a couple of lines."

There was a picture of Perry at a party, surrounded by famous people. The caption read, "PERRY HOLDEN (Enigma .Records mogul) chats with Beach Boy BRIAN WILSON and Eagle DON HENLEY at recent party given for ELTON JOHN." Page looked down the columns for Perry's name again. He read on: "FLEETWOOD MAC will probably play five or six dates in early fall in the Pacific Northwest. . . . Yet another rumor of a new BOB DYLAN tour is floating around New York recording circles, allegedly planned for Christmas. . . . THE EAGLES are also planning a tour to combat studio staleness, beginning this summer. . . . PERRY HOLDEN has reportedly signed to his Enigma label a new group that will accompany THE EAGLES on this tour. According to the Lake Geneva, Wisconsin, *Sentinel,* the five-man group of virtually unknown musicians is now recording its first record at nearby Ice Nine Studios, the location of several previous hush-hush Holden operations. An Enigma spokesperson said its most recent acquisition is a Texas group called JAMBEAUX, but would neither confirm nor deny any rumors. . . ."

"Now, I just don't hardly believe this." Page handed Holly the paper. The local newspaper was one thing, the *Rolling Stone* was quite another. They were an official rumor now. It made the hair on the back of Page's neck stand up. "Rock and Roll," he whispered.

"Rock and roll is right," Holly said. "What we've been trying to figure out is where they get their information."

"Must be a spy among us," Page mused.

Holly looked at Page and he fixed on her. At the same time, he noticed that the sound of jet engines had grown louder. He looked up and saw a small private jet coming in on a base leg to the Ice Nine landing strip. Goddamn, he thought, who would bring one of those things in here?

"You don't think . . ." Holly began.

"Butch!" Page hollered across the backyard, distracted from the airplane again. He had a suspect now. He tore the paper from Holly's hands and stalked across the patio. "Butch, you son of a bitch, come here and look at this."

"What?" Butch asked innocently. "What's the matter?"

"This." Page shoved the paper in his face. "That's what's the matter." Butch feigned innocence. Page continued to interrogate him, but Butch steadfastly denied any knowledge of the leak.

Link came over, and they decided that the only way to get it out of Butch was with truth serum. Page was no longer angry as they grabbed Butch and held him down. They were going to pour vodka down his throat to make him talk. Page had the bottle poised when he heard a laugh behind him that shot through him like an electric shock. He was so surprised that he accidentally dropped the bottle, cracking Butch across the nose.

"Don't let me interrupt," Jill said, laughing, her hands on her hips. "He's probably guilty, whatever it is."

Years later, when Steve asked about her visit, Page looked around the room as if he hadn't heard the question, then went on to talk about a completely different subject, about something that happened near the end of the first Ice Nine recording session.

A few weeks after Holly's barbecue, Perry had to rush back to California again, leaving Jambeaux alone. For the first two days, Link and Page needed the rest and just sat around the cottage watching daytime television or playing records, suffering *la cafard*. Then one evening they switched on the news.

It wasn't exactly a surprise—to most people it was just more history. But Page and Link had a slightly more intimate point of view. When Walter Cronkite came on and started talking, Page shot Link a quick glance and saw trouble. Cronkite said Nguyen Van Thieu had resigned as president of South Vietnam and had denounced the United States of America.

"Well, fuck that!" Link exploded out of his chair and stormed around the cottage. "Where the fuck does that Dink get off with that shit?" he hollered. "What in the fuck does he think *we* were doing over there, anyway, having a fucking picnic?"

As April drew to a close, Page and Link were glued to the set, listening with a deepening sense of depression as Cronkite told of "Big" Minh coming back to power with the Communists only five miles outside Saigon. Then, two days after that development, Link and Page sat watching a correspondent report a rocket attack so brutal and of such awesome proportions that they knew it was all over. Ton Son Nhut Airport took nearly two hundred rounds and the marines were barely holding, just waiting for that final dustoff, which President Ford ordered that very afternoon. Page and Link stayed up all night. The last of the choppers lifted off at around eight the next morning, and then it was over, all over, Vietnam, press it between the pages like a black orchid. There was no turning back.

That night Page and Link went out and got into a messy bar fight that landed them in jail. Page awoke in a cell. The first thing he saw when he opened his eyes was a familiar face. When he realized who it was, he just groaned and rolled over. He refused to talk to her, but nevertheless, the next day's paper carried a story by Darlene Powers, headlined: BAND MEMBERS JAILED. And if you wanted to document the precise starting point for the tone the press would take regarding Jambeaux, that was probably it, that story. In the vacuum of information about Jambeaux, the rumors that went unconfirmed, undenied, the press finally had a hook— Jambeaux, look out, these dudes are dangerous—and the search for their grisly history was on.

⊢21⊣

By the time they left Ice Nine, they were worn thin, you could practically shine a light through them. Yet the mood of Jambeaux was solidified. The record was done. There was a tape, you could hold it in your hand, you could listen to it. From Wisconsin they shuttled to Chicago, where they caught a 747 to Los Angeles. By the time they connected with Shelly, Page was just beginning to appreciate the exquisite diversity and monstrosity of the machine that was cranking up.

"Every step is crucial," Shelly told them. "You bungle one step and you might as well pack it up and go home." This was where the Silver Fox really started to earn his money, if he hadn't already proved how heavy he was by getting them on tour with the Eagles. Shelly told them all about how it worked. The end product of a recording session was a two-track tape—a stereo tape—of the entire record. When it met with Perry's satisfaction, it was taken to a mastering lab where one of Perry's mastering geniuses put the finishing touches on it. "EQ and editing," Shelly said, "EQ and editing, compressing and limiting, bass, midrange, treble, fiddle with the knobs until you like the way it sounds." This record, Lord willing, was going to be played on everything from Urei monitors to tinny, $4.95 Japanese transistor radios with one-inch speakers. So the final product had to sound good on any kind of equipment out there.

The band gathered at Perry's Malibu house one bright morning to hear a reference lacquer—a sort of proof of the record that could be played on a turntable.

"In the mastering session," Perry explained patiently, "there's a console similar to the one in the recording studio. Of course, anything that is done now is done to the entire record, because the tape is two-track. The mastering engineer can no longer isolate each of the twenty-four tracks you used. But simply put, he makes it sound the way he thinks we want it to sound. Kind of a final mix, if you will. And then he has a two-track player and a disc-cutting machine. He has a metal disc with a plastic coating on it. A diamond stylus cuts into the plastic to make grooves. He has to check it to make certain the physical setup of the grooves is correct. He inspects it under a microscope. Also, he must ask himself, Does it skip? Does it play properly? Are the grooves properly aligned? Is the groove depth correct? And, naturally, if you think about it, you'll see that the longer the record is, the less volume you can put out. The physics of record manufacture is very complex." Perry leaned back and sighed. The band members just sat in silence, listening to the old man admiringly. "It's a shame. Because the technology of recording is so much more sophisticated than the technology of record manufacture, that you lose a lot in the translation." Perry paused and looked out the window overlooking the ocean. "I don't know what to do about it. Maybe we'll bring some of those Europeans over here and start another pressing plant."

"What's the problem?" Page asked. "How come the quality is so different?"

"The process of pressing a record is similar to the process used in printing—up to a point. The lacquer is dipped into an electrolytic solution. A current is run through it and metal adheres to the lacquer. The end result is a negative image of the lacquer. That is then what we call the metal mother or the stamper. It is used to press the polyvinyl chloride of which the record is made. Well, there are a lot of ways to screw up that rather tedious and delicate process. And the end result is still only a lot of holes and wiggles that are there to shake a phonograph needle. It's very crude." Perry stood up and went over to the stereo set. "At any rate, we might as well listen to this lacquer. Once we approve one, I'll ask them to press maybe ten or twelve discs for us to hear." He smiled at them as he held the tone arm above the lacquer. "That way if something goes wrong, we won't have to eat twenty thousand records." He placed the needle on the disc.

Page couldn't get over it. The freaky, hollow sound he had initially heard in the studio had stretched out, grown up, it was like watching a gangly twelve-year-old girl take shape—you just turn around one day and there she is, five feet seven inches of woman, the braces gone with the arrival of other improvements. It sounded like the real thing: rock and roll. Not only that, but now, after so many years of having it trapped in his brain, it was finally trapped in plastic.

But Perry was not happy. He took it off halfway through the second cut, over loud, angry protests.

"Hold on, hold on." Perry smiled and held up his hands in a defensive gesture. "Here." He removed the disc and sailed it across the room at Butch, who had shouted loudest of all. Butch lunged for it as if Perry had tossed him an invaluable object of art—or perhaps a live grenade. "Take it home and listen to it carefully, you might learn something."

Perry didn't invite Jambeaux back until he had heard six more reference lacquers and was certain he had the right sound. Then, for their benefit, he invited the band members over and they listened to the disc all the way through. When the last guitar chord came down at the end of the last cut, they looked at Perry expectantly, unaware that he had already made up his mind. He solemnly put his thumb and forefinger together in a signal of approval, and then a whole other set of machines cranked up, an entire pressing plant, coughing out one hundred thousand shiny black vinyl discs in the space of a few weeks.

Meanwhile, Shelly's machine was out there working its magic. There was a big push, soliciting orders in advance and offering the retailers special deals (buy a hundred albums, get fifteen free). There were radio spots to prepare and the massive billboard above the Old World Restaurant on Sunset Boulevard. It said, quite simply, JAMBEAUX, in the enormous sunset-colored letters of their logo—no other explanation was given. Shelly was really doing his thing, motivating promotional men, hitting Perry up for more money for marketing and advertising, coordinating publicity that had been building since Darlene Powers first interrupted lunch.

"It has to hit like a chaotic but coordinated ballet." Shelly waxed poetic on the only subject he could truly get his teeth into. Print, television, radio, point-of-purchase display, greasing the critics (there, you would do anything it took to get them on your side), T-shirts sporting the new Jambeaux logo—a logo that would be with them from then on—penlights bearing the logo, electric dildos with the logo; anything at all you could imagine, Shelly could and would do it—it was the carnival business, for sure, and Shelly was out there, selling it to everyone who would stop long enough to listen, selling it with the fervor and conviction of a religious fanatic. For him it was a crusade, he wanted to convert the entire world to the Jambeaux faith.

When Page tried to recall it all later, for Steve's benefit, it was like watching something explode off a screen, "unreal." He didn't *do* anything, events "took place." He couldn't recall it logically or chronologically.

When Shelly showed Page the schedule for their upcoming tour, Page nearly flipped. "You gotta be fucking kidding, Shel." He laughed here. "We're gonna die." He read it over to make sure he was really seeing it correctly. "Listen up, here, you shitbirds, this'll knock your dick in the dirt." And Page read them the schedule—no, he read them one page of one *leg* of the scheduled tour, and it looked something like this:

JAMBEAUX
1975 Tour

June	Venue	City	Show Time
Wednesday, 4	Norfolk Scope	Norfolk, Virginia	8:00 P.M.
Thursday, 5	Richmond Coliseum	Richmond, Virginia	8:00 P.M.
Friday, 6	Capital Center	Landover, Maryland	8:00 P.M.
Saturday, 7	DAY OFF IN LOUISVILLE		
Sunday, 8	Fairground Stadium	Louisville, Kentucky	12:00 P.M.
Monday, 9	DAY OFF IN NEW YORK		
Tuesday, 10	DAY OFF IN NEW YORK		
Wednesday, 11	DAY OFF IN NEW YORK		
Thursday, 12	DAY OFF IN NEW YORK		
Friday, 13	University of Wyoming Fieldhouse	Laramie, Wyoming	8:00 P.M.
Saturday, 14	McNichols Sports Arena	Denver, Colorado	3:00 P.M.
Sunday, 15	Athletic Fieldhouse	Colorado Springs, Colorado	6:00 P.M.
Monday, 16	The Salt Palace	Salt Lake City, Utah	7:30 P.M.
Tuesday, 17	DAY OFF IN PHOENIX		
Wednesday, 18	Veterans Memorial Coliseum	Phoenix, Arizona	8:00 P.M.
Thursday, 19	Community Center Arena	Tucson, Arizona	8:00 P.M.
Friday, 20	University of New Mexico Arena	Albuquerque, New Mexico	8:00 P.M.
Saturday, 21	El Paso County Coliseum	El Paso, Texas	8:00 P.M.
Sunday, 22	The Coliseum/Texas Tech Campus	Lubbock, Texas	8:00 P.M.
Monday, 23	DAY OFF IN AMARILLO		
Tuesday, 24	Civic Center	Amarillo, Texas	8:00 P.M.
Wednesday, 25	Convention Center	San Antonio, Texas	8:00 P.M.
Thursday, 26	Tarrant County Convention Center	Fort Worth, Texas	8:00 P.M.
Friday, 27	Taylor County Coliseum	Abilene, Texas	8:00 P.M.
Saturday, 28	The Summit	Houston, Texas	8:00 P.M.

Then Shelly put them on an airplane to New York to meet with an Enigma V.P. who was setting up their big media party for the release of the record. None of them except Blye had ever set foot in Manhattan and when they saw it, their only impression was of some hideous Disneyland for adults—their kind of adults.

By then there was nothing left to stop them except proclivity and dire rumblings, old P.R. hype: "Those wacky guys who play rock and roll," you know the image, musicians are supposed to be laughable, lovable, zany characters up to fun and good healthy mischief. Except, then, of course, they'll turn around and rip the walls out of the Continental Hyatt House and throw the chambermaid out a tenth-floor window, and wind up in front of a judge who gives them a year's suspended sentence. It was always a problem with Jambeaux, discerning where the so-called natural madcap tomfoolery expected of all rock musicians left off and where the deep dark grisly took over.

When they located the building that housed the Enigma P.R. offices, a guard stopped them at the elevator.

"Can I help you?" he asked, looking at them as if they had just laid a large turd on his sign-in desk. When Page told him they were looking for Enigma Records, the guard asked if they had an appointment. Link would have sworn the guard smiled—smirked—as if he knew damned well these rangy kids didn't have an appointment.

"I don't know." Page turned to face Link, sincerely puzzled. No one had said anything about appointments. Shelly just said to show up.

"Well, I can't let you up there." The guard considered the matter finished.

"But they told us to come up there," Blye said.

"Who told you?"

"Perry Holden." Link was starting to get pissed.

"We don't have no Perry Holton here." The guard turned away again and Link, without another word, got into the elevator.

"Well, *fuck* him," Link said, and motioned for Page and the others to get in.

"What did you say?" The guard spun around angrily.

"I said"—Link stepped out of the elevator to face the guard—"your mother sucks off goats." The guard reached for his gun but went down so fast under Link's *impi uchi* that he didn't even get it out of his holster. When Page told the P.R. vice-president upstairs what had happened, the man said, "Oh, shit," only it came out in about eight syllables. "But that's a *crime*," the man whined, and they nearly wept with laughter.

"Auspicious beginnings," Page said into the phone half an hour later, talking to Jill.

"Can't you guys do anything without getting into trouble?" she screamed into the handset. "Look, from now on, you don't go anywhere without a driver at least. Possibly without a bodyguard, too, or a lawyer or something."

"Well, what's going to happen?" Page said.

"I don't know, Page, will you just do your business and go to your party and I'll talk to Perry? Don't worry about it, he'll straighten it out. But just please try to—" Here she stopped. Try to what? she thought. Try to change the entire pattern of your life? Try to form another band? Try not to be yourself? "Never mind," she said. "I'll talk to you later."

When they finally settled into the meeting with the P.R. vice-president, whose name was Dick, things took a little more time to get nasty.

"I'll just start by outlining the gameplan," Dick said, opening a large chart-pad that stood on an easel. When he said "gameplan," Link and Page looked at each other and shrugged. "We really feel Jambeaux has legs," Dick went on, "and there's going to be an all-out effort here, we're pulling out all the stops." Here Dick chuckled at his little music joke—pull out all the stops, get it? And Page looked at Link again, then at Blye, who rolled his eyes at the ceiling. "Now the primary reason for this dog and pony show, boys, is we're having, as you know, a really big party at Max's Kansas City tonight and we'd like to brief you on who's going to be there and what to say. The press is going to be there, and I mean *there in force*. We have pulled no punches, I say again, no punches, this time." Butch sighed and exchanged glances with Scoop, who shook his locks as if a chill had just come over him. "Now, as you know, you'll be playing two songs . . ." Dick droned on and on, flipping meaningless charts and actually using a pointer, until finally Page stood up and interrupted.

"Uh, Dick? Dick?" Dick poised himself, smiling, holding his pointer, attentive.

"Yes, Page, what is it?"

"Uh, Dick, listen, uh, where is this place?"

"Which place?"

"This Kansas place, what's it called?"

"Why, why," Dick blustered, "Max's Kansas City, it's *very* famous, *very* chic."

"Yeah, fine, fine, where *is* it?" Page hung his head as if he were very tired. Dick told him the address and Page repeated it.

"Why?" Dick asked as the band got up in unison. "Where are you going?" He looked totally baffled.

"We'll meet you there." Page had his back to the room and his hand on the doorknob. The group filed out and got in the elevator and left the building. There was a new guard there already.

⊢22⊣

Page sat in seat 1-F of the 747. The plane was still at the gate, awaiting rollback, as Page flipped through the *Rolling Stone* with intense concentration.

"Come on, it's gotta be here somewhere," he muttered to himself.

"Jill's gonna be pissed," Link said, leaning over to look at the magazine. Skipping the party had been bad enough, but when Jill had actually sent a driver-bodyguard to nursemaid the band, Page had dragged them out to Fire Island for several days—missing in action once again.

"I'm pissed too," Butch said, peering over the back of Page's seat. "Do you know how many people showed up at that party?"

"Shut up, Butch," Link said.

"Look!" Page stopped turning pages. "Here it is, man, I knew it, I *knew* it." He read the passage he'd been looking for. " 'In yet another twist of the knife in the ongoing story of Enigma Records' mystery band (going by the cryptic name Jambeaux), an enormous debut party for the Texas group's first album was thrown at Max's Kansas City as we were going to press. The twist? Not one member of Jambeaux showed up to greet the hundreds of guests who jammed the chic Manhattan club to hear them. Guests included Perry Holden, owner of the record company, who reportedly laughed and assured the press, "Oh, they exist all right." Also in attendance was *Rolling Stone* Editor-Publisher Jann Wenner. The new album, entitled *Jambeaux,* was played to the wild applause and cheering of a crowd described by Wenner as "normally quite jaded." ' "

"Well, fuck me dead," Link whispered.

"Wild applause and cheering," Page repeated. "Dig it, dig it, oh," and he knelt up in his seat in order to pass the paper back to Scoop. "Read it and weep, Professor, you're going to be a fucking star and people are going to be *looking at you,*" he taunted. Scoop squirmed in his seat. "Scoop, man, the entire fucking world is going to be *staring at you.*" Page stuck out his tongue and made a maniacal face.

"Hey, Little Buddy." Link pulled Page back into his seat. "Get strapped in, we rollin'."

Page had failed to notice that the plane was rolling along with a purpose. A two-hundred-ton machine, just like in the song, Page thought, watching happily out the window, transfixed and cool. "Oh, dig it, dig it, dig it," he kept saying. "Look at us, man, ooohhh." And the mammoth nose of the 747 rotated gently, oh-so-slowly ten full stories into the air, the great aluminum bird hunching horribly in a 150-mile-an-hour wind of its own making, out on a two-mile concrete strip, naked and exposed on two wings and a prayer, blasting out there on the genuine edge: there's your moment of truth for you, Page thought. There's no pretending now, everything is committed, like the long leap of a diver when his feet leave the board, no second chances. The still plane sits on the ramp like a monument, but down the runway, just before takeoff, it is almost animal in its effort to make the transition to flight.

The wide silver wings dipped low over the deck, an actual flapping elasticity. The engines shook and strained against their mounts and fired continuous kerosene shock diamonds into the chill morning air, and Lord, "Oh fuck oh dear, color me gone," aloft, flying, airmobile. "We have contact," Page muttered, but Link didn't even hear him above the roar.

"Like taking off a fuckin' apartment building," Link said. Page seemed so utterly unafraid and thrilled by it all that Link didn't notice that he'd slipped into another realm. There is a point where you go past fear to terror, past terror to panic, past panic to paralysis, past paralysis to acceptance, and then, wonder of wonders, past acceptance to really digging it, they had both been there. You just have to watch you don't go past digging it to addiction.

"Air fucking mobile," Page whispered as the giant wheels rumbled up the metal belly into the cavernous barnlike wells with a sound like the bowling halls of hell. "Mercy sakes, oh dear," Page said, watching a pasture full of tiny cows receding down there. "Look at all those Milk Pigs," he said.

"What?" Link asked.

"Oh, yes," Page said brightly, "Milk Pigs, no other way, taxonomy has to be revolutionized, and *now*. I have the perfect solution."

"Sounds like you *drank* the perfect solution." Link laughed.

"No, no, really, man, it'll simplify the world immensely if we just rename all the animals 'pigs.' See, you call your basic rattlesnake a Cordata Reptilia *Crotalus atrox* and you're just going to jack with people's heads. So instead, you just name all the animals pigs. Like a snake would be a Slither Pig."

"Well," Link said, "if you think so." He paused for a second and asked, "What would a pig be?"

"A ProtoPig, of course." Page folded his arms with satisfaction.

"Kangaroo," Link challenged.

"Pouch Pig," Page answered.

"Fish," Link offered.

"Water Pig."

"Bird."

"Air Pig."

"Dinosaur." Link thought he really had him this time.

"Um." Page thought for a moment. "PrePig."

"Gaw-damn." Link burst out laughing. "Fuckin'-A. What about people? *Homo sapiens.*"

Page's expression sharpened as the plane climbed through seven thousand feet at a steep angle. Finally he answered, "Long Pig."

Up at cruising altitude, Jambeaux retired to the upstairs lounge. "Will ya look at this saloon." Blye gawked.

"Gad Zooks." Scoop sat at the table. "A living room."

He cracked a pack of cards and started dealing blackjack hands to Butch and Link, while Blye measured off the dimensions of the room with his hand. "Fok! Do you realize how much drugs she could carry?"

Page went to the back of the lounge and lay down on the couch. The lazy, monstrous drone of the engines reminded him of the sound he used to hear on the road, trying to get some sleep in the backseat of a car zooming across country. He was just beginning to feel how tired he was. It was the same kind of exhaustion he had felt the last time he had really been on the road, five or six years earlier. Those nights, he thought, dozing. On the fucking road. Proto-sleaze motel C ration bivouac. Underfinanced cardiac emergency rock and roll shock troops, about as healthy a configuration as the classic snake eating its own tail.

He and Link had gone to L.A. to try to "make it," what a fucking goof. Straight out of one war and into the next, he and Link had actually thought they could just ride into town and *make* it out there. But all they had encountered were months of steady rains out in that desert community.

Somewhere along the line, holes had broken through the canopy of clouds that had plagued California that year and Page and Link had moved northward, instinctively migrating with the bad news. Dear L.A., color us gone. They had turned east at Interstate 80 for the cross-continental drive back to Houston, long-haul insanity, nothing finer, kamikaze butterflies made bright explosions on the car's windshield as they fought their way across America behind massive doses of cigarette and pot smoke, cold black coffee, luke-warm beer, peanuts, speed, and more cigarettes until their mouths felt as loathsome as their heads, like fully occupied Black Flag Ant Traps. The highway wind blew right through them, a low standing tremor, and the pulsing white flashes on the concrete mingled with white phosphorous memories, antihistory on the rock and roll deathways. Tincture of Americana, one drop in your morning coffee and your hazard neurons will sing for a year.

There were moments of beauty, too. One evening Page would never forget: where I-80 discontinued, they found themselves poised on the high ridge above Wendover, Utah, where the late rays of light burned up under the low, flat-bottomed clouds and reflected down onto the infinite expanse of shallow, liquid salt fields divided by roads into perfect geometrical patches of intense pastel shades. Green trapezoids abutting on tangerine isosceles triangles and wedged together by eighty-acre marine-blue paral-lelograms, and all of it shivering like one rich hallucination as the land gave up its heat.

Those were/weren't the days, Page thought. You *can* have it both ways. Another evening the sun hit the horizon with such force and they had smoked so many Alvin Surprises and taken so many Black Ones that later no one was certain if they were just very stoned or if the sunset had really been beautiful enough to make them stop the car along the highway and get out, screaming with laughter, to roll on their backs like dogs in the dust, burnished by the running sunlight. They never stopped to wonder about troopers who might ask what they kept in their suitcases or by what author-ity Link kept the Ithaca Auto & Burglar beneath his dashboard.

As Page listened to the steady dynamo roar and began to realize he was just riding in an airplane—this time on his way back there, for the real thing—he was overcome by an intense sense of confusion—elation and deep, steady grief—as if his reality sphincter had a bad nerve connection that made him incontinent with his dreams so that they ran together in puddles, psychic breakthrough bleeding. Once you have been out on the road for long enough, you never quite get off it in the essential way you must if you are going to live within the bounds of accepted human behavior. You begin to take the spirits home with you. On the road—war or rock and roll—all possibilities are yours, and home is just a reduction of options. Page had seen people who could never go home, and there was a facial expression they shared, one Page had never been able to identify until he visited the San Diego Zoo one day and saw the gorilla they had kept locked up there since 1949, a real prisoner of war. When Page saw that same expression on the gorilla's face—this ape just sat there, reacting about as much as a window does when light shines through it—he took a bad shuddering fit and his friends had to drive him back to the hotel.

And now he was heading for the big test—back on the road, for sure, but this was going to be a new twist, as if everything up to that point had been training and now it was time for the genuine contact—line of departure, as they said, no turning back.

In Los Angeles, Jambeaux continued to rehearse before the start of the big tour. The Big Tour, Page couldn't get over it. What would happen? The Big One. In preparation, they played a gig at the Roxy so Shelly could show them off to all the press and industry heavies—it was his way of making up for the episode at Max's Kansas City, and it actually turned to their advantage. "Marvelously successful," Perry called it. Because of the "mystery" that had been generated, reporters came from all over, "just to hear the beauty," Butch recalled.

At the party given after the Roxy performance, the band circulated through the crowd of reporters. Link smiled politely and called all the women "ma'am." Butch put the make on the wife of the president of a major recording company, which caused a minor ripple in the evening. Then he put the make on Perry's wife, Sandra, whom he had never met. When he found out who she was, he was so mortified he disappeared for an hour to compose himself, but Perry and Sandra just thought it was amusing. When Butch came back, he finally scored with a bartender, a woman who looked like a rather overweight Sophia Loren.

The reporters loved Blye. He told them sea stories, and almost every report that came out of that party was peppered with "beastly, bloody, flippin' splendid," and other such Blye-isms. Even Scoop came out of his shell long enough to spin a wild yarn for reporters, and Page was surprised to read it in a magazine afterwards. It was one of those true, lunatic episodes, involving a bar in Fayetteville, Arkansas, and a shootout in which Scoop and Page were defended by sixty Pachucos against a band of rednecks.

"Scoop," Page said after he read the story, "I don't recall that happening. I don't think I've ever *been* in Fayetteville, Arkansas."

"It didn't happen." Scoop smiled. "But I couldn't think of anything good to tell him so I just, you know. I made it up."

"Oh, Christ," Page said.

The night of the Roxy party, Page found in himself a capacity for excruciating shyness and wasn't put at ease until a reporter who had come all the way from Chicago took him aside and quietly interviewed him, leaving out all the stupid questions. She was a strange, thin lady, in her early thirties, who wore clothes that were more characteristic of San Francisco in the sixties than the Roxy in mid-seventies Los Angeles. She had a vaguely southern accent and when Page asked her where she was from, she said Missouri. Mmm, Page thought, one of Scoop's countrymen. Awfully good-looking for a ridge runner. Later that evening he discovered she had a cherry blossom tattooed on her shoulder. And hers was the only story that came out of that party that didn't play up the violent, grim world of Jambeaux.

⊢23⊣

"We had a sound check before the show," Butch said to Steve. "But the fucking recondo here"—he waved at Page—"got his ass lost and never made it."

"How'd you do a sound check, then?" Steve asked.

"We did it for him," Butch said. "It wasn't that big a deal."

"I'll tell you one thing," Page said. "When I first saw that stadium, it about blew me away."

"You'd seen outdoor concerts before," Cyndi said. "You took me to one."

"Yeah, but I'd never played one before. And I'd never been backstage at one."

"Must've flipped Scoop." Steve got up and brought three more beers from the bar.

"Just about." Page shook his empty beer bottle and accepted another from Steve. "Shelly was more nervous than we were, though." Actually, during the ride to that first big concert, his condition had been contagious. They'd waited for it so long, it seemed, none of them really knew what to do now that it was upon them. Rock and roll is made up of long stretches of boredom punctuated by moments of extreme intensity—some kind of furthest emotion for which there is no name. And they were traveling toward it now at a high velocity.

"Now, boys, boys," Shelly said, as they spooled along in the immense limousine, "I don't want you to be nervous. I know this is your first *big show,* and there are going to be *tens of thousands of people* there—"

"Will you shut the fuck up?" Scoop asked softly, his face hidden in his hands.

"Yeah," Link said, "Scoop'll have plenty of time to think about it when he hits that stage, Shel, look at him."

"Well, I'm just trying to help." Shelly looked baffled and maybe a little hurt, and Blye exploded with laughter.

"Haw! Fok! No danger of that, eh? Link, come on, lad, let's have a toke of that beastly reefer, now. I know you've got some. What's this, then?" Blye started digging in Link's pockets.

"I ain't studyin' no reefer," Link said. "Get outta there." There was a bucket with ice and champagne—standard operating procedure—and their new publicist, a woman named Michael, was sitting in the front seat with Scoop, stroking his head and calling into the backseat.

"Come on," she said, "somebody open the champagne, Scoop needs a drink." Page watched her slow, sloe eyes and still felt nervous.

"Shelly, whose idea was it to send only one car? It's too crowded in here."

"I know, somebody thought it was a single act," Shelly lamented.

"My mouth feels like the inside of a coat sleeve," Page said.

"Shuuut uuuup," Scoop pleaded. "Why doesn't somebody turn on the radio or something?"

"Haw! Yes!" Blye lurched forward and grabbed the knob on the little stereo console before him. He seemed to be the only one who wasn't nervous; of course that may have had something to do with eighty milligrams of methadone, but then, nothing made Blye nervous. "Beastly bleedin' ghastly bloody right!" he shouted.

"Shut uuuup!" Scoop moaned.

"Ohhhh Kaaay!!!!" The DJ came on the air, screaming in a flat-out orgasm of delirium. "That was Steely Daaan, we're gonna have the Stones for ya in a minute, also Stills, the new Dylan, and Lindaaa Ronstadt! But first don't forget I'm going to be at May Bell's Tuesday night from eight to ten slamming those hits to ya, so come on out and *Booogieeeee!* That's May Bell's Tuesday night eight to ten. And there are still a few tickets left in our Eagles Concert Contest, that concert is today, today at two o'clock, and it is *completely sold out!* So stay tuned because we're going to give away *two tickets* in the next hour to one of our callers and *two more* the hour after that." His voice lost its Methedrine-panic imitation-hots-for-ya quality and became confidential. "Now, also along with the Eagles today, you'll see this new group from Texas we've been reading all about—in their *first big concert*. The group is called Jambeaux and they really put down some bodacious sounds—"

"Will you shut that goddamned thing off?" Scoop whined.

"No, no." Michael was up on the seat back. "Turn it up."

"Shhh." Page leaned forward to hear.

"—and they're supposed to be some really cuh-ray-zee guys, too! We'll see about that, won't we? This afternoon at two o'clock at the Stadium, and now, let's hear them, this is their new record, it's called 'Jambeaux,' too, and so is the title track, I think you'll like it, I do, here it is, *Jambeaux*."

"Haw!" Blye exploded and grabbed at the champagne bottle, spilling watery ice all over Shelly's pants. Shelly brushed at it frantically, but it was too late, it looked as if he'd pissed himself.

"Oh, *man,* listen to it," Page whispered.

"See?" Michael grinned at Page. "I told you. Do you know that Cleveland is already hot on this record and it's barely *out?* And Memphis too, do you know what a fabulous breakout market Memphis is these days? I'm missing an est class to be here today."

"Jesus." Scoop's head came out of his hands for the first time since he'd gotten into the limo. "We sound pretty good."

"I'll fucking drink to that," Page whooped, grabbing the bottle from Blye. The limousine pulled into the stadium by a back entrance. There must have been eleven limousines there already, purring with their bored-looking drivers inside. Police lines had been set up and a huge truck was being unloaded by awful, blunt-headed characters who looked as if they'd kill you by hand for a free beer. They were hauling out great boxes of hot dog buns and cans of pork and beans. Another simian fellow was wheeling a dolly with ten cases of Budweiser on it.

"Looks like somebody's fixin' to have a little picnic," Link observed.

"That's food and stuff for the crews," Shelly explained. "You'll have whatever you need in your trailer."

When Page saw the stage, he had the same sensation he'd had seeing the nose of a 747—Oh, Christ, this is much too big, the same sensation he'd had the night Jill first picked him up in a limo, Oh fuck oh dear, this is much heavier than we'd imagined, isn't it?

This was one of the big outdoor concerts, a collection of thousands of fans stretching far and away in a baseball stadium, high up into the grandstands and down low to the very edge of the stage, where burly Andy Frain guards kept them at bay, a colorful, ragged, sunburned pit of humanity, all gaping at a spidery scaffolding in the infield, draped with the heraldry of rock and roll. Enormous letters spelled out the Jambeaux logo and stylized Art Deco vegetation hung on either side. The stage floor was suspended halfway up the scaffolding, perhaps twenty feet off the ground. As with everything in the world of rock and roll, overkill was the rule. The stage alone was the size of a grand ballroom. Holy Christ, Page thought, they could put the whole damned Riptide Rendezvous on that stage, the people won't even be able to see us.

When Jambeaux approached the stage behind, they were confronted by an unparalleled scene of noise and chaos—people rushing in every direction, shouting orders, moving equipment; virulent, piss-off, manic movement, reporters madly squinting into tiny notebooks, exotic Japanese motor-drive cameras cranking out the shots. And all the same, it was impossible to discern the object of such frantic activity, the scene revealed about as much of its inner secret as an anthill does when you kick the top off of it. Consequently, it came as a great surprise to Scoop when he realized that all of this·was directly connected to him. He went into hysterics, saying, "I can't do it, I can't do it," and Blye had to lead him off to the trailer/dressing room parked alongside the scaffolding.

"Come on." Michael took Page's arm. "I want you to meet some reporters."

"Later," Page said, looking up at the immensity of what he had done. Like a little kid, he had to see everything, touch everything, all at once. He was starting to feel like the people in L.A. who always touched each other—sometimes you just need to touch something to bring you around to reality again. And again.

Page and Link ignored suggestions from Shelly and Michael that they should all go to the trailer. Shelly seemed especially concerned. "Perry wants you in the trailer," he said.

"We'll be back," Link said, and they wandered off to dig everything. In the deep shade beneath the vast stage were the power supplies, big power supplies; talk about lining out your technology, talk about megawatt energy, it looked as if they could launch a full-tilt space war from beneath that stage. The black, blocky boxes were stenciled with the words FRAGILE, DELICATE ELECTRONIC EQUIPMENT and looked like some Easter Island number gone wrong, eight feet on a side, weighing hundreds of pounds each, apparently dropped there beneath the scaffolding by some giant, insect nightmare, with cables the size of Link's arm running out and up to the stage floor. Page drew in close to see what was in there. No wonder they said DELICATE, they contained Marantz 140s and 510s and big, heavy-looking Crown DC300-Rs.

At the back of the scaffolding, out of sight of the audience, a great wooden ramp ran up to the stage floor. Page gazed up it and felt smaller than he had ever felt, just as astonished at it all as he could be. He shook his head. "Ground Zero," he whispered reverently to Link. "The goddamned staging area." Then, almost like a prayer, "Rock and Roll."

Scores of roadies were moving around, grunting and shoving, wrestling and hogging enormous pieces of equipment into place, or else running up and down the ramp with everything from individual guitars to Leslie speakers and nine-foot Baldwin concert grand pianos, a five-man job to say the least. They all wore Teamsters buttons or caps or T-shirts and looked like something the sixties had coughed up—ragged ex-hippies down on their luck —though scattered here and there among them were some true heavies, serious Allied Van Lines types with muscles like docking cable and eyes like glass.

When they climbed the ramp to the stage floor, Page realized what all the power was for: suspended in front of and above the stage by what looked to be logging chain in blocks and tackle were eight of the largest speaker columns Page had ever seen. They were each fifteen feet tall and black—black seemed to be the standard color of rock and roll, no small coincidence there and no irony lost on Page later on—black on black on black, and if you can't make it blacker, then at least you can make it louder. The columns each had six woofers on the bottom and horns all the way up as far as the eye could see, blanketing the range of human hearing so thoroughly that no one would escape a single note played that afternoon. Looking out from Ground Zero, Page thought, Death from Above, no lie. And then he saw the people.

"Lookit, lookit." He grabbed Link's arm and wrestled him around.

"Scoop's gonna shit," Link said. "That scares *me*—"

"And you're fearless," Page added.

They shagged back down the ramp, dodging mean-looking roadies and dangerously heavy equipment. At the bottom of the ramp they were approached by a man wearing a badge that said BACKSTAGE SUPERVISOR.

"Excuse me," he said, squinting in the bright sunlight. "Do you guys have passes?"

"I don't believe we got any, did we?" Link asked Page. He turned to the supervisor. "Where do you get 'em anyway?"

"Well." The supervisor was unsure of what to say. "How did you get back here?"

"Limo." Page smiled.

"Who are you with?" The super was trying his best.

"Oh," Link said, pointing to Page, "I'm with him."

"Oh, no, motherfucker." Page turned on Link. "I'm with *you*."

"No, you don't, you ain't pulling that on me again. *I'm* with *you*." He jabbed Page in the chest with his finger.

"Look." The man realized he was being put on. "I'm going to have to ask you to leave if you don't belong back here."

"What do you think, Page?" Link asked casually. "Should we leave?"

"Wait a minute." The supervisor waved his hand. "Is your name Page?"

"That's what they call me."

"Then you're Link," the man said.

"Yep, all fucking day."

"Oh, shit." The supervisor shook his head and looked away. "Shit, oh, Christ, I'm sorry. Look, fellas, I mean, I didn't know who you were, see, and I'm supposed to keep people outta here to, you know, to *protect* you and—"

"If you think so," Page said, and they started to walk away.

"Hey," the man called, "sorry!"

When Page first spotted the boy coming out of the trailer, he thought he was hallucinating, it was like seeing himself loping through the crowds of people, grinning. When he realized what he was seeing he hollered.

"Hey! Hey, who the fuck gave *you* a pass?"

"Pass this." Steve shot him the finger and then grabbed his brother, pounding him on the back.

"Watch it, watch it, I'm a star, kid, you're going to injure my delicate fabric." Page held him at arm's length, examining him, and then asked, "Where the hell have you been?"

"Working in Oregon. Got a nice little band."

"What're you doin' here?" Page asked.

"I had to come see your first big move. Congratulations, I guess."

"Thanks." Page smiled. "I guess." And he felt just the slightest twinge of hesitation there, like, What have I done now? Years later he would tell Steve it was almost clairvoyant in its intensity, but they spotted Perry and it blew his concentration.

"Hey, *look*." Page grinned, pointing. "There he *is*, man, oooh, lookit him. Ain't he slick?"

Perry looked severely out of place in his suit, but he also looked as if he owned the entire scene, which, of course, he did. Page introduced Steve to Perry and they all started back toward the trailer.

"Where's Jill?" Page asked as they walked through the crowds.

"Dylan showed up," Perry said. "She's talking to him over

there." He pointed to another set of trailers on the far side of the stage, little private Eagle dressing rooms.

"Far out," Page said. "What's he *really* like?" He grinned up at Perry, who almost began to answer before he realized Page was putting him on. He just shook his head.

And then Page realized what Perry had said. "You mean Dylan's going to be listening to us?" He grabbed Perry's coat sleeve.

Perry smiled, as if to say, Gotcha, didn't I? "Every last note," Perry said.

"Fuckola," Page said, entering the dressing room.

"Link"—Perry took his arm before he entered the trailer—"I brought a little surprise for you."

"Can I smoke it now or should I wait until after the show?" Link asked.

"It's not that kind of surprise," Perry said, then extended his arm, indicating he wanted Link to go inside.

"Goddamn," Link breathed as he stepped in. Then he bellowed, *"Goddamn!"* as Judy jumped up and into his arms.

"You missin' the party, big fella," Judy said.

"So that's why you were so anxious for us to get inside," Page said to Shelly, who stood smiling in a corner. Scoop had apparently recovered his equilibrium, and so a regular little celebration started, with everyone jabbering away and Judy clinging to Link until Blye exploded again with laughter.

"What's so fuckin' funny over there?" Page called.

"Butch," Blye said. "Haw! Splendid!"

"What?" Shelly looked around, searching the recesses of the trailer.

"Beastly gone is wot."

"Like clockwork," Page said, "like fucking clockwork. Where is that shitbird?"

"Damned if I know," Scoop said.

There were moments of panic and there were moments of panic. They were supposed to go on in ten minutes and this moment held a fairly high mark on the panic scale.

There was a second trailer next door, which served as Perry's traveling office, though he rarely used it. When Blye suggested they look in there, Page and Link burst in to find Butch spread-eagled on the sofa with a young girl going down on him.

"Shame Butch is so fucking nervous about this gig," Link observed.

The girl wasn't embarrassed at all, she thought it was real sharp ("Butch says I'm Jambeaux's first groupie"), but Butch danced around, red-faced and bare-assed, trying to get his pants back on while Blye, who knew how extremely ticklish he was, poked him in the ribs.

"Two and a half inches of hard, throbbing steel," Blye taunted. "Look at him, lads." Finally, Butch lost his balance and toppled over, knocking out a lamp and scattering a great raft of phone messages. Link and Scoop and Page howled with laughter. They had to sit down, and the girl, too, just stood there giggling. Those wacky guys who play rock and roll.

A few minutes later they hustled up the ramp, and Page grabbed his guitar from among the rows and rows of guitars on their stands at the back of the stage. There must've been seventy electric guitars up there, lined up like headstones in some futuristic graveyard. Page shagged over to the front of the stage. He was small in real life, but up there he was practically invisible, at least he felt that way. He strapped on his instrument and then it hit him. Ground Zero. He thought it was going to stop his clock. The crowd opened like a flower of noise, a slow, vacant howl—it hardly mattered that Jambeaux was virtually unknown to them, The Show was beginning and everything became trapped in that sprawling rock and roll matrix.

Page looked out at this multidivision terror, its rainbow colors bathed in the sunlight, and knew, just *knew*—Jump Back, Jack!— these people are dangerous. Once you hear a crowd speak to you in a single voice like that, you never get over it. They love you and they want to tear you into small pieces, they'd probably eat you if you jumped down there among them, flat, fast panic up there, hold on real tight when it all comes down, how close can you get to someone who loves you? Page knew, Page knew they would drink your blood.

He felt an impenetrable calm come over him. So this is it, he thought. Well, I'll be a son of a bitch, look what we've done now. Link moved up behind him and touched his arm.

Page grinned at him. "Lock and load."

"Ready when you are, Little Buddy." Link giggled, high and out of character; he was definitely cranked and digging it.

Page looked around. The crowd was still going like one of those cartoons where someone accidentally drops a lit cigar into a crate full of fireworks, and Page cranked it right up, *Jambeaux.* He remembered the lazy, raking sound of his voice detonating across the beach (God, Galveston, generations ago now) but that had only been a squeak compared to what happened now, talk about blast radius. The sound of his singing carried for a mile. He felt as if someone on Mars could hear him it was so loud, brain-damage loud. And he looked out, listening to Link come in on the harmony next to him, and saw people down there dancing twenty feet below, fifty, a hundred, two hundred feet out, actually standing on the grass with their shirts off, dancing. *Dancing!* Dig it, a frightfully beautiful chick in the tiniest white bikini sitting on some guy's shoulders, jiggling her tits at them, Oooh, to have that pressing against the back of my neck, Page thought. And look, way up there in the bleachers, little brightly clad humans rocking back and forth. Page's song, Page's music, that sound, came rushing over him like the first fast flash of love when your knees want to let you go. He turned to look at Link, thinking, Lookit him, lookit, he's *beautiful,* listen to that *sound,* that hellgong pinging lightning bass and the warbling tenor.

And Page was in love, in love with Link, with Jambeaux, with the girl in the white bikini, with the entire vicious, delirious crowd, and most of all and for sure, with that sound. It went into him like pure heroin into the mainest line. Yes, *that's* why junkies commit murder. It made Page feel good enough to go out and kill somebody.

When the song ended, he leaped high into the air, throwing his head back and to one side, his hair flying out in a single crest to the left, his heels tucked up far enough to touch his ass. At that moment the woman photographer from *Rolling Stone* pressed the trigger on her motorized Nikon. It was the only picture of himself Page really liked, other than the poster from the Paris concert that hung on his wall at the Ranch. The *Stone* picture would always remind him of that first concert, the sheer unbridled jubilance of the moment, never forget it, nothing finer. You can only lose your virginity once, and it would never be the same. Like the moment when you wake up with a girl for the very first time, having slept alone for so long—wake up to the sun streaming in, the warmth of a body, the scattered hair on a pillow, the beauty, and you think, Take me, Lord, if you must, for I have lived.

Or maybe even like that time when you come out of training: there comes the first time you actually step into it, with real people trying to kill you with real bullets. You know you can never turn back from there, you can never *not have done it*, and you find out fast enough if you love it or hate it, probably both if you're like most.

As his feet touched the stage floor again, the crowd went into a frenzy. There it is, Page thought. He had heard that sound for so long in his head, suffered it all those years, slept with it, eaten with it, and now that it was made manifest, he was going to push it into the nation with fierce determination: they too would have to hear it, that mild irritation that results when an inconsequential nagging jingle from a cat-food commercial sticks in your head—he would make that sound stick in millions of brains, and it was going to be more than a mild irritation, more than just a jingle.

Page looked around and saw Perry and Judy clapping and hollering. That was all it took, it was on Page like a fever, and he put the band into another fast number, "When It Hits the Fan," a song about certain kinds of bills coming due ("You know I've got a lover in Texas / I've got one in L.A."). Then another and another, and by the time the whole thng was over, Page felt it had only just begun. Why do we have to quit now, when it's going so well? He didn't even realize they'd been playing for an hour.

As the band started to leave the stage, the crowd called them back with a rising "Ooohhhh!" Page could feel it in his feet, it was so loud, so adoring, so sincere, so bloodthirsty. Though he wasn't fully aware of it yet, strange things can happen to you when tens of thousands of people love you all at the same time so deeply that they want to murder you, it can change you—good or bad—and it was changing Page right then.

He already saw some of the paradoxes inherent in a rock and roll audience, the ultimate threat/provider, the essential friend/ enemy: their ghastly beauty could throw your diametric emotion switches so many ways at once that it could put you into hypnotic shock, the way flashing lights on the highway do to night drivers, take you straight into that bridge abutment at one hundred miles an hour. Page could see the fearsome concentration on the faces in the audience, the vague, distracted, locked-on, sexual-murderous focus, all aimed at the same spot, intersecting laser Manson eyes, crossing over into a fusion of energy right where he happened to be standing. He loved it, even though he knew it could vaporize human flesh, loved it the way an insect loves the light.

As the band returned to the front of the stage, following Perry's signal to do an encore, Page saw that even Scoop had it on him— who would have thought? Scoop was smiling and jiving. Page shot him an accusing look.

"I *love* it!" Scoop hollered above the crowd noise.

Page crossed the stage and embraced him. Forty thousand witnesses screamed that much louder, even though they had no idea why this little man was doing that—the sheer, un-self-conscious enthusiasm of Page's gesture was enough, it needed no translation.

"What're we gonna *do?*" Link was asking about the encore, but to Page the question couldn't have been more poignant or resonant with foreboding, like a half-lit tunnel into some surrealistic future. *What are we gonna dooooo?*

Page only thought for a second, and his smile widened. Speaking quite unintentionally into a live microphone, he said, "We're gonna ROCK AND ROW-WOOL!!" and beneath him the crowd went over the line to a level of hysteria that frightened him.

"You done it now." Link grinned, and they started into what Shelly called Page's "Schvantz Song," which was neither on the record nor on the schedule ("I can't have it removed or sell it / The sight of you is bound to swell it . . .."). As they came down the ramp off the stage, even the roadies were cheering them, slapping them on the backs as they ran by. Michael stood at the bottom of the ramp with the *Rolling Stone* photographer and a reporter, saying, "Page, Page," but he just shined it on, jogging, grinning, spent.

Shelly and Michael wanted Page to stay and hear the Eagles, but Page wouldn't hear of it. He felt like he'd been beaten up and Blye backed him up.

"The Eagles are lovely cunts," Blye said. "But look at me, *look* at me, I smell like a *buffalo.*" He was sweated so thoroughly that his clothes had turned five shades darker.

And anyway, Judy broke the tie, saying, "If you guys aren't going home now, Link and me are taking a taxicab back to the hotel anyway, so make up your damned minds."

"Page." Michael wrenched around from the front seat of the

limo as soon as they were roadborne. *"Rolling Stone* wanted to talk to you, now you've got to understand—"

"Not now." Page could barely talk at all, much less talk to a reporter. He was a little sick to his stomach and his face felt clammy. "I think I must be coming down with something."

"Oh, no." Shelly turned pale. "What is it?"

Page wasn't at all prepared for what he was really coming down with. Later, of course, he would see how obvious it should have been. Coming off the lurid sports in Vietnam, he had sometimes experienced such hideous depressions that he would begin to laugh hysterically, uncontrollably, with such unguarded, frightening madness that the other troops—even hardened Lurps—shied away from him, as if whatever he had contracted might be contagious. When Page crashed the night of the first concert, he went down so hard he thought it might break his bones. He hadn't been ready for it. Even after all the training, he still somehow thought rock and roll was supposed to be fun.

-24-

When Page thought about his star trip—when he turned his mind back to it all, quickly, as if for a shy, fast glance—he saw an eerie, panoramic scene, shot through with cocaine dust and marijuana smoke, shimmering like a hologram out toward some invisible horizon in an intense, white-phosphorous light and punctuated by the faraway clatter of light-assault technology. He saw people running and screaming, vast crowds of dislocated, stranded people, so totally stunned that it made him want to hold them so they could at least cry for a while and disperse some of it. He saw ragged lines of people, stretching away and out of sight. Some carried their belongings, others just carried tickets, and though something like a decade separated the two groups, Page was no longer sure there was a difference, no longer sure he cared if there wasn't. In both sets of events, his actions had slurred and smeared into a single, gross stroke of some awesome, obscene brush.

Asked what he had done that first year, all he could say was, "I became a star." He really had very little idea what he had done. It was as if he'd stepped on some invisible trip mechanism in time, a real black hole, and he came out the other end spinning and spinning.

So when he turned his mind back to that first tour, he would somehow arc over the years and the two frequencies would mix, like a bad cathode signal when you're too far away from (or too close to) the source. He saw a quick, deft series of brutal firefights, there was always smoke, intense action in blinding light and dangerous noise in dark places, screams and weird music—his own now—everything in his life shot forward at such velocity that the entire thing could only be viewed in retrospect or in the dread of foreboding. Sure, the rock and roll had been playing during the real firefights, but even though somebody had stopped the war, they'd forgotten to turn off the tape recorders and half the show went on. And on.

What they say is true, that music is like sex, a form of violence and pain—a cliché, to be certain, but an orgasm is only a cliché to those who are not experiencing one. That music had come and laid hands on such private places inside Page's clothing that he had fallen in love. But it had taken something the size of Shea Stadium to make him realize that music, too, was a personal thing, something close and tender or close and violent, the cut didn't matter, but sometimes he felt as comfortable playing to seventy thousand people as he would have felt copulating in front of them.

The language of these megaconcerts—of rock and roll itself— was about as sexual as the language of warfare was bloody, where a bomb that would shred hundreds of people and blow down an entire forest was described as having a "radius of destruction," a Claymore would "cause casualties," and something that could kill you if you went near it was called an "area denial system." Now Page was playing his music—that sound—so an accountant could tell him he had a "good bottom line" when he got back to the record-company offices. "A real fine draw," they would say. "We're moving a lot of units," he'd hear. "The gate was oversold." And some black people who were truly moved by Jambeaux represented nothing more in command lingo than a "crossover market." It made him want to seize the nearest handful of gold chain and maybe some of the chest hair underneath it and drag the man kicking and screaming out onto the stage.

But Page knew there was no way to communicate what it made

him feel. It was the purest kind of outrage, a hopelessness beyond words, a despair that made him just want to sit still and fold his hands and maybe shake his head. Or when it really got bad, when words like *awesome* and *hideous* no longer carried any freight, it made Page laugh, a laugh as hollow and ugly as the object of that laughter, a laugh that would draw his friends off and even turn away hungry reporters.

So to say he couldn't separate one concert from another in his mind, that he couldn't put the incidents in any chronological order, that they all seemed to have happened at once, was like saying he couldn't pinpoint the exact locus of any given orgasm in a love affair, any given bullet in an ambush. It hadn't been a slow application of thrills and horrors, but a single, wrenching explosion, critical mass, no process to it at all, just a point-image collection of everything that had happened to him during that opening year, and when anyone tampered with the strike mechanism, it blew him away in a very literal sense.

Sure, there was a calendar of events, a journalistic history to the story, but that bore as much resemblance to Page's reality as the tour schedule bore to the sound of music. You could go and look it up in the library if you wanted, or you could interview Shelly, if you could get to him. He'd explain the way the airplay picked up, the growing intensity of the song "Jambeaux," how it became a hit single and how the album sales soared after it. He could tell you about the trucks hurtling along the highways, delivering product to record stores in Minneapolis and Indianapolis and Butte, Montana; Phoenix and Huntington, Long Island; San Francisco and Laredo and Fargo, until the entire country was wild with it, high on *Jambeaux*, until the record actually washed over like a storm surge and went platinum. Shelly could tell you that his job, more or less, was to keep a howitzer pointed at the back door of Enigma Records to get it all done. He could tell you that he had to go in to deal with Perry when it became more than obvious that *Jambeaux* was going to sell beyond anyone's maddest expectations, that he had to overcome Perry's righteous enthusiasm and get down to the fine points of revising Jambeaux's royalties upward to a level in keeping with their new and growing star status. He could tell you about the problems of junking discs that had been pressed too fast and had warped. Or you could come down out of the stands to the front gate at some stadium and see the bone-malicious guards bind up a PCP-crazed fan with handcuffs so he looked just like a captured POW. You could see them at the gates, frisking people for booze or dope or fireworks or guns, the diametric indignities of rock and roll, so far away from the action on stage. But all this never really touched Page. He was out there, lost to Command.

He remembered a moment at some point during the Eagles tour, standing on the side of the stage after playing his show, listening to the Eagles perform. He liked them, especially this drummer with the frizzy hair. On that particular night, he just stood there looking out over the enormous crowd and listened to the drummer sing. He suddenly connected with the words of this song the Eagles had been doing now for weeks:

> You sealed your fate up a long time ago.
> Ain't it hard when you're all alone
> In the center ring?
> Now there's no time left to borrow.
> Is there gonna be anything left?
> Only stardust.

And he thought, Ain't that the truth. He couldn't believe he hadn't listened to the words before. When they went into the out portion of the song, chanting the word *Desperado* over and over, Page just looked back over the whole thing, from that first night with Link in Galveston—no, that first night slipping out into the tree line—and he couldn't believe it had happened to him. And later, when they were the main attraction, those lyrics became just that much more poignant.

Beyond the Eagles tour, it went into the fall in a blizzard of airplanes and limousines. Suddenly they were their own headliner, some newer rock and rollers (how new could you get?) in line behind them. And only months after that first concert, Page had lost all sense of time. It seemed as if they'd been doing it for years and yet that first moment on the big stage seemed to have happened yesterday.

Page could remember a hotel room. He could remember Jill, sitting there in her Japanese robe, cutting up rails on a marble table. She had come for a short visit, catching him on the fly. He had just played a concert and was killing the depression with cocaine and heavy vodka. Jill's assistant was there. Her name was Christie and she was lithe, vaguely pretty, and possessed of a tremendously overt concupiscence and an effortless grace of movement. Page couldn't take his eyes off her until she left.

When Christie was gone, Jill and Page removed all their clothes. They were making love in the giant bed when Christie came back in. Page started, but Jill held him there inside her, while Christie, without a word, undressed and got into bed with them. What, Page thought, does one do with two women at the same time? He never had to ask: they showed him. At the time Page was too ripped to think about it, but later he wondered: Had Jill planned it? If Christie just got undressed without a word, did that mean she and Jill had done this before? With whom?

There were other nights with Jill, but she always stayed only a short time—business, of course. She had been talking about starting her own label, perhaps under the auspices of Enigma, perhaps on her own. And each time she left, Page felt lost, sometimes found himself wandering from room to room in a hotel suite, unable to work or concentrate.

Then there was a day Page would never forget, a day clear as chrome, sober and free, a rare day off in Manhattan after a big concert. Jill was there and had insisted on taking Page to buy clothes. "You're a star, Page," she had said. "You have to have some new clothes."

"Numbah Ten, Jill. I hate clothing stores," Page had said. "Can't we have somebody come to *me?* Like Elton fucking John does? Come *on.* I mean, excuse me, but Elton fucking John is not the only star in the world, if you get my meaning." He shook his head, raising his voice on the street, drawing attention from people passing by. But of course, Page went. They were lugging packages out into the sunlight when Page asked the question.

"Would you have my child?"

"What?" Jill laughed, her sunglasses gleaming in the light.

"I mean it, I've always wanted a rug monkey, now I can afford to have one."

"But *Page."*

"No, no, really." Page was jive-stepping along. "Between your eyes and my eyes, it would be a gorgeous crumb snatcher. We could put it through my A-number-one, Special Forces child-training course. See, what you do is lock it up in the closet and dribble human blood under the door about once a week..."

"Page!" Jill shouted. "You are awful."

"No, come on, what do you say?"

"God, I don't know. Are you *serious?*"

"Hell, baby, Syria is halfway around the world." Page grinned and Jill gave him a dirty look. "Yes," Page said, meeting her eyes. "I am serious."

"Well." Jill fell silent. They walked half a block before she went on. "I suppose I've always assumed I'd have children someday." She looked at Page again. "I don't know, Page, I really have to think on that one."

"You do that," Page said.

And later that night, inside Jill, the minute point of pain produced by the nylon line attached to her intrauterine device reminded him that it would not happen, not now, not in any damn New York hotel room. Maybe never. Each time he moved and felt the sting of that cord, he was reminded of it, as much as he tried not to think about it.

When Page told Steve about that first year, he omitted any mention of Jill. There were plenty of things he would rather talk about before that. Yet it was Cyndi who brought it up only the second day she was in Michigan. Butch and Steve were playing again, and Page just didn't want to hear it, so he and Cyndi dressed warmly and walked away, out toward the woods.

"It wouldn't hurt you to play a little," Cyndi said, holding tight to Page's arm in the brittle cold. Their breath drifted away over the ice. "I don't think you ought to go back on your decision, but that doesn't mean you can never play again."

Page scanned the sky from pole to pole and said nothing. The day had come up thick and low, a sky like cooling paraffin. It definitely looked like they were in for some weather.

"You still blame yourself for everything, don't you?" Cyndi asked. "You really do, and I think it's stupid." Page stepped up his pace toward the tree line.

"Hey," he said, trying to sound cheerful, "what say we make a little H and I mission out of that G.R. city? Dive-bomb a convent or something. Get out the old Four-oh-one and go drunk flying."

"Page," Cyndi admonished, knowing he was faking it. But Page didn't respond. "All right, screw around if you like. But I mean it. I hate to see you chewing yourself over like that. There's nothing wrong. You're all right now. The whole thing's over, isn't it?"

Is it? Page wondered. Is it ever over? They could hear Steve calling from the house, and when Cyndi turned to look, Page wrenched her around a bit too roughly. When they crossed into the relative darkness of the forest she tried again.

"You told me never to bring this subject up—"

"Then don't." Page cut her off flatly, his humor gone.

"But I have to," she said.

"Then do."

"Children," Cyndi said softly.

"Then don't."

"No, really, what happened between you and Jill was a long time ago now. I know you still want to have children."

"Well, it's a good goddamned thing, now, isn't it?" Page shouted, whirling around to face her, disengaging his arm angrily. "I mean I really appreciate it that everybody knows what I want."

"Look," Cyndi said quietly, "I may be just one of the boys but that doesn't mean you need to treat me like that."

"Well, I'm really sorry." Page didn't sound sorry at all. "But let me tell you. I said not to bring it up and then you said you had to. And you did. Now what the hell do you want me to do about it? You're not exactly giving me a whole lot of selection, here."

"Well, I just want you to know," Cyndi said so softly Page thought she might be about to cry, "that there's nothing between us now. No diaphragm. No IUD. No pills. So the decision is yours." Page stared at her as if he'd just seen her for the first time.

They walked on in sullen silence and Page wished he had not shouted at her. More than that, he wished she had not brought it up—it just reminded Page of that much more he could feel guilty about. Blame myself? Of course I blame myself, where else can you take something so large and put it? An underground bunker in Kentucky wouldn't do the trick. It might hold reserves of nerve gas but it will never hold this. And who else can you blame? Jill for being one of them? What did you expect, she's a businesswoman. Are you going to blame Link then? Link for always taking care of me and everyone else with such meticulous concern that he never even thought to protect himself, that big, dumb fucker, always thinking he was invulnerable, nothing can happen to old Link— oh, no—he's been around too many blocks. Link's too Texas tough to have psychological problems, weaknesses; he's too big and dumb and funny and lovable to step into it so deep that he'll never get out again, the big dumb ape fucker....

"Shit," Page said softly. He just didn't want to think about any of it, but there it was. Cyndi kept quiet, feeling Page's arm go to a consistency like bone. She had come to know Page well enough to realize what she had done, quite unintentionally. There was a button on Page's console anymore that was like those heat-sensitive elevator buttons: you don't have to press them, they'll light up if you look at them slantwise. And she'd pressed it, opening the whole garden of flowers he'd tried so hard to plow under with silence and time.

⊢25⊣

When it came time to record the second album, Page insisted on Ice Nine Studios. Although the calendar said it was only the late winter of 1976, Page was experiencing nostalgia trips so young he felt he could have developed a genuine, heartfelt nostalgia for the future, that's how fast it was moving, that's how thoroughly it had heated up. And no one objected to a few weeks in the Wisconsin woods.

He came down hard on that second trip, sleeping for three days before someone woke him to say that they had this little record to make. When he came to in the cottage—his own this time—he realized it was Jill shaking his shoulder.

"Buzz," she said, smiling down at him, her hair suffused with the sharp winter sunlight.

"Yes," Page said. "Buzz," and it was another three days before anyone got the first track down, because Jill kept him in bed.

During the preceding months, his relationship with Jill had become a sort of Null-Squeeze—main love by coded comm line, long-distance quick feels—because both his and Jill's careers had washed over into the white region. Hers was lucent and giving off radiation in the invisible spectrum now, and Page was in orbit—the communication had been reduced to a litany: "Roger, negative contact, situation remains the same."

And now Page's three days with Jill were staged at the poles of unreality. When they weren't in bed together, she seemed to be living in a dreamworld of deals and points and figures, her existence came right off the planet and played itself out on the vinyl itself. And when they were in bed together—well, at first Page didn't even notice the absence of that tiny point of pain.

"Right on time." Jill smiled one morning during breakfast.

"Say again?" Page asked.

"You didn't feel it, did you?"

"Feel what?"

Jill laid it out for him, she had had her "device" removed and had come out to visit specifically at that time because she'd decided to have his child.

Page was instantly up and around the room, saying, "Man, oh, *man*," and slapping himself on the forehead, lighting a cigarette and gesturing wildly. "See, what we gotta do, right off, is get him up at odd hours of the night, wake the fucker up like three, four ayem. Get him used to night work."

Page entertained her all morning—just like old times—but a day and a half later, he found himself standing beside the windy airstrip, listening to the scream of the engines as the little jet spun around to face the wind on the runway beyond Ice Nine. The jets spooled up until the sound was almost unbearable, then the pilot released the brakes and in a few hundred feet the silvery plane angled out of there, color that woman gone.

Still, Page's new mood held. What if she actually got pregnant? he wondered. What would we do? He practically danced back to the cottage and in a fury of paper, wrote several new songs, changing the entire character of the schedule for the sessions. He recalled one in particular and dug through his belongings for old notes. Where had he made those notes? Yes, yes, of course. The Warwick Hotel in Houston, the very first night he had spent with her. He had almost forgotten about it. Mother Nature. It's an old, old song she sings.

By the time they got down to the business of recording, Page had worked it out with Jambeaux. Page wasn't the only one who had taken advantage of the week-long rest in the woods. Link had invited Judy up and she was able to stay for four days before her duties sent her back to the ranch. Butch had rented a car and driven to Kenosha, where, if his report was to be believed, he got "more ass than a toilet seat." Blye had gone to the lake after which Lake Geneva was named. He rented gear and fished on the ice with some of the old-timers for a few days. And Scoop. Well, Scoop practiced guitar. That was Scoop's idea of a vacation.

But they were all refreshed, feeling almost human now, and as they began their first day of recording one crisp morning, everything was already set up, and the process was familiar. Perry hit the COMM button and smiled at Page.

" 'Old Song,' " he said, "take one, tape is rolling."

Butch and Scoop went into the intro, slow and rolling, like some liquid that inexplicably flows uphill instead of down. Then Page took a small step forward and put his mouth to the microphone, so close his lips almost touched it.

> When I was five years old
> I heard Roy Rogers sing
> Back in the Saddle
> Home on the Range
> It's been a long, long time
> He and Dale have gotten old
> Now I never hear
> Those good old stories told.
>
> I can still remember
> A thing called Rock and Roll
> I was just a child
> Hurrying to school
> It's been and gone now
> The world is rearranged
> So I listen to the sounds
> That haven't ever changed.
>
> It's an old, old song
> Mother Nature sings
> A deaf man can hear it
> It's everybody's theme
> The heartbeat's your metronome
> Trees your tambourine
> Open your ears to it
> And you'll know what I mean.

Two hours later, they sat in the control booth listening to it, and Perry just nodded and smiled and then, in a very uncharacteristic gesture of jubilation, slapped Page's outstretched palm.

And they went after it with skill and glee, as Page learned yet another lesson about the quantum mechanics of rock and roll. The recording session seemed like an overnight visit, though it took fully eight weeks. Where the first album had been wrenched out of Jambeaux by a long process of pain and exhaustion, this second one exploded from the Wisconsin woods like a caged animal just waiting for someone to come and trip the gate. Link knew where all the energy was coming from. He had seen Page come out of his cottage those mornings with his arm around Jill.

One discordant memory stuck out in Page's mind years later, though he didn't think much about it at the time—a memory of Link, who seemed lost after Judy went back to Houston. Sitting one night in his cottage, after the record had been mixed and they were just about to leave. Link offered Page some of the brown powder, but Page refused. "I wouldn't mess with that. That's serious shit, Link, where'd you get it?"

"Aw." Link smiled and snorted the granules, wincing at the sting. "Just a little something to relax me, you know."

Page laughed at him. "Shit oh dear," he said. "Finally gettin' to old Link, eh? They finally got you, is that it, motherfucker?"

"I guess." Link grinned and chuckled hollowly, a low, rolling chuckle. "I guess they did."

"Fuckin' bear ate old Link." Page joked about it, but he wished at the time that Judy were there to cheer Link up. He didn't like the idea of what Link was doing, but then Page was too stoned at the time to care, and anyway, they had a plane to catch.

Back in L.A. they sat in Perry's living room listening to a reference lacquer. Perry rejected fourteen of them this time. But soon there were test pressings, cover proofs, and then one day they were holding another album in their hands. It was called *Entropy*, Page's word for the bottom line of the equation, some irrational number of rock and roll, a most esoteric science, if not an art. It would take the highs and ecstasy, the lows and dread, and it would even them all out in a hurricane stroke. Entropy. The only unexplained weirdity on the second album cover was a tiny notation that read

$$dS = dQ/T$$
$$S = k\ln P + c$$

and when the T-shirts were printed, they too bore these abstruse scientific definitions for the two forms of entropy.

The songs had taken on a hardened, giddy, lunatic quality, like that laugh that is more an anxiety tic than any kind of real laugh you'd ever hear at home. The difference between the language and sound of the first and second albums was the difference between the vacancy and utter distance in the blank stares of those who had seen some shit and the look of those who had *really seen it all come down.* There was a tightening of the imagery, like twisting something you know will break if you twist it again, and there was an urgency and tenderness that hadn't been there before, an urgency and tenderness and an underlying violence, as if to say, If you can't kiss it, eat it, if you can't eat it, fuck it, if you can't fuck it, blow it all away. When Page sat listening to it—after the album was done—it made him feel serene, it was so subtly evil and dangerous. It made him feel benevolent and harmless by comparison.

But he knew that another source of that serenity was the feeling that he was finally going home, a feeling imparted to him by Jill. If she was not pregnant this month, they would try again the next. And the next, until the deed was done. They would find a place to go, and maybe then he could achieve that thing he had wanted for so long now and was at last beginning to identify. "Teach us to care and not to care, Teach us to sit still."

Shelly said of *Entropy* that it was "shipped platinum." Page got off on the weird and delicate locutions rock and roll had generated, shipped platinum, it made him think of those slits in the walls of medieval cities through which they poured molten lead on visitors who had neglected to phone before stopping by. Imagine it, that silvery deadly thread of steaming metal snaking down toward you, and you going, Oh, shit! *Shipped platinum,* what a phrase, that was *Entropy.*

Enigma ran a full-page ad in the industry newspaper, *Radio and Records,* featuring the album cover (another simple group photo, only now the group looked as if it had been around some blocks). "JAMBEAUX explodes off the charts," the copy said, "with its new hit single 'Proud of My Sorrow' from the album *Entropy.*" The ad then listed radio stations that were playing it. The nation was hungry now, hungry for those heavy sounds ("Proud of my sorrow, baby, proud of my shame. I can't even remember your name"). In another section of the paper called "The Picture

Page," there was a photograph of Perry with other Enigma executives toasting the new record in the Malibu offices.

And then there was the phone call from Jill.

"Page?"

"Yes?"

"The rabbit died."

"Holy Schmidt," he whispered, and felt the blood run hot in his temples. "You sure?"

"It's a roger," she said happily. "T minus nine months and counting."

"Come on out," Page said. "We're going to San Fran."

"I can't." Jill sounded terribly rushed. "I really can't, Page. I just wanted you to know. I'll get out to see you as soon as things quiet down here."

And Page hung up feeling as if he had been reborn. So this is what those religious freaks go through, he thought. Time was still compressed for him, with no structure or function, and in a few weeks he was back on the road definitively, so that he couldn't put anything together, just the thrill of that knowledge. For the first few weeks of the tour, he had a new experience—the ultimate revelation that stardom could be fun. In a fury of creativity after Jill's call, he wrote several new songs, and even though it was not in the battle plan, Jambeaux began playing them, interspersed with their big hits and the songs from the new album.

The dead time between contact, when Jambeaux was not on stage, still weighed as heavily as ever on the band. But when Page stood out there in front of the people, he felt as if he were alone with Jill, singing just to her. The prospect of a normal life once again took him over in a wash of emotion. He envisioned a place up north somewhere, where he and Jill could rise with the sun, a mythical future place where hanging plants would grow indoors and snow would stretch away as far as the eye could see. There would be a warm bedroom with a big fireplace and they would lie in bed at night and drift off. By that time he imagined Jambeaux would have stopped touring and would just record studio albums from time to time, as superstars often do. No more all-night weirdness. And the kid, of course. A boy, naturally, one he would teach to hunt and fish the trout streams up there. In the mornings they would all saddle up horses and ride out into the tree line. Or maybe they'd cross-country ski along the deer trails. Maybe, Page thought whenever he was on stage, maybe Jan in Austin was not the only chance for that sort of thing. Maybe there was a better chance.

And when these thoughts were on Page, his voice and playing shifted up a notch, putting out clear laser power, and the effect was transfused into the entire band, making their concerts small, discrete ballets of pure rock and roll, the crowds went mad with Jambeaux and sales showed it.

"Proud of My Sorrow" took off, you could hardly turn on the radio without hearing it. And then the press really descended on them. Page had tried to avoid it—had, in fact, done less publicity than was expected of him, ever since the Roxy. But now, in his exuberant mood, he almost welcomed the contact he had with reporters. Of course, that got old fast enough when he saw what they printed. But not before there had been several interviews and some television time. And the way it shook down, much to Page's dismay, his face became the symbol of Jambeaux.

Without consulting him, Jill took the photograph of him jumping into the air, the one taken at that first big concert, and had a poster made from it. Soon it was plastered on record-store walls all around the country.

"Goddamnit," Page had shouted into the phone at her, "what in hell did you do that for?"

"Page, don't be a child," Jill said. "This is business. Show business."

"It's *my* business, too, damnit, I don't want people coming up to me on the street. It's just not fair. You know how I feel about my privacy."

"Oh, Page, don't be silly." Jill laughed at him. She just couldn't connect with it. She was far too wrapped up in show business. Page hung up feeling as if he'd been talking with a stranger. What happened to the other Jill? The one who had really identified with Page's trick brain? He sulked for a full day over it and got into a fight with Butch, who thought there should have been a poster of him, too.

But before too long, they were all in the same boat. Between the television, the pictures in *Rolling Stone,* the concert appearances, their faces became so recognizable that just going outside presented insurmountable problems.

"Look at this," Scoop said, handing Page a newspaper one afternoon in a hotel somewhere. It was a small item about Fleetwood Mac that talked about the SWAT team of guards that were deployed before each concert to keep the crowds back. It told how one member of the band arrived every ten minutes under heavy police guard, to keep down the hysteria and how, after the show was over, they dusted off in a chopper with their manager Gabe Arras.

"I'll be goddamned," Page whispered.

"I don't like the idea of that chopper," Link said.

"Haw!" Blye thought it was hilarious. "Yes, yes, splendid. Fok! That's what's going to happen, too, you realize that, don't you, girls?"

"Jesus," Butch whispered thoughtfully, "I think it's sharp. I'll bet helicopter pilots really get their share of snatch."

And Blye was right. Things changed rapidly. It wasn't long before they needed all the protection they could get. It was too big for them now, too scary to go alone. They were real stars, certified, tagged, stoned, and surrounded by people twenty-four hours a day, like some rare species come down from another galaxy for the first time. During that period, Page often remembered that first night with Jill in Houston on the way from Pino's, when he had reveled in the limousine ride. Now the limo had come to be a trap for him.

One evening in particular, during the spring of '76, came to mind. It was in Toronto, in an old, old hotel called the Windsor Arms. The band was sitting lazily around the suite, looking bored or angry, it was hard to tell which. Strung out all along Saint Thomas Street in front of the hotel and Sultan Street on the side in that chic little Yorkville area were a couple of hundred people, all watching the windows for signs of Jambeaux.

There was a very fat, very sad, adolescent girl, alternately wandering around in a hail of tears and sitting in a stunned, soporific trance. But Page knew, watching from the little hotel window, what it was. It was love, the mad, dislocated love of the rock and roll fan. That twisted love Page had come to know so quickly out there on tour, the love a carcinoma has for your skin.

"Fucking prisoners." Blye sat on the bed with a glass of dark rum, swirling it, looking into it, sipping it, swirling it again.

"Beastly flipping bloody fucking prisoners is what we are. I'm going starkers in here. I want to go *out!*"

"You can't," Page said evenly.

He was in a poor mood. He had been trying to reach Jill all day and could not get through. Her assistant, Christie, kept saying that she was really, really tied up and she would get back to him soonest. Page called Cyndi and learned that she had gotten through to Jill. So just who the fuck does she think she is, anyway?

Butch was reading a copy of *Playboy* in which he had been used for a fashion shooting, modeling clothes while surrounded by seminaked girls.

"How much money do you suppose I'm worth?" Blye asked thoughtfully.

"A lot," Page said flatly.

"Bloody load of good it's doing, eh?" He suddenly lit up and reached for his rum bottle. He poured a tumbler full and began talking intently. "See—haw! This is just the bloody *thing* we need. An adventure." Scoop drew in close to listen. "I mean one of those really heavy Peter Matthiessen–*Lord Jim*–Purgatory numbers, where you go so far away into the wilderness for so long under such brutal conditions that it just cleans you out, am I right? You come back with a white soul, burned smooth, annealed, lads. *Fused.* Haw! Fok! Like maybe someplace in Tibet. But before you go"—he became confidential now, having captured Scoop's attention and even drawn Butch away from his magazine—"before you go, you see, you've really got to get set, get prepared for it, because there's going to be no help there, girls. If anything should happen, you'll be on your own. So what you do is have all your teeth pulled out, because there won't be any dentists out there, you take extra sets of false teeth, see? Oh, yes, splendid. I can see it now. Then you have your appendix removed, because what if you eat some flippin' *snake* or something and get appendicitis, right? Am I right? And your gall bladder, natch, that comes out. You can't be mucking about with a beastly gall bladder. Also, kiss that spleen goodbye, no danger of that. And for good measure, let's scuttle one eyeball and a kidney, never can be too careful out there in the wilds."

Butch went back to his magazine, shaking his head, while Scoop stared wide-eyed, waiting for more, but Blye just held it in for as long as he could and then exploded with malicious glee. "Haw! Fok! Yes! Super." Those wacky guys who play rock and roll.

Page hadn't even turned from the window, and Link just chuckled softly from his position in one of the easy chairs.

Judy had come out to visit for two days away from her ranch, and she sat on the arm of Link's chair. "Blye, you are creepy, you know that? You're about the creepiest son of a bitch in this band." She smiled over at Scoop. "No offense, Scoop. You're creepy too."

"Look at this picture of me," Butch said dreamily.

"Grow up," Page muttered.

"No, man, really." Butch got up with the magazine. "Now isn't that a great sport coat? Do you think I ought to wear that tonight instead of this?" He touched the coat he was wearing. Page just ignored him.

"Come here, Butch, honey," Judy said. "I'll tell you what to wear."

It was eight in the evening and some of the fans had been out there for hours. The fat girl had been there since three, bumping dumbly into people, asking questions of strangers. Even in that crowd she was singularly forlorn, a rock and roll casualty, to be sure, and Page watched her with deepening depression, thinking, What is it about these people? What do they want? He tried to calculate in his mind how long it had been since he last saw Jill. She must actually look pregnant by now. He wanted to see it, to feel it. But she was out there, doing business. Then he tried to clear it from his mind. You fuck, he thought, you're doing business too. You want to see her so goddamned much, go see her. But of course he couldn't. Same-same. He looked back down to the girl in the street, who was now caroming off parked cars, and it was difficult for Page to comprehend that the gravity of her condition was in any way connected with him.

Then there was the man with the truck. The truck had a great blueberry waffle painted on the side. The man was thin and wore a handlebar mustache and a white uniform, like a soda jerk. Page watched him make menacing gestures at the fat girl, who backed away. The truck had begun to attract attention, and Page watched with growing disbelief as some of the fans actually began listening to it. They were putting their ears against it and listening to the goddamned truck. Page turned from the window.

"They're onto the blueberry waffle truck," he said.

"Shit," Butch said. "How're we gonna get to the gig now?"

"What'll we do?" Scoop asked. Scoop was concerned, for while he had become used to—loved, in fact—playing on the big stage, he still went a little crazy when confronted by a mad, hysterical mob of fans, which was a rather reasonable reaction in anyone's book.

"I'll call Shelly." Page went over to the phone. "Who do you have to fuck around here to get some coke?" he asked the room in general, dialing the phone. Link tossed him a little glass phial and Page fired two big spoonfuls up his nose while waiting for an answer. He watched Link take a separate phial from his pocket and, with his thumbnail, snort two scoops of his brown powder.

"Damnit, Link." Judy hopped off the arm of the chair. "That's not funny."

"I ain't doin' much." Link smiled vacantly. "Just now and again."

"Again is right," she said, her hands on her tight little hips. "Put that shit down."

"Well, how come Page can get high and not me?" Link asked.

"Page is not getting high on heroin," Judy said emphatically. She reached for the phial but missed and went over to sit on the bed, sulking.

"I'm fucking trying to quit," Blye said, watching, "and you're fucking trying to get hooked." He shook his head wearily.

"Don't worry." Link rubbed his nose and his eyes started to go to glass. "I'm just chippin' with it a little."

"Sure." Blye smirked nastily at him. "Riiiiight."

When Page got Shelly on the phone, he said, "They're onto the blueberry waffle truck." Page listened and then said, "All right, come on up." He returned to the window and drew back the shades.

"Link, come here, you're not going to believe this," Page said, but Link didn't move. He just stared into space. "Goddamnit, Link." Page dropped the shade. "You'd better be careful or you're not gonna be able to play." Then he just looked at Link, wondering. He had been seeing that blank, nodded-out look on Link's face much too often lately. He promised himself he'd have a talk with that boy.

"What I'm trying to tell him," Blye muttered. "Wanker."

"Shit." Page turned back to the window. The soda jerk was becoming nervous about these people *listening* to his truck; it was clear the fans thought *they* were in there. Suddenly, a very young boy who looked horribly drunk disengaged his ear from the truck and lurched belligerently into the middle of the street. He leaned back on his heels, almost fell over, and then squared off facing the hotel as if he were going to take a swing at it. He hollered at the top of his lungs, "Page, yew asshole! You're nothing but a bloody fucking asshole, Page!" He screamed it right at the window and Page recoiled visibly.

"I'll be dipped in shit," Page whispered.

"Haw! Fok!" Blye jumped up. "Sounds like one of me countrymen." Blye went over to look out the window. "Ohhh," he said, raising his eyebrows, "he looks fit, don't he? They *love* you, Page. Hear it? That's love. Unrequited love, that is."

"Goddamn." Page was shocked and let go of the curtain.

"Yew asshole!" The voice drifted up again. "Aw hate yew, Page!"

"Good bloody thing, too," Blye said softly, going back to the couch. Judy just stared at Link with growing anger but said nothing.

"Who the fuck told these people where we were?" Page looked out again and said, "Oh, no." The newsmen were arriving, three camera crews and numerous photographers and reporters. A few polite, ineffectual Toronto policemen had come to suggest that people behave in an orderly fashion, but no one paid any attention to them. Scoop got up and looked over Page's shoulder.

"Now how in hell did they find out?" Scoop asked.

"Probably a chambermaid," Shelly said as he walked in. "I've got it settled, though. Let me show you." Shelly crossed to the window and pointed out. "See that soccer field there?" Half a block down Sultan Street there was a space between two buildings and a large field beyond that, bordered by another street. Shelly told Page all about it.

At eight fifteen more police had arrived, but the crowd had grown to unmanageable proportions, and the reporters were yawning and looking at their watches. Jambeaux was assembled in the kitchen, the Pakistani busboys gawking at them. At a signal from outside, Jambeaux made its move. The door blew open as if from an explosion. As Page ran into the street, he glanced over quickly to see the entire crowd surround the waffle truck. The soda jerk went down under the weight of a hundred hands and feet. The camera crews were going mad in an informational feeding frenzy, trying to shoot the diversionary five-man group of roadies Shelly had sent to pose as Jambeaux. The poor roadies tried to hustle onto the truck, looking like combat troops reaching for the salvation of an escape chopper, but they were cut down in the crowd, cut down in that hot LZ hell.

Used to be the object was to find and engage the enemy, Page thought as he sprinted for the two buildings and the soccer field beyond. Now it's to avoid the enemy at all costs, we are definitely outnumbered here.

From the band's point of view the maneuver was successful— they made it to the auditorium without further incident. Later that night Shelly told Page that the soda jerk wound up in the hospital with a couple of cracked ribs. And when the band returned to the Windsor Arms late, the fat girl was still there, sitting on the curb, so bereft she didn't even have the energy to look up to see the object of her grief as it passed into the lobby. The next day Page couldn't help checking to see if she might still be there.

Command, as Page called the executive level of rock and roll, talked about its successes as if every step were monitored and directed with an accuracy and control far exceeding reality. They did telephone surveys in which they played a portion of the song, the "hookline," they called it ("It's an old, old song," for example), and asked the listener for a one-to-ten response. They would try to ascertain a song's "burnout factor." When Page heard language like that, he just laughed, burnout factor, freakola, he knew how really out of control it all was, he was on the fucking line. Some asshole would come around talking about the kind of orders Handleman and Lieberman were placing for K-Mart and Page would just blow vodka through his nose. Page knew how they got some of these groups off and running, "breakout," they called it. Those independent promotion men didn't work for the record companies, so it didn't matter if they kind of did a DJ a favor now and then. Page once asked a major network executive if payola still existed and the man said, categorically, no, quickly adding, "Of course you still get some of that with your black stations."

Command posture could be whatever it wanted to be ("Posture?" Blye would ask, feigning bafflement. "Posture? Here, bend over, there's a good posture, girls. Haw!"), the charts always looked good, the bottom line would buy you anything you wanted, but that didn't alter the matter when you stepped into the middle of it. Page saw that up close one night in some city when he stepped out of a hotel lobby and into a limousine. As the front car, carrying Butch and Blye, screamed away, Page's car stalled. It only stalled for a few seconds, but that was enough, primal neuronal terror. Outside the windows mad-eyed girls and evil-faced boys were literally trying to claw their way into the car, there were people on the hood, people on the roof, Page reached up and could feel it denting inward. Page's immediate reaction was to reach for his waistband, he forgot they no longer carried guns, and anyway, what was he going to do? Shoot his own fans? The driver tried to inch forward without killing someone (bad for the image, P.R. like that). Scoop covered his head and wept, it destroyed him. Link was stoned smooth out of his mind on some more of that bullshit he'd been sniffing. He just chuckled. "Check it out, Page, they love you."

"Shut the fuck up, will you, you big dumb asshole?" Page screamed, out of control. He turned on the driver next: "Run the fuckers over! Get me *out of here*." The chauffeur, calm as you please, kept inching forward until the crowd parted, and they sped away. The incident shook Page badly enough that he didn't sing very well that night. He couldn't stop the words going through his head, overlapping with that sound: "They're animals, they're animals, they're animals." And he couldn't stop marveling that this had taken place on a brightly lit street in a supposedly civilized city, and—most important—that there was *nothing they could do about it*. In other kinds of attacks, at least he had had some options.

After that Page started carrying a .45 again. Shelly talked him out of it, though, when Page did something with it that frightened everyone and got the band some more bad press. Page had been doing a lot of cocaine one night (seemed like every night now) and a reporter got into the dressing room, where something of a party was going on. Page went out of his mind.

"I told you to keep them out of here," he screamed at the bodyguard, drawing his pistol. The reporter got out of there fast, very fast.

"Oh, Page," Shelly said forlornly, "I'm afraid we've just made some more bad news." Shelly paused and looked at Page. "Page," he whispered wearily, "do you know you've done fifteen thousand dollars' worth of coke since you've been on tour?"

"Fuck 'em if they can't take a joke," Page said, and all the beautiful people in the dressing room laughed nervously. They hadn't heard Shelly, only Page. The scene was more than Page could tolerate. There were four vast tables with pâté and Perrier water, caviar, sour cream, chopped egg and onion, champagne, wine, and beer. People were wafting through the room as if they had no corporeal reality to them at all, as if they were pure spirit. There were wren-thin ladies in diaphanous gowns; you could see their *tits*, Blye would whisper. The people were so fey, marked by a gray light as if they might expire soon, Page wanted to toss a CS grenade in among them and see how fey they were then. Of course, his reaction to that reporter had almost the same effect. When he couldn't stand it anymore, he grabbed Shelly's arm much too tightly and Shelly grimaced.

"Get them out of here," Page whispered through clenched teeth. At that point Page was the only one who wasn't aware of what cocaine was doing to him.

"Who? Who?" Shelly looked around to see if yet another uninvited person had slipped in.

"Them." Page gestured with his chin. "*All* of them."

"Why, I can't do that," Shelly began, but seeing the expression on Page's face, he stopped and then said, "All right, all right. Just calm down."

Page was grinding his teeth when he went into the bathroom, while Shelly delicately told each person that Page was not feeling very well and could they perhaps come back after the show. The people didn't need to have it written out in longhand, they understood and left. And a number of weeks later when Page's mail was finally forwarded out to Michigan, there was a raft of get-well cards.

When Page came to the day after the incident in the dressing room, he realized how out of control he had been and felt profoundly embarrassed. Oh, Christ, what did I *do*? It put him in mind of that last night in Galveston. Then something else clicked into place: all these years, whenever Page lost control, Link had stepped in to take charge. Link had always been there, going, "Keep yer dick in yer pants, Little Buddy, you gone make it," or some such nonsense—anything to keep Page from going too far, directing him through these emotional minefields. But that night in the dressing room, Link just sat there, blanked out. And Page thought, Shit, between the two of us, we're riding for a fall. Somebody's going to have to start tapering down here, take a little control somehow.

Page knew what would help. He knew just what he needed. But when he finally got through to Jill, she said she simply couldn't come out now. There was too much going on. The old litany of nondelivery, things were too hot, new bands, start a record label, blah, blah, blah. And Page again tried to tell himself that her situation was no different from his, that he was too hot as well and as soon as he got off this damn tour, why, he'd shag out there and make his presence felt, you better believe it. Then they could start settling down. Hell, he'd even live in—gaa—Los Angeles, if that's what it took. No sweat, he told himself, no sweat, no sweat, no sweat. But, of course, that didn't do anything to solve either his immediate problem or Link's.

Page called Cyndi then. He didn't tell her Jill was pregnant—he wasn't sure how she would react and wouldn't have known how to bring up the subject anyway. But she could sense the urgency in his voice and agreed to come out the very next day. "I'll leave you a key to the suite," Page said. "I'll be there right after the concert."

When he arrived at about midnight—an early night for him—Cyndi was sitting in the living room of the suite, wearing a translucent nightgown and looking as stunning as she had ever looked. After the *pro forma* hugs and kisses, Page brought out a phial of cocaine. He cut up some lines on the coffee table and when she reached for the silver straw, Page smiled and held up his hand.

"What's the matter?" she asked.

"I want to show you something," he said and gently took her ankles, one in each hand, and placed them up on the cushion of the couch where she sat. She wore no underwear.

"What're you doing?" she asked, tugging her nightgown down over her knees.

"No, leave it," he said.

"What are you going to do?" she asked again, sounding a little worried.

"Watch, you'll like it." With one hand Page parted her lips, with the other, he took a generous mound of the powder on the tip of his finger and placed it deep inside her, allowing her lips to close.

"What *are* you *doing,* Page?"

"Wait," he said, taking her ankles and placing them back on the floor. He watched as Cyndi sat, still as a statue, and then suddenly brought her knees together.

"Oh," she said, letting out her breath. "Where did you learn *that?*"

"You pick up some weird things out here." Page smiled and then fired up two rails. He eyed her. She was stoned. They continued that way, Page administering to both of them, until dawn and then slept well into the afternoon. The next day Cyndi raised the subject on both their minds.

"What's going on between you and Jill?"

"I don't know," Page said. "She's really busy. I can't even get through to her anymore."

"I've talked to her and she sounded awfully strange," Cyndi offered.

"I know." Page wanted to tell her, wanted someone to talk about it all, but he couldn't, not yet. In the end he didn't have to. Cyndi said it for him.

"I don't know, Page," she started out softly. "Some women can do everything at once. They can have families"—here Page flinched visibly, thinking, How the fuck does she know? But Cyndi didn't even break stride—"they can have careers. They can stay soft and smooth and at the same time be hard as nails doing their jobs. But some others can never put it together in that way. I've never been a career builder. And now, the few times I get to talk to her, frankly"—she looked up at Page here—"and no offense— she's really acting like a bitch. She's just too immersed in her business, I guess. She used to be different, didn't she?"

"That's what I thought," Page said, relieved that Cyndi had said it, but bothered, deeply bothered. "I don't know what to make of it. The last time I talked to her, she had her assistant call me."

"Christie?" Cyndi asked.

"Yeah, then Jill came on the line."

"She did the same thing with me. I know she's busy, but I sure felt funny."

"Imagine how *I* felt."

Years later, when Cyndi brought up the subject in Michigan,

Page had no intention of discussing Jill. He was already getting a little edgy from having Butch and Steve around, always trying to talk him into playing again. It wore on him. It seemed that if they weren't nagging him about it, they were just staring at him oddly, as if he had cancer and the doctor had told them not to tell him.

But other times it didn't seem so at all. Butch and Steve must have seen that they weren't getting anywhere with Page or that if they didn't give him a little slack, he might just leave Michigan rather than go on listening to them (Page would never kick them out, they knew, he would only joke about it up to a point, then he would disappear himself, where they might never track him down).

One day they drove over to Muskegon and stopped at a bar on the edge of town, just to pass away the afternoon. It was a mid-western cowboy bar and the customers were all locals, deeply religious hunters and farmers who wouldn't have known who these kids were if they had shown their passports. And if they had known, they wouldn't have cared—rock and roll, what a bunch of shit. Country was another thing altogether: they took *their* music very seriously. This bar had a band and the customers sat with fixed, malevolent attention while a man sang with un-self-conscious intensity, "From thee-iss vaa-lee they say-ee yew or go-in. Ah wee-ll mee-iss yur bright Ahhz aind Shuite Schmal."

All afternoon Page and Steve and Butch drank the sweet, smooth, characterless draft beer and smoked cigarettes and talked in the warm darkness of that bar, listening to the singer and watching the locals come in stamping the snow off their boots and then go home a little lit. The pressure was off that day, neither Butch nor Steve was going to bug Page and he deeply appreciated it. It was like a reunion for the first time.

"I went to New York City." Butch was getting off a story for them, speaking in subdued tones. "And they had the Tutankhamen exhibit from Cairo there. It was terribly crowded with kids and middle-aged women, but I felt like I was all alone in there, it was so spooky, unbelievably weird, because all these things, these *artifacts*"—Butch said the word as if it translated out to "poison"—"were put there to guard the tomb, see, and to scare away or maybe even kill trespassers. And you could *feel* it, like a presence in the room. I felt like I was violating something sacred just by being there and like whoever took these things out of Egypt and whoever put them in glass cases for everyone to gawk at, well, they were definitely going to get theirs and it wouldn't be pretty when they did. Can you fade that?"

"Yeah," Page said.

"Wow." Steve took one of Page's cigarettes, and the three of them drew a little closer around the table, like small children who tell scary stories at night to get that hit, that rush and thrill of fear that will make you shiver and giggle; there's nothing in the world sexier than real danger or the giddy terror produced by it. The next best thing is to tell stories about it. And that day Page went home feeling very close to them again. Feeling lucky to have a brother and a friend and Cyndi waiting back there at the Ranch.

Page stretched out on the couch in his living room. Steve and Butch came and sat around the fire. Page was contemplating getting out the Sony video cassette recorder and watching *Dr. Strangelove* for grins when he heard the commotion. It sounded as if about twelve people were crashing through the back door, and Page shot out of his seat to see what was attacking.

The man came charging in, taut and squat, tanned and clean, shouting, "Haw! Fok! Super!" He grabbed Page and slapped him on the shoulders, grinning maniacally. "Christ's Wounds, lad, you're fucking landlocked, what gives? What beastly *gives* here?" And then he snorted and sputtered and exploded with laughter, as if they'd just played the dirtiest, meanest, most hideous and bitter trick of all on themselves. Page couldn't help being glad to see Blye. But when Red started bringing in his drum set, Page glared at Butch and Steve.

"Butch, you fuck, you engineered this idiocy, didn't you?"

"No." Butch opened his palms in a gesture of innocence. "Really, honest, I didn't. I mean, what's so *peculiar* about Blye visiting?"

"You fuck," Page repeated.

"Gettin' paranoid in your old age." Blye tried to suppress a laugh but it fractured out like a bad cough anyway.

"You lying little Saxon limey bastard."

"Naughty-naughty." Blye waved a crooked index finger at him. "Racial slurs, yet. You'd perhaps like some redskin humor?" He thought for a moment. "Let's see, now, how many Indians does it take to eat a possum? Right! Three, one of them eats the possum, two watch for traffic. Haw!"

"All right, all right," Page said.

"Listen, lad." Blye crept up to Page, hunched over, with his hands extended like claws. "We're going to get you, see? We have consulted Angels of Dread, Khmer Rouge, *brujos* from Arizona, lad, you're in trouble. Deep trouble. Just wait. We have dire things afoot, dire, dire, dire."

It was good to see Blye again, brain-damaged, sunstruck Blye. Cyndi came into the room just then and when Blye saw her, he lifted her off the ground, saying, "Ah, yes, yes, jiggling bottoms, give me *two* of these, here, lass." He put her down and grabbed her skirt to lift it.

"Let's have a look at the equipment, here." Cyndi giggled and slapped her skirt down. "Haw! Fok! No danger of that, eh?" Page stood wearily and announced supper.

"Freak," Steve said, sitting down to Campbell's tomato soup, a bacon, lettuce, and tomato sandwich, and potato chips. "Fucking freak. I have a freak for a brother."

"Fuck you guys." Page pulled up a chair. "This is the best chop in the world. Top chop. Fine, sustaining grits, man, eat, eat, and if you don't like this chop, you can walk home. Mmmm."

"Woo-woo!" Butch did a little dance step and grabbed a seat.

"Beastly health food," Blye said disdainfully, but he tore into it with a murderous vigor, slurping and making noises and gesticulating. He sprayed a fine pink mist of tomato soup with each explosive laugh.

"You should fucking talk." Steve waved a red spoon at him. "You're not even taking heroin anymore, you junkie freak, look at you."

"Tell 'em, brother," Page said, filling his mouth.

"Bit of a bother scoring at mid-ocean," Blye said, stopping to think about that. "Aw," he went on, "look at this! Look at all the rock stars at this beastly table, eh? Say, saw a rock star the other day. Made the mistake of going to a party somewhere out on Long Island. I'd anchored up at Annapolis, trying to sell the ghastly boat, and got seduced into a party. Well, so there's this kid, what's his name? Billy Joel, big star all of a sudden, right? And he's walking around like, 'Oh, I don't know why everybody's looking at me. I'm just acting normal. I act this way in the shower.' Really embarrassing, oh, never mind. Let's go out and set fires in the forest, wot?"

After supper, Steve pulled out a joint and said, "Let's get small."

He passed it around and then Blye went into the living room to set up his drums. Page watched, lacing his boots, thinking, Lord, fully three-fifths of Jambeaux is here. Add to that Steve's bass playing and voice and you had something. Something Page didn't want to think about just yet, his mind going, You low-life fuck, you wouldn't do *that* now, would you? Cyndi was right, it was stupid for him to blame himself. It was, in fact, a fair conceit for him to think he had control of anything at all in this whole mess. But he wanted it out of his mind, out of his house. He grabbed Cyndi and headed toward the woods.

"Page!" The voice calling from the house was hollow and dry in the icy air. Page and Cyndi just kept walking. "God's Body, Page, come back in here, lad!" Page laughed. "Come back here, you beastly, sniveling cunt!" The voice cracked against the tree line and ricocheted back, CUNT, cunt, *cunt.* . . . Page and Cyndi disappeared into the woods.

⊷26⊷

By the end of the *Entropy* tour, one of the problems Page was confronting was that his music—that sound—had to be played in such unacceptable places with such nightmare people that it was almost canceled in the equation. And by the same equation, he continually found himself wondering why he had done it, he didn't need fifty thousand people in order to make that sound, lop off four zeros, he needed five. Page remembered talking with Link when they first discussed forming the band. When Link asked about hiring horn players, Page had said, "I'm not goddamned Count Basie, you know." Page didn't know shit about it. It took thirty-five people just to operate a Jambeaux tour and that didn't count Command personnel back at Division in Malibu or L.A. or New York. That didn't count regional salesmen, truck drivers to haul records, the independent promo people with their little sacks of cocaine, the marketing dudes, accounting, wardrobe, P.R., airplane pilots, set designers, art directors, legal, or housekeeping. After all this time Page was just beginning to understand what Scoop was talking about the first day he approached him in the Burning Spear: Leave me to die in peace.

There couldn't have been a more fundamental conflict, a more immutable contradiction: on one side was the love of music—of an exotic, rare species of sound—and on the other was the ingrained loathing of the places in which music was played, the nightclubs and the auditoriums or stadiums, nests of vermin you wouldn't otherwise see even in your worst, backed-up paranoid coke dreams, dank pits a movie director would reject as "too rough," too depressing for the average audience. And when you lived that contradiction, the love and ecstasy of that sound alternated with a dry-heave revulsion, and in any given night on the job, the switch on those two feelings could be thrown back and forth so many times and at such speeds that you'd develop a Parkinson-like gait, a staggering, shuddering blankness, that would leave you unable to feel anything at all for weeks afterwards, Page had seen it happen all the time to nightclub musicians. Now he was seeing that it merely happened at a more accelerated pace and more severely to concert hall musicians, to stars, who had better access to the treatments for that condition—those medications whose side effects were often indistinguishable from the condition itself (Zen and the Art of Methadone Maintenance, Blye could tell you all about it). By then the rumors had already filtered back about Sonny—chilly silence and talk of hideous drug scenes—and Page wasn't sleeping through that too well, either, remembering his phone call to Phil Shorter.

After the last concert on the *Entropy* tour, Page was so numb he didn't even realize they were through, he just waited for the next gig until Blye took his arm. "We're done, through," he said, and Page squinted around, unbelieving. "We're going home," Blye said.

"Home?" Page asked, confused. There had been so much motion that no one had stopped to consider the fact that not one member of Jambeaux had a place to live (what for?). But Perry had the foresight to see that they would need some serious rest after this tour, so he had arranged for them to stay at the house Enigma kept in Beverly Hills for various guests and bands. Jambeaux had leased a plane by that time, and after Page boarded, he simply crashed, slept right through the flight. Link sat next to him, reading a magazine and singing softly, "Still you don't expect to be bright and bon vivant so far away from home," no shit, Sherlock, you better believe it. Page even dozed in the limousine that took them from LAX to Beverly Hills, past the Hills Hotel, up Beverly

Drive, then Cold Water Canyon Drive and on up winding Linda-crest Drive to the house. Only when the car stopped did Page begin to wake up, feeling as if he had been asleep for months—but it was only severe depression, the anxiety-trance reaction slipping over into narcolepsy. His emotion capacitors had been charged and discharged so often that he had no reaction whatsoever as he walked toward the gate.

Behind a high gray wooden fence, stone steps ran down to the house seventy feet below. The house was backed artfully into the hill and everything sloped accordingly, terraced ground cover all around, great sprawling tropical plants. Standing at the front of the house was an elegant, gentle black man named Albert who kept the place and served its guests.

"Gentlemen," he said as the band filed in, looking as chewed over as any assault team. He didn't react to the way they looked, he had seen it before—they had that two-click stare and looked shell-shocked, which of course they were, anyone would be after standing under a 130-decibel weight every night for hours. The sound alone was enough to put you under, never mind the rest, the mad animal crowds, hungry women, the black hole of success, hard drugs and liquor and irregular food, dehydration, hotels, oh, hotels. They had tried them all over the years—$200-a-night luxury penthouses and a buck-two-fifty dumps on the outskirts of nowhere—and it never changed. They had slept in doubles, singles, triples, duplexes, complexes, cabins, courts, high-rise, low-rent, seaside, lakeside, riverside, backside, outside, mountainside, desert, plain, salt flat, tundra, forest, downtown, uptown, midtown, small town, big city, with color TV, black and white (and black), built-in alarm systems, armed guards, lawn sprinklers, hot and cold running sores, free breakfast, no breakfast, swimming pool, cesspool; they had slept, fucked, shit, bathed, dressed, rehearsed, fought, nearly died, recovered; gone off the deep end on bad acid, shot smack, coke, firearms; been busted, bored, tired, sad, ecstatic. They had lived in these places until home or Houston or wherever they may have come from seemed about as close and recent as Arcturus or the Pleiades.

If anything had become clear, it was that these places were all the same. Getting a hotel room was a strict holding action, the hexagram of waiting, "Six in the fourth place means: Waiting in

blood. Get out of the pit." Stasis. Sleeping in a hotel was a negative act, some kind of null-sleep that exhausted you. Eating in one
made you hungry, drinking made you sober, more aware than ever
of the essence of hoteless. Music in hotels increased their primal
silence and the water in their bathtubs dried you faster than the
desert sun on bare bone. Dressing uncovered you in a first, basic,
sense, crying made you happy, laughing could break your heart.
And Jambeaux, like science-fiction space travelers who near the
speed of light, seemed to have gone nowhere by the time they
landed on Lindacrest Drive.

They were only just beginning to comprehend what Page would
try to convey to Steve years later, that the two ends of any spectrum are the exact same thing, just as the two ends of a circle are
the same point; the bow is tied with both ends of the ribbon, and if
you are a junkie wino on Forty-second Street in New York, you
have achieved the same goals as the junkie wino whose face is
pasted twenty-five feet across on a billboard overlooking Sunset
Boulevard. Staying in the middle is far more interesting because
you're either terrified of the short drop to the bottom or desperate
for the long climb to the top, so at least you can feel something.
Page had heard from a military man who went into the space
program that the astronauts who went into space—every last
Swinging Dick—had asked their boss to send them on a one-way
mission—anywhere, Jupiter, Pluto, Venus—because once you had
been *out there,* there was nothing left back in the World. Page
understood that. And now he came to Lindacrest Drive in the
same head as if he'd just arrived at a spot on a rock in the middle
of nowhere: he was annealed, just as Blye had promised he would
be, burned clean and completely empty.

Albert led them into the living room. On a glass table little
crystal glasses were set up with neat green wedges of lime, a fresh
bottle of Cuervo 1800, and a salt shaker.

"Ohhh, man," Scoop said when he saw it, "Old Available. My
favorite brand."

Then Albert brought trays of deviled eggs, caviar, stuffed mush-
room caps, vegetables to dip into some kind of cream-cheese
concoction. Scoop tried to sample everything at once. "Man, all
manner of divers grits has this cat brought us."

Page picked up the Cuervo bottle and examined it. "Intoxogrits," he said.

"Yes, of *course*." Scoop slapped himself on the forehead. "Why didn't I think of that? Intoxogrits. Me for some of that."

The radio was playing softly. Page listened to Jackson Browne sing about a fountain of sorrow—the song made sorrow sound like some delicious, pervasive poison. When the music stopped, a public service announcement came on, pleading with people to help out by taking a teenager into their homes temporarily.

"Gad Zooks!" Scoop jumped up. "I'll take a temporary teenager into my home anytime. Get that number down. Temporary teenagers, yes. Precisely what's needed here."

Butch had come in suffering deep road exhaustion. He quietly, almost methodically, swallowed a Quäälude and washed it down with a shot of tequila. Then another. Then a few more. Then a beer. Soon he was out cold in a corner of the living room. Blye crossed the room and began poking him and muttering to himself, "Mmm. Casualty." Poke, poke. "I'd set the danger of waking this lad at about zero, then." Blye raised his glass and toasted Butch. "Come on, lad. Health and stealth. Drink up."

"Man," Link said, looking all around. "What a pad. What a goofy, freaky pad they've got for us. I wish Judy was here."

Scoop continued to stuff his face with food. "Mmm, grits. Green, crunchy grits, Yard Pig grits."

"Yard Pig?" Blye asked.

"Chicken," Page said absently. He wasn't paying much attention to them. He wanted to speak to Jill. In fact, he had half expected her to be there to greet them. He left the room, looking for a phone. He found one in the library on the second floor and made himself comfortable at the desk before calling her.

"How are you feeling?" he asked. "Come on over. We're back." He couldn't think of what to say. He felt as if she were a light year away, and she sounded speedy and disconnected. She explained that she had too much to do. He had heard that so many times since she visited him at Ice Nine during the *Entropy* sessions that he couldn't remember the last time he had seen her. She said she finally had it together to start her own label and one of her new bands was coming into town to sign with her. She had to—just had to—be there. But she'd come by soonest, she said.

When Page signed off, he realized that he hadn't even asked her the most important question of all, but he was in no condition to deal with it now, just business, he told himself, after all, everybody's got work to do, just because he shows up in town doesn't mean the whole city's supposed to drop everything and say hello, right? Right?

And he put it out of his mind. He had another piece of business to take care of, an urgent one: he needed a place. This little house in the California hills was all right but it was not home, not in any sense. It was a more elaborate hotel, that's what it was, a hotel with a butler. And Page knew exactly the kind of place he wanted. He picked up the phone again and called Perry. Miraculously he got him first try.

"What're you doing, fuckin' off today?" Page asked.

"Whatever do you mean, Page?" Perry sounded truly puzzled.

"You answered the phone." Page smiled. It was good to talk to Perry. Good old Perry.

"Welcome home anyway," Perry said. "Now I want you just to relax and have fun. We're all going to leave you alone for a while. You all ought to go do something, separately. You've been together too much, I think."

"I'm going somewhere all right, that's what I'm calling about."

"Where?"

"Well, I've got to ask you something. Do you think I can afford a house, a really nice house?"

Perry laughed out loud. "Well, I haven't talked to your accountant, but I think you might swing that."

"I want you to help me find a house in Wisconsin. I know I shouldn't be asking you to do this, but I don't know who else would know. Can you help me?"

Perry thought for a moment. "Yes. In fact, it's funny you should ask that, because I know someone who just moved to Montana and has a place for sale. If you trust my judgment. You see, it's not in Wisconsin, it's in Michigan, but it's beautiful, truly beautiful."

"Look, Michigan is fine," Page said. "I love Michigan. Would you live in it?"

"Yes, in fact, I've been tempted to buy it but I don't think I could take the move. Clutter, you know."

"Check it out, will you? I trust your taste just fine and I *need* a place."

"How much do you want to spend?" Perry asked.

"Who cares?" Page laughed. "Who fucking cares?"

"I'll call you when I've found out, then."

When Page returned, Link was popping deviled eggs into his mouth. Page was feeling better and slapped him on the shoulder. "Well, how about that shit?"

"Motherfucking ate the bear, didn't we?" Link grinned, his mouth full of disgusting, masticated egg material. Link seemed fairly straight this day, but Page noticed that he had lost weight, his cheeks had become slightly sunken, and his color was always a little waxy. That ruddy, robust athletic appearance he'd always had was gone.

Across the room were two sets of curtained French doors that opened onto a balcony overlooking the hills. On the other side of the valley Page could see more houses nestled into the arid desert slopes. He walked out onto the balcony and looked down. "Oh, man, a *pool*," he whispered. He spotted a volleyball floating there and turned to Link. "Let's play some Riverine Death Soccer," he said conspiratorially.

"Fok! Yes, super." Blye jumped up.

Page organized the game with the three conscious members of the band and explained the rules. Riverine Death Soccer, like *mano fría,* was one of the few games in which you received points for inflicting disabling injury or death on your opponent. After a while in the pool, it became clear that Link and Page were going to kill Scoop, if not Blye. So they got out to let the Captain have it off against the Professor. Link and Page sat on lawn chairs sipping beer and looking off across the valley.

"You know," Link said, squinting out at the glass-walled houses across the valley, "with my little Remington Two-seventy, I'll bet we could really keep their heads down over there."

"Yeah, and with an M-Sixty and a bipod we could pin down the whole fuckin' valley for a couple of hours before they brought in the choppers."

"You know," Link continued casually, "with a LAWS rocket launcher or even an RPG-Seven, I'll bet we could put the hurt on that little green house real good."

"True, true." Page tried to sound serious but it wasn't working. "With an eight-inch gun and a small surgical nuclear warhead we could simply blast the entire hill back to the pleistocene with one shot."

"Yeah, but a nice forty-kiloton airburst right about there"—

Link pointed—"would definitely put these L.A. assholes in their place."

"Certainly ruin their afternoon," Page said—those wacky guys who play rock and roll. Page drank off his beer and went to get another. He was turning around to Link when he spotted Butch.

Butch stood up on the balcony like six feet four inches of slimy cadaver, weaving around dangerously and squinting down at the pool, trying to figure out what on earth had happened. Where was he? On tour? Did they have to play tonight? Whose house was this?

"Wuzit?" he asked. Scoop looked up and laughed at him. "Whozit?"

"Better get Damage Control," Scoop said.

"Fucked up like a soup sandwich," Link observed.

It was funny right up until the moment Butch fell off the balcony. He just smiled weakly, weaved once, and toppled like a great log over the wrought-iron railing, end over end toward the deck below. When his feet hit in the pool's deep end a plume of water shot high into the air, shattering crystals in the sunlight, and Butch slid to the bottom without so much as touching concrete. To call it miraculous would be misstating the case: it was an impossible fall, and there was ample terrace space where he could have sustained a nifty fracture or worse.

Blye dove before Butch even hit the water and was there when he reached the bottom. There was a moment of panic such as they hadn't seen in months, which ended abruptly when Butch exploded out of the water, sputtering and coughing.

As Link and Page and Blye pulled Butch from the pool and laid him on the side, Butch just wheezed and muttered breathlessly, "It's OK, everything's under control." And that did it.

"Under control!" Blye screamed, practically hysterical. "Under beastly *control!* Oh, Good Bloody Thing Too!!"

Jambeaux had not selected the card that read CONTROL, it wasn't even in the deck, they might come up with five aces, but not control. Page watched it by candlelight, up in Link's room late that night, when everyone else had gone to bed. His nervous system sang to him those dreadful Bolivian cantatas. He felt as if the light in the room—yellow, jumping candlelight—was emanating from his own eyes, that's how intense the high was, his nose didn't exist anymore: frozen off. He felt his spine, like that of a cooked fish, could simply be lifted out with two fingers and a gentle pull and it would come away, segmented, white and intact, drawing with it his entire rib cage. Page was extremely stoned.

Link held the spoon over the candle flame and the powder in the spoon melted. With a sterile hypodermic needle, Link drew off the liquid, and then found a vein right in the crook of his elbow. He drew back the plunger and blood mixed with the liquid, pink, dead lock-on target signal, and he squeezed it off, fired it home, and then quickly ripped off the Velcro tourniquet from his bicep. Wham! Page had seen it happen in the slaughterhouse, you hit the pig across the nape of the neck with a little eight-pound sledge and it'll go down like, like, like—like a dead pig. Link just grinned and dug it, oh, great, nothing at all to it. Nothing finer.

"You fuck," Page said, watching him. "You're going to stop doing that, do you know that? I personally am going to stop you."

Link just chuckled slowly. "You ain't high at all, are you, Little Buddy?"

"You fuck," Page repeated.

Control was not a byword in that inner-inner circle; the whole show had gotten hot and dangerous, the joking was really over.

⊢27⊣

There is a type of cold up in Michigan in the centerpoints of winter that is so brutal and unrelenting that no amount of clothing can scare out the wind and keep it from sneaking in somewhere to rummage around in your pile of bones. When Page and Cyndi returned from one of their walks in the woods, they were shaking so hard from it that they could barely talk. They just sat by the fireplace, waiting for their engines to start again.

Page sat there, watching Cyndi, who was wind-red and lovely. He heard the back door open, and Lilly burst in, wagging her tail excitedly. Page reached down to scratch her neck.

"Colder'n a rat's tit," Red said as he came in.

"Where are my children? My blessed flock?" Page asked. Cyndi got up and went to the couch to lie down, looking spent.

"Went roarin' off in the little red truck." Red shrugged, running a hand through his icy hair. " 'Cept Steve." He turned to leave the room. "He's been upstairs on the phone with Perry for an hour."

"Perry?" Page squinted at Red, who was turning to leave the room.

"Yeah," Red said, leaving Page to wonder. He thought he had it all figured out. Maybe he'd better give Perry a call himself, he thought, find out exactly what's going down. He watched the failing overcast light beyond the windows.

When Steve came downstairs, Cyndi was asleep on the couch, and Page put his finger to his lips and motioned for Steve to come out into the kitchen where they could talk.

"I heard Sonny's playing a concert in G.R.," Steve said. "Everybody's going, want to come?"

"That might be all right," Page said. He wanted to ask Steve about Perry, but didn't. Steve said nothing for a few minutes. He took Page's cigarettes and lit one.

"Want a beer?" He got up to look in the refrigerator.

"Nah," Page said.

"Say, what're you doing for your birthday?" Steve sat down and opened his beer.

"Gettin' older." Page smiled sadly. "Just gettin' older."

"I thought since we got those two assholes up here, we might have a little party, if that's all the same with you." Page could see right through Steve's nonchalance.

"What *kind* of party?"

"Shit, I don't know. It was just a thought."

"Yeah, well, we'll see." Page paused. "Where were you thinking of having this little party?"

"Come on, man, I'm just asking. You *are* my brother, remember?"

"Yeah." Page smiled, narrowing his eyes. "I remember."

Steve dropped his eyes, then changed the subject. "Say." He leaned in confidentially. "I meant to ask you. Blye *is* cleaned up, isn't he?"

"Far as I know," Page said. "Has been for quite a while."

"Yeah, that's what I thought." Steve considered it for a moment. "Goddamn, remember when he was busted? Jesus, that was some shit. Heap big news for the old renegades, eh?"

"Yeah, well, that was just about all it was too. News. In fact, the bust was just exactly the least of what was going on then."

"Run that by me again."

Page didn't particularly want the subject brought up at all. He sighed and went to get a beer—what the fuck, might as well talk to the kid. He'd gone this far with the story.

"See," Page began, popping the cap off a bottle, "the only thing the public ever knew of that story was that Blye was busted, right? The rest of us were really going through some changes, too. The reporters never saw that, though."

Page lit a cigarette and bubbled the bottle, thinking back on it. Yeah, sure, it was a good story, anyway. There are no surprise endings; if you're ever surprised by one, it just means you were asleep that year. Light's on but nobody's home, as Link once said.

The period following Jambeaux's stay at that Lindacrest house was the first time in over two years that the entire band hadn't been together. Thanksgiving was coming, and each of them had something he wanted to do. Besides, they all knew they needed some time apart. Page laughed now, remembering Link talking to his mother on the phone.

"Mama," Link had whined, "how'd you git this number?"

"Link," the old lady had said in her cracked, Texas voice, slowly measuring her words, "every since your daddy died, I've been a-keepin' track of you and don't you think just because you get you put on the television that I can't steel do it."

"But Mama, I'd a called you, you know that." And Link covered the mouthpiece, embarrassed, while Blye made a mime of playing a violin and the others giggled. "What do you want, Mama?"

"Link, it's time you come home fer Thanksgivin'. You ain't been home for no Thanksgivin' since you done got back from Veet Name and thet was eight years ago. Link, I don't care if they're a-writin' you up in the papers, you gotta come home for Thanksgivin'."

"All right, Mama, all right." He covered the mouthpiece and hollered at Blye, "Cut it out, Blye, I'm not kidding," then went back to the phone. "All right, Mama, but you gotta let me bring my girl home, too."

"Link, every since your daddy died, I ain't never tolt you not to braing none of your friends home, now you just be here, you hear?"

"Yes, Mama," Link said, and he hung up.

Oh, and did the shit fly around Lindacrest. Butch got out of the way fast and Scoop stumbled over a table trying to get up the stairs. Drinks scattered, crashing in a spray of crystals. Link was like a bull let loose, tearing around, trying to grab someone—anyone—shouting, "You cocksuckers, you think you're so fucking smart, just because you never *met* your mothers . . ." until they finally got him down and sat on him (it took all four of them, one on each arm, one on each leg) and then, of course, he began laughing too. He left the next day to pick Judy up at her ranch and from there went to his mother's. But not, Page explained to Steve, without first stopping in Houston to see some old friends.

Butch refused to leave Lindacrest. "You double-dip mother-fuckers think I'm leaving now that I'm finally up to my asshole in nookie? You guys are nuts!" Ultimately, Butch was the only one who ever liked California, and even he grew tired of it eventually. But at that time, Thanksgiving dinner for Butch was going to be warmed in its own natural juices, he would practically drive Albert insane—basically sound, used-to-anything Albert—with the steady stream of groupies he brought through there between the time the other band members left and the time they returned to the re-alization that they could never, ever stay at *that* house again. Every girl under twenty-one within a thirty-mile radius knew the address, and it had even shown up on the maps of the stars that kids sell to tourists along Sunset Boulevard. In fact, shortly after Butch left, Enigma canceled its lease on the house because even the record-company executives couldn't use it for fear of being attacked by lust-crazed teenage girls, and it was certainly off limits for any other rock band.

Not that Page was surprised by what Link called Butch's "shit-tin' where he sleeps." What had surprised him was the gradual change in Scoop's personality. Perhaps it wasn't his personality that changed, perhaps it was just one facet of it, in the sense that anyone's total personality is a prism of contradictions. For Scoop had become addicted to performing in front of massive crowds, the bigger, the better. Somewhere in his ridge-runner heart, Scoop had recognized the ultimate safety and security of the big stage. No one could touch him, it was just him and that sound. The audience was just a vague, undulating color pattern, a movie taking place on the far wall, they might as well have been on Mars. Back at the Burning Spear, the stage had been two feet off the dance floor and the audience was so close he could smell it. Scoop had been shouldered off that stage more than once when things got wild—a fight or just a dancer out of control could do the trick. One night he'd seen a trumpet player get his front teeth knocked in when a hard-boogie couple lost its balance and reeled into the man's horn. But at Shea Stadium or Madison Square Garden or any of those high-elevation rock and roll palaces, the audience would need some pretty sophisticated long-range weaponry to so much as touch you. And where Page reacted to the audience response—the wildness and applause, the screaming and full-channel frenzy—Scoop was soothed by the absence of any response, for Scoop only recognized response in the form of physical injury, or at least the danger of it; the fact that the people were hysterical and dangerous and loud intruded on Scoop's frame of mind about as much as any mad animal in a zoo would have. Scoop was far more hysterical, far louder, and much more dangerous than they were. And anyway, you couldn't even hear them when you played over those incredible banks of speakers. Scoop was completely and totally (and singularly in Jambeaux) a player, with no other motivation, no other moves in his repertoire.

It was fitting, then, that Scoop's vacation time was taken up with a concert tour. Sonny had pulled up from the bleak serious and had asked Scoop to join him in a short series of concerts, reminisce about those old cockroach days.

Page hadn't seen Sonny since Jambeaux signed with Enigma. He felt too embarrassed, couldn't shake the feeling that he'd had a hand in Sonny's troubles—maybe he'd had no choice at the time, still no excuse for amputating on a friend. He was grateful that Sonny was back in the World, it was simply a miracle he hadn't gone down in the obits of believers with Joplin, Hendrix, Morrison, or face down in the pool like Brian Jones.

No big surprises in Blye's choice of vacation, either. He flew straight to Key West and bought himself a boat, a classy old fifty-foot ketch with all the brass fittings, even brass oil lamps in the saloon and two new diesel engines. He named his new boat *The Maggot*.

Page waited at Lindacrest until the call came from Perry. Perry told him to catch a flight to Chicago and change for Grand Rapids, Michigan, where a car would meet him and take him to that house. He said Jill would meet him there, that she had actually set up the deal. He said she decorated the place herself for some reason. Page smiled, he knew why. He thought he knew why. He was so far away from reality at that point that it didn't even occur to him that if his assumption was correct, everyone else would have been able to tell why too. The last time he had seen Jill, she was—by his calculations—five months pregnant with his child. It didn't even occur to him that her shape should have changed, how could he know? He had never had children before. Later he would attribute his blindness to shell shock. Like a bad lens, his resolution was shot, he saw only foggy outlines, suspicious but never completely revealing. So when he finally came into focus, it happened so fast and close to the face, he thought he could catch the reek ten time zones and a decade down the line. When Page opened himself to the revelation, it blew him right into the future.

His reaction was paradoxical: he laughed. Oh, yes, he thought, this is certainly how it happens, it was so bitter it was almost delicious. How could he have been so stupid? There it was, the exquisite moment, knock you off your horse in a flash of light. He had seen it once before, some grunt (was it at Fort Sill?) just back from Vietnam, his wife there to greet him. She looked slim and trim and tan and the grunt hauled back and hit her so hard it broke her neck. Page learned later that she had written him that she was pregnant and he had arrived, finally, expecting to see her just about eight months pregnant.

Oh, Page, Page, he thought to himself, how could you fall for that one? No wonder Jill had avoided him. She'd said it was her new groups, her embryonic record company, and so he hadn't thought about it, and Jill hadn't told him either and now they were standing there in this house in Michigan somewhere, and she looked as trim and neat in her skin-tight blue jeans as she had always looked.

"I realized I had to do this thing," Jill said. "We can still have children. We can have children anytime, but a chance like this . . ." She could see it in his face and knew she'd better not say anything else.

If Page had gone a little crazy with joy when Jill visited him at

Ice Nine or when she called him with the news, if her report that she was pregnant with his child had set him on an emotional level above any he had experienced before, now the news and full flash that she had changed her mind and had gotten an abortion in order to do her business more efficiently, her complete innocence of what she had done, the grim fullness of the joke came down on Page with such force that he was paralyzed by it. He didn't even have the strength to raise his hand against her, and a good thing too, because when he opened his hands out to her, in a baffled, bereft, helpless gesture, a wordless gesture empty of any suggestion of aggression, both his hands were quickly and brutally bound behind him.

"Let him go," Jill said angrily, and Page's hands were released. "It's all right," she said to the man. "You can wait outside." And another, even funnier realization shuddered through Page.

For while there was some part of Jill, some still-human part, however perverted, that wanted to be the one to tell Page, to have this last, final moment with him, another part was moving, implacable and neuter as some cathode scanner, along the line of her career. Children would not get in the way and neither would injury from an unfulfilled boyfriend. And this man-driver, companion, assistant, whatever you called him—was her hedge against what she might not know of Page's personality. She didn't understand that early on Page had opened himself to her in a way he had never done before and that in doing so, had made his own penalty that much greater now that she had finally opened herself to him, opened the petals of that black flower. Line of departure, Page thought, Rock and Roll. Black is the color and you can't make it blacker. The flower only opened for a split second before its gunmetal petals slammed shut, but Page saw enough to last him for generations.

Their conversation after the man went outside was almost comical, or so it seemed to Page. There was nothing she could say (she was actually telling Page they could do it again in a few years if he still wanted to) and all Page had to tell her was that the house was fine, it would do just fine and if she would just leave, he would be fine. But Page had already sent his car back, thinking he would get a ride with Jill, and so she asked in all innocence, "How are you going to get back?"

Back! Haw! Page nearly busted a gut, talk about inappropriate, metaphorical foot-in-your-mouth questions, talk about timing! How am I going to *get back?* Good fucking question, you tell *me,* deep-space probe maybe? How am I going to get back? Oh, just go, go. . . .

And she left, saying that she still wanted them to remain friends, but Page didn't even know what she was talking about by then. He sat down on the couch and listened to the car drive away and watched out the vast windows as a bird flew over Thousand Moon Lake behind the house. He made one decision, anyway: he wasn't going to run (where to?), fuck it, he had no attachments to this house other than the most immediate and obvious one. Let it be my Taj Mahal, then, I'll play the Shah Jehan, who gives a shit? If he had been burned clean before, even his ashes were scattered now, he felt as if he weighed nothing at all, like a faint scent on a low breeze.

He crashed so hard he slept for nearly five days. And when he awoke from it one morning, not even aware how long it had been, he looked at the startling brilliant winter light pouring in and he finally saw the house for the first time. Jill had furnished it well (her consolation prize, Page guessed) just as Perry would have, except for that canopy bed up in the master bedroom, but what the hell, leave it like it is.

Page felt calm now. He hadn't cried or lost control, only hardened up fast, lyophilized to about the consistency of ruby; something deep inside him froze, basic survival move, once again, because it was that or let them siphon you off in a bucket. His heart closed like a crypt, nothing was going to get in or out. And to say it changed his point of view would be like saying napalm changed the complexion.

There were also intellectual realizations. Page knew what the bodyguard had meant (he was born at night . . .) and it really took him back, back to the Burning Spear and two gangsters talking to Ritchie with fierce animation, took him back to a lot of images he didn't care to contemplate, but there they were nonetheless, sometimes you don't have much selection about the movie you watch, even when you own the whole damned film company.

Page might have stayed out there indefinitely if a driver hadn't shown up one day with a message from Perry. Page just packed a little AWOL bag and headed out with the man, what the fuck, might as well get my feet wet. And Page went back to L.A. to receive the news that Blye had been busted, busted badly. Specifically, boarded within U.S. territorial waters carrying something like a pound of nearly pure heroin.

Perry dressed Page down in that same, sweet, nerve-gas way of his, quietly, almost ploddingly. "Page, I thought we had reached an understanding. I remember clearly charging you with the responsibility and I also clearly remember you protesting vigorously that Blye was reliable, that we all have our hang-ups, is that not correct, Page? Does my memory fail me? Am I senile or am I correct, Page? Page, please speak to me, I want to hear your side of it, Page, because this is going to cost us a small fortune." It went on interminably and Page just smiled mildly, it didn't even reach him, poor Blye, brought under in his prime. Well, Page thought, how many more lives can you drag through this swamp before it all ends, before entropy really sets in and someone comes to collect all the tickets?

The way Perry solved the problem woke Page up quickly and also completed the circuit that lit the light bulb above his head, epiphany central. Perry let Blye stew in some coastal jail just long enough, and then he got him out so fast and definitively that Blye didn't know whether it had been a nightmare or a real bust. Perry didn't just get him out of jail—that was simple. He got the whole case dropped. The attorneys went to the first pretrial hearing where arraignment was to take place and the judge dismissed the case. Lab reports, he said, were inconclusive as to whether or not the substance seized was heroin, and the sample had been destroyed by fire and therefore there was no evidence with which to make a case.

"Say again?" Page asked when he was told, and again he could feel that thing inside him, it was almost a comfort, it was so solid, like some large crystal, brilliant in its clarity, some Hope Diamond of despair, so hard Page thought nothing could thaw it now, which meant nothing could damage him. It wasn't the first time Page had been wrong.

But for the moment—having been dragged from his exile in Michigan to be called onto Perry's carpet—Page simply listened and watched with growing amusement (fucker's so fucking slick . . .).

"Now, Page, you know I want Blye off heroin. Completely off. But this little misadventure has been very bad for us in so many ways that I don't even care to enumerate them. So I still implore you to do what you can for him, but where you are unsuccessful, at least we can have Blye keeping out of this sort of scrape. From now on it's Blye's decision. We have for him an inside source if he wants to go that way, a source of extreme discretion and incomparable quality. His name is Merlin. Blye also has his source of overcoming this habit if he wants that. So I consider the matter settled until there is further trouble, at which point Blye can count himself out of this operation and Jambeaux can begin looking for another drummer." Perry paused and tented his fingers. "Are we speaking the same language, Page?"

"Can I go back to Michigan now?" Page asked, finishing his beer. And Perry stared at him with the same bafflement he had that very first day Page had come to Malibu and told him the story about losing his government-issue watch in a land-mine explosion.

⊢28⊣

Steve was squinting hard, as if he had been burned badly on a stove, setting his teeth in an expression of pain. "I never knew that, man, I never realized that had happened."

"Fuck it," Page said, "it was a long time ago." He paused. "Besides, it was good for my writing." He didn't have much more to say about it. He had returned to the Ranch after Blye's bust, thinking, Out of one war, into another, and another. And another. These people really are all the same, aren't they? A reliable source of heroin, eh? Extreme discretion and incomparable quality. Fine, fine. Page did nothing for a solid week except look at the colors and patterns made by the lazing prism of crystal that had formed. Fascinating.

He didn't even notice when Christmas passed, to him it was nothing of the sort. It was just another day, snow, brilliant winter light, ice, a deer stepping across Thousand Moon Lake or a woodcock exploding into the woods. He sat in the big living room and watched the fires he built. He listened to records. And he felt fine, even when he thought about it. He reacted to the input about as much as a tree.

Being so completely alone was a new, trippy experience for Page. He began to think his former life had no reality of its own, that it was just something he'd imagined, and now he was at some hunting place where his stepfather had taken him. And left him.

He made coffee in the mornings and sat watching the birds fight on the balcony beyond the double glass doors. He put out stale bread for the squirrels, one of which he started calling Blye because it had a lopsided expression, a squint like Blye's. ("C'mere, Blye, you junkie squirrel, take your bread now. . . .") Then he would sit in the living room and watch the fire again, the woods and the lake. The place to him became some kind of suspended animation, and he started talking to himself, not a bad sign as people say, at least you're talking.

"My little ranch," he would say sometimes, he actually began to dig it. "Rancho space station, Null-X, Enigma." And one day he called some workmen at the lumberyard in town and had them erect a sign of rough-hewn timbers. It read ENIGMA RANCH, with a big brand X below. He was sitting in the living room the night that it was completed, enjoying the notion of it, when the phone rang and nearly scared him to death. He hadn't heard it ring since he'd been there. It was Perry and he wanted another record.

"Have you written a word?" he asked testily.

"Not so's you'd notice," Page said.

"Do you know one of the things in your contract is a live album?"

"Yes," Page said flatly. Tour again, eh? Might as well get my feet wet.

"Well . . ."

"I'll have you ten songs soonest," Page said. "For a non-live album. Then we'll talk live albums."

"If you think so," Perry said and hung up. He hadn't sounded happy.

But Page didn't even think about it for another week. "Spaced." He did, however, start taking long walks deep into woods he didn't know. Little look-see. Reconnaissance patrols. Then he would come back and take hour-long hot showers to kill the chills. Page wasn't aware of how much time passed, but he could mark the moment that started him working again. He remembered something he hadn't thought of for a long time, an incident that had, in a way, embarrassed him.

Page remembered a series of takeoffs and landings coming out of Vietnam, a string of landing strips, airfields, seat-belt webbing cutting into him, discomfort, and that blank, dreamless sleep of someone who can't face even the best of his nighttime visions. He ended up at Fort Sill, one of the biggest bases in the country.

America, home soil, free at last, free at last. While he knew he had loved it over there, loved and despised it like nothing else in his life, it was still good to be back in the World with two nuts, two eyes, four limbs. He was so giddy with it that he didn't even stop to think when he left the base, against orders. He had a craving that he hadn't even realized he had. It had gone so deep that it was like a distant pain long forgotten, something you live with. On the ride to Lawton, Oklahoma, Page just grinned stupidly about him, what a trip! The U.S. of A. He felt he personally had won the war, even though as he rode, boys just like him were taking grease back there. Home, home, home, he'd never even seen Oklahoma before and he felt like he was in the womb.

He found the Mexican restaurant he'd been told about. He'd heard of this happening. Butch's daddy had been in World War Two and Butch had told him this story about the old man coming back from the Big One in 1945 and going straight to the first restaurant he could find in San Fran. He ordered a head of lettuce and a jar of mayonnaise, and just *ate the whole fucking thing*. C's will do that to you after a while.

Page entered the restaurant and sat down with a sigh and a smile. He ordered a Dos Equis and drank it off, studied the menu, and ordered another beer. He got a stack of warm tortillas, some beans and rice, chopped pork and beef, a dish of hot peppers, enchiladas, mounds of lettuce and sliced fresh tomato, and he went on like that, wallowing in it, ordering beer after beer, delicacy after delicacy, until he could barely breathe. And then he started on the tequila.

He drank two, then four, eight, sixteen, until the motherly waitress became concerned. She continued to bring him the jiggers until finally he began sobbing uncontrollably. He had a look in his eyes like he might kill someone—no, like he *had* killed someone, that ultimate vagueness of someone who has no more edges to him, whose own persona is bleeding off him so fast he has no center anymore and so no balance, nothing left to conquer. Frame of mind? He had no frame anymore, the picture went right off the paper. The waitress saw this when she put her hand on his face, and he broke down completely like a child. She took him by the shoulders, calling him *"Pobrecita,"* and then drove him all the way back to the base. In a military town the size of Lawton, it wasn't the first time she'd seen that.

By that time, the spooks who were supposed to debrief him were a little crazy, because he had disappeared—U/A—but when he got to the Colonel and the man saw his face and the note on the documents that he was one of *them,* a real superstar recondo, he just cussed Page out good and proper and sent him off to bed. The Colonel had seen it before too.

When Page remembered the incident, he saw that what he was doing up in Michigan was just the same. It at least gave him a starting point, some underpinning for what he was going to write for their next album. He sat down as if he had memorized it all before and he just spilled his guts this time; in two weeks it was done. Some of it went like this:

> We're doing our penance in these mountains.
> There was no need for it to happen this way.
> 'Cause you went back on your word
> Spoke it to all of us (it was so clear)
> But we were too callow
> And life was so much fun (we could not follow)
> Now, ladies and gentlemen, we are
> The Queens of the Quick
> Deacons of the Dead
> Barons of the Barrenness
> Right here on our own homestead.
> We're the rulers of this radioactive rain.
> And we're never gonna get that word again.
>
> Once we were so young I can't remember.
> We'd just sit in the grass and play.
> That seemed like such a thrill.
> But later the ladies (sooner the lies)
> The drugs and desperation
> Funny colors in the sky (we rushed right to them).
> Now friends and enemies, we are
> The Patrons of Pestilence
> Dukes of Disaster

Emperors of the Emptiness
We feel in our bones.
We're magicians who pull dead birds out of thin air.
And we're too far down that road to care.

He delivered it up to Perry as a *fait accompli,* lyrics, music, arrangements, harmonies, voicings, everything, including the title for
the album: *Recondo,* a word so resonant to Page that it almost
exploded off the manuscript, literally recognition, recon, reconnaissance, and of course, by phonetic extension, recondite: in-
comprehensible to someone with ordinary understanding or
knowledge. Page actually looked it up in the dictionary, there it
was, from *condere,* "to store up." That's right, he thought, store it
up and then recognize it, if you think you can stand to, *Recondo,*
Rock and Roll.

It was the first time Page had mixed his war imagery into anything at all. In these songs, his experience in combat mingled with
all the other things that went into a song, some venomous, cross-
bred mutation, so subtle and so delicately threatening that not even
the critics who looked for such things could put a finger on what
made the music seem so "demonic" (their word). But it certainly
had the desired effect on the crowd, at least the effect Page desired.
Rock and roll, they had always been right about it, it was evil, it
made people kill. The lyrics and literal meaning of a song didn't
have to be satanic to make the song seem so, Page knew. The first
time he had heard the Electric Light Orchestra sing "Sweet Is the
Night," he thought it was a very grisly song, perhaps about someone who committed suicide in a particularly tasteless fashion. In
part, that was due to signal-to-noise ratio, the telephone game
effect: he had misunderstood two key lyrics. Where Jeff Lynn sang
"Cartier," referring to a wristwatch, Page had heard "cardiac."
And Page heard "razor morning light" where the actual words
were "rays of." Page preferred his own image when he finally
understood the lyrics correctly, but even so, the song continued to
sound demonic to him. It was good rock and roll, it was monstrous.

And the whole story was right there for anyone to see, right
inside that poster—*Les Beaux Jams,* the Big One, Paris, 1977.
You could see it all right in that frame. For whatever was casting
that searing white light, whatever laser energy could reduce Jam-

beaux to that insect level, was certain proof that behind the Day-Glo rock and roll exterior there was yet another lurid tale to be told. Yes, the music had the desired effect, Page had achieved his end, somehow, in an ineffable, ugly way. Or, more likely, the end had achieved him. The sound that had haunted him for so long now haunted an entire generation and Page thought he had done it start to finish, with willful and wanton malice aforethought, the charges were mounting, there was far too much evidence now, he couldn't possibly get a fair trial, because there it was, right inside that poster. Page may have thought he made the music but really the music made him.

⊢29⊣

Page looked out at the forty thousand people and felt the hair stand up on the back of his neck. He stood behind and to one side of Butch and he could see Butch was feeling the same exact thing. The man stood lazily back from the intense circle of light with the bright golden Selmer tenor saxophone hanging from a neck strap. Behind them, Blye pumped against the cymbals, crushed into the drums and the low, throbbing sound comforted and relaxed Butch more than any drug could have. Page smiled, seeing that Butch was locked into it. It was warm up there in the sunfire spots with the steady, rhythmic sounds all around, a living thing that enveloped and protected them, it was like going beyond sex, through it to a womb. Page looked out just past the footlights and saw a beautiful girl with curly brown hair and an adoring smile and he just wanted to take her and put his head between her legs.

Link's bass line described the raw chords, the basic meaning of the sound. Scoop's guitar fills made bright incandescent explosions, diamond punctuations throughout, and Page closed his eyes, feeling it all wash over him. He could actually see what Butch was feeling, that was one of the reasons he had always loved being on stage with that ungainly monster. It was almost like telepathy up there, Page could read his mind, read his heart and soul, too, and now he saw that Butch couldn't have been more content or richer, he was in the actual mine, the ore was all around him, all he had to do was refine it.

Page eased out the broad, solid chords. He felt the vowels release from his throat, a litter of strapping healthy notes in the
nighttime green first fields of creation, organic miracle under a
bone-white moon. The chorus came to its end and Butch stepped
casually into the hot circle of arclight for his solo. Here he comes,
Page thought, watching him, knowing it was going to be right,
lookit him, Butch placing the bamboo LaVoz reed to his lips,
listening, licking it once, now twice, now three times with his
tongue, then inhaling deeply, his abdomen expanding, *Oh, lookit
him.*

The notes popped out of his saxophone so strong and bright and
clear they were practically visible. Some were very round and had
a deep luster like pearls of different sizes and of colors no oyster
ever knew. Butch heard the audience's amazement, the thousand-
channel sigh of approval, and he went on with that much more
determination. The golden bell of the saxophone emitted shapes
with such fluency that the effect was like watching someone blow
molten copper bubbles from a pipe. Butch shifted his stance and
embouchure and another series of notes came out, this time with
finely cut angles to them, fracturing prismatically in the spotlights,
transuranium mutations, undiscovered jewels, stones blown out as
if by an explosion from within the ore itself. The intersecting fields
of light carved the bell of the horn into a bladed shape, and the
whole instrument seemed to change its form as he played the
magic morphology. Page just watched with his mouth open, his
eyes wide, as Butch stepped delicately back out of the light and the
notes trailed off like small asteroids failing in the distance of deep
space, incinerated there, and the applause was like having someone
put warm fingers around a most private anatomy.

For a few moments, no one was in the naked circle of light. The
sound appeared to have no source, it was *omni*, other, pure sound,
as Link dropped his bass line clean and true as a plumb bob to
hell. Blye clocked out decades of rhythm in each stroke, Page's
chords fanned out ahead, and then, through the sound the people
made—the almost cooing roar that came up from the pit—Scoop's
laser guitar cut a wrenching, jagged hole, out of nowhere or out of
every direction at once, atomic sabers clashing in the air.

Scoop moved into the bleached circle of light, pouring it out at
them in a steady stream of concentrated energy—monumental,
hysterical, jubilant piss-off, ecstasy, and anger—and the people

moved it one notch tighter, seriously in the red region with it. Page watched as the matches started lighting, now a few here, a few more there, that orange light above each head, pentacostal in some dark, saintstorm religion. When Blye struck a handspun Turkish brass cymbal with a sound like the monsoons breaking at broad midnight, the already spooky arena filled with an unbearably eerie light as the music worked the people.

Jambeaux played and played, and neither money nor chemicals nor the power and the glory could have drawn them off the moment, because whatever else pained them, whatever threatened, was dispatched in a single wave. It was magic and it moved them hard and together.

Scoop finished with an electric flourish that split the night like a rabid stitch of lightning walking down the night sky, and he stepped back out of the circle of light. The song re-formed, took another shape, and wheeled around like a galaxy on its axis. Page stepped forward to sing it out, his open vowels bursting in air like floral shells of sound. When he finished and heard the fast, escaping breath of ecstasy from the audience, the slipping, dysphoric beauty of it, and saw that fully three-quarters of the people were signed with that holy-ghostly orange light, that ultimate salute, he leaned into the microphone and screamed it out, *"Rock and Row-Wool!"* and the Enigma staff photographer hit the trigger on her motor Nikon, catching Page alone in the circle of light and the supremely spooky rock and roll salute from the audience.

The crowd stormed the stage. Page, high on it, beyond it, moved toward them, not even realizing the danger there. He stepped right up to the edge of the stage, feeling as if he had just made love to every one of them, forty thousand orgasms, only when he got to the footlights, he could see they were serious and it shot into focus so quickly he thought later he could actually hear the bones cracking as the crowd surged, surged again, and the beautiful girl with the curly brown hair and the adoring smile went under.

Page saw the first foot go onto the girl's neck and he didn't need to see anymore, his stomach lurched against his ribs and his initial instinct was to jump off the stage to help, but that would have been suicide. It only came to him then that they were after *him,* and then he saw the second and the third foot go down on the girl's shoulder, ribs, back, and it was perfectly clear to anyone who cared to look that she was dead.

Jambeaux got out of Paris quickly after that concert.

It wasn't, Page explained to Cyndi, to Steve, to anyone who cared to hear, his idea of some morbid joke to have the live album cover feature that picture, or even to have the poster made of that album cover or to go then and take the trouble to frame that poster and hang it in his living room. *Les Beaux Jams* seemed as good a title as any for a live album by a group named Jambeaux, and if that was the best picture Page had seen, and if it happened to have been snapped only seconds before that girl was trampled to death, well, that didn't necessarily mean that Page was being morbid or that Jambeaux as a whole—as a band or a concept or even, as one clever writer had called it, a dysplasia—was evil. But then again, Page admitted, smiling his shy smile, there may have been some kernel of ultimate bitterness in there to top it off, yes, perhaps that was the Jambeaux message after all—that it is so hot that if you touch it, you will die. "Seductively evil," one review had called them, fine. The hexagram of Ko, Revolution, nine in the third place means: *Starting brings misfortune. Perseverance brings danger. When talk of revolution has gone the rounds three times, One may commit himself, And men will believe him,* you better believe it. Page knew that people didn't exactly run the bulls at Pamplona because it was cheaper than trucking them across town. So there it was, fuck 'em if they can't take a joke.

"You're evil," Steve was saying. "You are, do you know that? You're really evil, that's the answer."

"Then you're brother to evil." Page smiled. He didn't regret the picture. The picture hadn't killed anyone. It was just another piece of evidence.

But now there was no time to continue the discussion. Blye and Butch had returned, boiling into the room with enough fury for ten people, half drunk and making noise. Suddenly Page thought, I know, I know how can I get rid of these people, all of them except one, but can I really do that? Maybe Steve is right. Maybe I am evil. Maybe I've just come to the point where my survival is more important than the survival of others, or maybe it's always been that way, maybe that is the answer.

"Teach us to care and not to care, Teach us to sit still." Page looked up and saw a hunched figure straggling in with such apparent difficulty that at first Page thought the man was injured. He entered the hallway, covered with snow like a scarecrow long after the harvest and well into winter. And Page knew a kind of resolve he hadn't felt in years. Even that late in the game he still thought he was controlling events.

⊣30⊢

After Jill left him at his ranch, Page never again used cocaine. There was no conscious effort. In fact, it didn't occur to him that he had quit until he was back out on the road, where cocaine was plentiful. He just stopped. *Finis la coca.* It was another facet of the crystal that had hardened within him. With that going, drugs seemed superfluous. But now, on this snowy night at the Ranch, with Steve and Cyndi, Butch and Blye there, and Scoop's arrival topping it off, Page decided, What the hell, and popped the small ball of hashish into his mouth, just for old times' sake.

When they tried to get Page to play, he didn't have to refuse. He was crawling around on all fours on the living-room rug, giggling and talking nonsense. Hash, when eaten, can have that effect. It crept up silently and took Page from behind. He was watching and listening, going, No, it can't be, what's this? It was like watching a movie, some old playback, another kink in time: OK, there's Butch on piano, no mistaking that sound. And Blye, of course. Then there's Page—no, that can't be Page because Page is on the floor under the coffee table. Wait, there's that hellgong bass line, Link. Link!

No, that's not Link. Of course it isn't. It's Steve. That fucker. That's fucking Steve, playing fucking bass. Well, I'll be dipped . . .

And here comes Scoop's guitar, those ecstatic science-fiction fills, and sure enough there it is, Jambeaux, that's Page there singing, I'd know his voice anywhere. No, no, no, Page is fucked up like a Mexican astronaut. That's Steve, old double-threat Steve.

It went on like that until Page fell asleep. Somehow Cyndi got him up to the bedroom ("Proof," she said the next day, "that a man can have an erection while in a coma") and they awoke together in the first light of morning. Page's first thought was, Goddamn, somebody tried to kill me last night. Fuckers attacked me with a lethal chemical substance. I'm going to have to get these guys out of here and fast.

The snow had stopped and the sun was out, but it had dumped a significant quantity in the night and they were snowed in—not even Page's tricked-out trucks would get through this depth, and it would be at least another day before the county plows could clear it out. Page went downstairs with Cyndi to make coffee, and he thought of the last time he had been snowed in—truly snowed in. It had been right after the new year of 1977, right before the Paris concert.

When Link came back from spending Thanksgiving with Judy and his mother, he was different. Very different. Page didn't like it at all. He tried to break through and talk to Link, but the man was not responding. About the only person Page saw Link talk to in those days was that guy named Merlin Shea, Perry's incomparable inside source. Page kept trying to get Link to stay away from him, but it was no use. And once the *Recondo* tour started, the chaos level shot up to the point where they couldn't talk about it. When it got to the point where Link was actually screwing up on stage, forgetting the words to songs, missing notes, dragging—when it touched his music, too, Page talked Shelly into letting them cancel several concerts so that they could have a few days off. Page had practically kidnapped Link to get him to Michigan.

The day they arrived at the Ranch it had been snowing for fourteen hours and there was no sign that it would stop. As soon as they settled in and Page made this observation, Link began to get nervous. For the first time since Link had returned from seeing Judy, he became talkative.

"Does it snow much up here?" Link asked, and Page laughed. "How come you moved all the way the fuck up here?"

"Yeah, shitbird, it snows a lot." Page was glad that Link was at least saying something. "Sometimes it'll snow several feet."

"What do you do then?" Link glanced around, looked out the windows over the lake. It was snowing so hard that he couldn't see the other shore. "How do you get around?"

"Oh, well, you don't get around." Page grinned. "You just stay in here where it's nice and warm and healthy." Page let that settle and then added, "A man could die out there in weather like this."

"Shit," Link said, and he started fidgeting, scratching himself and darting his eyes this way and that. He went into the bathroom for a while, and when he came out he was all right again. It was so transparent Page didn't say anything about it, just waited until

Link was nodding a little and then rifled his luggage. He took the heroin he found and flushed it down the toilet, thinking, Well, that's one decision we won't have to make. Cold fucking turkey. The next morning Link was already starting to get sick and the snow was still falling. There was going to be no way in or out of that ranch, not today, probably not the next day either. Link was going to have to ride this one out on his own.

When Link discovered what Page had done, he didn't blow up as Page had expected. He broke down and cried, which took Page completely by surprise. Page had never seen Link in that condition, so open and uncontrolled. Something had taken the callus off him and there was no protection left. Page brought him a tumbler of whiskey to try to calm him down.

"Link." Page felt horrible about the way Link was carrying on, felt personally responsible, but he knew something had to be done. "Link, come on, man, somebody's got to stop you before you kill yourself. Don't you realize what's going on? Jesus." He grabbed Link by the shoulders and shook him. "Come on, drink this bullshit."

Link drank some of the whiskey and gradually began to quiet down enough to talk. He hadn't told anyone up until then. He'd just kept it for himself, his own private cache of misery. And now he gave it to Page, it was simple: while he was at his mother's house, Judy had caught him shooting up once too often, and she had left him.

"And that's why you're shooting so much more." Page stood up and put his hands on his hips. "Well, that makes a fuck of a lot of sense, doesn't it? Maybe if you just stopped altogether, she'd come back."

"She got married," Link said, and then he broke down again, partly from simple release, simple grief, and Page could see how much in love Link was. It wasn't a term Link would have used and he certainly didn't show such feelings the way other people did —he wasn't the type to go moaning around like a sick cow or bouncing off the walls the way Page might. But Page had known it, had seen it now for years. And taking Judy away from him was at least as bad as taking away his drug. Page wasn't sure Link could withstand the two at once.

As he watched Link, he could see that the undeniable effects of heroin withdrawal were setting in, the spidery crystal tentacles shooting through and calcifying, where they could grip him and shake his tree until he fell right out of it. Page knew people could die from it, love or drugs, but he had no idea how lightly or heavily Link was addicted at this point. It was a simple error in judgment.

"I'm sorry, man." Page sat next to him, unsure what to do or say. "I'm really sorry." Link got up unsteadily and went to the bathroom.

Page could hear him vomiting. He came back looking gray. "But that doesn't mean I can let you kill yourself. We've got to stop this somewhere. It's just got to stop somewhere."

By afternoon, Page was aware that he had underestimated the situation. Link couldn't get up off the floor and he sputtered at Page, "I've got to get something or I'm gonna *die*."

Page didn't know whether or not that was true, but he knew he wouldn't be able to watch Link go through any more of this. Maybe he really would die, Page had no way of judging. And he got up, his face flushed red with outrage. Damned if he did. Damned if he didn't. Damned, condemned, shit. And beneath all that: Who got Link into this in the first place? Page knew, he knew. At least he thought he knew.

By the time Page got the local doctor on the phone, Link was writhing so violently that Page was worried he might go into convulsions if something weren't done. By arguing and shouting, pleading and cajoling, Page got the doctor to agree to see what he could do. Then Page sat on the floor with a bowl of ice water and a cloth, trying to keep the fever down. An hour and a half later a teenage boy showed up on cross-country skis, covered from head to foot with big, wet snowflakes. He had a package, which Page ripped open. He took out the styrette of morphine and assembled it as quickly as his shaking hands would allow. He had a great deal of trouble giving Link the injection because Link's muscles were cramping and twitching and Link couldn't prevent himself from thrashing around. He finally got the needle into Link and fired it home. The boy who had delivered the package just stood there in mute wonder at the macabre thing he'd just seen. Page tipped him heavily and told him to get lost. And there it was: Link got well so fast he went to sleep for twelve hours. The withdrawal had worn him smooth.

The next day Page got one of his friends in the area to snowmobile in and get them out of there. They arrived in Los Angeles in time to pick up the tour where they'd left off, and although Page convinced Link to start trying that methadone Blye had used, Link just seemed lost without Judy. By the time they returned from the Paris concert, he was back on the point again.

And every time Page saw Link with Merlin, he felt a chill like ethylene glycol running through his veins. That low-life fuck, in his fancy clothes with his Cajun accent. Page flew into a homicidal rage one night when he saw Merlin slipping Link some more heroin and Butch and Blye had to hold Page down to keep him from killing the man. Finally, desperate for something to do, Page called Judy.

"Page, I don't want to hear from you again," she said, her Texas accent as flat and dry as a prairie. "I've got a home and I'm pregnant. I don't want to hear anything about it."

"Oh, God," Page said. Pregnant. She'll never come back. "Link's gonna kill himself without you," he pleaded.

"Page." He could hear her voice crack at the other end of the line. "Don't you understand anything? Why do you think I left him? I couldn't watch him destroy himself. Page, I tried. God knows, I tried with him. How long was it, anyway? Two years? More than two years, Page, and then at his mother's house, he was at it again. I couldn't stand it any longer. I'm in love with him, don't you realize that? And I just. Can't. See him." There she broke down and hung up on Page, who stood holding the phone for the longest time. He didn't even hear the dial tone. A high-pitched squeal from the phone shook him out of it.

Near the end of the *Recondo* tour, after the Paris concert, Page sat in Link's room one night. They were at the Plaza Hotel in New York, preparing to go to Madison Square Garden for a concert. Their last of the tour. Link asked Page to leave the room so he could get ready.

"Ready, my ass," Page said without humor.

"What's wrong with you?" Link asked defensively.

"Go ahead and do it, Link," Page said. " 'Cause I'm not leaving." He could see the big beads of sweat coming off Link's brow and hitting the carpet.

"Fuck." Link tried to laugh, but it wasn't happening. "I'm cool. I'm just gonna get dressed and shower."

"And when the fuck did it ever bother you if I was here when you took a shower? I'm not gettin' into the shower with you, if that's what's worrying you."

"Aw, come on," Link said weakly. "You're just paranoid."

"All right." Page got up angrily. "All right, then." He started going through Link's suitcase.

"What're you doing?" Link jumped up.

"If you're so goddamned cool, what do you care if I look in here?"

"OK, OK." Link went back to his chair and put his head in his hands. "I've got some bullshit. I just don't want you to watch."

"Well, fuck you!" Page whirled around to face him, the veins standing out on his forehead. "I mean it, fuck you, Link. If you're gonna do it, you're gonna do it now. Because I'm not leaving and we have to go to the Garden in twenty minutes." Page looked down at the floor, breathing hard. He reached under his vest and pulled out a small revolver. "Here." He threw it onto the couch. "There you go, Link. Why don't you just fucking get it over with."

Link took the Velcro tourniquet and tied off, trying not to look over at the revolver on the couch. Page watched him as if he were watching Link cut off his own leg at the knee. Link wouldn't meet his eyes. He fired off with such grudging, vicious determination that Page had to stop and wonder for the first time since he'd known Link if maybe there was a lot more he didn't know about this man. If there was something beyond that possessed him. Maybe Link's traditional poise and seeming invulnerability covered the same layers of undischarged malignancy that blew Page down the chute so frequently. Maybe Page just had a better sluice for it all, and Link filtered and stored those poisons so efficiently that they were finally killing him. Maybe those shuddering fits and old, regurgitated shell-shock reactions were good for Page, and where Link didn't have them as openly, he had to burn them off in a more private, far more devastating manner. Page thought of the stackfires in Texas City, where the refineries steadily burned off the volatile chemicals by lighting a flame above the chimneys. If they didn't do that, the gases would settle over the area and the minute someone struck a spark, the entire town would disappear from the face of the earth.

An hour later, sitting in the dressing room at the Garden—the dismal cinderblock room that had so little character it could have been part of a military installation—surrounded by strange fey bodies, out star-fucking for the evening, Link was well again, his illness gone, and he tried to talk to Page, to apologize for the thing that had embarrassed him so profoundly.

"Shut up, man," Page said flatly, his anger gone now. "I don't want to hear it. Just see if you can get through the gig."

"Aw, come on, Page, now really," Link began, but Page just glared at him so steadily that Link turned and went to sit and sulk in a corner.

Now Page could hear the crowd, even through the layers of ferroconcrete. They had been doing this from time to time ever since the release of *Recondo* and it scared Page, putting him in mind of some awful pagan game, a game in which only the shedding of blood could determine the outcome. Riverine Mobile Death Soccer had been just one of the jokes once, but now all the jokes were over. The crowd was howling out the phrase Page wished he'd never given them. He shivered, listening.

"ROCK AND ROLL! ROCK AND ROLL!" they chanted in a single dissonant voice, and through the floor Page could feel the stamping of their feet. "ROCK AND ROLL! ROCK AND ROLL!" over and over until Page started hearing something altogether different, he had come full circle, he thought, there was no stopping now, he was beyond that imaginary line of commitment, and he just resigned himself to it. Fuck it, he heard himself saying. Might as well get my feet wet.

And now Page was snowed in again in Michigan, but this time it was the beginning and end of all sorts of stories for him. This time he had Cyndi there, three of his fucking band members—or former band members, depending on which side of the story you chose to believe. And just as soon as that road was clear, he was going to get rid of them. Nothing personal, just a basic survival technique he apparently learned too well, long ago. The previous night, crawling around zonked on hashish, listening to that sound—the real thing, distilled essence of Jambeaux—Page had come to a simple realization: sure Steve was his brother, his own flesh and blood. But he had come asking for it and, well, what the hell, it was an old story, Cain and Abel at least. But Page still didn't know shit about it. Cain and Abel, he'd forgotten, only did what God intended.

At the moment, however, he hurried Cyndi so they could get out before the maniacs awoke and started trouble. He would call Shelly when they got there, if Shelly weren't already out on the road. Page knew what was going on (he was born at night . . .). Those wacky guys who play rock and roll. We'll see, he thought, we'll see.

He and Cyndi locked on their cross-country skis and were out into the woods before eight in the morning. By ten they were far away having a hot breakfast of eggs and bacon and biscuits at the cabin of one of the local boys, where a fat cast-iron stove put out a comforting heat after that long trek.

Off and on, Page tried to reach Shelly, but they kept telling him Shelly was out and they didn't know where he had gone. Page knew that was a load, they knew damned well where Shelly was, they knew when Shelly farted. He tried Perry then but they said Perry was on an extended trip and Page thought, What is this shit? He had his plan, now what was theirs? Maybe Cyndi was right. Maybe he just needed the illusion of control so that when things went wrong, he could blame himself. Self-abuse is better than no abuse at all.

Page and Cyndi didn't return to the Ranch until well after dark, and as they approached, Cyndi stopped Page, pointing through the trees a long distance away to an intense splash of light on the snow.

"Page, what's that in there? By the house?" Page took a fast look and it didn't compute at first. He thought he must be seeing something out of a science-fiction fantasy. Then he refocused on the weird machinery, the harsh pool of light.

"Oh, my God," he whispered. "I don't believe it."

-31-

After the *Recondo* tour was over, in early 1977, Page finally put his foot down, hard. Link had bought a pad high on a hill in L.A., not so much because he wanted to be in L.A., but because he always found himself there. Page pulled up the winding drive, through the security gate, and stepped out into the sunlight with a

briefcase. Link greeted him at the door, looking pale and wasted
—diminished, as if from a lingering disease. Page was all business
and in a downright hostile mood.

"What's happening, Little Buddy?" Link asked, smiling.

"Don't give me any of that Little Buddy shit." Page pushed past
him. "Is anyone else here?"

"Just me," Link said.

"Come here," Page said, setting the briefcase on the table. "I
just want you to know what I'm going to do before I do it."

"What's that?" Link was truly puzzled.

Page opened the briefcase and said, "See these? Know what
those are?"

"Jesus shit," Link whispered, "what'd you do, rob the fucking
marines?"

"I asked do you know what they are?"

"Well, Christ, Page, of course I know what they are, they're
white phosphorus grenades, where in hell did you get them?"

"Well. . . ." Page didn't answer his question. "I'm going up to
Merlin's house and I'm going to blow his shit away. Burn it right
down. I heard he just got in a new shipment and it's never going to
leave his place."

"Page, have you lost your mind?" Link looked to see if Page
was joking and saw immediately that he was not.

"Yes, I guess you could say I've lost my mind." Page closed the
case. "Anyway, I just want you to know what I'm doing."

"Page." Link grabbed his arm, but Page pulled away. "Hey,
man, I'm gonna have to stop you. You'll go to jail forever if you
do that."

"I'd rather be in jail, then." Page turned to leave, and Link
followed.

"No, Page." Link went after him out the door and down the
patio toward the driveway. "Hey, listen, man, come on."

"I just wanted you to know what you've started here, Link. You
think about that when you read the papers tomorrow, because
Merlin's going to be DOA and I mean that."

Page had reached his car and opened the door when Link
grabbed his arm. Their eyes met and they froze like that. Link had
known Page for enough years to realize that he was crazy. And
surely if he was crazy enough to go and find white phosphorus
grenades, he was mad enough to use them.

"Is there anything," Link asked, "anything I can do to make you stop this?"

"Yes," Page said flatly.

"All right." Link hung his head. "Tell me. I think I know already, but fucking tell me."

"Come to New Orleans with me." Page let his shoulders fall, visibly relaxing for the first time. "That place where Sonny went. I'll go with you. I'll help you through it. We'll get you fixed up once and for all."

"I'm scared, Page," Link said. "I've never been scared like this in my life, but now I'm scared all the time." Page looked at Link and saw in his face a sadness he hadn't seen for years.

"I'm scared too, Link, scared shit," Page said, shaking his head. "But we been scared before, so let's just fucking do it."

"All right. Let's give it a shot anyway."

"No shot about it," Page said. "This is the last chance. If I didn't know that, I wouldn't have pulled this shit."

Page took a little place in the Quarter and went to the hospital every day. The time went slowly there, and Link was not doing well for a while, but sometimes in the middle of the pain and exhaustion he would grin up at Page—hard sweating defiant grin —and say something that would make Page laugh and know he was now determined to get through it. "I want you to git that doctor," Link would say, grinning maliciously. "I want you to tell him to come in here and pull all my teeth out without an anesthetic. It'll take my mind off it."

As it got better, Link and Page could be found sitting in the courtyard in the Louisiana sun, playing two guitars softly.

"Come on, asshole," Link would say, " 'Buffalo Gals,' it's my favorite cowboy song."

"Cowboy shit." Page laughed. "I want to do 'Red River Valley.' "

"That piece of crap?"

Link's color came back. His face filled out again and he started to gain weight. When he was released into Page's "custody," they knocked around town, watching it all come down: spring in New Orleans, nothing finer. They both felt cleaned out, purified, almost holy.

They sat on the terrace by the river, just south of the farmer's vegetable market, and drank chicory coffee and ate crispy powdered-sugar beignets. The sun was brilliant and the day warm. They were digging the gorgeous New Orleans women who passed the little restaurant, and even the tourists with cameras, who kept coming up to ask if they could take their pictures.

"You're from Jambeaux, aren't you?" they would ask.

"No, ma'am," Page would say. "I'm John Dean and this here's my main man, H.R. call-him-Bob Haldeman." The people would laugh, and then Page and Link would pose for them.

"Lord," Link said after one particularly beautiful woman had walked away, "I'd ventilate her in a hot minute." And Page looked up, because Link hadn't expressed interest in a woman for such a long time. Page knew he was getting well.

"Listen," Page said at the end of the morning, "we've got some work to do. I've got a whole new concept for our next album. I've been working on it every day now. A new sound, man, a whole new thing I've been hearing. And I want to go up to my ranch and work out the way it's gonna be. This time I want you to help me write it."

"Is it still snowing up there?" Link asked, squinting at him.

"Shit." Page laughed. "Yeah, sure, snows all summer."

"I hear they've got some bodacious trout fishing."

"Browns, man, enormous browns."

Link sighed and leaned back. "Well, I could go for some of that, wouldn't mind that at all. Maybe even go back to that Ice Nine studio up in Canada."

"Wisconsin," Page corrected.

"Same difference." Link grinned.

A few days later Link sat in the copilot's seat of the Cessna 401 and grabbed the microphone. He depressed the switch and started chattering away in military lingo, "Roger, Medallion, we mark your position, I scramble all after position, Ranger two-five-seven-five, one-seven-niner, bracket and fire for effect . . . ," and then making explosion sounds until the ground-control personnel threatened to send out the air marshals. Page leaned over and slapped at Link, trying to get the microphone away from him. "You shit, come on, turdbird, let's get this fucker on the road, I gotta be wheels-in-the-wells by twelve-hunnert if we're gonna make it back in time, now cut it the fuck out."

"OK, OK." Link chuckled and handed Page the microphone. "Gimme the checklist, numbnuts, let's go."

"Cowl flaps," Link barked.

"Open," Page responded.

"Cabin door."

"Locked."

"Wing flaps."

"Up, zero degrees."

It went on like that, Page did his engine run-up and then they were gone, airmobile. They arrived late at the Ranch and sat around drinking beer and looking over some notes Page had made on the new songs he wanted to write. It was about one in the morning when Perry called.

"Hey!" Page said happily. "How they hanging, Pear?"

Perry, however, did not sound so happy. He wanted a live album. Page's face went dark—mockingly so at first. He looked over at Link and made a swirling motion at his temple, as if to indicate that Perry was insane.

"Well, listen, man, me and Link are up here writing a whole fucking new studio album, so just don't worry your pretty gray head."

But Perry was not amused. He wanted a live album and that meant a tour, coordinated with a mobile recording studio. It meant gearing up for a multiregional sweep of the nation, a full-scale operation, and Page's mood grew less jubilant with every word Perry spoke. This dude was serious.

"Page, do you realize that we're coming out with a greatest hits album?"

"Well, shit, so what?"

"All these things have to be coordinated, Page. Shelly has talked it over with me. Don't you realize that your last album has grossed over ten million dollars already? We have to move now. The time you and Link spent in New Orleans has set the schedule off tremendously but we can pick up now. And none of the live material we've taped to date is usable, do you understand what I mean?"

"No, I'm afraid I don't." Page's mood had completely deflated now. "What *do* you mean?"

"I mean, Page, no offense, but half the time the live material was recorded while you were out of your mind with the gentleman you refer to as the Bolivian Consulate. The other half, Link was out of his mind on the other thing we discussed. Now, Link is recovered. You are recovered. And we need a live album with material that lives up to the quality control Jambeaux is famous for. Am I making myself clear *now,* Page?"

Page said nothing. Link was jiving around the room, since he hadn't heard the harangue. But when he saw Page's expression, he stopped and gave Page an inquiring shrug. Finally Page spoke.

"Yeah," was all he said.

"So we'll see you in Los Angeles in, say, seventy-two hours at the latest?"

"Sure," Page said and hung up, thinking, You've got to pay the cost to be the boss.

"What the fuck was that?" Link asked.

"We just got orders."

"What orders?"

"Live album, remember? I'd forgotten all about it."

"Shit," Link said. "Now? Right now?"

"Right fucking now."

Page saw it clearly in retrospect. Hindsight, as they say, is twenty-twenty. Of course, he saw it then too, just as he'd seen it in Houston that night in the limousine for the first time with Jill. Just as he'd seen it and ignored it a thousand other times. He could have just said, No, fuck you, no, no, no, but he still had some learning to do, expensive learning. The next morning, Link read him that checklist again, and a few hours later they were met at O'Hare Butler Aviation by an Enigma company Learjet. And then they were on the road again, line of departure, Page standing in that bolt of light, screaming once more, *"Rock and Row-Wool!"*

-32-

As Cyndi and Page approached the house on their cross-country skis, Page shook his head. The two Hughes 500 helicopters were parked in the snow and Page touched one with his gloved hand.

"What's going on?" Cyndi asked.

"Come on," he said as they unsnapped their skis. "Fucker's slick," Page muttered, heading for the door. "Slick, slick, slick."

"Who?" Cyndi asked, but she was silenced by the trite refrain that echoed around the vast room as they entered.

"Surprise!" everyone shouted at once.

"Some fucking surprise," Page said, shedding his heavy weather gear. " 'Bout as subtle as an airstrike."

And Jambeaux cranked into it—a violent guitar introduction to the old Beatles' song:

> You say it's your birthday
> It's my birthday too, yeah
> You say it's your birthday
> We're gonna have a good time

Page stared at Steve, who sang it out, meeting his brother's eyes. Page just shook his head, thinking, I might have known he'd do something like this. Then he felt a hand on his shoulder and whirled around to face Perry.

"I know what you're thinking," Perry said. "But it wasn't his idea. It was mine. Steve just did a little legwork for me."

"You?" Page asked. "You set this whole thing up?"

"I cannot tell a lie," Perry lied. And Page thought, What? What's going on here? And then he saw something that almost made the party worth it. There he was, that translucent angel, ambling over like a ballet skeleton with those long pink fingers opening and closing and the shocking cascades of white hair.

"Sonny." Page hugged him, while Sonny held his head as if it were going to explode.

"Page, Page," Sonny said, almost out of control. "Man, look at all the *pussy* here, man, oh, *man!*" Page just laughed and looked around. Indeed, they had brought enough women so they could really light that hard boogie light.

"What do you want to get for your birthday?" Shelly asked, taking Page's hand.

"I want to get *down!*" Page said.

"Listen to them." Perry tilted his head in the direction of the band. "What do you think?"

"Just like old times." Page squinted at the man, thinking, Is he going to do what I think he's going to do? Beat me to the goddamned punch again? Very slick. But Page couldn't think clearly yet, there was too much input. Holly came over and embraced him, man, Holly, nothing finer.

"How'd you get all these people here?" Page asked her. He

knew she'd had a hand in it, since Perry had hired her away from Ice Nine when Jill left to go on her own. "I had to cross-country ski out this morning."

"We ferried everyone out in the choppers," Holly said. "Had to make several trips, but it was only to G.R. and back."

"Goddamn." Page looked back over to the band again, to Steve, who was singing it out. It doesn't matter, then, does it? Page thought. It really doesn't make any difference at all what I do. Jambeaux was its own organism all along, now simply regenerating like a starfish, one limb drops off and another grows back to replace it. Page thought he had quit. Quit! Haw! Man, that's beautiful. He thought he'd form a band and a band formed him.

"Let me show you the cake," Shelly said, taking Page by the arm. He took him to the table. The sheet cake was a true work of art, big enough to feed eighty people. The inscription said, in baroque confectioner's letters, *I was born at night, but it definitely wasn't last night*.

"All right now!" Butch said through the microphone. "Let's quiet down, please." The room began to settle. A girl rushed up and hugged Butch.

"Hello, Butch."

"Hi, Lauren," he said, leaning down to place a kiss on her forehead. He turned back to the mike. "Shelly?" He signaled and Shelly produced a Dunhill lighter to start the candles. Another girl rushed up to kiss Butch. "Hi, Karen," he said, leaning away from the mike again to kiss her. Then Steve hit that hellgong bass and everyone sang the song.

Happy Birthday, dear Paaaaage! Happy Birthday tooooo youuuuuuu! And Page blew out the candles as Jambeaux launched into "Sixteen Candles."

As the evening wore on, it became obvious that Page would have to have a conference with Perry and Shelly about the new development. Some old bills had come due and everyone knew how Page was going to pay them. The three men wound up in the kitchen.

"One last time," Perry said wearily. "We can go right ahead from here, just like nothing happened, if you'll change your mind and get on with your work. Jambeaux has a lot of potential left in it and you know I'm not going to see it go down the drain."

"Yeah." Page hung his head. "I know you're not. But I'm sorry. I'm finished with it."

"Then I guess you've figured out the alternative."

"Yeah, I started thinking about it as soon as he arrived."

"Well," Perry sighed. "He's certainly agreed to play with Jambeaux, but he still thinks I'm going to convince you to come back on as lead singer, rhythm guitarist, composer, and so on. He was planning on just being part of the group."

"Yeah, well"—Page shook his head—"guess you can't think of everything." There was a long silence and then Page stood up. "Guess I'd better get him in here and let him know about his new career."

"I guess," Perry said. Shelly had not said a word. Now he spoke.

"You'll still write some songs for Jambeaux, I hope."

"If you think so," Page said and left the room. The band had stopped playing, and Page cornered Steve and took him outside. They stood by the garage in the cold still air, talking. Steve was sorry Page wasn't going to join them, but he couldn't disguise his unbridled giddiness at the notion that he was going to lead this world-famous band. And Page thought, once again, There's going to be only one way for Steve to find out on his own. There was one last story, too, maybe one that would change his mind, but screw it. Page wasn't about to tell that one. Steve would just have to go through it.

"I need a drink," Page said when they'd finished talking.

"Rock and Roll," Steve said.

And Page joined the party then, for sure and for real. He drank himself senseless, but no matter how much he drank, something Steve had once said kept ringing in his mind: *You're evil, Page, you know that, don't you?*

And that one last story was still going around and around in his head, long after the choppers had reared back and lifted off one last time, leaving Page and Cyndi waving up at them, arm in arm. That one last story.

It started right when Page and Link were pulled away from the Ranch to go back on the road for that live-album tour. They had been on it for five weeks and knew damned well they were going to have enough material for the purpose. The band was sounding better than ever and the recordings were some of the best live material they had heard. The preposterousness of the situation, however, was taking its inevitable toll: on the road. Page and Link had been straight the entire time. Page remembered standing on the stage at the Convention Center in San Antonio, Texas, singing his ass off, and Link stepping up beside him to sing harmony:

> You will never know when it's coming
> But you'll sure know when it's passed.
> Everyone behind you is running.
> And they'll catch you if you last.

> It's a real revelation
> It can really ice you, man.
> What a terrible, beautiful moment,
> When it all comes down,
> When it hits the fan.

Then they were back at the hotel, eating, talking about getting out.

"I'm about to go fucking rock happy," Link said.

"Comin' unwrapped here," Page said.

"If only we could go out and do something." Link poked a fork at Page. Blye and Butch came in, leading Scoop.

"Thank you," Blye said, grabbing a potato off Page's plate and eating it like an apple.

"Get outta here, you creepy strange-o." Page slapped at his hand.

"Man," Butch said, "we've got the perfect thing, here." He turned to Scoop. "Show 'em." Scoop shyly held up something that looked like a toilet seat with an electric guitar neck affixed to it.

"What the fuck is that?" Link asked.

"The ToilaPhone." Butch smiled.

"The Commodiola," Blye announced.

"He made it himself." Butch pointed to Scoop.

"Suitably gross," Page allowed.

"And now for something completely different." Butch did a little dance step.

"Such as?" Page asked.

"I'm gonna get me some pussy," Butch announced proudly. "I found this great little chick."

"How old?" Page asked. "Nine?"

"Man," Link said, "I'm so horny I'd fuck a snake."

"You?" Blye laughed. "Haw! You'd fuck a rockpile if you thought there was a snake in it."

As Page listened to them banter back and forth, he realized that Link was really well now. The whole band, every one of them, had gone through the hellfires and look at them: they seemed normal.

At the depth of Link's tailspin, he had told Page that he hadn't had the desire even to look at a woman for months. And Page thought back to that day in New Orleans, sitting at the little café. Yeah, if Link was starting to chase skirts again, he was definitely out of the woods this time. Rock happy and horny, how deliciously normal.

The next day Link mentioned it again. "Don't you worry," Page told him, "we gonna get you laid three ways."

"Which three are those?" Link smiled.

"Long, deep, and frequently."

As the limousine pulled through the gates, taking them to work, Page made the driver stop. Michael was riding in the front seat and Page pointed out the window.

"See those two girls?" Page said.

"Which two?" There were only about four hundred of them.

"The ones right there." Page pointed. "See the girl with the silver jacket?"

"Yeah."

"Give her and her friend passes."

"Why, whatever for?" Michael feigned innocence.

"What the fuck do you think for?" Link chuckled.

The driver pulled up to the stage door and Michael went back out into the crowd to find the girls. After the concert, the girls came backstage, so excited that Page and Link knew they'd picked the right companions. Sandy and Kathy were their names. They rode back to the hotel in the limo, saying things like, "I can't believe it," and giggling a lot.

Up in Link's suite, they drank and partied until the early-morning hours. Out came the Quaaludes, naturally, and various other goodies that such girls carry. Then more booze, and at some point Page, barely able to walk, lurched back to his own suite with Kathy, while Link and Sandy continued to boogie. Page saw the hallway twist and turn and revolve on its side and knew he had taken far too much of everything.

When questioned, Page said he could remember seeing Link and Sandy a little later—when and where wasn't clear in his mind, but they had all gotten back together and had a few more drinks, perhaps more drugs too, he didn't know. There was cocaine, there were Quāāludes, a lot of whiskey, under questioning it was all smeared and blurred through the dawn. Link was having the time of his life, too. Kathy and Page returned to Page's suite and screwed into the morning, and that was all Page remembered.

In the morning, when they found Link dead from an apparent accidental overdose of depressants and alcohol, the girl named Sandy was gone. When they got the maid to open Page's door, Page was in a profound sleep and the girl named Kathy was not there either. In Page's mind, the girls' faces were nothing more than vague Zapruder Film memories, and no one ever found out who they were. In his condition, it was no wonder Page thought he was dreaming, the police photographers snapping pictures of Link asleep in bed, how strange. Each time the flashbulb went off, a searing pain shot into Page's cortex. What are they doing, they're going to wake him. No danger of that. Somewhere in the halls people were running and shouting, something was going on. Page couldn't remember much more of it. And that didn't matter anyway, because he sure wasn't going to tell that one to Steve.

⊣ 33 ⊢

It was about three days later, something like that. Dawn in a cemetery and Page was having an unreal conversation with the two men who had the backhoe. They were big men, not trained in the graveside manner, and they didn't give a shit what Page thought about it.

"I'm telling you," Page said evenly, "you're not going to dig this hole with that thing. I'm going to do it myself. With this." Page held up the shovel.

"Now, son," one of them began, trying to be sympathetic, "I know how you feel, but you just can't do that. It'll take you all day. Anyway, there's union regulations."

"How much are you getting paid?" Page asked.

"Twelve an hour," the man said.

"Here." Page took out a wad of bills and gave each man two fifties. "Now get that damned machine out of here." And without another word Page stepped on the shovel blade and began digging. The two workers shrugged and backed their machine away, shaking their heads.

It was almost dusk when Page finished, but the hole was dug, with square corners, just the way it was supposed to be. The next day he was so sore he felt as if he'd been beat up. He found himself standing in the brilliant sunlight, thinking, Man, it's so cool, what a day. The wind had picked up and was blowing hard, but the sun was shining. He looked around and saw Perry, sleek and tightly buttoned into a coat, then Jill, next to him, in black, Cyndi also in black (black is the color . . .) losing control of her clothing in the piss-off winds that seemed to come from all directions at once. The Silver Fox stood in a black trench coat, holding his collar closed. Jambeaux was there, the whole band, a second-long flash of Scoop's straw-colored hair standing straight up in the virulent gale, some lightning-struck scarecrow, and Page recoiled from the image. (Wait, wait, can't we just talk this over?) Blye seemed deeply disappointed. He had his arms folded against his barrel chest and looked neither here nor there, simply endured the lashing wind and sunlight. Butch held a long coat about him with both hands, his head turned away from the wind, the storm whipping his hair in streaks around his face so that no expression showed, but he was still as a stone. Beyond him, Page saw the field of monuments and gravestones, and he felt a detachment enter him like a spike, as if he were in a dream.

Then he saw the statue. It was a massive monument with a large angel on top. The angel had its hands stretched outward and down toward the grave beneath it, and the angel's right hand had been broken off at the wrist. Page looked over and saw Link's mother, and then it all came back to him. He looked past Cyndi to Jill, up front then, to Perry, he saw Scoop turn to look at him with such forlorn and desperate bafflement that it went through him like a shot. He watched Butch holding against the bright razor wind. Blye turned slowly, gazing at Page, and Page just nodded, there it is.

There was even a preacher there. He was a young man, flat and faceless as a painted plank, stiff in his black cassock that did not stir, as if by some special dispensation he was immune from weather and wind.

He recited psalms without referring to the book, each word a phonetic thistle lodged in the throat, his voice as dry and echoless as a prairie. Page started at his first words; it was almost as if he'd known who Link was: "They gaped upon me with their mouths, as a ravening and roaring lion. I am poured out like water, and all my bones are out of joint: My heart is like wax; it is melted in the midst of my bowels. My strength is dried up like a potsherd; and my tongue cleaveth to my jaws; and thou hast brought me into the dust of death. For dogs have compassed me: the assembly of the wicked have inclosed me: they pierced my hands and my feet. I may tell all my bones: They look and stare upon me. They part my garments among them, and cast lots upon my vesture. But be not thou far from me, O Lord: O my strength haste thee to help me. Deliver my soul from the sword; my darling from the power of the dog. Save me from the lion's mouth: for thou hast heard me from the horns of the unicorns."

Page wanted desperately to go at that point, he knew what was coming next, but that was an old move. So he stayed, he listened, the words whipping through him like the wind through his clothes: "The Lord is my shepherd; I shall not want." The humor was gone out of it, ancient as the earth, Page had seen it written across too many discarded flak jackets. "He maketh me to lie down in green pastures: He leadeth me beside the still waters. He restoreth my soul: He leadeth me in the paths of righteousness for his name's sake." He does? Page wondered. Is that what He does? Well, it's a good goddamned thing, too. "Yea, though I walk through the valley of the shadow of death, I shall fear no evil, for thou art with me; thy rod and thy staff they comfort me. Thou preparest a table before me in the presence of mine enemies: thou anointest my head with oil; my cup runneth over. Surely goodness and mercy shall follow me all the days of my life; and I will dwell in the house of the Lord for ever."

"If you think so," Page said under his breath, and walked over to hand the shovel to Link's mother, who threw the first clods of soil onto the casket. As Page threw the second and then the third shovel full of dirt in, the people looked at him oddly, but said nothing. Then Page felt a hand on his shoulder and turned to see Judy there.

"I'll do it," she said, but Page went back to filling the hole. "I'll *do* it," she said more firmly, and for a moment Page thought of telling her to go fuck herself, that the time was long past when she could do anything to help, but he stopped himself again. He knew it was far more complicated than that. For the longest time he just looked at her and then he handed her the shovel and walked away, listening to the steady, hollow thump of the dirt hitting the casket.

The crowd was stringing out away from the hole, toward the cars. Page rode with Cyndi in a long black limousine with an android driver cut off from them by a glass partition. Cyndi said nothing until they got to the airport, and then she asked where Page was going, didn't he want some company? It wouldn't be good to be alone.

Page just smiled. No, it wouldn't be good to be alone. He should have thought of that one years ago. It sure wouldn't be good. He told her he had some business to attend to and left her with a kiss on the cheek. After a couple of days, she called but there was no answer at the Ranch. Perry called too. No one was able to reach Page. This went on for a week before someone decided to go out there and see where he was. Blye flew out with Cyndi, but a search of the house revealed nothing. The phones had been systematically ripped out of the walls. Nothing else was disturbed, and there was no sign of Page. Any footprints into that place or away from it had been meticulously wiped out by someone who knew woods and jungle, someone who had been there, some superstar recondo, because they could find no trace of him.

What they didn't know was that when Page arrived back on the Ranch after the funeral, some glacial crystal had thawed inside him and begun its implacable downward movement, he could barely contain himself, couldn't sit still for five minutes without breaking into tears. So he'd go outside, often deep into woods he'd never seen before, acting out old, frozen dreams of terror eight thousand miles and a decade away, sleeping the night in the leaves, seeing Link in his sleep and starting awake so suddenly and violently that he could hear the animals wake and move away. It was a rare time, rare that the agony could take him so exquisitely that he would wake up howling like a dog, shot through with grief, and the oldest songs played in all innocence could shake his cage uncontrollably, "Take another little piece of my heart, now, baby." Tears in the forest, tears in the street, real tears and tears inside, broken-hearted, stop-on-the-sidewalk-to-lean-against-a-build-ing tears, completely un-self-conscious now for the first time in his life, the grief whipping through him like wildfire winds through pine and sumac until he couldn't hear a sound (forget *that* sound) without practically flipping, he thought he would, too: he found himself one bright, gorgeous stark Michigan morning sitting on the side of the bathtub with the barrel of a .44-'40 saddle rifle clenched between his teeth, up against the roof of the mouth there, and he had even taken up the slack on the trigger. But he thought, No, no, remember the audience? The rock and roll hounds? They *want* you to do that, it's just what the dogs want, and I won't give it to them, won't give them the satisfaction. Line of departure. Unload. Disperse, finally.

And then that old music, that old sound, came in clear as winter light through the chaos of sorrow. "Look what they've done to my song." Fever and frenzy, yes, a long, lurid trip, and there was that same old sound, still playing after all the years and miles. The music came roaring in at new, unprecedented levels that the great Northwestern banks of speakers could never match. It went be-yond the ear. And Page knew he had to wait in order to achieve some kind of silence in those woods. Otherwise it would blind him and deafen him and kill him.

So Page backed off. He pulled back enough to go on. The day he sat on the rim of the tub with his rifle in his mouth was prob-ably the day he realized that going on in any real sense meant refusing to go on in another, more literal sense. He knew then that he was going to survive—at all costs. By All Means, as the saying goes. It only took him months to get over it, like centuries—fuck it, finally, yes, ultimate Darwinian Outcomes: survival of the most persistent, persistence sometimes meaning a lot less than meets the eye, submit, submit, submit, it's bigger than we are, much bigger, old Lurps philosophy there.

Page began walking on the earth with great care. One step at a time. And the crystal began to solidify inside him again, freezing inward from the ragged edges like a pond glazing over late in the season, or like scar tissue forming over a wide wound, inviting you to test it. And all around, rock and roll was cooling too, the old wars were really over now, at last and for sure, the beginning and end of all sorts of stories, wrapped up in those days of exile, old blood, bad blood, new blood, mixing endlessly, stay in a crouch and keep your hat on, and whatever you do, don't look back. The sound itself even started to fade, free at last, free at last, burned clean.

And having tested all the cures, now that the Minister of Remedies was gone, there was only one left: "Teach us to care and not to care, Teach us to sit still." Page was going back now, retreating to some kind of unexplored ocean trench, bathyscaphe survival of the spirit, but at least down there it was quiet, with phosphorescent fish and killing pressures, but silence. Only the clanking of his own internal mechanisms bore witness that anything was happening at all.

He came out of it feeling as if he'd shaken a bad, backed-up minor flash of someone else's life—that never happened to *me*. I know that, because I wouldn't have survived it, and look: here I am. Amazing what a little distance and time will do for you. So it was almost too much of a coincidence that Page found himself leaning against the garage by the sprawling house the day his younger brother Steve showed up. It was like a premonition.